A queer coming-of-age about a grieving teen whose plan to move abroad and find his own "Neverland" is derailed by community service, only for it to lead him on an unintentional journey of self-discovery — navigating love, coming to terms with his demisexuality, and redefining what home truly means.

Haunted by the car crash that took his family, eighteen-year-old Aaron is on the brink of fleeing London for Australia. Inspired by his late sister's dream of working in a wildlife park, he searches for a fresh start — a place he can finally call home.

But on the eve of his departure, Aaron is caught with weed at a party, arrested, and sentenced to community service cleaning up the grounds and reviving the gardens of a neglected local retirement centre, anchoring him to the very city he longs to escape.

At the centre, Aaron meets an eclectic crew of misfits, including Landon, a fellow young offender with a reputation for trouble. As Aaron spends more time with the group — especially with Landon — he begins to feel a sense of belonging he never expected. Beneath Landon's tough exterior, Aaron discovers a kindred spirit, someone who sees beyond his scars, both physical and emotional.

Through sleeplessness and late-night conversations, a connection sparks unlike anything Aaron has ever known. For the first time, he feels attracted to someone.

Just as Aaron begins to embrace his demisexuality, Landon's difficult past resurfaces, threatening their fragile relationship. Torn between honouring his sister's memory and staying with Landon, Aaron must decide where his true "Neverland" lies: in Australia or right where he is.

WE MAY BE FRACTURED

JESSICA LASCAR

A NineStar Press Publication
www.ninestarpress.com

We May Be Fractured

First Edition, August 2025

ISBN: 978-1-64890-852-1
Also available in eBook, ISBN: 978-1-64890-851-4

CONTENT WARNING:
This book contains sexual language and content that is fade-to-black. Depictions of PTSD, past trauma, panic attack (on page), death of close family members (flashback), grief, survivor's guilt, child abuse (past, off page), child sexual abuse (past, off page), self-harm (past, off page), scars, smoking, confrontation rapist/abuser, smoking—cigarettes and marijuana.

Chapter One

Neverland

[Now playing » Somewhere I Belong—Linkin Park]

Aaron's cheek scars tingled as he got lost one last time in the Barbican Centre's maze. But the pendant pressing against his chest gnawed at him more—a haunting reminder of the night he'd survived and a promise waiting to be fulfilled.

He yanked his hood low, adjusted his earphones, and claimed his usual spot on a low wall. With one knee hugged to his chest and the other leg dangling, his faded black canvas trainers tapped out a rhythm in the air above the deserted courtyard. Surrounded by the stillness of the fountains and the ghostly playground, the song's melody began to untangle his thoughts, knotted like the strings of his hoodie.

In less than twenty-four hours, he'd be in Australia, soaking up the magic of the Southern Lights and taking care of koalas and other wild critters. It felt unreal that the trip was happening after being on hold for what seemed like forever.

First, he'd completed school, then exams, and he'd even hung around for those A levels and uni interviews. Not that he was into it, as he couldn't care less. It was all to keep Aunt Olivia off his back. She was convinced he was taking a gap year, after all. But the truth? He'd be leaving for good, with no plans to return.

As the last notes faded away, muffled silence swallowed Aaron. The eerie calm, a stark contrast to London's typical hustle, amplified the very thoughts he'd been attempting to quiet.

He grasped his necklace, fingers tracing the jagged edges of the pendant's glass. The uneven texture grounded him.

Taking a deep breath, Aaron pulled out his phone and opened the call log:

Tori

Tori

Tori

Each unanswered call echoed his growing desperation. Shivers ran down his spine. A name shouldn't wield such power.

But it did.

With a shaky thumb, Aaron pressed the call button and held the phone close to his chest, waiting. Once again, Tori's familiar voicemail message greeted him.

Hey there, it's Tori. Can't find my phone...as usual! But leave a message after the beat and maybe—just maybe—I'll get back to you!

The chorus of "Something Just Like This" by The Chainsmokers and Coldplay hummed in the background. Not his favourite tune, but its catchy melody often played on a loop in his mind.

"Hey, Tori, it's me, Aaron," he said, his voice rough and choked as if he'd downed a shot of vodka. "I keep hoping you'll answer one of these days. I wanted to tell you that tomorrow, I'm leaving and not coming back. I'm heading to the place we always dreamed of, far away from everything and everyone. You remember, right? Our Neverland." He paused, his throat tightening as memories of that imagined future flooded back. "I wish you were coming with me, but—"

An incoming call cut off his message, and Cliff's image, grinning as he clutched a bottle of tequila, flashed on the screen.

After a moment's hesitation, Aaron answered the call with, "What now?"

"You sorted for tonight's party?" Cliff's voice buzzed with excitement, and Aaron pictured him bouncing on the balls of his feet.

Oh, right, the costume party. It had slipped Aaron's mind as his great journey loomed over everything.

"I'll pass," he replied curtly.

"Don't be such a mood killer! Afraid you'll bump into your *ex*?" Cliff teased.

Aaron straightened, feet planted firmly on the ground. "For the last time, she wasn't my girlfriend. We hooked up. Once." It wasn't even that great.

"Come on, mate. It's your last night here."

"I'm off to Australia tomorrow, and—"

"All the more reason. One last *wild* night. See you in a bit."

Without waiting for a response, Cliff ended the call. He was always the life of the party, always pushing Aaron out of his comfort zone.

But as Aaron's gaze lingered on the Barbican Centre's vastness, a hard realisation struck him: this was, indeed, his last night in London.

Aaron sighed, something between giving in and gearing up hanging in the crisp air. He stared at the three huge concrete blocks cutting sharply against the sky, their jagged edges slicing through the fluffy clouds above.

He'd always been fascinated by those brutalist giants, with their bold, no-nonsense lines. They took him straight to the world of sci-fi movies as he got lost in the grid patterns of the surrounding buildings, scanning the balconies arranged in a gravity-defying architectural ballet.

The place never got old, no matter how many times Aaron came here.

He'd often scratched his head over the maze-like layout. He could see where he wanted to go, but getting there always involved a mad dash of ups, downs, and loads of twists and turns. He figured some genius had dreamed up the structure, an endless loop that always spat him back where he started. The sky-high walkways didn't make things any easier, linking identical buildings, distinguished only by the occasional plant hanging on the railing.

How odd to see bits of green in such a grey landscape. It seemed out of place. Much like himself.

But for Aaron, the combination of green and grey had its own charm. It made him think of places from myths and bedtime stories reminiscent of the Hanging Gardens of Babylon. A place as fantastical as Neverland.

A brief smile crossed his face, but it didn't stick around for long.

It was time to say goodbye—to the city, to this life, and maybe even to Tori.

His phone buzzed again in his pocket, but this time, a message from Aunt Olivia flashed on the screen.

Aunt Olivia: *Coming back for dinner?*

Dragging his feet, Aaron made his way towards the exit. He couldn't help but chuckle when he passed a bewildered group trying to navigate the maze of pathways.

Once he stepped outside, the familiar noise of the city hit him—the constant buzz of traffic, bursts of laughter spilling out from nearby pubs, and the occasional distant wail of an ambulance siren.

Heading to the Tube station, Aaron moved mechanically, phone in hand to swipe through the turnstile, a quick dash down the left side of the escalator, and an agile pivot towards the platform where the train would whisk him back to Aunt Olivia's.

*

As he entered the Greenwich area, Aaron breathed deeply, taking in the first teeth-baring bite of the autumn evening air. Leaves crunched under his quick steps as he continued into quiet side streets, all lined with red-brick houses. After a series of lookalike facades, he stopped at a black door.

This had been his *home* for the last three years.

Aaron slid his key into the lock and, with his other hand, held the slightly shaky, still-not-fixed doorknob. That little inconvenience had always bugged him, but now, something weird twisted in his gut. This was it. He wouldn't have to deal with the dodgy doorknob any longer.

He stepped inside to the sound of a film on the telly seeping along the corridor, the usual romcom Aunt Olivia loved.

Aaron slipped off his shoes and crept up the stairs, taking them two at a time, careful not to make any of the steps creak.

He retreated to his room, which was as cold as the half-full mugs of peppermint tea he often forgot around the house, and was relieved to find everything as he'd left it that morning: his messy bed with bunched-up sheets, an empty duffle bag on the edge of the mattress, and the wardrobe doors flung wide open. Aaron grabbed the few garments he owned—white T-shirts, grey hoodies, dark jeans, and joggers—and tossed them into the bag. Most of his clothes, worn from too many washes, needed replacing. Yet, as long as they held together, he kept them.

While he continued to fill the bag, a light tap on the door forced him to stop for a moment. Out of the corner of his eye, he caught a glimpse of long brown hair as Aunt Olivia slipped inside.

"I'm crashing at Cliff's tonight." He didn't bother to turn around. "It's easier to get to Heathrow from there."

"Have you taken everything you need for your trip?" Aunt Olivia asked eagerly, her voice light and playful as she came closer, dragging her bare feet on the carpet. It seemed as though she was the one going.

Aaron mumbled in agreement and kept arranging his belongings silently, then closed the zipper with satisfaction.

"I'm so excited for you!" she chirped, plopping onto the edge of the bed and crossing her legs. The bedframe creaked slightly as the mattress dipped under her weight, making the bag tilt. "A little adventure with Cliff before uni is exactly what you need. I can't wait to hear all about the beautiful places you'll visit in Australia!"

Aaron glanced at the pictures on the wall, which showed all the beautiful places his sister had wished to see, including koalas and the Southern Lights. He stiffened and grabbed the collar of his shirt, pulling hard to let air pass, then slipped underneath to scratch the itchy, damaged skin on his chest.

"Aarie." Aunt Olivia grabbed his arm. "Pause for a second and sit down with me."

His agitation eased at her touch. He set the bag down and slumped beside her, hunching forward with his face buried in his hands. Breathing in and out rhythmically, he attempted to steady his hammering heart and prevent it from bursting forth from his chest. The comforting warmth of his aunt's hand on his back grounded him to the present, gradually stilling his trembling.

Aaron lifted his face, letting his hands come to rest on his thighs. He scanned the room, seeking another grounding point. He settled on the shelf above the desk, brimming with books. One spine caught his attention.

The awful shade of green stood out. Green like the pendant he wore, green as the leaves that seemed the same to him every season, green as the hope that had fractured within him after the accident.

"Aarie"—Aunt Olivia called him by his nickname—"both good and bad things happen in life. You can't avoid it. And running away from what you can't face won't lead you anywhere. This kind of race is not one you can win."

Those words echoed ones he'd heard in that haunting hospital room three years ago. If Aaron closed his eyes, he could still smell the sharp scent of disinfectant mingling with the delicate aroma of flowers.

His phone chimed with the upbeat tune of the *Super Mario* theme song, the quirky sound clashing with the tension of the moment. Aaron ignored it and turned to look Aunt Olivia in the eyes. They were as dark as his, but they didn't hold the same shadows.

"It's all right," he reassured her. "You've already said it. This trip will be good for me."

She gave a small, hesitant nod, her wrinkled forehead betraying her scepticism. "I only want you to be happy."

Aaron abruptly rose to his feet. "Happy or not, I'm *still* here. Isn't that enough?"

"Aarie, what matters is having a purpose, a direction. You can't drift like a twig in the stream. It's fine to feel lost at times, but remember, you have the strength to swim through the current. I've told you this before, and I'll say it again. There is more to life than just living."

Aaron lifted his bag, only to set it back down on the bed. He unzipped it and rummaged through its contents, blatantly dodging an all-too-familiar conversation, one that cut too close.

It wasn't that he didn't appreciate Aunt Olivia's concern. She'd been a solid rock when the world had crumbled around him after the accident. But there were places in his pain she couldn't reach, dark corners he hoped she'd never have to see.

The phone's persistent ringing flirted with Aaron's last nerve, tempting him to throw it out the window.

"I'll let you crack on with your packing," his aunt said quietly, standing up. She handed him a small notebook.

Aaron took it, a bit hesitant. The dark, leathery cover had loads of tiny constellations embossed on it, arranged in a pattern painfully familiar. He hovered a thumb over the stars but stopped short.

"Early birthday present," she explained. "You're always doodling on books and scraps of paper. Figured it'd be nice to have a proper notebook to draw all the wild animals you'll see, the scenery, and the Lights..."

Aaron held the little notebook but didn't open it, unsure if he'd ever use it. "Thank you."

"Remember to call now and then, okay?" Aunt Olivia added, and then she was gone.

Aaron chucked the notebook into his bag and zipped it up. Adjusting the shoulder strap, he looked around the room one last time.

Here, unlike at his parents', he'd been able to plaster the walls with posters of his favourite bands, films, and snaps of Australia. But even with all his personal touches, the room never really screamed 'Aaron'.

Just a house. Never a home.

Aaron wandered over to the shelf above his desk that held the green book. The sun's slanted rays illustrated the spine and the title, *Peter Pan*. Below the words, a cascade of tiny golden stars sparkled.

When he first picked up that book, the embossed stars on the cover had a pleasing, comforting texture beneath his fingers. Now, he imagined they'd burn like scorching hot metal.

Whispers from the past buzzed in his ears, dragging him back to that bloody hospital room.

"This is for you, Aarie." Tori had spoken with laboured breaths, pointing to a flat, rectangular package on the bed. *"Things in life don't always go as planned. But it doesn't mean you can't move forward. If you ever feel stuck or lost...try to look in here to find your way home."*

But Aaron never opened that damn book.

He didn't want to remember the happy times he and Tori had spent reading it together or the sound of their joyful laughter that he couldn't bring back anymore. He was worried that, instead of pointing him anywhere, the book would remind him of a happiness that was out of reach now.

Ever since his sister left, Aaron had lost a reference point on the map of life.

So, he'd decided to shoot off to the other side of the world, placing oceans and continents between his past and present. And like Peter Pan, he'd fly towards his Neverland, even if no happy thoughts were driving him. Only a desperate need for something different. *Anything* different.

He hesitated, his gaze locked on the book. Part of him longed to grab it, but the other was repulsed. The pendant around his neck throbbed against his skin, its weight both a burden and a comfort.

His phone, ringing non-stop, yanked him back, dragging him from a vortex of feelings and 'what could have been' thoughts. Now wasn't the time to lose himself in the past. Tomorrow was waving him over, hinting at a new beginning.

He had to get moving. Life, as he'd painfully learned, waited for no one. It marched on, even as personal worlds crumbled. And it was high time he marched with it.

Stepping away from the desk, Aaron pulled out his still-ringing phone.

"I'm ready." He straightened his posture. "Wait for me."

Chapter Two

The Night of Errors

[Now playing » All These Things That I've Done—The Killers]

There it was again.

Every single time they attended a party, Cliff would vanish on him within seconds, on the hunt for someone to snog.

From his spot in the kitchen corner, next to a counter cluttered with empty bottles, used cups, and half-eaten snacks, Aaron had no trouble spotting Cliff. He was impossible to miss in that awful Squid Game jumpsuit he claimed was bright red, though it looked like a dull brown to Aaron. He stood out even more while having a full-on face-sucking session with a vampire girl. *Classic Cliff.*

Aaron huffed. A mere half hour in, and he was done. His plan to enjoy some drinks and snacks had been ruined, the good stuff gone. The only available option was a sad bowl of vile-tasting crisps, a pickled onion abomination that not even the sweet Pimm's could wash away.

He leaned against the cool wall, seeking some comfort. The dim lights almost lulled him towards a nap, but the loud booming music and chatter kept his eyes open.

Giving up on trying to blend in with the kitchen mess, Aaron glanced around.

The room buzzed with the heat of too many bodies, a palpable layer of pheromones hanging in the space between them. The mingled scents of smoke and pot tinged the thick, booze-soaked air. Some people played a blindfolded drinking game, while others tried a different version of beer pong using a clementine as the ball. A few danced clumsily, and others, like Cliff, were simply enjoying themselves.

Aaron could've gone down the same path, found someone to kiss to pass the time. Like that girl from the last party he'd ended up with, who somehow got the idea she was his girlfriend. But the very thought of kissing for the sake of it was even more boring to him.

As he watched everyone lost in their own little bubble of pleasure and fun, a pang of envy struck Aaron. He felt so empty. He'd been feeling like this ever since the accident.

Aunt Olivia and his short-lived therapist had said it was expected, that grief hits everyone differently. But he'd always been a bit detached, even before anything had happened.

Aaron never understood why his mates were so keen on snogging and shagging. Their wild tales had him curious, sure, but half the time, he wondered if they were trying to one-up one another or maybe recreating scenes from Netflix shows.

His experience with kissing had been pretty average, not terrible, but definitely not mind-boggling like he'd assumed from romantic films. No fireworks, no sparks. And sex? Even more underwhelming. Whether with girls or boys, each experience felt meaningless. His body was there, but his mind always drifted elsewhere, never fully engaged. It felt as though he was trying to satisfy a craving he didn't quite have, like eating food without being hungry. He could appreciate the flavour, but the appetite, the passion, just wasn't there.

Aaron should have seen it coming, really. Another way he didn't fit in.

Being colour-blind was the first clue that he didn't see the world like everyone else. It made sense, then, that his bisexuality also strayed from what was considered typical.

Still, it stung, always missing a piece of the bigger picture.

Looking down at his Squid Game contestant costume, he let out a dry laugh. It was all too fitting: caught in a game and unclear on the rules as if everyone else had a cheat code he lacked. The secret to wanting someone.

Aaron swallowed hard and made a quick move towards the corridor. He aimed for the staircase at the entrance, hoping to find some quieter space upstairs. But getting to it proved to be more difficult than an obstacle run.

First, his jacket got snagged on an angel costume's wings, slowing him down and leaving him with a few stray feathers as souvenirs. After freeing himself, he barely dodged a tipsy ballerina's elbow. And to top it all off, the clementine from the beer pong game flew right into him, splattering into someone's drink and splashing both their outfits.

"Aaron?" A guy sporting a large straw hat and an unbuttoned waistcoat called to him from the bottom of the stairs. Based on his get-up, he made a decent Luffy from *One Piece*.

It took Aaron a moment to place him. They'd hooked up. Once. Sort of. But it hadn't been anything memorable. He'd even ignored the guy's friend request on Instagram the next day.

As he brushed past him, Aaron gave a quick nod and a brief half-smile, not slowing down. Reaching the first floor felt like snagging a win, even if he was now a hot, soaked mess with dark splotches all over his tracksuit. But at least he was finally a world away from the bedlam down there.

Hunting for an empty room, Aaron stumbled upon one with a small balcony attached. After a mini-battle with a stubborn French door, he made it outside. The night unfolded before him, with the back garden below and a dark, empty canvas above, not a star in sight.

Urban life often concealed the full majesty of the night sky, but Tori had taught him to use constellations as guides to always find his way home. Now, she was the one who had strayed, leaving him feeling like an outsider in his own reality.

Aaron's hands started shaking, a result of the crisp, cold air and his bubbling frustration. He fiddled with the little rings on his chain, reaching for the pendant, then let his hands drift down to his pocket to grab his phone. He was about to call Tori but nixed the idea. Instead, he went for a cigarette, more about doing something with his hands than actually wanting to smoke.

"Hey, Aaron," came the same voice as before from behind him.

Luffy. He'd be damned if he could remember his real name.

"Hey," Aaron replied, keeping his voice flat.

Luffy leaned against the balcony railing beside him, cradling a big cup. "Still playing Ice King, huh?"

His words held a provocative edge, a bait Aaron wasn't willing to bite.

"Heard you're off to Australia tomorrow. That right?"

"It is."

A sly grin slid across Luffy's face. "Why not have a little *fun* before you jet off?"

"Thanks, but no thanks," Aaron shot back, his tone leaving no room for argument. "I'm not interested."

Feigning surprise, Luffy's eyes still held a persistent glint. "Come on. You can't pretend there wasn't something between us."

"It was nothing," Aaron clipped out, wanting to end this conversation here and now.

Luffy's grin only widened. "Playing hard to get, are we? That's what's so...*intriguing* about you."

"I'm not playing anything."

Luffy tilted his head, his gaze lingering on Aaron before that ever-present smirk returned. "We could always give it another go..."

Aaron exhaled slowly, watching his breath form a misty cloud in the air. He wished he could disappear into it. "How about you go find someone else to bother tonight?"

Luffy took a slow sip from his cup, never breaking eye contact. He edged closer. "You know, you should've come as Five from *The Umbrella Academy*. An old soul in an eighteen-year-old's body." He sounded displeased now. "You're such a bore. Do you even know how to have fun?"

Aaron rolled his eyes internally. Here we go again, just because he wasn't into wild parties or making a scene didn't mean he didn't know how to have fun. "I do. We have different concepts of fun."

His idea of a good time involved a solid night in with a series, a killer video game, or a book.

Luffy fished a small joint from his pocket. "Here." He extended it towards Aaron. "Maybe this will help you loosen up."

Aaron narrowed his eyes slightly. "Where did you nick that?"

"Look at you, choir boy. Afraid that if you let loose, you might have *real* fun?"

Aaron tensed. Without hesitation, he scrapped the cigarette and snatched the joint. He placed it between his lips. A brief flicker of flame from Luffy's lighter momentarily illuminated his devilish grin before the tip caught fire.

Drawing in deeply, the familiar warmth snaked through Aaron's lungs. He kept his gaze fixed on Luffy as he released a stream of smoke into the night.

Luffy reclaimed the joint and inhaled with casual ease before his eyes flicked towards Aaron's right cheek. The one with the scars.

"Did some gangster mess you up, and now, you have to take off?" Luffy prodded. "Or is this some sort of romantic escapade?"

Aaron had anticipated the question. The last time, Luffy hadn't asked, too busy with his mouth full while making out, but Aaron had sensed the unvoiced curiosity lurking then.

He snorted, half laughing. "Told you. Love's not my thing."

"So, you weren't lying when you told me you don't want to be with anyone."

Aaron shook his head, taking the joint back before it went out.

"Too bad," Luffy said. "I was hoping to crack your shell."

"There's nothing to crack."

"*She* gave you that, didn't she?" Luffy pointed at Aaron's pendant. "This whole trip, it's to be with *her*, the girl in your voice messages. What's her name again?"

Aaron tightened his grip on the joint. "Look, we hooked up, but that doesn't give you the right to stick your nose in my fucking business."

"Hit a nerve, didn't I? You wouldn't be this fired up if I was off the mark."

"Just drop it, okay?"

Aaron took another drag from the joint, then blew a cloud of smoke directly into Luffy's face. His lips twitched upward as Luffy coughed and squinted through watering eyes.

This guy knew nothing about him and Tori. No one did. Aaron had never found the courage to share that part of his history with anyone. It was too raw, too deep. An injury that time refused to mend.

But Luffy was right. The pendant was a promise to her, a promise Aaron fully intended to keep.

Just as Luffy tried to pull himself together, Cliff showed up, his timing perfect. He stumbled towards them, almost tripping over his own feet. With a decisive shove, Cliff squeezed himself between them, nearly sending Luffy toppling.

Cliff's eyes, bleary and bloodshot, zeroed in on the joint, which he quickly grabbed from Aaron. "Why didn't you lads tell me the party was out here?"

As strong as the weed smell was, Aaron couldn't ignore the unmistakable blend of vodka and sweat emanating from his friend. Cliff appeared messier than when they arrived, with greasy hair and one sleeve of his jumpsuit dangling behind his back.

"I'll go, then." Luffy took the opportunity to remove himself from the tense situation. He started towards the window with heavy steps but paused, turning back to face Aaron.

Their eyes locked in an intense, silent exchange that Aaron couldn't understand.

Then, Luffy extended two plastic bags of weed towards him as a peace offering. "Looks like you need this more than I do."

"Keep it," Aaron declined, still annoyed by their exchange.

"Oh, come on. Take it," Cliff chimed in. He swiftly pocketed one bag, while sliding the other into Aaron's. "Might come in handy, you know."

Before Aaron could make sense of what just happened, Luffy leaned in, his tone soft yet pointed.

"Have a good trip, Aaron. Whatever, or *whoever*, you're looking for, I hope they're worth it." He paused, holding Aaron's gaze with a peculiar intensity. "And for the record, it didn't work for me either. You kiss like a straight guy."

With those parting words, Luffy left the balcony, leaving them to freeze in the frosty air. Aaron frowned, confusion and annoyance brewing inside him. What was that even supposed to mean?

"What's wrong with you?" Cliff asked, elbow propped on the railing as he tried to keep himself upright. It was remarkable, though, how he managed to steadily hold the nearly burned-out joint between his fingers.

"Nothing," Aaron replied, his eyes still lost beyond the glass.

"You said goodbye to an easy shag."

"Seriously?" The guy didn't appeal to Aaron, but that didn't make Cliff's comment any less shallow.

"I mean...You two hooked up at Henry's party, right?"

"So?"

"So, it would've been easy to go for another round."

"Doesn't matter. Sex isn't my top priority."

Cliff stared at him with that same baffled expression as if he were talking to someone from another planet.

"Come on, Aaron, you've got twice the playing field as I do. Blokes, gals..." He had that glint in his eyes, half envy, half confusion. "You mean to tell me, out of everyone here tonight, not one person's caught your fancy? You're too picky, mate!"

Aaron shrugged. It wasn't a matter of preference, but indifference. Despite what Cliff thought, being bi didn't guarantee more opportunities. It just expanded the range of people he wasn't attracted to.

"Man, you're such a drag," Cliff grumbled, visibly disappointed.

"I'm good. I don't need anything or anyone," Aaron insisted.

Cliff sighed, then tried to rally. "I hoped you'd have a bit of fun on your last night, you know?"

Aaron pulled out his phone and earphones, flashing the screen at Cliff to show the TV series on his list. "This is my kind of fun."

Shaking his head with a resigned look, Cliff took a final puff and flicked the stub onto the path below. He punched Aaron playfully on the arm before heading off to chat up someone else.

Alone once more, Aaron could finally relax. Before starting the series, he glanced at the four numbers ticking away in the corner of his screen. For most, they just tracked time, but for Aaron, they counted down to a new chapter. In a few hours, he'd be on his way to Heathrow, boarding a flight to Australia.

Despite what he'd told Aunt Olivia, Aaron was tired of drifting, feeling like a shell filled with nothing but a consuming emptiness. Light as a cloud, like the smoke he'd released into the night air earlier, it filled him up, leaving no space for anything bright or joyful.

As the episode played out some ordinary life scenes—well, as 'ordinary' as any scripted scene could get—Aaron found himself yearning for simplicity of waking up to the smell of fresh coffee, days packed with laughter and friends, treating himself to burgers and junk food. More than anything, he yearned for a place he could fit.

Somewhere to belong.

Home.

Aaron had been so absorbed in his show that he only noticed Cliff's return when his earphones were yanked out.

"Police! Police! Police are here!" Cliff panted, his eyes wide and wild. He grabbed Aaron's arm, pulling him towards the door. "Bloody cunt next door.... We need to leave. Now."

Dread prickled through Aaron. His costume reeked of booze and smoke, the smell clinging to the fabric, making his nose wrinkle. He just wanted a hot shower and a warm bed.

Trailing behind Cliff, he manoeuvred down the cluttered staircase, sidestepping toppled cups and forgotten food. However, their exit wasn't to be so easy. A policewoman blocked their path at the bottom of the stairs.

"Not so fast, boys." She eyed them suspiciously. "Are you both eighteen?"

Cliff's laughter cut through the tension. Despite being legal for a while, his youthful appearance often invited such questions. "It's the Japanese-Korean genes," he'd often joke. "I'm destined to look like a teenager until I suddenly Yoda overnight." It was as if he was always going to be either way too young or way too old, with no in-between.

"We're both of age," Aaron snapped, trying to edge past the policewoman towards the exit. "Can we just go home?"

"I'm afraid not." She stood firmly in their way. "You both look underage and stink of booze and weed."

"We're not underage. I've got IDs," Cliff slurred, fumbling with his jacket. As he yanked the cards free, the bag of weed hit the floor with them.

"Well, well, well," the policewoman said, bending to pick it up. She gave him a look that was half strict, half amused. "What do we have here? Care to explain how you got this?"

Cliff blinked, too far gone to answer.

Aaron's heart raced. If they searched him next, they'd find the other one. He shifted back a step.

"Where do you think you're going?" the policewoman said sharply. "You're next. Hands where I can see them."

"I don't have anything," Aaron insisted, but she was already patting him down.

"Well, well, well," she repeated, more seriously this time, as she pulled the second bag from his jacket. "Two supposed minors with drugs."

"That's not mine," Aaron blurted, just as Cliff mumbled, "We're not minors."

"Are you carrying more? Were you planning to sell these?"

"Wait, what? No—" Aaron stammered. "I didn't even use it."

"Doesn't matter. Possession of cannabis is still illegal."

Sweat beaded at Aaron's forehead. "Listen, I'm just caught up in this." He spun on Cliff. "This is *your* fault. *You* stuffed it in my pocket."

Cliff's head snapped up. "What the fuck, Aaron? You throwing me under the bus now?"

"*You*'re the one who took it and insisted I hold it," Aaron shot back. "You always do this—get shitfaced and drag me down with you because you can't handle being bored for five minutes. But not this time. I've got plans."

Cliff squinted at him, swaying. "Oh, right. Your *precious* plans. You've always had something more important going on."

"Yeah. I do. You've got nothing but the next party."

"God, you're such a wanker," Cliff spat, trying to look mad but struggling to keep his balance. He aimed a punch at Aaron, but it was so weak it barely landed.

"Boys," the policewoman cut in. "Maybe save this for another time. You're both in a bad spot already."

Aaron turned to her. "Oh, please. Just take him. He's the one who's clearly wasted."

Cliff's second punch hit Aaron's shoulder, still sloppy but enough to shock.

Aaron, more frustrated than hurt, simply pushed Cliff back. It wasn't hard given Cliff's state. Drunk and high, he was no match for Aaron.

"Enough." The policewoman pulled them apart and called over another officer to help, especially with Cliff, who was still trying to punch Aaron in the face.

She then crouched to scoop up their fallen IDs. "*Cliff Jung*," she read, scrutinising the first card. Then she examined the second. "*Aaron Walsh*."

Hearing his surname sent a chill down Aaron's spine, a reminder of a family that no longer was.

The officer's gaze flicked between them a few times, stern and assessing. She pocketed the IDs and, with help from her colleague, escorted Aaron and Cliff outside.

They went quietly at first. But as they neared the police car parked at the kerb, panic set in. Aaron couldn't afford any delays, not with his flight to Australia, his new life, just hours away. A summer job waited for him, a home, and the Southern Lights that Tori had always talked about.

He'd *promised* her.

With a swift motion, Aaron unzipped his jacket and prepared to run as fast as he could. But the officer was quick, and a slippery puddle didn't help. Aaron threw an elbow, managing to hit the policeman's stomach, but he was swiftly pulled back towards the car.

"You're making a mistake," he insisted, struggling. "I've nothing to do with this."

"We'll decide that after a nice chat at the station," the policewoman replied, unflappable as she opened the car door and gestured for them to get in the back.

Once they were inside, Aaron didn't give up. He lunged for the door handle, trying to escape, but it was no use; the door was secured. Cliff, on the other hand, sat quietly in his spot.

The officers settled into the front seats. The policewoman, gripping the steering wheel, finally broke the silence, staring at them in the rear-view mirror.

"Jung and Walsh," she said, emphasising their last names with what sounded to Aaron like a bit of satisfaction. "Looks like your party's over."

Chapter Three

Stranded in London

[Now playing » Dreamin ft. blackbear—The Score]

It had all gone from bad to worse, real quick.

A night that was supposed to be forgettable had turned into a giant mess.

Maybe Aaron wasn't as lucky as everyone said when he'd survived that car crash. Maybe surviving was the real curse. Perhaps he had it coming.

Perched on a frost-kissed bench in Greenwich Park at the break of dawn, Aaron held his phone in hands going numb from the cold, feeling the chill even through his trousers. He had almost nothing left, no mates around, hardly any cash, and nowhere to head to. The unused ticket to Australia mocked him from his lock screen, a brutal reminder of his missed flight.

By now, he should have been on his way to the other side of the world. Instead, he was stuck here in London. Alone. Homeless.

Well, in theory, he could go back to Aunt Olivia's and plan everything again, but shame and the thought that she believed he was already on a plane held him back. He didn't want to be a burden to her again. She'd done enough.

Aaron released a foggy breath and fiddled with his phone. Idle swipes took him through Instagram, where, among the selfies and happy snaps, he stumbled upon photos of the Southern Lights.

It should've been him posting something like that, sitting beneath an aurora-lit sky rather than the cloudy one above him, as grey as the pigeons bobbing around his feet. He was meant to see those lights with his own eyes, feel the magic they whispered about, not squint at them through someone else's lens.

Aaron recalled the first time Tori had shared the secret of the Lights with him as kids. It had been yet another of those evenings filled with their parents' heated arguments, the walls not doing their best to muffle the harsh words. They'd found refuge in Tori's room, where they'd turned pillows into forts and blankets into barriers, reading books or playing games; inside, it felt like they were miles away from all the noise.

"Aarie, guess what? I've found something cool," Tori had said, her eyes sparkling like the stars he'd often seen in her space books. *"Imagine we're in this huge place, bigger than any park we've seen, and the sky is glowy and dancing with all sorts of colours, like...like a giant night light, but cooler!"*

"Colours like what?"

Tori had hesitated, her smile faltering. *"You don't have to see it the way others do. Actually, it's even better if you don't. It's more about the feeling than the colour. You know when we play in the sea, how it feels all cool and splashy? That's the blue. And green is the grass we hide in, all tickly and fresh. And you can see blues and greens meeting in the sky."*

"So, it's like...like magic in the sky?"

"Even better! It's this special thing called the Southern Lights, all

the way in Australia. Legends say that the Lights are a bridge from this world to the next, and that if you make a wish while looking at them, it will come true."

"Really?"

"Maybe. Who knows? One day, though, we'll be there, watching those lights, wishing for a better future, and there'll be kangaroos and koalas around us. It'll be our magic place." She'd turned on a small lamp that changed colours beneath the sheets, making their blanket fort glow in different shades. She waved her hands around, pretending to paint the air. *"See? Like this. It's not just about the colours. It's the air, the stars, the light dancing, way bigger and in the sky. It's like...the best show in the world, only for us!"*

Aaron had nodded, wide-eyed and full of belief. Tori could turn any story into an adventure. And in the hush of her reading, with the pages whispering tales of far-off lands, he'd found a peace that felt like...well, love.

Those childhood dreams were now mere fragments, as shattered as the glass that had scarred Aaron on that dreadful day, both on his body and deep within his heart.

With a shaky finger numbed by the cold, he scrolled through his contacts and tapped on Tom's, his would-be flatmate down in Australia. As he hit the call button, a stark warning flashed on the screen: 10 percent battery remaining. Aaron ignored it.

"Aaron, mate! How are things?" Tom's voice, cheerfully oblivious, contrasted sharply with the storm brewing in Aaron's chest. "Shouldn't you be on your way here by now?"

Aaron hesitated. "Hey, Tom, I, uh...kinda hit a bit of a hiccup. I've missed my flight."

There was a sharp intake of breath on the other end. "Oh, man. Grabbing another one, then?"

Another pause, longer this time. "Well, um...not exactly. I might have been caught with some weed last night and hit an officer, so they slapped me with community service. A hundred hours over four months."

"Bloody hell, Aaron. So, you're not coming, then?"

Clearing his throat, Aaron tried to keep his voice steady. "Need to sort this shit out first."

"Oh, right," Tom said, a heavy dose of disappointment in his tone. "You know, I was counting on you being here. I held on to that room just for you, but this changes everything. I *really* need to find a new flatmate now."

A knot of panic tightened in Aaron's stomach. "Wait...are you telling me you can't hold the room for me anymore?"

Tom let out a long sigh. "Wish I could, but I've got bills to pay."

"Shit," Aaron muttered to himself.

"Call me back when you're ready to come. I'm sure we can figure something out then. But for now, the room's gone."

"What about the summer job at the wildlife park?"

Tom hesitated long enough for Aaron to sense the incoming bad news. "About that...they won't wait for you either."

Aaron cursed again.

"Look, Aaron, I get it. This isn't just a trip for you. It's about Tori, and I understand you wanted everything to align perfectly, the way you two had planned. But you've been waiting a long time, a few more months won't be the end of the world."

But it was.

At eighteen and a half, Aaron was exactly the age Tori had been when the lethal car crash stole her dreams and her future; it had been right after she'd won a scholarship to her dream university in Sydney.

Every day, Aaron felt as though he was walking in her shadow, haunted by the life and opportunities she'd never experience while he continued living. If he hadn't switched seats with Tori in the back of the car, perhaps she would still be here. The doctors had told him his spot was why he'd made it.

It wasn't fair, him being the sole survivor. If someone in his family had to survive, it should've been Tori. She was special; he was nothing.

"The Lights, Tom. It's the last chance to see them before summer comes in."

"The Lights aren't a one-time event. They'll be back next winter."

"Yes, I know that, but—"

"Aaron, you know I loved your sister, right?" Tom's voice wavered, betraying his own pain. He, too, had lost someone special. His girlfriend. "I miss her every day too. And she...she'd want us to see the bigger picture. Finish what you have to do in London, and then come. There'll be other jobs, other opportunities. We'll figure it out."

"You don't understand. I have to..." Aaron choked out. The last dregs of his battery had finally given out, leaving him surrounded by silence and unsaid words.

Clenching his teeth, he slammed his hand on the bench. Some pigeons, too close to him, scattered in a frenzy. He'd always found those birds annoying; in this moment, he loathed them even more.

As they bolted, Aaron's head started to spin. His heartbeat thudded in his ears, his legs about to give out any second. Aaron buried his face in his hands, his whole body quivering with frustration. It was as if the universe was messing with him on purpose, making his already washed-out world even duller.

He toyed with the pendant hanging around his neck, each edge a sharp reminder of what he'd lost and what he still needed to find. This very piece had been wedged between his and Tori's clasped hands as the car flipped, coming to rest upside down on the motorway.

The past seeped through the scars, pinning him here: wide awake, unable to move.

"Hold on to a happy thought, and we'll fly away to Neverland, okay?" Tori had somehow managed to whisper amid the wreckage, her hand never leaving his. *"Don't let go."*

But holding on to a happy thought without Tori was hard.

Clutching his dead phone, Aaron mumbled, barely audible even to himself, "Tori, I'm so, so sorry. I tried...I really did."

Leaves rustled and shuffled around him. A massive, bear-like black dog bounded up, nosing and licking at his knee, perhaps catching the scent of stale booze and crisps from last night's party. Its owner, a woman all neat with her hair up, tried to haul it back, but the dog wasn't having any of it.

"Oh, I'm so sorry," she half-smiled, apologetic but warm.

Aaron managed a shrug and patted the dog, feeling a twinge of something bittersweet. Once, he'd asked his parents if they could keep a stray cat he'd found, but pets were off-limits at home. Everything had to be in order, with no room for chaos or mess.

"Are you okay, love?" Her tone held genuine concern as she gave him a once-over.

In his stained Squid Game tracksuit, scars crisscrossing his skin, and likely with bags under his eyes, Aaron must've painted quite a picture.

"Yeah, I'm okay." The lie slipped smoothly off his tongue, a reflex born from years of secrecy with his parents. "Just partied a bit too hard last night and thought I'd walk off the hangover."

"Oh, to be young and reckless," she commented lightly. "At least it's a beautiful stroll here. Taking in the view, are you?" She waved a hand at the trees surrounding them. "It's a pretty time of year, autumn."

Aaron swept absentmindedly over the fallen leaves while she talked about how autumn lifted spirits before winer rolled in with its cold, grey grip.

When she and her dog moved on, he sighed, his vision slipping out of focus.

Why did people always wax lyrical about the fall colours? To him, it was all just a greenish-brown hodgepodge. Kind of like his life right now, all muddled up with this bloody community service he'd got roped into.

Aaron let out a long breath, mumbling under his breath, "Everything sucks."

♫ Shit Happens

[Now playing » Podcast, Ep. 10—Shit Happens—Don't Listen To Me]

Some days, everything feels like a giant pile of shit.

Or perhaps it's been like this for a while now.

It's as if the world has a grudge against us. Maybe all the misfortunes that befall us are nothing but the result of karma for some wrong we've done.

Well...let me tell you: The world doesn't give a shit about us. Not even one bit.

There's no karma or conspiracy plotting against us. We are insignificant, and what happens to us, just happens, period. It comes about, and all we can do is take a deep breath, flush the crap, and move on.

Someone wiser than me, Lao Tzu, once said: "Instead of cursing the darkness, it's better to light a candle." Simple, right? Why the hell didn't I think of that earlier?

Now, I don't know if these philosophical nuggets genuinely serve any purpose or if they showcase my secret collection of aphorisms on Pinterest. What I do know is that complaining leads to nothing, and nothing's going to go right unless we decide it should.

So, let's roll up our sleeves and put on those ridiculous fluorescent vests. It's work time.

Today's soundtrack is "Welcome To Paradise" by Green Day.

And as per usual, no thanks for tuning in, loser.

I'm Psycho, and this is "Don't Listen To Me."

[♫ Closing » Welcome to Paradise—Green Day]

Chapter Four

A Bunch of Misfits

[Now playing » Welcome to Paradise—Green Day]

Aaron sure didn't see this coming.

First day of community service, and here he was, smack in the middle of a jungle pretending to be a garden, all under the watchful eye of a once-fancy Victorian building.

Weeds towered like sentinels, barring the way as he navigated through a graveyard of forgotten memories—rusted appliances, mould-eaten mattresses, and sad, decayed remnants of what was once furniture. The building's worn facade added to the gloom, occasionally interrupted by chaotic graffiti, the lone heartbeat in this place.

He'd hoped, maybe naively, to be picking up litter by the Thames, not wrestling with...whatever this mess was. This was a job for more than a day, more than one person. And they expected him to do it alone?

"Off to a pretty lousy start, kid," his supposed supervisor declared in a distinctive Brummie accent. Broad-shouldered, arms crossed, and with an unimpressed arch of her brow, she cut an imposing figure. "Twenty minutes late on day one isn't the best look."

"It's not my fault," Aaron started, phone still in hand, the map app glaring back at him. "I couldn't find the—"

"Nope, save it. Everyone else found it just fine," she interrupted, not sparing him an ounce of sympathy.

"Everyone else?" He flicked his eyes around, spotting a cluster of young people hanging out near a graffiti-splashed conservatory not too far away. He didn't recall the community service package coming with a group deal.

"Meet the team," she pointed out. "You're stuck with one another every Saturday for the next few months."

Fantastic. Just what he needed—bonding with a bunch of criminals.

"Workday's nine to five. Lunch at noon. At the end, you get a slip for your hours," she recited, her monotone indicating she'd said it a hundred times before. Her expression alone spoke volumes of boredom and disinterest.

Digging in her bag, she pulled out a glaring fluorescent jacket and tossed it his way.

Catching it, Aaron frowned. "What's this for?"

"Hi-vis jacket. Wear it. Always."

Aaron unfurled it, his gaze landing on the bold 'Community Payback' printed on the back. "For keeping tabs on us or public shaming?"

"Your choice of perspective. Put it on." She gestured dismissively towards the group. "Now go and mingle while we wait for my colleague."

"So, your colleague can be late, but I can't?"

"He's not the one with a record," she shot back, a hint of smugness evident.

With a huff, Aaron put the jacket on and walked over to the group.

As he reached them, a girl with a head full of skinny braids closed in on him. Her suede boots, knee-high, left little marks on the ground, scattering pebbles with every determined step she took. A whiff of sweet vanilla preceded her.

She stopped right in front of him, sizing him up with big eyes framed by long lashes, her gaze hovering over the scars on his face. Aaron braced himself for the usual routine he'd nicknamed 'The Gaze Game', or that moment of shock, the blend of curiosity and pity, followed by the inevitable awkward glance away. But she threw him for a loop, steadily holding his gaze.

"Hi, I'm Maeve," she said with a big, wide smile, twirling a braid around her finger.

Aaron focused on her long pointy nails, which were so shiny they made his hi-vis jacket seem dull. He was impressed at how she managed not to snag those talons in her braids.

"First time?" She pushed for a conversation.

He nodded, wishing it would be his last too.

"On my third go." Maeve blew a bubble with her chewing gum, letting it pop before laughing casually. "They said one more theft, and it's straight to jail next time."

Aaron nodded again, baffled by her candidness. He wasn't here to make small talk. He just wanted to do his time, get it over with, and get back on track with his life.

Maeve leaned in, eyeing the scars on his right cheek. Ah, there it was—the next phase of 'The Gaze Game' only a few had ventured to play. Popping her gum, she grinned. "You in a gang or something? Those scars sure shout 'bad boy'."

Aaron traced the twin lines trailing down his jaw. Comments like these weren't new to him, and they never got easier to hear. He wished he could wipe the constant reminders off his face and mind.

As he tried to come up with a smart comeback, another voice piped in.

"Thank God, you're not ugly! I was hoping for a fittie to join the team."

Turning, Aaron found himself face-to-face with a full-blown sensory overload. Before him stood a tall guy in a Barbie hoodie that was practically a pin cushion as a chaotic collection of quirky badges covered it. And if the hoodie wasn't statement enough, his heart-patterned trousers screamed for attention. He clutched a phone in a rainbow case, and cloth bracelets wrapped around his wrist, each one frayed, braided, or beaded.

The bold stranger's eyes briefly settled on Aaron's scars. No one was immune to 'The Gaze Game'.

"You have...an *interesting* look," he commented, taking a step closer than Aaron might have liked, clearly not one for personal space. "I'm Nyle, with a *Y*, by the way."

Raising an eyebrow, Aaron replied, "And I'm Aaron, with two *A*'s."

A high-pitched laugh erupted from Nyle. "Interesting, and has a sense of humour. Totally my type. How old are you?"

Was this guy hitting on him? Why were people here so upfront? "I'll be nineteen soon."

"Oh, same age as Maeve. I'm starting to feel very old surrounded by *babies*."

"Drama Queen, you're only twenty-one," Maeve chimed in, then leaned towards Aaron. "And ignore him. Any bloke with a pulse is his type."

"As if you're any less slutty than I am," Nyle shot back.

"YOLO, right?" she laughed.

"Anyway, to prove I don't just go for anyone, the other newbie is *definitely* not my type. He's so basic," Nyle pointed out.

Following Nyle's gesture, Aaron's heart dropped a beat.

There, with his unmistakable glossy black hair, was Cliff. They hadn't spoken since that disaster of a party. Now, justice had them both doing community service together. Aaron's gut told him they couldn't avoid their past forever, especially not with Cliff. Yet for now, Cliff seemed unaware of him, deep in conversation with a girl, both of them wearing the hideous jackets.

"I didn't get much chat time with him," Maeve mused. "But if he's choosing *her* over me, he's probably a snore."

Aaron's focus shifted to the girl in question—petite, with platform high-tops peeking out from under a flowy floral skirt, and pale, undoubtedly dyed hair pulled back to reveal an undercut of a much darker shade.

As she chatted animatedly with Cliff, a black rose tattoo peeked out from her wrist with every gesture.

"Looks can be deceiving," Maeve murmured, leaning closer to Aaron, her breath tickling his ear. "Ria might look like a delicate flower, but trust me, behind that angelic face, there's a fire. Cross her, and you'll see a switch flip from cute kitty to full-blown tiger."

Aaron blinked, studying her. Beneath the facade of a delicate bloom, that girl might be more of a carnivorous plant, hiding a bite. She was there for a reason, after all.

But when their eyes met, he was taken aback as Ria sent him a radiant smile, not a casual, polite one but a beam that pierced right through his scars and defences.

Nobody, except Tori and Aunt Olivia, had ever given him that kind of look. For a second, Aaron felt like a deer caught in headlights, Ria's intense focus blinding him, pushing him to the edge.

He held the connection with her for a couple of heartbeats, but then a wave of unease crept in, pulling his gaze to someone lurking in the background.

There, against a dark, graffiti-adorned wall stood a guy enveloped in black clothes from head to toe. No hi-vis jacket on him; he was hiding in the shadows. The only betrayal of his anonymity was the eyebrow piercing that occasionally caught and reflected fleeting glimmers of the surrounding light.

Hands nonchalantly tucked into his oversized hoodie, the guy seemed uninterested in mingling, his eyes lazily scanning yet sharply observant of the surroundings. Aaron could relate; Maeve's non-stop talking had turned into background noise for him too.

But something denser clung to the guy's aura, a palpable indifference that he wore as one might a well-worn coat. When their eyes met, unlike Ria's earlier warmth, he offered nothing but a chillingly detached stare.

"'The Psycho,'" Maeve continued after catching his attention with a cough.

"What?" Aaron looked back at her, disoriented, having missed part of her conversation.

"That guy who just gave you a murderous look—they call him 'The Psycho'. Best to steer clear if you want to stay safe. He's completely nuts."

"Don't call him that," Nyle interjected.

"Why not? Everyone saw how he lost it at the pub the other day, punching that dude just for glancing at Ria." Maeve's voice trailed off as the supervisor waved everyone closer with a languid hand.

"Gather 'round, kids."

The group obeyed, forming a semicircle around her. It was then, amidst the shuffle, that Cliff locked eyes with Aaron, his expression twisting into a disgusted scowl.

"For the newcomers, I'm Sarah." She half-heartedly pointed to a faded nametag on her jacket. "I'm here to make sure you do your job. As you can see"—she gestured around—"this care centre garden needs some *serious* attention. You're all part of the community payback revitalisation project, and in the next few months, your goal is to revive this sad-looking place."

"*Our*," corrected the man standing behind her. "*Our* goal is to revive this place."

Sarah shot him a bored, exasperated look. "Yeah, whatever..."

In stark contrast to her, the man radiated enthusiasm, his polished outfit oddly out of sync with the gardening project ahead.

"Hi, everyone, I'm Muhammad!" He greeted them with a wide grin and a self-aware chuckle as he smoothed down his well-combed hair. "I know I'm a tad overdressed, but trust me, I can get my hands dirty. We've got a bit of a mission ahead with these pesky weeds, cleaning up graffiti, and sorting out the old resting areas. This isn't just any garden, okay? This patch of greenery holds a lot of meaning for the care centre. I think we can turn it around, make it a nice place again for everyone who needs it."

Sarah, visibly unimpressed, interjected, "All right, let's get organised. We'll start with weed removal first. After that, some of you will help Mr. Fancy Gardener with the plants, while the rest will be on graffiti removal duty."

Muhammad, gesturing towards a shed with lively enthusiasm, declared, "Everything you need is right in there. Kit yourselves out, and later this afternoon, I'll lead the plant team."

Fluttering her eyelashes, Maeve chimed in, "Fingers crossed I land in your squad, Muhammad."

With an eye roll, Sarah retorted, "Enough. Grab your gloves and shovels, and let's get moving, shall we?"

The group dispersed, each person showing different reactions about the work ahead. Maeve, though, had stopped, her attention drawn to a big withered tree in the centre of the garden.

"What's wrong with that tree?" she asked.

Aaron, following her gaze, studied its pitiful state with its twisted branches, chipped bark, and curled leaves.

"That cherry tree?" Muhammad sighed. "No one knows. On the surface, everything seems okay with it, yet it clearly isn't thriving. But despite its appearance, it still shows signs of life."

"Can't we do something to revive it?" asked Ria.

"We've tried, but nothing seems to work. You know, nature has its mysteries, and this tree keeps its secrets well."

"We should get rid of it." Cliff scoffed, giving the tree a disdainful once-over. "If this garden is meant to revive, then why keep this monstrosity right at the centre?"

"Well, it's a commemorative tree, planted in memory of Lily, the late founder's daughter. Unless it dies naturally, we're not going to kill it," Muhammad retorted, clearly on the defensive.

"It's an eyesore. And it looks as good as dead anyway."

Aaron silently agreed. The gnarled, twisted tree seemed well beyond salvation.

Sarah clapped her hands together. "All right, enough drama about that old tree. There's an entire garden waiting."

As everyone scattered to get to work, Cliff spared both Aaron and the tree another disgusted look. Aaron didn't give him the satisfaction of a reaction, but Maeve beelined straight to Cliff, probably hoping to pry some juicy gossip about whatever was going on between the two of them.

Meanwhile, the guy in all black—'The Psycho'—lingered, eyes glued to the tree. He stood there, all solitary-like amid the bustle, deep in thought before he quietly faded into the shadows.

"Bailey," Sarah shouted at him. "Don't make me beg every time, and put on the damn jacket!"

The guy stopped in his tracks, his face a fortress, giving nothing away. He didn't look back at Sarah or say a word, just slipped on the jacket, keeping behind as everyone else marched ahead.

Aaron passed him and picked up one of the few shovels left. It didn't take him long to figure out the others had snagged the better ones, leaving the scraps. So, he opted for the only shovel with an intact handle and without tape or string holding it together. But he stopped a few inches from grabbing it when heavy footsteps approached.

The Psy—Bailey—had caught up to him, and from the way he looked at the tools, Aaron could tell he wasn't thrilled either. As Aaron reached for the shovel, the other guy did the same. However, Aaron, a split-second quicker, snatched it first.

"First come, first served," Aaron taunted, gripping the handle firmly, refusing to be pushed around.

The guy said nothing, did nothing, but his stare was brutal enough to make Aaron step back. It was like a blade in his gut; that was how razor-sharp the vibe was. Still, Aaron held his ground, lifting his head slightly to meet the guy's gaze, unshaken by the silent threat in those clear eyes.

Their silent standoff was brief. Bailey grabbed the remaining shovel and stalked away, his Docs emphatically hitting the ground.

*

After three hours of hard work, the entrance pathway was mostly clean. It turned out far more exhausting than the group had bargained for, even more so because of Maeve's minimal effort. She had the nerve to blame her freshly done manicure, which earned her a few muttered curses.

When they were finally given a break for lunch, relief and cheers broke out. Aaron hung back, torn between following the majority towards a shaded area or mimicking the broody guy who'd chosen to stay near the conservatory.

"Come with us," Nyle said, ending his dilemma.

After a brief moment, Aaron shuffled over to join them at a low stone wall. Everyone else dug into their packed lunches like it was some sort of picnic. Aaron just sat there. He hadn't brought anything.

All the while, Cliff kept shooting him dagger looks.

"So," Nyle said, sensing the thick tension, "you two have a bit of history?"

"More than I'd like," Cliff muttered, his jaw clenched. "Tell me, Aaron, how can you even sleep at night after what you've done?"

"Easy. I count sheep."

Cliff's hands shook slightly. "If karma doesn't catch up to you, I might."

Sarah stepped in swiftly, placing herself between them. "Enough. Knock it off, or I'll make your lives even more miserable."

Cliff retreated but kept giving Aaron the stink eye while munching on his sandwich. Aaron did his best to ignore him.

"You not eating something?" Nyle asked, glancing over.

"Not in the mood," Aaron replied, but his growling stomach said otherwise. His recent diet of protein bars wasn't holding up well.

"Here." Nyle offered half of his BLT. "Take it."

"You keep it," Aaron replied, but Nyle persisted, placing it next to him.

"Don't bother," Maeve quipped. "If he's got a death wish, let him be."

Aaron raised an eyebrow. "What's that supposed to mean?"

She tilted her head in Bailey's direction next to the conservatory. "You might want to tread lightly around Landon."

Landon. Bailey. Landon Bailey. The threatening guy finally had a name.

"And why's that?" Aaron asked.

Maeve leaned in. "He's spent some time in juvie."

Aaron took a bite from the sandwich before replying, "And what? We're all golden boys and girls here?"

She rolled her eyes. "You know what I mean."

"I really don't."

"Word is, he killed someone," Maeve added, perhaps hoping to scare him.

"If that were true, he wouldn't be here with us pulling weeds, would he?"

Ria piped up, breaking away from her conversation with Cliff, "Wasn't it about drug possession and assaulting a police officer?"

"No, no, I told you already. Landon ended up inside for robbery," Nyle corrected.

Maeve waved him off. "Whatever…just steer clear. The guy's mental."

"I'm not scared of him," Aaron informed her, finding the topic already boring.

"You should be."

"Let's get one thing straight," he said, turning to look her in the eyes. "I'm not used to doing what others say. I can judge people for myself. Besides"—he pointed at her—"who's to say I'm not the more dangerous one here?"

"Oh yeah? And tell us, Aaron Walsh, what dark deeds brought you here?"

"He's been a dick," Cliff replied. "Aaron's the type to watch your back, then stab it. He's right when he says we might have more to fear from him."

"Fuck you," Aaron retorted.

"No thanks. I had enough when you screwed me at the party."

"That would be enough for me too." Nyle chuckled to break the tension.

"Stick to your fantasy rainbow world, 'My Little Pony'," Cliff snapped at him.

"Hey." Ria tugged at him. "There's no need to take it out on Nyle. He was joking."

Sarah approached, clapping to get their attention. "Seriously, kids? Can't behave for a few minutes?"

"It's him." Cliff pointed at Aaron, who continued eating his sandwich as if nothing had happened.

"Walsh," Sarah sighed. "You're walking a fine line, like Bailey. Don't push it. Go cool off somewhere else."

Aaron quickly finished his sandwich. He pulled out a cigarette and headed over to where he'd last seen the *scary* guy—Landon. As he got closer, Landon's glance at him was fleeting, almost dismissive, as if Aaron was nothing more than an annoying fly.

Small, insignificant, harmless.

It caught Aaron off-guard that Landon hadn't given a second glance at his scars. Maeve and Nyle had obvious reactions to them. Even Ria had taken a brief pause before offering her radiant smile. But Landon? He hadn't flinched, as if the scars weren't even there.

With the cigarette dangling from his lips, Aaron studied him.

The others had painted a picture of Landon being dangerous, maybe even deadly. But as he stood there, relaxed against the wall, puffing out smoke, he appeared like a bored dragon whose tail they'd tried in vain to cut off.

Aaron fumbled for his lighter, only to be met with disappointment when it didn't work. He caught Landon's eye and mimed the action of lighting the cigarette with his thumb.

Landon followed the motion with a lazy glance but made no move to help. Instead, he took his sweet time with his own cigarette, blowing smoke in Aaron's direction with every puff. When he was down to the last embers, he dropped the stub and crushed it beneath his shoe.

Without a word, he walked off, once again with a decisive stride.

Aaron, cigarette still unlit in his mouth, watched him go.

For all the rumours and tales about Landon, only one word summed up Aaron's impression: wanker.

Chapter Five

Point Nemo

[Now playing » You'd Be Paranoid Too (If Everyone Was Out to Get You)—Waterparks]

The afternoon went by as they painted over the graffiti-covered walls at the entrance.

Sarah had split them up into two groups of three. Maeve, to her delight, had been paired with Nyle and Cliff to take care of the plants under Muhammad's supervision. That left Aaron in a team with Ria and Landon.

He was glad to be away from Maeve and Nyle's constant chatter. Ria and Landon were much quieter, especially Landon. The guy hardly said a word, just the odd grunt here and there. But he did work fast. He was like a machine, clearing off the graffiti at a seriously impressive rate.

Considering their earlier run-in, Aaron was surprised by how focused Landon was. He'd expected him to be trouble, but watching him now, it was clear the guy was committed to the job. It was quite impressive.

"That one's kinda cool," Ria commented, pointing to a mural that featured large, dramatic animals rendered in stark black and white. "Street art is so captivating."

He wished his parents could have heard that. They'd never seen art in graffiti, let alone his sketches. Hell, they used to roll their eyes whenever they caught him doodling away. Every time they passed some street artist, they would make sure to hint that Aaron might end up like them, selling scribbles or tagging walls. They had these grand dreams of him in a crisp suit, maybe as a doctor or a lawyer—the kind of jobs they could brag about at family gatherings.

And here he was, wiping away the very graffiti they turned their noses up at, thanks to a community sentence and a shiny new criminal record. They would've been so ashamed of him. The irony of the situation brought a wry smile to his face. But as quickly as it appeared, it faded. Despite everything, he missed his parents. Or maybe, it was the idea of them.

Aunt Olivia had tried her best to be there for him, to fill the gap they left. She was always supportive, even when he put his drawing on pause after the accident. Maybe he should have been honest with her about his plans to move away.

He swiped his brush over a snippet of art, and his thoughts wandered to the notebook she had gifted him, still tucked away in his bag. Still empty.

As the day wound down, Aaron's team managed to clear off most of the graffiti, but Maeve and Nyle had done more chatting with Muhammad than plant work.

Sarah clapped her hands together. "Good job today. See you all next week. And Walsh," she added, making Aaron pause, "don't be late next time, yeah?"

With a quick nod, he set off. It was still early, so he figured he had some time to kill before finding a place to crash. He whipped out his phone and scrolled through a couch surfing app—his lifeline for the past week. As he was about to message someone for a spot to stay, Nyle sidled up to him.

"Hey, Aaron, fancy joining us for a bonfire tonight?" he asked.

Aaron glanced at Ria, Maeve, and Cliff behind him, surprised to see even Landon in the mix. "Who's 'us'?"

"Just *us* and a few others," Nyle replied. "Got grub and some bevvies."

The thought of free food appealed to Aaron, especially since he didn't have any other plans. And who knew, he might even manage to crash on Nyle's couch afterwards.

"All right," he finally said.

Nyle looked pleasantly surprised. "Stunning!"

As they all made their way to the Tube station, Maeve shot him a cheeky wink, Ria offered a kind smile, and Cliff eyeballed him. Landon, though, remained expressionless, but Aaron could have sworn annoyance flickered in his eyes.

*

Spread over three floors with four bedrooms, Nyle's place was much more than Aaron had imagined.

On the Tube ride over, Nyle had nonchalantly mentioned that he owned the place. Aaron hadn't questioned it, though he remained sceptical. Owning a house like this, even on the outskirts of North Greenwich, seemed like a stretch for someone so young.

As they stepped inside, a corridor opened up into a spacious living area, with the kitchen off to one side, a sofa on the other, and a large window framing a view of the sprawling back garden.

They dropped the beers they'd picked up onto the kitchen island. Landon and Ria set to work prepping the drinks, while Nyle disappeared into the garden to sort out some wood for the fire pit.

Maeve dove into the fridge and snagged cheese, dips, grapes, carrots, celery sticks, and mince pies to place on the counter. She then dumped bags of crisps into bowls. Aaron clocked how everyone seemed to know their way around, clearly not their first time here.

"Are you a veggie or vegan?" Maeve asked as she fiddled with the food.

"No."

"Any fancy diet?"

"Not really, no."

"Would you like a cocktail?" offered Ria.

"Sure."

Ria mixed a few drinks together, garnishing the result with mint and lime. "Here you go." She offered the drink to Aaron.

He sniffed it, catching mainly mint. "What's this?"

"Just try it," Nyle suggested, coming back into the room. "Ria and Landon used to be bartenders."

Aaron took a tentative sip and found he liked it.

Not long after, Nyle's friends, a cheerful couple, came in. They did the rounds of hellos, then launched into a lively discussion about movies and TV shows. Aaron caught snippets about their shared frustration with the change of main actor in their latest favourite series, strong feelings about another getting axed after only two seasons, and buzz around some new superhero movie coming out.

Another guy stepped in, proudly showing off artsy beer cans he'd brought, some craft brew he seemed keen on sharing. He appeared older than the others, likely in his thirties, and had a distinctive hairstyle with shaved sides and a lone tuft of hair in the centre. But Aaron found his T-shirt to be the most interesting thing about him. It sported the unmistakable silhouette of the Mandalorian helmet. A fan of the series himself, Aaron silently approved.

The atmosphere grew cosier and cosier by the minute. Chatting, laughing, and the mingling scents of mint, lemon, and beer filled the room. Aaron drifted between groups, eavesdropping here and there, quietly soaking in the overlapping dialogues without adding his two cents. He preferred being an observer.

Needing a break and some fresh air, Aaron headed outside. He found himself pulled towards the bonfire, like a moth drawn to a light.

Standing there, he lost himself in the flames as they leaped and swayed. Even when he blinked, the dance of the fire lingered, painting bright patterns on the inside of his eyelids.

The fire's warmth contrasted greatly with the chilly evening air. But even that warmth couldn't stop a shiver as memories of a similar fire at his parent's house when his mum had burned his drawings, calling them "dirty old paper." He'd tried to save them, but all he got were the gnarly burns on his knuckles.

Nyle's booming voice from the living room snapped Aaron back to the present.

"Luz, you made it!"

A blonde girl had just arrived, and everyone was all over her with cheerful heys, hugs, and kisses. A tall, skinny guy trailed behind her, who didn't get the same enthusiastic reception.

When he introduced himself, it became obvious he was as much a stranger to the group as to Aaron. The way he said his name—Jean or Jacques?—had a French ring to it, making Aaron guess where he might be from.

"And who's this?" the girl asked, zeroing in on Aaron as she marched over. "Another one of your *dates*?"

Before Aaron could get a word in, she stood right in front of him, pointing a finger at him. "If you so much as hurt my brother, you'll wish you never met him. Understand?"

Brother? That made Aaron do a double take. Nyle and the girl had the same blond hair and similar eyes—were they blue? Green?—but unlike Nyle's loud style, she wore a simple white dress.

"No, I—" Aaron began.

"So, what is it? A one-night-stand thing?"

"Luzanne!" Nyle cut in, sounding strained. He hurried over to them. "He's not like that. He's from my...*other job*."

The way Nyle stressed the last words led Aaron to believe he perhaps didn't intend to reveal too many details in front of her date.

"Oh." Luzanne seemed to understand. "The *other job*."

"What other job?" French guy piped in. "Luz said you work at the science museum. Do you do something else?"

"Volunteering," Nyle said too quickly, as if he wasn't comfortable with the lie.

"Ah, *magnifique*," French guy said, impressed. "Are they all from your volunteering?"

Nyle hurriedly introduced everyone and then steered his sister's date towards the kitchen. Landon didn't seem too keen on interacting with the new guy, even brushing off a question he asked.

After more time spent chatting and enjoying snacks, Nyle motioned for everyone to gather around the fire. One by one, they sat on cushions and blankets Ria had laid out on the grass. Aaron ended up not so randomly sandwiched between Nyle and Maeve.

Off to the side, Landon kept to himself, his back against the fence, cigarette in hand. He seemed even more annoyed than he'd been all day, his eyes frequently darting to Luzanne. Each time she shared a kiss or a whisper with the French guy, Landon's expression soured more, as if he'd tasted something bitter.

"Get a room, you two," Nyle joked when their kiss lingered a little too long. "Between movies and series, I see enough *straight* stuff. I don't need a live demo."

"Hey, no *heterophobic* comments allowed," Luzanne shot back with a grin.

"Well, as the only gay person here, I'm in the minority."

"Hey," French Guy called out, raising a hand, "I'm bisexual."

"Of course you are." Nyle gritted his teeth. "It's a French thing to appreciate both the *baguette* and the *brioche*, right?"

The glare Luzanne gave him cut off any further remarks.

Ria jumped in. "Don't forget I'm pan."

"Oh, right," Nyle commented, not too convinced. "Doesn't count if you keep dating only cishet men."

"You're one to talk about inclusivity. Who I am isn't about who I date," she teased in a friendly tone as if they'd had this conversation many times. "Guess I'm used to being excluded from any community."

The Beer Guy, with a casual tilt of his can, joined the conversation.

"Why do kids nowadays feel the need for all of these fancy labels? Seriously, the LGBTQ-plus acronym's getting as long as my niece's Christmas list—endless and full of stuff I've never even heard of."

Ria shot him a sharp look. "Edging on being a hater, Fell?"

"Far from it," Fell defended, holding up his beer as a peace offering. "Just saying. Sometimes, less is more, you know?"

Nyle chuckled and nodded. "He's got a point. I'm two hundred percent gay. Totally into dudes. Easy-peasy."

Maeve nudged his arm. "Count me in on the easy-peasy-label club. I'm straight and all about dudes."

"And I'm all about the ladies," Fell chimed in, raising his can with a grin.

Cliff agreed with a clink of his drink, and the two shared a silent *cheers*.

"What about you?" Nyle asked, looking directly at Aaron. "Playing for a particular team?"

Aaron shifted uncomfortably, avoiding eye contact. He didn't hide his sexuality, but even after figuring things out, he felt like a player perpetually benched, never truly part of the team. "Why does it matter?"

"Oh, oh, *oh*." Nyle winked. "No pressure. But just know you're among friends."

"More like strangers. I've only known you all for a day."

Nyle clapped his hands. "Perfect time for a 'Rapid-Fire Questions' game to spice things up."

Everyone nodded and cheered in agreement. And just like that, Aaron picked up some fun facts about the others: Nyle was a fashion design dropout, Maeve grew up as the only girl among six brothers, Fell had an encyclopaedic knowledge of classic rock, and Ria boasted a collection of six different *Blue Peter* badges.

Then it was Ria's turn to ask a question. "What's one place you've always wanted to visit but never have?'"

"Point Nemo," Aaron replied. He enjoyed the puzzled looks that followed, quite satisfied with his cheeky answer.

Nyle furrowed his brow. "What?"

Aaron wasn't surprised Nyle didn't know about Point Nemo. It wasn't exactly common knowledge, and he liked knowing something others didn't. Tori had introduced him to it, always sharing cool facts about space, koalas, and geography.

Maeve leaned in. "Most people would say Fiji, Maldives, or maybe New Zealand, and here you are with this imaginary location."

Nyle looked contemplative. "You're so much fun, Aaron. Makes me wonder what else you've got there."

"Point Nemo is a real place," Aaron protested.

Nyle chuckled. "Of course. Named after the cute Disney fish, right?"

Before Aaron could reply, a different voice cut through the air. "No, it's not after a Disney character. Point Nemo is named for Captain Nemo from *Twenty Thousand Leagues Under the Sea*."

Aaron turned his attention to Landon. It was the first time he had heard him speak at all. His voice, surprisingly deep and measured, had a distinctively posh accent as if he came out from the royal family, perfect for a book narrator or a meditation app. He had the kind of voice that would be soothing in another context. But in that moment, it touched Aaron's skin.

"So, what's Point Nemo?" Aaron asked, challenging Landon.

The slight arch of Landon's pierced eyebrow conveyed his disbelief at the question. "It's the most remote point in the ocean, farther from land than any other place on Earth." He sounded like a living Wikipedia. "Interestingly, when you're at Point Nemo, you're closer to astronauts in space than to anyone on land. No wonder it's become a space junkyard, where they send old satellites and spacecraft to die. Fascinating, isn't it?"

Everyone seemed impressed by Landon's detailed rundown, Aaron included, even though he already knew about Point Nemo. That place had always fascinated him, more for its closeness to the stars than the sea. As a kid, he dreamed about escaping there, imagining a portal to a parallel world where, maybe, he'd find the perfect family.

"Well, that was a trip down the Discovery Channel rabbit hole, both enlightening and slightly creepy. Thanks for that," Nyle said with heavy sarcasm. Then, he turned to Aaron. "Come on. Isn't there a more touristy spot you'd want to visit?"

"Australia," he murmured, fiddling with the pendant around his neck. "I'm planning to move to Sydney in a few months."

A few comments followed from the TV series enthusiasts, as they had visited Sydney and were full of advice to dispense. Aaron listened with little interest but pretended to be grateful for the suggestions.

"Since you've joined us, Landon"—Ria sent him a curious smile—"what's your place, then? The one you've never been to but always wanted to go?"

Landon's gaze drifted off for a moment. "Riverdreams Wonderland."

Nyle's eyes lit up. "Oh, the theme park? I loved their massive rainbow candy floss!"

Luzanne rolled her eyes. "Really, Nyle? The highlight was the haunted house."

"Yeah, it was brilliantly creepy," Fell added. "It's a shame the park didn't last."

Nyle nodded. "Lanny's still gutted because he'd saved all his pocket money for it, but it shut just the day before he could go. What a bummer."

Landon winced at the nickname but didn't say anything.

Aaron remembered the buzz when Riverdreams Wonderland opened. He was thirteen at the time, and like many, he dreamed of going there. But, like Landon, he never had the chance and ended up with only second-hand tales of its wonders. Now, all that remained were the derelict structures along the Thames, a playground for daredevils.

"Still, that's not a proper place, either, but at least it is reachable." Nyle glanced at Aaron. "Let's move on to less ambiguous questions. Favourite colour?"

This time there was no need to be enigmatic. Aaron answered honestly. "Black." It was the only colour he was always sure about.

A stifled chuckle sounded from Landon.

"You find that amusing?" Aaron turned sharply towards him. "You haven't even joined us properly."

Landon, unfazed, threaded his way between Ria and the Fell. Sitting cross-legged, elbow on his thigh, and chin cradled between fingers, he said, "Black isn't a colour." The flatness of his tone mocked Aaron as his earlier chuckle had.

"I'll take no colour critique from someone wearing all black from head to toe."

Landon's intense stare bore into Aaron, an unspoken challenge lingering in the air.

Perhaps sensing the escalating tension, Nyle jumped in. "I'm a fan of all colours. Rainbow's my favourite."

"Rainbow isn't a colour either," Luzanne pointed out. Then, it was her turn to pose the next question, even though Aaron was next in line. "Let's spice things up. When and how was your first time?"

Aaron's irritation spiked, not just at the clichéd question, but because it was supposed to be his turn. "Why's everyone so obsessed with 'the first time' thing? Does anyone even have good memories of all their firsts?"

Luzanne shrugged. "No, but first kisses, first time you have sex—these are kind of a big deal, right?"

Aaron scoffed. "Your firsts were all fireworks and magic, then?"

"Hell, no." She giggled. "First times are usually awkward messes."

A collection of "Yeah" and "True that" went around.

"So why are we making such a big deal about them?" Aaron challenged.

"Isn't it like...the gold standard?" Luzanne said. "Everyone needs to have something to compare to, right?"

"Maybe we're all just looking at it wrong. Why not rave about our *best* times instead of the firsts? Think about how cool that'd be."

Ria came on board, clapping. "Preach, Aaron!"

The others had mixed reactions; some seemed to mull it over while Nyle and Luzanne just wanted to move on.

"Okay, mood killer over here. New game, anyone?" Luzanne proposed.

"Got booze involved?" Nyle asked, lifting his beer can.

"How about 'Never have I ever'?" Luzanne suggested.

There were some groans, some cheers, but everyone was game. Surprisingly, even Landon, Mr. Too-Cool-for-School-Games, didn't back down.

Chapter Six

Sex

[Now playing » Pumped Up Kicks—Foster the People]

"I'll start," Nyle said, his gaze landing on Aaron. "Never have I ever… been with a guy."

"Here we go again," Luzanne muttered and sipped her drink.

Aaron froze, his drink in mid-air inches from his lips. Sure, he'd hooked up with a guy, but they hadn't gone 'all the way'.

"Define 'been with'," Aaron blurted out.

Nyle blinked. "Wait a minute… Do we have a virgin here?"

"Seriously, Nyle?" Ria interjected with a hint of annoyance. "Virginity is such an old-school concept. It's just more baggage society dumps on us."

"What are you talking about? It's rather simple. You've either had sex or you haven't."

"And what counts as 'having sex'? Who gets to decide that definition?"

"Come on, Ria. Don't turn everything into a philosophical debate or, worse, an excuse to organise a protest." Nyle groaned. "That's how you got into trouble last time."

Luzanne raised a hand to silence him, showing she was interested in what Ria had to say.

Ria pressed on. "You know, traditional definitions of 'virginity' are so limited. It's usually about a penis and a vagina. But what about other forms of intimacy? Or people who might never do the whole 'penis in vagina' thing? Do they not count?"

A few nods of agreement spread around the circle.

"I meant *penetrative* sex, then," Nyle mumbled, trying to defend his initial statement.

Meeting Aaron's gaze, Ria clarified, "To answer your question, the definition of sex can be whatever you want it to be. The focus should be on how you *feel* about your experiences. Not labels."

The group sat in an awkward, reflective silence.

Breaking the quiet, Nyle quipped, "Wow, Ria. This Christmas, I think I'll gift you a jumper that says 'I'm majoring in Gender and Sexuality Studies'."

"And I'll give you one that says 'twat'," Landon shot back.

"Thanks, Lanny."

"He's not wrong," Ria playfully added.

"When do you ever not side with Landon?" Maeve remarked, her voice tinged with bitterness.

"You three," Nyle pointed his beer first at Landon, then Ria, and finally Aaron. "Next 'party-pooper' intervention, you're out. This game is for fun and getting wasted."

Landon leaned back with an air of casual confidence, sipping his cocktail. "You should've laid out these winning rules from the start."

Nyle shot him a mock-stern look. "There are no winners in this game."

"Maybe there are though." Landon shifted his gaze to Aaron.

Luzanne chimed in, "Never have I ever...had *penetrative* sex."

Aaron shot Luzanne a 'seriously?' look as he drank. She was definitely calling him out.

"So you're not a virgin after all," Nyle teased him.

"Never have I ever..." Jean continued, "...thought about sleeping with someone here tonight."

Surprisingly—or maybe not—one by one, they all drank.

All but Aaron.

As the rounds continued, Aaron picked up on the trend. Every single "Never have I ever" was about sex. As in, never have I ever...had a quickie in a public loo, had a friends-with-benefits situation, or used glow-in-the-dark condoms.

So, while everyone's drinks kept disappearing, his stayed mostly full.

Catching on to Aaron's sobriety, the group, mainly thanks to instigator Nyle, switched things up. Using titbits they'd picked up earlier, they started throwing out softer pitches, such as never having sailed to Point Nemo or not visited Sydney.

As expected, Cliff threw a curveball into the mix. "Never have I ever...backstabbed a mate."

Maeve chuckled, glancing around the circle with an 'I know what that's about' expression.

That stung, but Aaron wasn't about to let Cliff see it. Meeting his challenging stare, he lifted his drink in a 'cheers to that' gesture.

Finally, it was Aaron's turn. Taking a deep breath, he looked round at everyone. "Never have I ever...tried to pick on someone in this game just to get them wasted."

Nyle took a dramatic swig of his drink, and a few others joined him. Ria and Landon, however, didn't.

"You're not upset, are you?" Nyle scratched his head. "We're just messing around."

"It's cool," Aaron replied. "I'm not bothered. But seriously, what's with all the sex questions?"

"Because it's fun?"

"I think sex is overrated."

Nyle frowned. "Are you for real?"

"He is," Cliff said, jumping in. "The dude's bi, and yet he's not using it to his full potential."

Aaron shot him an annoyed look. "There's more to life than sex, you know."

"Like what?" Nyle challenged. He seemed sceptical and curious at the same time.

"Like jamming to music, bingeing an entire series in one night, diving deep into a book, or just...running until you're tired."

"Sounds to me like you've never had a good fuck," Nyle commented instantaneously, perhaps without malice.

"Sounds to me like you want to go fuck yourself, and not in the way you might like," Aaron retorted, instead, *with* malice.

"If you want, I can make it enjoyable for you, too."

Luzanne sighed. "Nyle's being Nyle again."

Aaron grinned, unimpressed. "I got it, thanks. Not interested."

Nyle pouted, gesturing at himself. "You're refusing a hottie like me?"

"Yeah," Jean quipped. "Even I have to admit Nyle's a great catch."

"Hey," Luzanne protested, playfully slapping his arm.

"*Mon amour*, he's your brother." He kissed her cheek. "Beauty runs in your genes!"

A few people laughed. Aaron paused to really look at Nyle—his delicate facial features, chiselled jawline, and a lean body that hinted at regular gym visits. He could see why others might find him attractive, but for Aaron, Nyle's over-the-top approach overshadowed his looks.

"Offer's always on the table if you ever want a taste." Nyle leaned in a little too close. "I know how to make the good guys bad for a weekend," he sing-songed, casually lifting his drink. But his hand faltered, tipping the contents onto Aaron's hoodie.

Accidental or not, it was unwelcome.

"Ah, shoot," Nyle murmured, extending a hand to pat the stain on Aaron's chest, dangerously near the scars Aaron kept hidden away.

"Don't," he snapped, firm but controlled, masking the discomfort surging.

Nyle paused, his hand still mid-air. "Sorry, I was just—"

"I said don't," Aaron interjected again, more firmly this time, catching Nyle's wrist in a tight but measured grip. "You've got three seconds to remove your hand before I make sure you can't use it again."

The mood soured in an instant. Ria and Landon shared a look of concern, while Nyle withdrew his hand.

Standing up abruptly, Aaron strode towards a quiet part of the garden, each step a firm punctuation to his harsh words. The weight of everyone's stares felt like darts against his back as he moved away.

Subdued chatter immediately rose, but Maeve's voice emerged clearly.

"Maybe he was right. Maybe it's not Landon we should be afraid of anymore, but him."

Without turning around, Aaron slipped behind the summer house that loomed still in the corner, its door fastened with an old padlock. This place had either been forbidden or forgotten, and Aaron used it as a shield from the others.

Patting down his pockets, he found a crumpled cigarette. Out of habit, he placed it between his lips but sighed as he still had no lighter. He plucked it from his mouth and rolled it between his fingers.

"I don't think it will light itself if you keep staring at it," a soft voice remarked behind him. "Unless, of course, you're hiding special powers, like laser vision."

He turned to Ria, her height only reaching his chest. She could pass for a minor, and he wondered if she, like Cliff, suffered from a similar age-defying spell.

"Got a lighter?" he asked, half hoping.

She shook her head, her ponytail swinging from side to side. "I don't smoke. But if you want, I can ask Landon to lend me his."

Aaron glanced behind her, spotting Landon among the group, the guy he might've accidentally stolen the 'intimidating' crown from.

"Never mind…" He put the cigarette back in his pocket. "I should probably cut down anyway."

"Nyle made quite the impression, huh?"

"That's one way to describe it."

Nyle's bubbly energy perfectly mirrored his appearance—lanky, exuberant, and nuanced. He looked like someone who never met a stranger, only friends he hadn't made yet.

Ria tilted her head. "Nyle's all bark and no bite. But you know what they say, it's the quiet ones you have to watch out for."

"Then you better run," he told her, but without any threatening inflection.

"Who said I wasn't talking about me?"

"In my opinion, the creepy award of the evening goes hands down to your friend 'I dress in black because it's the *non-colour* of my soul'."

"Landon?"

"Yeah, Landon." Aaron tested the name on his tongue.

"Landon knows how to be silent, but he's also noisy when he wants to draw attention."

Thinking back to how Landon had ignored him after Aaron had asked for a lighter and the distinct sound of his boots on the ground, Aaron mused, "He's like a cat, isn't he?"

Ria burst out laughing. "Oh my god, that's spot on! I've never thought of him like that, but you're absolutely right!"

It took a while, but in the end, Ria managed to convince Aaron to give another chance to the evening, which continued with toasted marshmallows and less-intrusive games.

When the bonfire died out, the guests left one by one. Luzanne and Jean, hand in hand and giggling, headed upstairs. Landon's gaze followed them until they vanished beyond the stairwell, and then he stepped out into the garden, cigarette pack in hand.

In the dim glow of the living room, Aaron hesitated, the couch-surfing app open on his phone.

"Hey." Nyle approached cautiously after saying goodbye to his friends. "If you're looking for a place, you're welcome to crash here."

Aaron looked at him suspiciously, wary of his real motives.

Nyle tilted his head towards Aaron's phone. "Saw you checking that app. It's not some weird move. Promise."

Aaron obscured his phone screen and stared at him, annoyed.

"I'm sorry about what happened before," Nyle continued. "I was trying to flirt, especially after finding out you're bi. Seriously, you're fit and...intriguing. I mean, sure, your fashion sense could use some work, but you're attractive. Can't blame a guy for trying."

"Just because you find someone attractive doesn't mean you should make them uncomfortable."

"True. But I hoped you would be down for a shag."

"Told you already. Not interested."

"All righty." Nyle raised his hands. "I got the message. You can still sleep here though. We have an extra room that's empty. If you wait, I can sort it out and—"

"No, there's no need. The couch is fine for one night."

"Really?"

"Yes, I'm used to it by now."

"Stunning! Stay here. Don't move." Nyle ran up the stairs.

After a few seconds, a loud noise followed an equally loud curse as if Nyle had dropped something. He came limping back with a pile of sheets, blankets, and a pillow.

"The loo's down there." Nyle motioned with his head. "If you're thirsty or hungry, you know where the kitchen is, and there's a socket by the sofa for your phone. Anything else, give me a shout." He handed Aaron everything and disappeared around the corner.

After quickly setting up his makeshift bed, Aaron flopped down.

He'd barely closed his eyes when the rhythmic thudding from upstairs began, each beat accompanied by the occasional "Yes" and "Oui." He groaned.

Of course this would happen; Luzanne and Jean had been all over each other the entire night. Thankfully, their nocturnal symphony was brief. Silence soon blanketed the room, sleep not far behind.

Aaron shuffled, trying to get comfortable. Just as he managed to settle, a floorboard creaked. He opened his eyes, recalling Ria's words about Landon. But instead of Landon, a small black cat with one glossy eye and a tattered ear appeared.

"Hey there," Aaron said softly, sliding from the couch and crouching in front of it. He stretched out his hand and waited, letting the cat come closer at its own pace.

It hesitated, then sniffed and nuzzled his fingers.

"Couldn't sleep either?" Aaron muttered, returning to the couch. He patted a spot beside him.

The cat considered the invitation. Then, it jumped up next to him and curled up into a soft fur ball. Aaron petted it until they both fell asleep in the quiet of the night.

Chapter Seven

Crumbs of Lies

[Now playing » Wolf in Sheep's Clothing—Set It Off]

Of all the couches Aaron had ever crashed on, Nyle's was hands-down the most comfy.

He would've stayed buried in its cushions all day if it weren't for his *Super Mario* ringtone blaring, yanking him out of sleep. He groped under the pillow and pulled out his phone.

"Hello?" His voice, thick with sleep, was a dead giveaway. He quickly cleared his throat, trying to sound more awake.

"Aarie? How's everything?" Aunt Olivia's voice was crisp and energetic on the other end.

Knowing the time difference and Australia's weather by heart, Aaron had become a pro at spinning stories. It was a skill he'd picked up as a kid to keep his parents off his back, and now it came as easily as breathing. He wove tales of his 'adventures' in Australia, describing places he'd supposedly visited and food he'd 'tried', while his aunt hung on every word, occasionally reminding him and Cliff to stay safe.

As he chatted away, Aaron found himself wandering into the kitchen. He never could stay put on a call. He was about to hop onto the kitchen counter for a more comfortable chat when he spotted a figure lurking near the fridge.

"Uh, Auntie, I have to go, dinner's ready here." He hastily ended the call, eyes fixed on the shadowy figure now staring back at him.

It took him a second to register Landon standing there in the dimly lit kitchen. Ria wasn't wrong about him—silent one moment, noticeable the next. More than a cat, he seemed like a panther ready to pounce. Landon wasn't just sizing Aaron up. He gazed at him intensely, almost like he was trying to peel back layers of secrets Aaron himself might not even know.

Their eyes met and held, stretching into what felt like forever. Aaron's gaze then drifted to Landon's arms, the tattoos an unexpected discovery. Last night, they'd been hidden by a long-sleeved hoodie. But now with him in a T-shirt, they stood out, covering every visible inch of skin from hands to biceps. Perhaps even beyond. The maze of designs told stories Aaron couldn't make out but was curious about.

"Aren't you a bit old to lie to mum and dad?" Landon teased, starting to work with what looked like a fancy espresso machine.

"Wasn't talking to them; they're not around anymore. I'm on my own," Aaron corrected quietly.

Landon arched a brow, his piercing glinting as he poured a bag of coffee beans into the grinder. "Oh please, everyone in this house has some sobbing backstory. You're not special."

The loud grind distracted Aaron from Landon's jab. Still, he couldn't shake off a twinge of irritation as he watched Landon get a bottle of milk and two mugs, one of which had a Grumpy Cat print on it.

A soft meow broke the tension. The same cat from last night hopped onto the counter.

"Hey, buddy," Aaron said, offering his index finger. The cat sniffed it before butting its head against his hand, asking for some pets.

Landon observed their interaction, his face unreadable, then went back to the coffee-making. "Cappuccino?" His tone was neutral, as if he might have only asked because he'd prepped the machine for two servings.

"No, thanks. I don't like coffee."

"So, lack of taste isn't limited to clothes."

Aaron tried to formulate a retort, but before he could, Nyle burst into the room with all the subtlety of an elephant.

"Good morning, Sunshine! Sleep well?"

His vibrant aura was even flashier than the unicorn on his jumper that proclaimed, *I'm not strange. I'm a limited edition.* A dishevelled Luzanne trailed behind him, her long hair in a tangle and her pyjamas crinkled.

"Ugh... How can you be so upbeat in the morning?" She groaned, reaching for the kettle.

"If you rise, you might as well shine." Nyle quipped.

He leaned over the counter towards Landon and casually ordered, "A Latte, please," as though he was at his favourite coffee shop. He then plucked a banana from a bowl and gestured with it at Aaron.

"I've given it some thought." Nyle paused, enjoying the suspense. "And I think you should stay here."

Landon's scoff sliced through the noise of the steaming milk.

Even Luzanne rolled her eyes. "You're so predictable."

"But Luz, shouldn't you be supportive of another *potential* housemate romance?"

"Dude, he's not into you," Luzanne shot back. "And I can't believe you're mentioning that. My 'housemate romance' never got a happy ending." She grabbed some tea bags, throwing Landon a sour look.

"That's because it was straight," Nyle countered playfully. "Gay love stories have better endings."

Landon interjected, "Depends on the story."

"Killjoy," Nyle retorted, continuing to brandish the banana at Aaron. "But really, you should stick around."

"Why are you offering me a place to stay?" Aaron asked, confused.

"Because you need one."

"I have options." He had none. As a jobless teen with no credentials or rental history, finding a place was a tough ask and other short-term solutions way out of his budget.

"Look, we've had a room free since our last housemate left, and we're willing to offer you a mates' rate."

"I have an aunt in London. Was just on the phone with her moments ago, and she said I can crash at hers," Aaron replied, perhaps a tad too hastily.

Landon chuckled, working on the frothy milk for his latte art. "Sure."

"Listen." Nyle nudged the banana tip against Aaron's chest. "I'm all for helping someone in trouble. From the second I saw you, it was clear you're going through a rough patch. There's no shame in that. We've all been there. And I sure wish I'd had someone to offer help when I needed it. Don't be too proud to accept a hand when it's offered."

"I'm not a charity case."

"Just listen to Nyle," Luzanne intervened, pouring steaming water into two cat-shaped mugs. "He's got a real soft spot for *lost causes*." Her eyes flicked to Landon again before she headed back upstairs.

Landon didn't say anything. He just slid the freshly made latte towards Nyle with a smirk playing on his lips.

Aaron felt the dig, meant for both him and Landon, but before he could dwell on it too much, the cat brushed its cheek against his palm, drawing his attention. He smiled at it, momentarily soothed by the soft fur under his fingers.

"Weird," Nyle observed. "Kat doesn't like strangers. It took me almost a year to get her to stop biting and scratching me. Look—" He raised his elbow, showing a faded mark. "This was a bad one, bled a lot. But she seems to like you."

"Cat?" Aaron questioned.

"Yeah, but spelled with a *K*. You know, a bit of wordplay. Clever, huh?"

No, not really. Why was he so fixated on spelling? Aaron watched as Nyle reached out to pet Kat, but she hissed and skittered away.

"See? She's got zero love for me. The little traitor." Nyle looked both offended and genuinely puzzled.

"You can't just go in for a pet because you want to. It's all about the approach. You need to wait for her to come to you." Aaron slowly extended his hand, and Kat headbutted it, then hopped onto his lap and curled into a ball of fur. "Boundaries, you know?"

Nyle caught his eye as if they both knew Aaron was talking about more than just the cat. As Kat started purring loudly, Nyle laughed.

"Look at her," Nyle exclaimed in surprise. "She's purring. Oh my god, that's a sign you should stay."

"And since when does Kat have a say in potential housemates?" Landon remarked with a dry tone.

"If it were up to you, we'd never have any housemates. So, I've started relying on Kat's judgement. Besides, I've noticed anyone she likes, you don't. Just confirms that Aaron's a good fit."

"What kind of nonsense theory is this?" Landon scoffed and took a sip of his coffee. The Grumpy Cat image on the mug mirrored his expression almost perfectly.

"Kat doesn't like Ria, for example. But you do."

"Ria's allergic to cats."

"Whatevs. Point is, Aaron's welcome here."

Aaron opened his mouth to speak, but Nyle's enthusiasm swept over his objections like an avalanche of alphabet-shaped potato bites. He knew he didn't have much of a choice.

"Okay, I'll stay," Aaron conceded, reluctant gratitude threading his tone. "But just so we're clear, it's only until I've served my community service hours. Then, I'm off to Australia."

"Stunning." Nyle's smile didn't wane; if anything, it grew warmer. "Stay for as long or as little as you need."

"Just don't end up like our last housemate," Landon remarked with a hint of menace, walking away to rinse the milk jug and coffee handle.

"What happened to him?" Aaron asked, curiosity piqued.

"I killed him and buried the body in the garden." Landon pointed to a spot beyond the window.

"Aha." Aaron didn't even glance at the spot he'd indicated. Instead, his attention was captured by the extravagant print on Landon's socks. "Right. And I suppose the broccoli on your socks is part of your killer wardrobe?"

Landon glanced down, then shot Aaron a sharp look.

"How about a house tour?" Nyle suggested, slicing through the tension.

Aaron agreed with a nod. To further emphasise his nonchalance, he grabbed a banana and began to peel it. As he was about to take a bite, Nyle tried to warn him, but it was too late. The bitter taste of the unripe banana filled his mouth.

"Haven't they taught you that green bananas aren't ripe?" Landon couldn't resist the opportunity to comment.

"I like them this way." Reality was he couldn't tell the colour difference. Green and yellow always mixed him up.

"Bollocks." Landon circled the island and strode out of the kitchen.

"Come on, let's go." Nyle tugged at Aaron's arm.

Aaron turned back to pick up his bag and loop it over his shoulder, then followed Nyle down the corridor to a room next to the entrance.

Landon's footsteps on the stairs resonated through the walls, each one forceful, as though Landon was trying to leave an impression on the creaking wooden boards. But soon, the sound faded, growing distant until the upper level swallowed it.

"This is where our last housemate stayed," Nyle gestured around the room. "I know it looks a bit bare right now. The guy cleared out all his stuff."

Aaron took the sight in. The snug room, its walls unadorned, had a bow window overlooking the street. A two-seater sofa and desk sat in one corner, a lonely shelf hanging above them.

"Don't worry about the sofa. It pulls out into a bed. We just need more sheets. But I'm off today, so if you're free, maybe we could head to the shopping centre and pick up some things you might need?"

"Are you sure about this?" Aaron asked. More than him, he worried about Landon's chilly attitude. "I don't want to cause any trouble."

"Just steer clear of Landon, and you'll be fine."

"Was there a problem with the guy who stayed here before? Did he and Landon not get along?"

Nyle hesitated, then said, "It's not just Landon. Keep your distance from Luzanne too."

Aaron thought back to Luzanne's comment about a not-so-happy romance with a housemate, and he'd picked up on some tension between Landon and Luzanne.

"Landon and Luzanne..." he mused aloud, trying to piece the puzzle together. "Were they...you know, involved at some point?"

Nyle's eyes went comically wide, and a look of pure horror crossed his face. "No, no, and a thousand times, no. Gross!" Seeing Aaron's obvious confusion, he added quickly, "Landon's my cousin."

A soft "oh" escaped Aaron's lips. It made sense now, why the two lived under the same roof and also why Landon tolerated Nyle. The two of them couldn't have been more different—Nyle, bursting with life, from his wardrobe to his personality, and Landon, all in black, quiet, and introspective. Nyle would chat up a storm, while Landon measured his words. It was like comparing day to night.

"You're probably wondering," Nyle said, "how we can be related, what with him being Black and Luzanne and I being white. But we're blood cousins. Our moms are sisters."

That hadn't exactly been on Aaron's mind, but he let it slide.

"So? Shopping? We can buy some new clothes," Nyle suggested with an exciting squeak.

Aaron pointed at his shoulder bag. "I'm good with what I have."

Nyle sized Aaron up and down with exaggerated scrutiny. "That bag can't have too much. A new T-shirt or two wouldn't hurt. With looks like yours, you should be dressing to impress. Trust me, you need a wardrobe refresh."

Choosing not to react to Nyle's comment, Aaron let himself be shown the rest of the house. As they reached the first floor, Nyle led

Aaron to a door which revealed his own room. It was everything Aaron had anticipated. A corner rack held a variety of extravagant clothes, and posters of some actors and singers added character to the walls. And the bed, oh the bed! An army of plushies covered it, each one looking as cheerful as its owner.

Next, they moved on to the bathroom. A couple of hair care products, beauty creams, and candles took up the bathtub's edge. Their spicy scent reminded Aaron of a Starbucks pumpkin spice latte.

"We'll be sharing the bathroom. Luzanne and Landon each have their own, en-suite." He pointed towards a closed door across the hall, indicating Luzanne's room.

As they were about to go back downstairs, Aaron pointed to the stairs leading up. "Aren't we checking out the second floor?" He already took a step towards it.

"Wait, Aaron, hold up!" Nyle's voice cracked with a hint of panic, but Aaron had already reached the door at the top with a stark black sign reading *Fuck Off*.

Nyle hurried to get in front of him, a nervous half-smile on his face. "That's Landon's room. Best to think of it like the west wing in *Beauty and the Beast*. Off-limits, unless you have a death wish. Oh, and the summer house in the garden? Same rules apply."

Far from being deterred, Aaron's curiosity spiked. His parents had always been strict about what was off-limits, which only made forbidden things more tempting to him. But Nyle was already ushering him back downstairs.

For the time being, the mysteries of the upper floor and the summer house would have to wait.

When they returned to the kitchen, Kat brushed up against Aaron's leg, seeking some attention.

Aaron bent down to scratch her chin. "Where did you find her?"

"Oh, no, it wasn't me who brought her home. It was Landon."

This surprised Aaron. Given Luzanne's earlier comment about 'lost causes', he'd assumed the cat belonged to Nyle.

"He found her caught up in a catfight near the station," explained

Nyle. "She lost an eye and half an ear in that mess."

Anger bubbled up at the thought of the other cats that had hurt her. Aaron was grateful that Landon had stepped in. The idea of what could've happened if he hadn't intervened saddened him.

"I'm going to take a quick shower," Nyle said. "Once I'm out, you can hop in. And hey, try my argan oil shampoo. It works wonders on curls like yours." He winked, an easy smile playing on his lips. "Once we're both freshened up, let's head out to the shops, yeah?"

*

By lunchtime, Aaron seriously regretted his decision to accept Nyle's invitation to one of the biggest and most chaotic shopping centres in London. In a shopping whirlwind, Nyle pulled Aaron into pretty much every store they hit. And it wasn't just the spree itself. Nyle turned every changing room into his own personal catwalk, constantly taking selfies and posting them on socials.

"Got to keep my followers in the loop," he'd say with a grin after snapping another photo.

Aaron stood there, half-amused, half-overwhelmed, watching Nyle do his thing. The guy was some sort of beauty and queer fashion influencer, and it was wild to see him in action.

"You'll look good in these." Nyle shoved a pair of black jeans and a stack of hoodies into Aaron's arms. "They're so you."

A little thrown by the whole thing but trusting Nyle's eye for style, Aaron ended up at the till, handing over his card. He hoped the colours were as Nyle described.

More floors awaited them, and Aaron was starting to feel worn out. The distant whines of kids being nudged along by their parents somehow matched his inner cry. Browsing racks and hopping from one store to another wasn't his thing, especially without a clear purpose. So, when Nyle suggested going to the cinema, relief swept through Aaron. It meant a break from both the shopping and the nonstop conversation. Nyle was decent, sorting him out with a place to stay and even suggesting some new outfits. But he talked too much.

When their day wrapped up at a burger place, Nyle kept teasing that it felt like a date. Aaron chuckled to himself—if this was Nyle's idea of a romantic day, he was easily pleased. Especially since he'd spent most of the time grunting and nodding or answering in monosyllables, not paying much attention to him.

As they dug into their burgers and crinkled cheese fries, Nyle started talking about how tough it was to sync up schedules with Luzanne and Landon for some quality family time.

"So, what is it that you do again?" Aaron asked, wiping burger sauce off his hand.

"I work at the science museum in the kids' section. I get to do all sorts of cool experiments. Days off vary though. But Luz has it even wilder. Front desk at a fancy hotel, with both morning and evening shifts, and her hours are always changing. Landon's the only one with the most consistent schedule."

"What's his job?"

"He's a tattoo artist."

That took Aaron by surprise for the second time that day. With Landon's evident skill in making cocktails and coffee, he'd assumed he worked in a swanky bar or cafe. But a tattoo artist? That explained all the ink on his arms.

"You know," Nyle said after swallowing a final bite, "I asked him to tattoo me once. Thought I'd snag the 'family discount'. But the git said no."

"Oh? What were you after?" Tattoos intrigued Aaron, though he wasn't sure they were for him. His skin already bore enough marks as it was.

Nyle rolled up his sleeve, revealing his bicep. "A massive Chinese dragon, right here."

"A Chinese dragon, huh? Any special reason?"

Nyle shrugged. "Thought it'd look sick."

"Seems like a pretty big decision for just 'sick', doesn't it?"

Nyle blinked. "You sound like Landon. That's exactly what he said."

"Well, sounds like he had a point, then."

*

Back home, Aaron was finally left alone. As Nyle's footsteps headed upstairs, a sigh of relief escaped him. He toyed with the idea of an evening run, but given Nyle's non-stop chatter earlier, he felt more like winding down with a movie.

Walking into his room, though, something seemed off. His bag sat by the desk, just where he'd left it, but the strap was flipped the wrong way. Heart racing, he checked inside. Nothing seemed amiss, but he was certain someone had been through it. And that someone *had* to be Landon.

Aaron left the room with clenched fists and considered heading to the second floor to confront him, but a noise from the kitchen redirected him. Glancing through the slightly open patio doors, he spotted the faint glow of a cigarette in the garden.

Landon leaned against the fence, just as he had the previous night.

Aaron approached him, stopping a short distance away. "Why did you go through my stuff?"

Landon simply took another drag of his cigarette, not turning to face him, then said, "Did I?"

Frustrated, Aaron pressed on. "I noticed my bag was moved. Why?"

Landon exhaled a plume of smoke into the already cloudy night, still not looking at him. "Just checking."

"For what?"

Landon finally looked up, his eyes narrowed. "Are you part of a cult?"

"What? No!"

"Drugs?"

Aaron frowned, not sure where he was heading with those weird questions.

"Or are you some rich kid looking for a thrill?" Landon continued.

"Why are you asking me all of this?"

"I don't like you."

"That's mutual."

"You know, Nyle trusts easily. But me? Not so much." Landon took a step closer to Aaron. "You have an aura, something off. Can't put my finger on it."

In a swift move, Aaron snatched the cigarette from Landon's hand and inhaled deeply. Landon merely shook his head at the bold move.

"Did you kill your parents?" Landon asked him, his tone casual, as if discussing the weather.

"Why? Have you?"

Landon fixed Aaron with a look that bordered on boredom, ready to move on.

Aaron's frustration simmered. "Why am I the only one answering questions here? That's not fair."

"Life, Aaron, isn't about fairness."

"Didn't take you for the philosophical type."

"Just goes to show, doesn't it? No need for questions. You're learning about me without them."

"Actually, I've heard two or three things about you," Aaron said and took a deep drag from the stolen cigarette.

A ghost of a smile played on Landon's lips. "And now you've heard one more."

"Is what they say true?"

Landon stared at him, frowning. "Elaborate."

"They warned me about you, say I should steer away because you're dangerous, a *real* criminal, maybe even a killer. How much of that is true?"

"If I were, wouldn't you be playing with fire right now? You're either brave or just daft."

Aaron tilted his head. "Presumption does not suit you."

"Maybe they're right. I've been in a scrap or two. Might be wise to listen."

But Aaron, having grown up in a household where appearances were deceiving, could easily read between the lines. His parents had been masters at painting a picture of a happy family to the outside world, with the reality at home far from it.

Landon was a puzzle, no doubt, but Aaron recognised his

defensiveness and something familiar in his gaze, a certain well-known darkness.

He knew all too well that shadow which hinted at a life lived too hard and too fast, nourished by a steady diet of anger and distrust. They were cut from the same cloth. He wasn't intimidated.

"I don't only go by what I hear," Aaron said. "I like to get the full story. And if you're lying, well, that's on you."

"Speaking from experience? You seemed quite the actor this morning, Pinocchio."

Aaron huffed. "I'm not buying it."

"Honestly, I couldn't care less what you or the others believe."

"Not even if it's your family? Nyle also told me to be careful around you."

"Nyle's barely family. He's just my birth mum's sister's son."

Aaron paused, processing the roundabout explanation. "Still."

"Maybe you should follow Nyle's lead if you're planning to stick around a bit longer."

Aaron grinned. "Who says it's not you who should be wary of me?"

Landon surveyed him. "What did you do? Nicked some gummy bears from a candy shop?"

"Who knows? 'I've been in a scrap or two. Might be wise to listen'."

Landon snorted. "Parroting is childish," he said and started walking towards the house. "Time for bed, Aaron. Night's for the grown-ups."

But Aaron wasn't about to let it go. "Don't underestimate me."

Landon shot back, "I could say the same to you."

"Know the story of *Little Red Riding Hood*?"

Landon hesitated and turned towards him, a puzzled expression on his face.

Aaron continued. "It isn't always the scary ones you need to worry about. Sometimes the real danger comes in disguise. It's the seemingly kind ones that'll get you."

"If you think you're the wolf, you've got the wrong character."

"And who would I be then? The girl in the red hood?"

Landon took back the cigarette, now just a stub. He drew the last long puff, then flicked the butt in a cup on the ground, his eyes not leaving Aaron's. "No, you're the fucking grandma."

The words hung in the air as if they'd been shouted, even though they'd been anything but loud. They kept ringing in Aaron's ears as Landon retreated into the house without so much as a backwards glance.

Aaron stood frozen, the sting of defeat hitting him like a gut punch. He'd stepped into the garden ready for a confrontation, fists clenched and chin up. But he found himself thrown off balance. Not so much by what Landon had said but by the challenge unspoken between them.

Watching Landon disappear into the house, Aaron knew one thing for sure: this little game between them was only getting started.

Chapter Eight

Unexpected Kindness

[Now playing » Monster—dodie]

In the following days at Nyle's, Aaron did his best to adjust to the odd vibe in the house.

A tense atmosphere hung around, as if everyone was treading on eggshells. Nyle tried hard to bring the family together, but it wasn't taking off, especially with Landon. The guy preferred his own company, always ducking out to his room or hanging in the summer house.

Luzanne, though generally getting along with Nyle and Aaron, was hardly around due to her odd hotel shifts. But she definitely wasn't on Team Landon. Whenever they bumped into each other in the kitchen, she'd shoot him deadly glares or annoyed scoffs.

So, more often than not, Nyle and Aaron ended up alone at the dinner table.

And things between Aaron and Landon weren't exactly that great either.

They butted heads more often than not, and it felt like Landon was trying to spook him. But Aaron wasn't one to back down easily. In fact, he made it his mission to get under Landon's skin, just like Landon did to him.

On his third morning at Nyle's, after a refreshing run, Aaron walked into the kitchen to find Landon perched on the counter casually eating breakfast, a box of cereal on one side of him and a bottle of milk, carelessly left open, on the other.

"Morning," Aaron greeted, more for politeness than anything, as he made his way to the sink.

Landon, true to form, continued stirring his spoon in his mug, not bothering to look up. Aaron noted yet another quirky design on the mug—a black cat sipping coffee with a caption that read *That's what I do. I drink coffee, I hate people, and I know things*. Pretty fitting. How many other funny mugs were around? And were they all Nyle's doing?

Maybe that would explain Landon's socks as well, the only break in his otherwise all-black attire. Aaron couldn't make out today's pattern—donuts, maybe?—because he got distracted by the soggy cereal in Landon's mug, drowning in milk.

"Ugh, disgusting," Aaron commented as he took a sip of water.

Landon finally glanced up. "You're not exactly a pretty sight either." He gestured at Aaron's sweat-stained T-shirt.

"You know, cereal doesn't need to be soaked like it's pasta," Aaron joked, trying to keep the mood light.

Ignoring him, Landon stirred his mug even more and then drank the contents with obvious enjoyment. Aaron watched, half annoyed, half amused, as Landon's Adam's apple bobbed exaggeratedly with each swallow. Landon's theatrical sigh after finishing confirmed to Aaron that he was being provoked.

Deciding to play his game, Aaron grabbed a mug, poured in some milk, and tossed in the cereal bit by bit, getting it just damp. He made sure to chew loudly, crunching down on each bite.

Landon put up with the performance for a couple of seconds, then hopped down from the counter and headed out of the kitchen. Once he was out of sight, Aaron chuckled to himself and leaned on the counter. These silent battles were odd but strangely satisfying.

But Aaron found times where he dared to push the boundaries further.

That night, when he went out to the garden for a quick smoke, he couldn't resist sneaking a peek into the summer house through its small window. He only managed to catch a glimpse of a desk, a laptop, and what looked like a sketchbook, all shrouded in darkness. Maybe it was some sort of secret art studio. But before he could see more, Landon popped up out of nowhere, startling him like an unexpected camera flash going off in his face, leaving Aaron blinking and disoriented.

"Curiosity killed the cat," Landon whispered right into Aaron's ear.

That sent a shiver down Aaron's spine. But as he stepped back and scrutinised Landon, with his weary expression, he sensed something deep and complex under the surface. Everyone told him Landon was bad news, even his own family, but Aaron had a feeling there was more to him than what people saw.

"But satisfaction brought it back," he retorted, trying to keep his cool before turning to leave.

Despite standing his ground, the encounter left Aaron with a bitter aftertaste and a knot of unease in his stomach. Landon had an undeniable air of intrigue that puzzled him. Why was Aaron so captivated by someone like him?

*

The end of the week had already rolled around, and Aaron hadn't managed to land a job. His mornings had been a relentless quest across the city, seeking any work to make up for the missed flight and the fine for weed possession. He remained cautious about draining his savings, which he needed for his planned new start in Australia. While crashing at Nyle's had helped him save on rent, Aaron knew that luck wouldn't cover everything else.

He'd been everywhere—cafés, shops, anywhere that might need an extra pair of hands, willing to take on any role that didn't require specific qualifications. But he only met a string of rejections.

As Aaron trudged back to Nyle's place that evening, he started to lose hope.

He had half a mind to collapse into bed and escape into a TV series, but as he approached the house, the blaring of a television greeted him. He kicked off his shoes and shed his hoodie at the entrance, then continued to the living room.

Nyle lounged on the sofa with a salad bowl on his lap, absorbed in a reality show where fit people in bikinis and swim trunks yelled at one another on a tropical beach. In the kitchen, Landon was busy making a beast of a sandwich with his headphones on. The amount of filling he'd stacked up seemed like a challenge to the two slices of bread trying to contain it.

"Hey, Aaron," Nyle greeted him loudly, his voice competing with the show. "How's it going? You catch up on some sleep? Grabbed any dinner yet?"

Not even a minute in, and Nyle bombarded him with questions.

"Why's the TV so loud?" Aaron asked.

Nyle put his half-eaten bowl on the coffee table, snatched up the remote, and muted the show. Pointing to the ceiling, he cupped his hand to his ear. A series of noises from upstairs broke the silence, sounding like furniture being shuffled and something thudding against the wall. Then, unmistakably, moans filtered down through the ceiling.

"Luzanne and Jean?" Aaron guessed.

"Yeah, they've been at it since they came back an hour ago," Nyle said, cranking the TV volume back up and looking resigned. "Quite the noise, huh?"

"Doesn't it bother you?"

Nyle shrugged. "She's having a good time, I guess. And honestly, I've probably made more noise myself at times."

Aaron didn't know what to say to that, so he sank into the seat next to Nyle. Kat jumped onto his lap at once, purring and demanding some affection.

"So," Nyle prodded again, "where've you been all day?"

"Job hunting." Aaron petted Kat absentmindedly. "Total waste of time though."

"You were actually out looking for a job?" Nyle sounded genuinely surprised.

Aaron nodded. "I don't have a resume. Figured I'd try my luck in person. Don't need a resume to wait tables, do you?"

Nyle shot him a look full of amusement and pity. "Darling, this is London. Jobs don't exactly fall from the sky."

"I thought showing up might help."

"Any luck with that?"

"Everywhere I went, it was the same story. Either 'apply online' or a flat 'no' after one look at me."

Nyle didn't comment. *I told you so* was written all over his face.

"Any chance there's an opening at the museum or maybe Luzanne's hotel? I'm willing to give anything a go."

Landon snorted softly and placed a bowl on the floor for Kat. Quick as a flash, Kat hopped off Aaron's lap and made a beeline for it. "Right, so Nyle's what, now? A letting agent and a job centre?"

Nyle sent Landon a glance that said *enough*, then focused back on Aaron. "Wish I could help, but there's nothing going at the museum right now. And the hotel? They're pretty picky about how you look. Luzanne can't even wear her hair down or have a nose stud. It's all about keeping up appearances, you know."

Aaron responded with a low grunt, not exactly shocked but still feeling the sting. He was well aware his scars didn't exactly make for a warm first impression, but each reminder felt like a new jab.

"How did you get those scars?" Nyle asked, his curiosity finally having the best of him.

Aaron was about to give one of his practised, dismissive answers. But then, the brakes of a car screeched outside, the sound piercing through the room like a siren from the past.

In an instant, Aaron wasn't in the room anymore. In his head, he was back there, upside down on the hard asphalt. He traced the scars on his cheek like a map of that night, while he clenched the pendant at his neck in his other hand. His T-shirt clung tighter around his torso as the room's temperature skyrocketed. He needed fresh air. Now.

Without a word to Nyle, Aaron bolted from the sofa, through the door, and outside into the garden. Despite the chill in the air, his body reacted as if he were in a sauna, and he panted heavily, his heart thumping wildly.

Bending over, he tried to steady his breathing but to no avail. He picked up a leaf, crushed it, then dug his nails into the soil, anything to keep his mind grounded.

A rustling sound made him spin around, and thinking it was Nyle, he snapped, "If you're out here to give me a pep talk, I don't—" His eyes landed on a pair of donut-patterned socks.

"I didn't come out here to cheer you up," Landon said.

"And here I was thinking you didn't like me."

"I don't." Landon lit up a cigarette and took a deep puff. "But I believe no one should be judged solely on their appearance."

Aaron eyed him. Was Landon talking about him or about himself? "So, you're not going to ask about the scars?"

Landon exhaled a puff of smoke, his expression thoughtful in the dim light. "Do I look like Nyle? If you wanted to talk about it, you would've already."

Aaron bit his lip and tasted a metallic tang. "I should be used to it by now. Scars always invite questions."

"You don't have to answer them." Landon blew out more smoke and scrutinised Aaron. "Though, I'm surprised you haven't used this as a chance to tell another story."

Aaron smiled, stretching the scars. "The classic 'I tripped down the stairs' doesn't really cut it."

"Who knows?" Landon's gaze remained unreadable in the night. "Sometimes, people are so dense they might not believe you even when you're telling the truth."

They fell into a comfortable silence, the night enveloping them like a soft shroud.

Finally, Landon spoke up again, flicking his cigarette away. "Tomorrow. Ten a.m. At the front door."

Aaron took a moment to process the cryptic invitation. "What? Are we having a cowboy duel at high noon or something?"

The corners of Landon's mouth lifted slightly. "Or something," he replied, locking eyes with Aaron.

With that, he disappeared back into the house, leaving Aaron alone with his thoughts. What was Landon planning?

Chapter Nine

Bourbon and Custard Cream

[Now playing » Turn—The Wombats]

At ten sharp, Aaron was at the front door, punctual as ever.

He didn't have to wait long before Landon showed up. They walked together to the station, wrapped in silence. The Tube ride was no different, the quiet only broken when Landon offered Aaron one of his earbuds.

At first, it seemed a nice gesture, but as he listened, Aaron caught on to the tunes: "Bad Liar" by Imagine Dragons, "Fire, Ready, Aim" by Green Day, and "Two Birds" by Regina Spektor. All about lying. Silently, he handed back the earphone, unimpressed by the not-so-subtle jab.

Stepping out at Camden Town station, he followed Landon through the busy streets, passing all the funky shops. He had a feeling they were heading to Landon's workplace, and sure enough, they halted in front of a large sign for tattoos and piercings.

As they stepped into the shop, the bold black theme dominating the décor struck Aaron immediately. From the walls to the furniture, everything had an edgy vibe. Despite the starkness, the place felt alive, especially when they were greeted by two cheerful guys at the reception. Their smiles brightened up the room.

"Hey, Lanny!" one of them called out, his hand adorned with rings waving in the air. "Got a customer waiting already."

Aaron and Landon glanced towards the sofas against the wall, where a girl in a school uniform sat cross-legged, hugging a backpack that was practically exploding with cute plushies. Nyle would have totally adored that bag.

"And who's this?" the other receptionist asked, eyeing Aaron curiously.

"Just someone looking for a job," Landon said, then headed over to the girl, gesturing for Aaron to follow.

Aaron tagged along behind Landon and the girl into a small room at the end of the corridor; the drawings covering the walls made it less gloomy compared to the rest of the shop. More sketches lay sprawled across tables, alongside bottles of ink.

"So? What can I do for you?" Landon inquired as the girl took a seat on the central couch.

She bit her lip, a trace of lipstick coming off, and turned, tugging down her shirt collar to show the back of her shoulder. "I, um, want a heart tattoo with my boyfriend's name in it."

Aaron had to hold back a laugh. Talk about a tattoo cliché. But Landon was all business, face expressionless as he listened.

"How long have you been together?" he asked.

"One month."

Landon offered her a small, knowing smile. "Listen, I get where you're coming from, but tattoos are permanent. It might seem perfect now, but it's a big decision, especially if things change."

"We won't break up. He's my soulmate."

"Maybe just give it a bit more thought?"

"I've thought about it, and I want his name on me."

The back-and-forth went on, with Landon calmly explaining the implications and the girl adamant about her choice. Eventually, realising Landon wasn't going to budge, she stood up in a huff and stormed out, her complaints echoing back from the reception area.

Soon after, a long-haired man decked out in tattoos and piercings appeared in the doorway, looking none too pleased. "What's this I hear about you turning away customers?"

"I'm not going to tattoo a whim she'll likely regret," Landon said firmly.

"The girl wants a tattoo. You're here to do tattoos," his boss countered.

"But—"

"No 'buts', okay? You're an apprentice, meaning you're here to gain experience. You've got talent, sure, but this attitude of yours won't get you far. If you won't do the tattoo for that girl, then Sam will. She seems more keen on practising and less on arguing."

"You can't be serious? You can't support that girl's absurd request. She'll regret it."

"I can do whatever I want. This is *my* studio," the guy retorted, getting angrier. "As long as you stay here, you do as I say. End. Of. Story."

Landon remained silent, frustration evident in his posture as he watched his boss leave the room. He slumped onto a table, twirling a marker in his hand.

"I didn't know you were such a moralist," Aaron taunted, amused by the altercation.

"It's not about morals," Landon replied sharply. "Every tattoo I do has my signature on it. I don't want my work to be some impulsive decision someone regrets."

"Well, that's unexpected. Thought you weren't the sentimental type either."

"It's not sentiment," Landon snapped. "It's about pride in my work. Not just doing whatever to keep the boss happy."

Aaron nodded, already aware from Landon's refusal to tattoo Nyle that he took his profession seriously. He scanned the sketches plastered on the walls. "All these drawings...are they yours?"

"Yeah," Landon replied, as if it was no big deal. Aaron studied them closer, surprised at how detailed and unique they were. It was wild to think that a guy as apparently cold as Landon could put so much heart into these lines.

"Why did you start tattooing?" Aaron asked.

Landon ran his fingers over a sketch on the wall, one that resembled the drooping rose on Ria's hand. His expression softened. "I've always been into drawing. There's something about creating from scratch, bringing out more to what you see."

Aaron related to that. He used to love sketching out his fantasies, even considered going to art school, but ditched the idea because of his parents. Now, seeing Landon's art, a flicker of his old passion burned inside him. He wanted to get back into it.

"Why don't you tell your boss to screw himself and open your own shop? You're really good."

"I almost forgot how young and clueless you are about how the real world works."

"You're not exactly ancient yourself," Aaron retorted. Considering they were both in a youth community service program, Landon couldn't be much older. "What are you, twenty?"

"I'm twenty-two," Landon said flatly.

"You didn't answer my question though."

Landon sighed. "It takes a fair bit of cash to start a shop, and banks aren't exactly queuing up to throw money at someone with a record."

That clicked for Aaron. Maeve's words came back to him. "Maeve said you did time in juvie?"

Landon offered only a noncommittal shrug. "You ask too many questions."

"And you seem pretty good at dodging them."

"It's not the questions I have a problem with," Landon shot back, his eyes flicking with something harder. "It's the answers I'd rather not give."

*

The morning slipped by quietly in the shop, with no further customer rejections. Aaron didn't get to see Landon tattooing anyone, but he quietly observed his consultation sessions. He was still puzzled about why he was there. He had no experience in tattooing, and Landon didn't know about his interest in drawing.

Everything started to make more sense at lunchtime when Landon took him next door to a vinyl shop with the sign *Revolutions Per Minute*. The name was pretty cool, but the shop was a different story. As soon as they stepped in, a mustiness combined with the strong scent of over-brewed coffee hit Aaron. They weaved through tightly packed shelves crammed with vinyl records, arranged in a totally random order. The chaotic setup of the place was overwhelming.

In the back, a guy lounged in a chair, buried in a book, with his foot up on the counter and a fancy beer can beside him. A woolly cap hid his face. He didn't even glance up as they approached.

"Fell," Landon said, breaking the silence as they got closer. "This is Aaron, the guy I told you about." Turning to Aaron, he added, "And Aaron, meet Fell, the shop owner."

Fell looked up then, and Aaron instantly recognized the Beer Guy from the bonfire party.

"Aaron," Fell acknowledged with a nod, clearly remembering him too. "Landon mentioned you're looking for work. As you can see—" He gestured around the cluttered shop. "—there's plenty to sort out here."

Aaron chuckled nervously as he glanced around. He doubted whether his few remaining months before heading to Australia would be enough to sort this mess out.

"Before we start, I need to do a quick interview to see if you're the right fit," Fell announced, standing up. He grabbed two biscuit packets from the counter and held them out, one bourbon and one custard cream. "Which one's your jam?"

Caught off-guard, Aaron hesitated. His parents had spun a tale about food allergies when he was a kid, and he never got around to tasting them. Even after he found out it wasn't true, he never developed a taste for sweet things. "Uh, I haven't had either, actually."

Fell paused in surprise. "Wait, you've never tried a bourbon or custard cream biscuit?"

Aaron chuckled, a bit embarrassed, as both Fell and Landon stared at him like he'd just admitted he'd never used a smartphone.

"You're missing out," Fell remarked playfully. He carefully detached one half of a bourbon biscuit and one half of a custard cream, then pressed them together, creating a unique combination. He took an experimental bite, nodded in approval, then assembled two more hybrid biscuits.

"Here, try this," Fell offered, extending one to Aaron and another to Landon.

Aaron took a bite and, to his surprise, found it quite tasty.

"Well? What's the verdict?" Fell asked.

Mouth still full, Aaron approved. "Yeah, it's pretty good."

Fell clapped him on the back. "Welcome to the weirdo club."

"He was already in, biscuits or not," Landon quipped.

"So, when can you start?" Fell asked.

"Like, now?"

"Brilliant." Fell pulled out a key and handed it to him. "No strict hours here. If it's closed when you get here, just open up, and same deal for closing."

Aaron held the key tight, feeling excitement and nerves. This was all kicking off faster than he'd expected.

"Right, but first, let's grab some grub. Landon and I usually hit the market for a bite," Fell said, already heading for the exit.

Aaron tried to picture Landon and Fell as lunch buddies. As they made their way to Camden Lock Market, he watched in amusement as Fell greeted almost everyone they passed. From shopkeepers to stall vendors, it seemed Fell was a local celeb. His easy-going and friendly nature contrasted sharply with Landon's more withdrawn personality.

After weaving through the noisy market crowd, Aaron found a moment to lean in towards Landon while they waited in a queue for food.

"Thanks, by the way," he murmured.

Landon didn't let on he heard, didn't react, didn't say a word, not even a nod. But later, after they finished eating and stepped aside for a cigarette break, Landon silently extended his lighter towards Aaron.

That small gesture felt like a quiet acknowledgment. Aaron couldn't help but smile. Perhaps hanging out with Landon wouldn't be as challenging as he'd initially thought.

Chapter Ten

Colour-blind

[Now playing » Spectrum—Florence + the Machine]

Aaron's second Saturday at the retirement centre saw him back on graffiti duty with the same team as last week.

Ria attacked the graffiti with a vengeance, while Landon remained his usual quiet and focused.

Meanwhile, Maeve, Nyle, and Cliff worked plant duty with Muhammad. Or better, Muhammad was the one getting his hands dirty. Voices carried over to where Aaron worked, with Maeve saying something about "not a single speck of dirt on my shoes," and Nyle whining over his now less-sparkly jumper.

Aaron shook his head as he picked up a brush. The lot may be a quirky bunch, but he was starting to appreciate the variety—a welcome distraction from his own troubles.

He still hadn't heard back from Tom about a second shot at the wildlife park, and rebooking his ticket to Australia was pending. The Southern Lights were pretty much off the table now, and Aaron had stopped fixating on every new photo that popped up on his socials. Just a few more months, and he'd be back on his feet. This was only a bit of a blip.

"So, Aaron, what's your deal?" Ria asked as she scrubbed at some spray paint. "Are you done with school? Got any uni plans?"

"Nah," Aaron replied, working on a patch of graffiti. "I'm off to Australia soon. I'll be working at a wildlife park." At least, he hoped so.

"Oh, right, you said that at Nyle's, didn't you? What's it gonna be, wrestling kangaroos or hugging koalas?"

"More of a koala guy." Aaron cracked a small smile, though nothing like the sheer joy Tori always had for the furry critters.

"They're adorable, aren't they?" Ria glanced at him, her brush dancing over the wall.

Landon chimed in without looking up. "Cute, but they're like prickly cacti personality-wise. Not as cuddly as they seem."

"I like a challenge," Aaron replied.

Landon huffed and went back to his scrubbing, but Aaron swore he saw the slightest uptick at the corners of his mouth.

"Did you know koalas have fingerprints almost like ours?" Aaron added, remembering one of Tori's fun facts. "So similar, you can barely tell them apart, even under a microscope."

"Really?" Ria paused, her brush mid-air, a spray of droplets flying. "Imagine using that at a crime scene. 'Wasn't me, officer, must've been a koala.'"

Aaron laughed. "And what about you, Ria? What are you up to when you're not scrubbing walls or sparking debates at parties?"

"Well, I'm majoring in Gender and Sexuality Studies. Big into the LGBTQ plus community too. That's sort of what landed me here."

"Oh yeah? How come?"

Ria leaned on her brush, taking a breather. "A group of us were protesting for queer education in schools. We wanted LGBTQ plus topics included in the curriculum, you know, to teach kids about all the different queer identities and histories."

Aaron remembered Ria being quite vocal about sexuality at the bonfire. "And then what happened?"

"We were doing our peaceful thing when this anti-LGBTQ plus lot turned up. They started kicking off, shouting all sorts of rubbish at us. Police stepped in, and next thing you know, I'm in handcuffs."

"That's rough," Aaron sympathised.

"It's the way it goes sometimes," Ria replied, diving back into graffiti removal. "It's all about making a change, isn't it?"

"The only change I want to see is these walls looking pristine." Sarah's voice cut through the air. "Enough chatting. You lot were my favourite because you're quiet. All the chatterboxes are with Muhammad. But I'm starting to doubt that..."

They all got back to it, the vibe shifting to more focus, less talk.

As lunchtime approached, the two groups took a break from their tasks and met outside the conservatory. Landon quietly slipped away, heading towards the withered cherry tree at the centre of the gardens.

As Maeve joined them, she continued her lively chat with Muhammad. "You know, Muhammad, you have a way with plants. It's almost magical." She touched his arm. "Are you always this eager to get down and dirty?"

Muhammad coughed and leaned back. "It's just years of practice, Maeve. Nothing magical about it."

Behind them, Nyle appeared less amused. "Great. There's dirt everywhere." He groaned, picking at the fabric of his jumper. "This is going to be a nightmare to clean."

Then Maeve shifted her attention from Muhammad to Landon. "Hey, look at Landon over there, brooding away."

They all turned to him.

Cigarette hanging from his mouth, Landon appeared quite angry at the tree as he stripped away pieces of bark and scuffed the soil around its base with his combat boots.

"Is the psycho planning to chop that down?" Maeve asked.

"I'd help him if he was," Cliff joked. "Can't figure out why they've kept that awful thing around."

"Nobody's chopping anything down without my permission," Muhammad intervened. "Let's focus on lunch now, shall we?"

The group moved off to find a spot to eat, but Aaron hesitated, watching Landon. Something about the way Landon stood there made Aaron think there was more on his mind than just the tree. Did he want to get rid of it, or was something else bugging him?

*

Somehow, they ended the day with a visit to a nearby pub, which Nyle jokingly referred to as Aaron's initiation into the world of twenty-somethings.

Aaron wasn't keen—he just wanted to crash at home—but everyone else, even Landon, was on board with the idea.

As they entered the pub, the smell of stale beer hit Aaron, the air thick with it. His trainer's sole kept sticking to the carpet with each step.

They squeezed their way through the crowd, trying to make themselves heard over the pop music blasting from the speakers and the constant hum of chattering people. The place was packed, every table occupied.

"There's one free over there!" Maeve pointed to a secluded table at the back just as its occupants stood up.

"Quick, before someone else grabs it," Ria urged, leading the charge.

Landon hung back, letting the others pick their spots first. He then smoothly took a seat in a corner, his back against the wall. Aaron eyed that seat with annoyance and curiosity, the perfect spot offering a clear view of the whole place and an easy way out if needed. Plus, it'd be ideal for keeping his phone screen to himself. But Landon, already settled in, left Aaron no choice but to sit opposite him.

As everyone debated what drinks to order, Maeve decided Landon should do the honours, seeing as he was closest to the bar.

Without a word, Landon jotted down the orders and made his way to the counter. Aaron watched him for a bit, then, acting on a whim, followed, figuring he could lend a hand.

Landon gave him an annoyed glance. "Go back. I don't need help."

"Maybe not. But I want to make sure you don't poison my drink."

"That's insulting." Landon replied, laced with humour. "If I were going to get rid of you, I'd at least do it fairly."

"So, you've thought about killing me like your ex-housemate, huh?"

"It's crossed my mind a time or two."

When the bartender placed all the drinks on the counter one by one, Aaron was surprised to find a cola among the beers. No one had mentioned it.

"Don't you drink?" he asked.

Landon looked at him, puzzled. "What do these look like to you?"

"I meant alcohol."

"You don't need to drink alcohol to socialise."

Aaron was about to say more when the familiar tune "Something Just Like This" filled the pub. He quickly helped Landon with the drinks, his mind swirling as they returned to the table.

He sipped his beer, hoping to loosen the knot in his throat. It was stupid, how a simple song could trigger such intense emotions. His necklace felt too tight, the pendant pressing into his skin. Aaron considered going back to the bar for a peppermint tea, though he doubted whether it would be enough to settle him.

The rest of the night blurred into jokes, beers, and chit-chat. Aaron sat there, his mind miles away, replaying old memories.

Across from him, Landon also seemed in his own world, half glued to his phone, half zoning out. Aaron couldn't figure out why he even tagged along if he was going to be so out of it. Next to Landon, Cliff worked on slowly getting sloshed, his head bobbing as if on a spring.

"Hey, how about we grab some gelato?" Nyle suggested. "Someone I work with at the museum, who's actually from Italy, told me about this amazing place just around the corner. Says it's proper Italian."

Maeve's eyes brightened at the suggestion. "Gelato? Count me in!"

Despite not being into it, Aaron agreed to go along with the rest of the group. They all finished their drinks, then shuffled out, with Landon trailing behind, looking like he'd rather be anywhere else.

On the way, Nyle quipped, "I think Landon's the only person on the planet who doesn't like ice cream."

Landon, hands deep in his oversized hoodie, shot back, "It's not that I don't like it. Just not my thing."

"So, are you gonna have any with us tonight, then?" asked Nyle.

"Nope."

"You're an odd one, hun. Likes his sweets, but gives ice cream a miss." Nyle then turned to Aaron. "What about you, dear?"

"Not my thing either, but I'll give it a try."

Nyle sighed in frustration, but as they reached the gelato shop, he peered excitedly at the display. "Look at all these. What's everyone having? I reckon the hazelnut praline's calling my name. And that pistachio—so green."

Aaron scanned the crowded array of swirls, crumbled toppings, and shiny drizzles. Most of them looked the same, impossible to guess without the labels. Whatever Nyle was raving about didn't look all that tempting.

Maeve, sensing his hesitation, nudged him. "Got a favourite, Aaron?"

He hummed, not sure what to pick.

"How about something with chocolate? Like stracciatella? Can't go wrong there."

"Don't bother, Maeve," Cliff cut in. "The weirdo's allergic to chocolate."

Nyle's eyes nearly popped out as he looked back and forth between Aaron and Landon. "Seriously? You two are the oddest people I've ever met."

"Not because we have criminal records?" Aaron joked.

As the group piled into the shop, Aaron and Landon hung back, finding a quieter spot away from the queue that snaked outside.

Landon eyed Aaron suspiciously. "So, you're allergic to chocolate." Though neither a question nor a statement, Landon's tone bordered on an accusation. "I don't recall seeing you agonising after eating chocolate biscuits the other day."

Uh, oh. Aaron shifted uncomfortably. "Well, it's a bit...compli-cated."

Landon's eyes narrowed as he stepped closer, crowded Aaron against the wall. Resting his hand on the brick wall beside Aaron's head, he leaned in, studying him intently, eyes locked on Aaron's. "You still don't square with me. I don't like it."

"Apparently, you don't like much of anything," Aaron retorted, try-ing to hold his ground.

"Indeed. But liars claim the top spots."

Now, inches apart, Aaron caught the scent of coconut and cigarette smoke on Landon. This close, he should have felt intimidated, but he didn't.

Aaron met Landon's gaze firmly and didn't budge an inch. He tried to convince himself he was standing up to him, proving he wasn't a cow-ard. But what if pride had nothing to do with it? A weird flutter stirred in his stomach whenever Landon came close or paid him attention.

Aaron liked the thrill of getting a reaction out of Landon, breaking through his usual indifference. Or maybe, as Maeve had pointed out, Aaron's sense of self-preservation was somewhat skewed.

"It's just that, um, my parents always told me I was allergic to choc-olate," he explained. "And even after knowing that wasn't true, I never dug into it. I don't want to explain everything to people, so I stick with the allergy story." The admission made him feel foolish.

Landon studied him as though attempting to decipher the truth just by looking at him. "And what about Australia? Is that for real, or is it another tale you've spun?"

"No, Australia is real. It's been a dream of mine to go there for a long time now."

"Mm." Landon didn't seem entirely convinced. He took a step back and fished out a cigarette. "Just so you know, me helping you out doesn't mean we're mates or anything."

"Never thought we were," Aaron replied coolly.

"You see, our last housemate was a pathological liar. Said he needed money for his family, spun a story about bad luck, and even brainwashed Luzanne. Turns out his family was fine. He was just blowing cash on gambling. Can't have you playing the same game, not with Nyle this time. He's weak, especially for pretty faces."

Aaron didn't know what to think of both Landon's comment about 'pretty faces' and the hint of a protective streak. "So, you do care about your family."

"He's my cousin."

"I thought he was just your 'birth mum's sister's son'."

Landon huffed. "So, parroting is your thing, uh?"

"What can I say? I live to impress."

A cloud of smoke framed Landon's face. "I don't think you're a pathological liar like him. But you...you have a way of bending the truth. Maybe it's a coping mechanism or something. Makes things more interesting, doesn't it?"

Discomfort twinged at how much Landon had seen through him. "Maybe," Aaron conceded, not quite meeting his eyes.

As Landon took another drag of his cigarette, Aaron spotted a tattoo of a bone on his middle finger. Quite clever. But the letters across the knuckles of his other hand really grabbed his attention: TNEY.

"What's that stand for?" Aaron nodded them.

Landon used the glowing tip of his cigarette to point at each letter as if spelling them out. "Mind. Your. Own. Business."

Aaron chuckled. "Not exactly subtle, is it? If you didn't want people asking, you could've picked a less obvious spot."

"My hand, my choice. Not like I'm questioning your fashion sense."

Aaron glanced at his outfit—a dark grey hoodie over a light grey T-shirt, paired with black jeans. "What's wrong with this?"

"That brown hoodie and the washed-out pink tee? Not exactly a fashion statement. Even the mice in Cinderella could do a better job."

Aaron looked down again, thrown off, transported back to that classroom, surrounded by laughter, his artwork with a purple sky and brown grass on display, and the sting of embarrassment when others pointed out his odd colour choices.

Quietly, he admitted, "I'm colour-blind."

Landon wrinkled his forehead. "Bullshit."

"I'm not lying."

Landon took the last puff of his cigarette, then crushed the butt under the sole of his shoe. He crossed his arms on his chest and threw Aaron a challenging look. "What colours am I wearing?"

"Black hoodie and black jeans."

"So, you can see."

"Being colour-blind doesn't mean being blind. Black is the only colour I'm sure of, but I struggle to distinguish others because they're similar."

"What colour is this?" Landon pointed to the sticker attached to the wall behind him.

Aaron rolled his eyes; that question again, the same one they always asked. Every. Single. Time. He understood the curiosity, but the teasing and jokes? Not so much. He'd hated when kids handed him unlabelled crayons or tricked him into thinking his clothes were the wrong shade, just for a laugh.

"I'm not into the 'what colour is this' game," Aaron said. "I know the colours, but I see them differently, or sometimes I mix them up."

"Not sure if I buy that."

"Colours are just a trick of light anyway."

"Next, you're gonna hit me with 'there is no spoon' too?"

Aaron barely laughed at the *Matrix* reference. "No, but colours are deceptive. Take the sea, for example. People say it's blue, but that's just how we perceive it."

Landon fixed him with a narrow gaze, challenging his point as he had done back at the bonfire. "Bad example. The sea's tricky in more ways than just colour. It's what you don't see that's the real danger."

Aaron couldn't resist a jab. "So, what are you afraid of not seeing, Landon?"

"I'm not afraid, just easily annoyed. And you excel at that."

"I thought nothing bothered you."

"Minus one" was Landon's cryptic answer.

Aaron, puzzled, waited for an explanation.

"In old-school video games, you get three lives," Landon explained. "I'm giving you three chances before I lose my patience. You just used one up."

Aaron caught the playful yet serious look in Landon's eyes. "And if I hit minus three?"

Landon's expression softened slightly, now seriousness with a playful edge. "You'd better not find out."

♫ Under My Skin

[Now playing » Podcast, Ep. 15—Under My skin—Don't Listen To Me]

So, I've got this vocabulary, right? I'm talking beyond your average words—even the quirky ones that haven't made it into the Oxford Dictionary yet. I like to think I have the right word for every situation. But, here's the thing—there's this guy, and for the life of me, I can't nail down what it is I feel about him.

Saying it's irritation doesn't quite cut it. And hate? That's strong, isn't it?

But man, does he know how to get under my skin. It's like he's this annoying pimple you can't stop poking at. It keeps bugging me, you know?

You'd think I'd be scared of him. There's clearly something eating him up inside, and that kind of thing can make people unpredictable, can make them dangerous.

But the other day, I caught a real good look in his eyes. And you know what? I didn't see the threat I was expecting. Instead, I saw someone kind of like me. And that's what's throwing me for a loop.

So here I am, lying awake at ass o'clock, trying to make sense of this weird, tingly feeling I get every time we bump into each other. Will he be the end of me?

[♫ Closing » loneliness for love—lovelytheband]

Chapter Eleven

Date Night

[Now playing » loneliness for love—lovelytheband]

Over the next week, Aaron found himself slipping into a surprisingly comfortable routine.

His days kicked off with a morning run, followed by a hearty breakfast, and then it was off to work in Camden Town. Lunch breaks with Fell and Landon were always a bit of a giggle, full of banter and hilarious stories, and dinners with Nyle were just as fun.

But his favourite times were the Tube rides with Landon.

Unlike Nyle and Fell, Landon didn't feel the need to fill every silence, something Aaron appreciated. He often found social interactions draining, but the time spent in Landon's company recharged him.

They weren't exactly 'mates'—Landon had made that pretty clear—but things were getting easier between them.

It was all right, actually. Even in their quiet moments on the Tube, Aaron started noticing things about Landon that drew him in.

For one, they shared a similar taste in punk and rock music, although Landon's liking for Taylor Swift surprised Aaron. During their commutes, Landon was always absorbed in a book, its cover torn off. Aaron tried to sneak peeks, but the title remained a mystery.

"Why doesn't your book have a cover?" Aaron asked that morning on their way to Camden Town.

Landon closed the book with a swift motion and held it up for Aaron to see. "Can you guess what it is now?"

"Nope."

"Exactly," Landon said with a slight smile.

Aaron thought maybe the book had got messed up, with spilled coffee or something. But clearly, Landon had ripped the cover off on purpose. "You're a savage," Aaron accused playfully.

Landon's sweet tooth had also caught Aaron's attention.

Landon frequently shared snacks like biscuits and chocolates with Fell, who indulged him with an almost uncle-like affection. In some ways, Fell reminded Aaron of Aunt Olivia. One minute, he was all chill, and the next, he'd drop in some serious life advice.

Just a few minutes earlier, Fell had shared his thoughts about songs from artists who were no longer around, yet left an indelible mark on the world. He spoke about how, through their art and memories, they continue to live on. That made Aaron reflect on how much of Tori still lived within him and his desire to carry forward her dreams.

He could see why Landon liked him.

But those two could not be any more different.

Fell, a big extrovert, would chat up anyone and everyone, making friends left, right, and centre. Customers would wander in, aimlessly browsing, and before they knew it, they'd be spilling their guts to Fell. But they rarely bought anything. Fell, for all his friendliness, wasn't exactly smashing it as a shop owner.

The guy was super laid-back, maybe too much so. He'd spend hours chilling in the shop, either lost in a book, playing Pokémon, or deep into videos about brewing his own beer. He knew his stuff when it came to music, though, and even got Aaron hooked on some old-school vinyl, educating him about the legendary bands from back in the day. But when it came to the shop itself, Fell didn't seem all that fussed.

As Aaron rummaged through a pile of vinyl records, his curiosity won over. "Why run this place if it's not your thing?"

Fell put his book down and leaned back. "It was my dad's shop. Didn't mean much to me until he was gone, and it ended up being mine. It's less about making sales here—online does well enough for that. It's more for the vibe, the memories, and talking music with folks who get it. I used to dream about being a rockstar, had a band and everything, but it didn't work out. So now, I'm here, selling the dream in a different way."

Aaron's interest increased. "You were in a band? Are you on Spotify?"

Fell chuckled, shaking his head. "Yeah, we're on there, but I'm not about to spill the beans on that."

"I'll ask Landon, then," Aaron teased.

"Not even he knows. Kept that part of my life under wraps."

"So, are you, like, famous, then? Would I have heard of you?"

"Who knows?" Fell replied, turning back to his book.

*

On Thursday, after a very quiet day at RPM, right around closing time, an unexpected visitor came in.

"Heya," a voice called out cheerily as they stepped through the door.

Aaron, turning, instantly recognised Ria in a long dress that reached her calves, her bright smile lighting up the room. "Hey, what brings you here?"

"Just swinging by to say hi," she replied, her eyes sparkling. "Landon mentioned you'd started working at the shop with Fell. Had to see it for myself. We've been nagging him for ages to get some help."

Ria's gaze wandered over the shop, her fingers lightly trailing along the rows of neatly organised albums. "This is amazing. It's like a whole new place."

Aaron shrugged modestly, gesturing towards a sizable pile of items near the counter. "Still loads to sort out though."

"Looks to me like you've made a cracking start."

"I've been his guide," Fell declared, pushing himself up from his chair with a hint of pride. It was the first time he'd gotten up that morning. As he moved towards Ria, he stumbled slightly, his legs probably numb from sitting too long.

Standing beside her, Fell had to bend his head down nearly a foot to make eye contact, the height difference between them remarkable. Even Ria's platform high-tops did little to bridge the gap.

"Here for a date with Landon?" Fell asked with a casual air.

Ria nodded. Surprise flicked through Aaron.

He'd noticed that Landon and Ria were friendly, but the thought of them being an item hadn't crossed his mind until now. It nagged at him as he'd pegged Landon as someone who, much like himself, wasn't into the whole dating or sex scene. Or was it the idea of *them* being together that bothered him more?

Just then, Landon walked in. "Hey," he greeted everyone with a casual wave.

Ria spun around, her smile blooming at the sight of Landon.

Though they seemed polar opposites, Landon and Ria balanced each other. Landon was like a cloud on a sunny day with Ria, the ray that could pierce through it, chasing off even the gloomiest spaces.

Landon's eyes flicked between Aaron and Fell. "All right, catch you guys tomorrow," he said.

Aaron's stomach twisted as he watched Landon and Ria head out together. Why did it bother him so much?

He shook his head to clear his mind and finished arranging the last albums. He was ready to go home and hole up in the quiet of his room to watch a series.

*

Aaron pushed the door open to Nyle and Luzanne's raised voices booming down the corridor. He froze at the entrance. The echoes of their argument bounced off the walls, not just of the house but within his mind as well. Soon, their shouts morphed into the all-too-familiar shouts of his parents.

Aaron closed his eyes and slid down to the floor, back in that house again, a scared little kid with hands pressed over his ears, trying to block out the yelling from the kitchen. It was always the kitchen.

Deep breath in, deep breath out.

He tried to get a grip, to remind himself he wasn't that kid anymore, no longer stuck in that house. But he couldn't stop shaking, and try as he might, he couldn't tune out the sounds of the ongoing argument down the corridor.

"...and why should I put my love life on hold 'cause Landon gets ticked off? That normal to you?" Luzanne said, her frustration obvious.

"That's not what I'm saying," Nyle shot back, his tone high but less confrontational.

"Then what are you saying? You always take his side. How many more times are you gonna bail him out?"

"Stop, it's not like that. I'm not defending him."

"Oh really?" Luzanne shouted back sarcastically. "Then explain how you both ended up doing community service together?"

"It was both our fault."

"Bullshit. You took the fall to keep him out of jail again. Maybe he should've gone back."

"You don't mean that," Nyle said, wavering.

"I do. My love life's a mess because of him. He even threatened to break Jean's hand the other day just for wanting to braid my hair after I said no. Now Jean's terrified of him."

"It's his way of being a protective brother," Nyle said, trying to reason.

"Brother? Landon doesn't know the first thing about being a *brother.*"

"And after everything, can you blame him?"

"Don't start with that. He's been this way forever, even after coming back home. Not even two days in, he hit Mom's boyfriend."

"Do you really wanna defend that drunkard? Landon was right to step in."

"What about my ex, then? Did he deserve a beating too?"

Aaron, unable to stand the shouting any longer, abruptly stood to leave. But in his rush, he got all tangled up in the coats and bags hanging by the door. The whole lot came tumbling to the floor with a clatter.

"Oh, shit...Aaron," Nyle blurted out from the corridor, obviously taken aback.

Aaron sidestepped the pile of clothing and ran back out the front door.

He had to get away as soon as possible. So, he ran aimlessly through the streets, passing shops and people, until he reached the riverside. The biting cold wind against his skin soothed him, helping shake off the awful memories clinging to him like sticky sweat.

Before he knew it, he'd run a fair distance and ended up in front of a familiar sign by the Greenwich meridian, pointing across the river towards Canary Wharf.

The sign read *Here 24,859*, indicating the miles needed to circle the globe and return to that very spot. Aaron wished he could travel twice that distance if only it meant having Tori back by his side.

"I love you 24,859," she'd said once as they passed the sign.

"Only that much?" he had asked her, disappointed she'd put a number on it.

"It's not little. It means that my love can travel huge distances but will always find its way back to you."

Aaron pulled out his phone and called Tori, only to be greeted once again by her voicemail and the familiar background song.

"Where the hell are you, Tori?" he asked desperately. "Where the hell are you..."

*

When Aaron got back, tired and sweaty, he found Nyle waiting in the living room, looking worried. It was just the two of them, plus Kat sleeping on a chair, Luzanne nowhere in sight.

"You heard all that, didn't you?" Nyle asked, scratching his arm.

"Yeah, more than I should have," Aaron admitted.

Nyle sighed and headed to the kitchen. "Fancy something to drink? Coffee? Hot chocolate? Beer?"

"Got any peppermint tea?"

Digging through the tea bags, Nyle found one and turned on the kettle while Aaron settled on the sofa.

They stayed in awkward silence, broken only by the sound of the boiling water.

After a couple of tense minutes, Aaron braced himself and asked, "Luzanne...she's Landon's sister?"

Nyle exhaled heavily as though he'd just put down a set of weights. "It's a bit of a story." He poured the hot water into two penguin-shaped mugs. "But, yeah, Landon and Luzanne are blood siblings."

Aaron took the tea Nyle offered, but stayed quiet, unsure if he wanted to dive deeper into this.

Nyle seemed to take Aaron's silence as a cue to go on. He plopped down next to Aaron on the sofa as if he had a heavy burden to unload. "Aunt Lucy was seventeen when she had him. A fling with a tourist. My grandparents wanted her to get rid of the pregnancy, but she stuck with it, said she wanted to keep the baby."

Aaron breathed in the minty aroma of his tea. Why was Nyle spilling all these family secrets? Did he trust him, or was he just being open?

"For a while," Nyle continued, "she managed, doing odd jobs here and there. Then she met this bloke, moved in with him. Seemed like a decent guy, treated Landon all right. They even talked marriage. He fooled everyone because when Aunt Lucy got pregnant with Luzanne, he did a runner. Took most of her savings too."

"What a complete arsehole." It made Aaron think of his own family, how they'd been masters at putting up a front. Smiles in photos, the perfect little family at gatherings. But behind closed doors, it was arguments and cold silences. If something seemed too good, it usually was. He knew that all too well.

"Aunt Lucy struggled enough with Landon. But two kids? Her

depression got worse. She turned to booze and ended up losing them both."

"So, they gave Luzanne and Landon away?"

Nyle nodded. "Neighbours called social services. Somehow, my parents managed to take in Luzanne and raise her like a daughter. That's why I think of her as my sister."

"And Landon?"

"Couldn't take him too. He got put into foster care, bounced around *a lot.*"

"How much is 'a lot'?"

"Twelve homes. He's always been...problematic. So, they kept moving him."

Aaron winced. He'd had a rough time with just one family; bouncing between twelve was unimaginable. "So, technically, Luzanne's your cousin?"

"Yeah, but blood doesn't matter to us. I love them both the same. Landon, though, he sees things *differently.*"

Aaron thought back to what Landon had said about Nyle being hardly family and referring to his mother as his birth mum. Pretty clear they weren't exactly close. "What about Landon's mum?"

"She's living up north last I heard. Landon and her, they don't talk. He tried living with her, in between foster placements, but it didn't work out. He lost it with her new partner, and that landed him back in care until he was eighteen. After that, he was pretty much on his own. Then our gran died, left us this house in her will, so we all ended up moving in here together."

It all made sense now, why they were all under one roof.

"It's a bit of a madhouse sometimes," Nyle continued. "We try to get along because it's convenient. But Luzanne reckons Landon resents her for staying with us while he got chucked around. She thinks he's out to sabotage any relationship she tries to have."

Aaron took another deep breath of his tea, trying to piece things together. It was hard to picture Landon, Mr. Apathy himself, getting a kick out of ruining someone else's day. There had to be more to it than being jealous of Luzanne.

"Speaking of Landon..." Nyle said, glancing around. "Didn't he come back with you?"

"Nah, he's out with Ria."

"Oh, right!" Nyle didn't seem surprised. "They do their thing every other Thursday. Like clockwork. Almost makes me jealous. Landon never hangs out with me. But good on him for finding someone to, you know, let off steam with. Sometimes, you need to...let it go." He winked. "It's not healthy keeping it all to yourself."

Aaron sensed a jab there.

"Funny thing, though, Ria's never stayed over, never been in his room or the summer house. It's like Landon's got his own little forbidden kingdom. Not even regular flings are allowed, only Kat gets the grand tour."

"Maybe he's hoarding a pile of gold in there, Scrooge McDuck style," Aaron joked.

"Who knows..." Nyle shrugged.

Having finished his tea, Nyle went to the kitchen and popped the mug in the dishwasher. Aaron followed, not having touched his but feeling more chilled out thanks to the mint. A shower was next on the agenda.

As he was about to tip his mug into the sink, Aaron's gaze landed on the fruit basket.

"Odd, huh?" Nyle said. "Landon's taken to sketching on bananas, like paper wasn't enough."

Aaron picked one up, examining the detailed drawing on the skin. It reminded him of the tattoo sketches he'd seen at the shop.

"Yeah, just the ripe ones. Who knows why," Nyle mused. "Guess he's not into green as a canvas. Or maybe his doodles stand out more on yellow."

Aaron tightened his grip on the banana. Had Landon started marking them because of him?

The idea sent a weird but warm flutter through Aaron's chest.

Chapter Twelve

Second Chance

[Now playing » Human—Of Monsters and Men]

The next Saturday at the retirement centre, Maeve, Nyle, and Ria really got into the Halloween spirit with their outfits.

Maeve wore a gothic dress, her nails and makeup dark, looking like she'd stepped out of a Tim Burton film. Nyle had put in vampire teeth with a smear of fake blood near his mouth. Ria chose a cute style, wearing cat ears.

Aaron hadn't bothered with a costume, but his mood perfectly aligned with Halloween's dark and gloomy feel.

Waking up to photos of Tom enjoying his life on Bondi Beach hadn't helped. It reminded Aaron of missing out on the life he'd envisioned. A life that felt painfully distant while he was stuck here, far from his dreams.

As he mused over his situation, Cliff stalked past in his reused Squid Game jumpsuit.

"Remind you of something?" he asked with a snarl.

Aaron scanned his costume. "Yeah, you're giving off some serious *Orange Is the New Black* vibes. Quite fitting, don't you think?"

Cliff flipped him the finger. "You're such a dick, Aaron. No wonder you befriended the local psycho."

"Fuck off," Aaron fired back.

Aaron turned to Landon behind him, who seemed completely unfazed by the names people called him. That indifference made Aaron angrier.

"You're not dressed up?" asked Landon.

Aaron pointed to his scars. "These make me look spooky enough all year. What's your excuse?"

"Oh, but I *am* dressed up." Landon leered. "Serial killer. They look just like everyone else."

Aaron snorted. "More like a 'cereal' killer, with your soggy breakfast fascination."

A hint of a smile tugged at the corner of Landon's mouth, revealing a faint dimple. Had it always been there?

"All right, let's get moving," Sarah announced in a flat tone, looking bored as usual. She briefly scanned Maeve, Nyle, Ria, and Cliff, taking in their costumes, clearly not impressed. "Chop, chop! Time to start!"

They were all on plant duty that day. So, one by one, they geared up, pulling on gloves and grabbing tools, ready to dive into the work. Landon, though, seemed to have a different plan in mind.

He approached Muhammad, and they exchanged a brief conversation, which prompted Muhammad to quickly leave and soon return with an armful of boxes filled with all sorts of gardening gear. Landon scooped them all up and headed straight for the old cherry tree.

Sarah watched Landon's departure, annoyance crossing her face. She opened her mouth, probably to tell him off, but Muhammad stepped in.

"Leave him, Sarah," he said calmly. "We need more young people like him, caring about our community. He should be rewarded."

Sarah looked like she wanted to protest, but instead, she let out a resigned sigh and turned to the others. "You lot, focus on the flower beds and hedges." She gestured towards the other parts of the garden.

Maeve sidled up to Muhammad with a grin. "Hey, I'm all about community spirit too. Do I get a special reward for my hard work?"

Ria rolled her eyes at Maeve's antics and joined Aaron. Together, they silently made their way to the garden's edge, where they picked out a spot to start their work.

Aaron stole a glance back at Landon. He stood, examining the cherry tree with an intensity and care that Aaron had only seen when Landon worked on his tattoo designs.

It struck him how Landon's gentle, focused attention was so different from the aloof, tough persona he usually displayed as he gazed at each branch and leaf, suggesting a deep, silent connection to the tree.

Aaron wished the others could see this side of Landon too, not the 'local psycho' or the tough guy with piercings and tattoos, but someone who cared, deeply and quietly.

*

An hour into working with the plants, Aaron's patience had worn thin.

He'd mocked Nyle and Maeve for their persistent whining over these tasks. Yet, he was no better off, complaining about everything, his hands fumbling and dirty. This is not where he was supposed to be. He was meant to be on that fucking beach with Tom, watching koalas, maybe even learning to surf.

He should have been making a wish under the Southern Lights already, hoping for a better future. Instead, here he remained, knees deep, not in sand but dirt, struggling with plants he barely knew the names of, under a blurry grey sky.

This whole gardening thing was pointless. Why couldn't they hire professionals and let them do something simpler? None of them had any experience with this stuff. Apart from Ria.

She seemed to be in her element, moving with a certain grace around the plants, always smiling, always cheerful. It had started to get on Aaron's nerves. How could she be so perpetually happy? And how did Landon, of all people, put up with her?

"Aaron, could you add some more mulch here?" Ria asked him. "We need to finish this bed."

He trudged over, the bag heavy in his arms. "Where do you want it?" he asked, trying to keep his growing irritation in check.

"Sprinkle it around the peonies." Ria pointed, still smiling.

Aaron bent to spread the mulch, but his movements were too rough, too hasty. The bag slipped, spilling mulch everywhere but where it was supposed to go.

Nyle burst into laughter, clapping his hands. "That's one way to mulch, I guess!"

Cliff, grinning nastily, added, "I've seen toddlers with better coordination."

Aaron stood there, surrounded by the mess, wishing he could disappear into the mulch he'd just spilled.

When lunchtime finally rolled around, he brushed his hands off and stepped away from the group, needing some time to himself. As soon as he found a quiet spot away from the gardening chaos, Aaron pulled out his phone. His fingers trembled before he pressed Tori's contact info.

"Hey, Tori, it's me. I'm here again at this stupid community service thing, and honestly...it's a mess. I'm supposed to do something good with these plants, and I just— I don't get it. I can't see the point in any of it. They're getting free labour out of us."

He paused, a deep sigh escaping him. "Every day that passes, I feel like...like all those dreams we had are fading away, slipping through my fingers. Sometimes I wonder if I'll ever make it to our Neverland or see those Lights you were so excited about. It's tough, Tori, really tough without you here..."

After he finished recording, Aaron typed out a message to Tom.

Hey, any updates on the job? Really need some good news right now. Let me know if you've heard anything. Thanks.

He slid his phone back into his pocket and cast a look over the garden, feeling trapped. In a sneaky move, he stripped off his hi-vis jacket and started tiptoeing away from the group. Maybe no one would notice his absence for the other half of the day. After all, Landon was off doing his own thing with the cherry tree, away from the rest of them.

"I wouldn't do that if I were you." Sarah's voice, right behind him, stopped him in his tracks, her tone unusually serious.

Aaron turned to face her.

She regarded him with sternness and understanding. "You walk out now; you're just making it harder for yourself."

Aaron hesitated. "I just...I can't deal with this right now."

Sarah sighed, then offered him a cigarette. "Not the best habit, I know, but it seems like we could both use one."

Aaron nodded, accepting it.

"Look, I know you don't want to be here," she continued as she lit their cigarettes. "Even I don't want to be here. But walking away won't solve anything. You've still got hours to complete, and avoiding them won't make them disappear."

Aaron slumped, the weight of her words hitting him. They echoed what Aunt Olivia had said to him before he left.

Sarah took a deep puff, her eyes never leaving Aaron. "Listen, Walsh. You're a decent kid. First time here, right? And for something pretty daft, if I remember correctly. But let's be honest, I don't want to see you back here once you're done. You're young; you've got your whole life ahead of you."

Aaron took a drag, thinking about the new life he was supposed to have started living if not for this setback.

"You're in a better spot than a lot of them here," she added, motioning towards the others. "Most of them have a pretty hefty record, and they're not much older than you."

Aaron's gaze automatically shifted to Landon.

"Yeah," Sarah nodded, following his gaze. "Bailey's one of them. And Maeve? She's practically a regular. I've seen plenty of kids like you come through. Some of them manage to turn things around. Others...well, let's just say they have a harder time. It's up to you which path you choose. So, what's it gonna be?"

Aaron released a cloud of smoke, still focused on Maeve and Nyle, who were goofing around.

"I've got to say, I like him," Sarah remarked, nodding to Nyle. "He adds some spark to this dreary place."

"Yeah, sometimes maybe too sparky," Aaron mumbled.

"Are you finding it hard to gel with them?" Sarah probed gently.

Aaron shrugged half-heartedly. "It's all right, I guess."

Sarah took one last drag, dropped her cigarette, and crushed it under her boot. "You should try to open up. Keeping everything bottled up is not doing you any favours. You gotta deal with whatever's eating at you. The sooner you get your head down and work through this, the quicker you're out of here."

She paused with a knowing look. "And hey, you never know, you might find a silver lining in all this mess," she added, her tone softening before she turned and walked away.

Aaron stood there, watching her leave. Her words resonated, stirring something inside him. With a deep, steadying breath, he picked up his jacket and headed back to his task.

Ria approached him, her cat ears slightly askew. "Hey, something wrong?" She looked genuinely concerned.

Aaron glanced at her, guilt nipping at him for not being helpful or friendly. "Just tired of all of this."

"I know this isn't the best situation, but have a look around." she said, gesturing to their surroundings. "Think about how lovely these gardens will be once we're done."

Aaron found it really hard to picture, especially as he surveyed the chaotic scene before him—Nyle battling a hose that seemed to have a life of its own, Cliff awkwardly planting flowers, either burying them so deep they might never see daylight or leaving them too shallow to take root, and Maeve appearing to mistake weeds for flowers, inadvertently yanking out a few blossoms as she tried to clean up the beds. Finally, his attention drifted over to Landon, wrestling with the cherry tree, its branches snapping back with each cut.

"Looks more like a war zone than a garden," Aaron remarked.

"Good things take time, Aaron."

"Suppose so. But it's tough to see the point right now."

"They also look messy before they get better," Ria added. "When I gardened with my nan, she'd always say the real beauty is in the process, in doing something and then patiently watching it bloom. There's something truly satisfying about seeing your hard work pay off."

Aaron's gaze drifted back to Landon and the cherry tree. "He's putting a lot of effort into a tree that looks half-dead. Why bother?"

"Just because something takes effort doesn't mean it's not worth it," Ria replied gently. "Maybe Landon sees something in it. You know, he has a way of seeing potential where others don't. He looks past the surface."

Aaron remained fixed on Landon and the cherry tree. It clicked right there. That tree, battered and worn, still stood and fought for life.

He walked over to Landon and observed him quietly. "I get it now," he said, "what you're doing with this tree."

"Wow, a detective in the making," Landon muttered, half-joking. He didn't even look up.

Aaron crouched beside him and observed his forehead, shiny with sweat, and his nails covered in dirt. "You're really into saving it, huh?"

Landon finally looked at him. "This tree's been neglected. It's got a fungal infection, probably from all the damp weather we've had. If left untreated, it suffocates the tree, stops it from blooming. It deserves a second chance."

Aaron smiled slightly. He knew there was more to Landon's words than just the tree. Landon's life had been a series of challenges, moving from one foster home to another, never quite finding his place. Now, here he was, giving this tree a chance he rarely got himself.

"All right," he rolled up his sleeves. "How can I help?"

"You?" Landon said, incredulous. "Help with this?"

"Sure, why not? I'm no expert, but there's always Google." Aaron pulled out his phone and did a quick search on treating tree fungal infections. "Here, it says we need—"

"Got it covered already." Landon dropped a pile of tools at his feet. "We need to trim the roots and improve the soil."

As they started sorting things out, Ria came over. "So, what's the master plan for the tree rescue, team?"

"There's no plan." Landon shook his head. "And there's definitely no *team*."

Ria ignored him, her eyes already sparkling with excitement. She slipped on a pair of gardening gloves and crouched. "We're saving it, right? My gran showed me a few tricks."

Landon nodded, approving. "Well, at least one of us knows what they're doing."

And so, they got to work. Aaron, Landon, and Ria, an unlikely trio, united by a mission to revive an old, forgotten tree.

Aaron found himself immersed in the task, frustrations fading into the background. Sarah's words echoed in his mind; maybe it wasn't so bad after all.

Chapter Thirteen

Tea and Cigarettes

[Now playing » Nightmares—Palaye Royale]

Aaron woke up abruptly in the dead of the night, heart racing and skin slick with sweat.

It felt as if thorns lined his lungs, each breath scraping painfully against them. Trying to calm down, he massaged his chest, but the scars on his torso burned where the T-shirt, now two sizes too small, touched them.

The same nightmare haunted him: the backseat of the car, the escalating argument in front, the sudden, terrifying screech of brakes, the world flipping upside down. His mother's screams pierced through his memory; Tori's hand desperately gripped his in the chaos.

Then came the crash.

Metal crumpling like paper, a sickening sense of weightlessness, and a shower of glass shards cutting into his flesh, just as real as they had been on that fateful day.

Every time, he hoped the dream would end differently, but it never did. Tori's hand always slipped away, leaving him alone with a piece of glass in his palm.

With effort, Aaron sat up, gripping the bed sheets. He looked around his dimly lit room, trying to ground himself in the present, but he wasn't sure where or *when* he was. Time seemed distorted, like in his dreams. These nightmares weren't just in his head; they seeped into his body, making his arms and legs feel like heavy weights.

It took Aaron an eternity to get out of bed. When he finally managed to plant his feet on the rough carpet, he reminded himself where he was—and, more importantly, where he *wasn't*. But he knew it was only temporary relief. The demons of the past would come back to haunt him as soon as he let his guard slip. Years and miles apart made no difference; they'd always track him down, no matter where he hid.

He focused on his breathing, trying to calm his trembling hands. He kept at it until his heartbeat slowed and his breaths came out normal again. Still feeling shaky, Aaron tiptoed out of his room and crept through the dark corridor, using the light from his phone to find his way to the kitchen. The clock showed three in the morning—his usual wake-up call, the so-called 'witching hour'. He didn't buy into that kind of stuff but couldn't deny feeling like he was cursed.

Drinking glass after glass of water didn't do much to ease the bitter taste filling his mouth. So, he headed to the front door, slipped on his shoes, and stepped out into the night, ready to run until he couldn't anymore.

*

Returning an hour later, Aaron found Landon in the kitchen, heating skull-shaped crumpets in a pan, a leftover from Halloween.

"What are you doing up at this hour?" Landon asked as he transferred the sizzling crumpets to a plate. He then proceeded to smother them with an absurd amount of Nutella.

"Couldn't sleep," Aaron replied, propping his elbows on the kitchen island. "Went for a run."

"Right, because a midnight run in freezing weather is a sure way to knock you out," Landon said, dripping with sarcasm despite his sleepy look.

"Better than a sugar coma," Aaron remarked, eyeing the crumpets with disgust. "You can't sleep either?"

Landon didn't answer and offered Aaron the plate. "Want one?"

Aaron shook his head. "I'll pass."

Landon shot him a look that screamed 'your loss' and finished his snack without another word. Then, he turned on the kettle, grabbed two mugs, and rifled through the stash of tea bags. "Any preferences?"

Aaron paused before answering. "Peppermint."

Once the water boiled, Landon filled each mug, then, nodding towards the garden, suggested, "Let's take these outside."

The chilly November air greeted Aaron again as they stepped out, the grass cool and damp under his bare feet. Landon wrapped himself in a ginormous wool blanket and settled down by the fence.

Aaron hesitated for a second before joining him. He closed his eyes, taking in the minty smell of his tea. The aroma, along with the heat from the mug, started to relax his tense muscles.

The weight of something warm and soft over his shoulders made him open his eyes; Landon had shared his blanket with him. The small, unexpected gesture made the night seem less harsh.

Aaron turned to thank him, but Landon was already lost in his tea, slurping away.

Under the dim street lights, Aaron studied him.

Something seemed different about Landon tonight, a kind of softness not usually there. Perhaps the oversized hoodie and baggy joggers made him seem less sharp, or maybe it was his bare face without the usual piercings and the sleepiness still lingering in his eyes. A single, messy curl tumbled over his forehead, adding to this gentler image... made him look...kind of cute, actually.

Aaron realised he'd been staring too long when Landon cleared his throat, breaking the silence.

"Staring is rude. You're making me feel all twitchy."

"Sorry." Aaron shifted his gaze to his bare feet in the grass. He knew better than to stare at people.

Landon fumbled in his pockets and took out a pack of cigarettes. He pulled out two and offered one to Aaron.

As Aaron placed the cigarette between his lips, the flame from the lighter cast a brief glow on Landon's tattooed hand, the letters 'TNEY' still a mystery.

They both took a puff, sending swirls of smoke into the air, their other hands clutching steaming mugs. Tea and cigarettes, an unusual pairing. Just like the two of them.

"Insomnia or nightmares?" Landon asked.

"Just a bad dream. How about you?"

"Insomnia."

Aaron took a drag while smiling slightly. "Fascinating."

"So, were you running away from your nightmares?"

"Are you avoiding yours?"

Landon continued smoking, but Aaron wasn't fooled. There was a difference between not being able to sleep and avoiding sleep altogether.

"What are you running from?" Landon asked, his eyes fixed intently on Aaron.

Aaron hesitated. "What makes you think I'm running from something?"

Landon stifled a laugh, exhaling more smoke. "I seriously wasn't expecting an answer from a rabbit like you."

"I'm not a rabbit."

"Come on, you have nowhere to go, and you constantly lie to your aunt. You're always on edge, flipping out when someone gets too close, and you get panic attacks. There's something haunting you, and it's the same thing that keeps you awake at night."

Aaron turned to look in another direction. He hated to admit how accurate Landon's observation was.

"One thing I've learned is that going far away isn't enough to leave behind what you don't like," Landon added.

"I'm not running away," Aaron protested.

"Keep telling yourself that. What's your plan after this? Australia? It's literally on the other side of the world."

Aaron spun around, surprised. "How do you remember all this about me?"

"Don't flatter yourself. It's just that I understand more than you might think about fleeing from demons. But you can never escape what's in your mind, no matter where you go."

Landon's words struck him harder than the chilly air. An undeniable truth lay in them, an unexpectedly disarming rawness. It made him think back to Sarah's suggestion about opening up.

His parents had always emphasised the importance of being strong, never revealing any weakness. But witnessing the strength in Landon's vulnerability, the bravery in his openness, made Aaron question that belief.

In the quiet, under the soft glow of the lamp lights, with mint and smoke and Landon's candidness filling the air, an unexpected sense of security flowed through Aaron.

Though unfamiliar territory, this feeling of wanting to open up, the risk might be worth taking, a step towards something real. Maybe he could let someone in, even if only for a little while.

"Ever had a dream that felt so real, you weren't sure if it was just in your head or something that actually happened?" Aaron asked.

Landon paused, took a sip of his tea, and nodded.

"Sometimes, I think if I could remember properly...if I could remember what exactly happened the night I got these"—he gestured at his scars—"maybe I could get over it, you know?"

Landon's eyes momentarily clouded. "Or maybe you'd wish you could forget it altogether."

"You saying there's no way out?"

Landon shook his head, scratching behind his ear. "I don't bother too much about dreams. Real life's got enough crap as it is."

"Wow, profound. Why didn't I think of that?"

"I'm not joking," Landon said more seriously. "Dreams are...brain noise, aren't they?"

"Yeah, but you don't know that when you're dreaming."

"True, but facts are facts, right?"

"Facts are a luxury for when you're awake."

"So, change what bugs you when you're awake."

Aaron barked out a short laugh. "If only it were that simple..."

"It can be," Landon insisted, turning to face him. "Just focus on what keeps you grounded. Find something real to hold on to and use that against the stuff in your head."

Aaron absentmindedly brushed his thumb against the pendant on his necklace. The familiar comfort it usually brought was off tonight.

He took one last drag from his cigarette and savoured the minty scent of his lukewarm tea. Next to him, Landon put out his cigarette butt and casually tossed it into his mug. A low, melodic hum escaped his lips.

"What's that tune?" Aaron asked, intrigued by the softness in Landon's voice.

"'Mr. Sandman'. You know, the song? Maybe if you call on him, he'll help you sleep," Landon said with a half-smile.

Aaron frowned in confusion.

"Mr. Sandman's a character from folklore," Landon explained. "They say he brings good dreams by sprinkling magic sand in kids' eyes while they sleep."

"Does it work?" Aaron asked, half-joking.

Landon shrugged. "Can't say he's ever paid me a visit."

"How do you know all this stuff?"

"I read a lot," Landon replied. "Books, usually. They sell them in shops, have them in libraries, even on Amazon. You might find reading one interesting."

Aaron smiled at Landon's playful jab. This kind of teasing felt inclusive, a shared joke rather than a jibe aimed at him.

He was about to make a witty comeback when a blood-curdling scream shattered the quiet night, jolting them both. It sounded like it was coming from down the street.

"Foxes," Landon declared with confidence as the screams persisted. "They're mating."

"So, you're into nature documentaries as well as books?"

Landon shot him a look. "Didn't you grow up around here?"

"I've never heard foxes going at it," Aaron admitted. The continued shrieking made him wince. "It's awful. Sounds like they're killing each other."

Landon chuckled. "Believe it or not, they're having a good time."

"Well, good on them, I guess…" Aaron tried to mask his discomfort with a chuckle. Even the foxes had a better sex life than him.

Landon narrowed his eyes. "So, how do you normally get to sleep?"

The sudden shift in conversation threw Aaron, but he figured Landon was just fishing for tips. "Usually, a long run does the trick."

Landon made a noncommittal sound and got to his feet. "There are other ways to wind down, you know."

"What, like our fox friends? Getting busy until exhaustion hits?"

Landon shrugged, a hint of a smile on his face. "Doesn't have to involve anyone else. Sometimes, a bit of self-love does the job better. There's plenty of science backing that up."

Aaron stood up, too, chuckling. "I'm learning a lot about you tonight—folklore expert, bookworm, and now a sex therapist."

"What can I say? I live to impress," Landon quipped, heading back inside.

Aaron shook his head. Who was the parrot now?

He returned to his room, his head and chest lighter, where he threw himself onto the bed, the sheets, once itchy and warm with nightmares, now fresh and soft. Aaron closed his eyes, trying to relax.

His peace, however, was short-lived.

The sudden buzz of his phone jolted him. Picking it up, he frowned at seeing Landon's name on the screen. But his confusion quickly gave way to warmth in his chest as he read the message.

A link to a song: "Mr. Sandman" by SYML.

Chapter Fourteen

Interesting

[Now playing » Flaws—Bastille]

From that night on, things changed between Aaron and Landon.

They didn't speak much during their Tube rides, but Landon had started sharing his playlist with him. A small thing, but it added a layer of intimacy to their...friendship? Aaron wasn't sure what to label their growing bond. He knew, though, it was something special.

Their text exchanges had also become a regular part of Aaron's day.

Landon would send anything from hilarious cat videos to gardening articles, each message bringing them closer. Aaron couldn't help but smile whenever his phone buzzed.

Aaron had been sorting some Christmas albums at RPM on Wednesday when Fell nudged him.

"You're always chuckling at that phone screen. Spill, is there *some-one* in the picture?"

Aaron snorted dismissively. This reminded him of Aunt Olivia, always poking her nose into his life, asking about crushes, especially after she found out he was bi. Aaron kept telling her he wasn't interested in anyone, but she'd smile, saying he'd change his mind once he met *the one.*

"There's no *one*," he replied, wrinkling his nose. "And I don't chuckle."

But his denial was short-lived.

A new message from Landon made him burst into laughter, his elbow accidentally nudging the stack of vinyl records, sending them crashing down in a cascade. Landon had sent a photo of the girl who'd gotten her boyfriend's name tattooed on her shoulder, now back for a cover-up. The irony wasn't lost on Aaron, and Landon's choice of soundtrack—"Critical Mistakes" by 888—was the cherry on top.

Trying to compose himself as he picked up the fallen albums, Aaron realised how much these little exchanges with Landon meant to him. They'd become a bright spot in his days, a connection he hadn't expected.

But Aaron and Landon truly connected during the quiet nights.

Whether due to insomnia or unwinding before bed, their tea and cigarette breaks had become an almost sacred ritual.

With only the distant sounds of seagulls or buses as a backdrop, they would open up and talk.

Really talk.

*

On Friday night—technically early Saturday morning by the clock's standard—Aaron and Landon found themselves side by side on the grass. With their backs against the fence, they each held a cup of tea in one hand and a cigarette in the other. The usual nightmare had jolted Aaron awake, but this time, the comfort of Landon's nearby presence was enough to dissuade him from his typical, post-nightmare run.

"What's the big deal about Australia?" Landon broke the quiet. "Why are you so set on going there?"

"I've told you before, haven't I? I'm planning to work at a wildlife park in Sydney."

"But can't you work with animals anywhere? There's a zoo in Regent's Park."

"Yeah, but they don't have koalas, do they?" Aaron countered.

"You can find them in other zoos, I guess. But it's not about the koalas, is it?"

Aaron shifted slightly and inhaled his minty tea. "No, it's not. It's also about the Southern Lights. They're...sort of a dream of mine."

Landon looked puzzled. "Aren't those the Northern Lights?"

"Yeah, same kind of phenomenon, but in different places. The Northern Lights are commonly seen in the northern hemisphere. Auroras in the southern hemisphere are known as the Southern Lights. What's special about them is their rarity. They're less known, more elusive, like...like the best show in the world, for your eyes only."

"Still, seems like a long way to go for some lights in the sky. You could head to Iceland for the Northern ones. It's a lot closer." Landon took a sip, then a drag.

Aaron whipped out his phone and flicked through his Instagram. "Here, look at this." He handed the phone to Landon.

A magical scene of the Southern Lights lit up the screen, with arcs and swirls of light weaving through the star-studded sky, creating an ethereal, otherworldly display. Even if he couldn't make out every shade—some blending, others washed out—the slow, hypnotic motion turned the night canvas into something alive. The darkness of the trees below only added to the mystique.

If it looked this mesmerising to Aaron, it must have been even more breathtaking through Landon's eyes.

Landon examined the photo, then glanced up at Aaron. "Okay, that does look incredible."

"That's why I want to go. Imagine being there, under those dancing lights." Aaron sighed, retrieving his phone. "If not for this community service, I would have watched them at their best before summer kicked in. I have to wait for next year now."

"Can you even see them?"

Aaron chuckled. "Yes, Landon, I can see them."

"But can you see the colours?" Landon's tone was more curious than mocking.

As Aaron pocketed his phone, he looked up at the clouded sky, exhaling even more clouds. "Well, I might not see them as vividly as you can, but yes, I can still make out the lights. Different, probably, but still beautiful."

"Doesn't that bother you?" Landon asked. "Not seeing everything?"

Aaron shrugged. It did bother him. "Yeah, a little bit, but I've learned to live with it, to focus on details others might not even notice so that I'm not completely missing out."

Landon looked at him. "You're not. Sounds to me like you've got a superpower instead."

Aaron snorted. "A superpower? How do you figure that?"

"I'm serious," Landon insisted. "As you said, you see things differently, not less. Just because you don't perceive colours like everyone else doesn't mean you're missing out. Maybe *we* are the ones who are missing out on the smaller details."

Aaron considered Landon's words, the concept slowly sinking in. "Never thought of it like that."

"We all see the world in our own way, colour-blind or not. It's about perspective, isn't it? We can be staring at the same thing and still see it completely differently."

Aaron found a sense of comfort in Landon's words. What if his different way of being bi was another part of what made him unique?

"But there's got to be more to Australia than just koalas and the Lights, right?" Landon asked.

Aaron took a deep minty breath. "I made a promise to someone...someone very important to me. I *have* to go there."

"I see." Landon inhaled a long drag. "And this person...where are they now?" he asked gently but probing. "Is this the same one you've been leaving those voice messages for?"

"Um, I..." Touching the glass pendant hanging from his neck, Aaron's thoughts drifted to Tori's words, telling him to find his happy thoughts and fly to Neverland. Was he any closer to that place? Or was he losing his way? And even if he got there, what then?

He didn't realise he was shivering until Landon wrapped his blanket around him.

"Hey, it's all right. You don't have to go there now. You've shared enough," Landon said softly. "Let's call it a night, okay?"

They snuffed out their cigarettes and headed back inside.

"Landon..." Aaron hesitated in the corridor, still draped in the warmth of the blanket, wanting to say more. He knew he could trust him.

Landon stopped at the foot of the stairs, waiting. His gaze encouraged Aaron to speak, but the words wouldn't come out.

Finally, Aaron managed a quiet "Goodnight."

"Goodnight, Aaron," Landon replied, then turned and disappeared upstairs.

*

Their growing bond hadn't gone unnoticed by the rest of the group. That Saturday, as Aaron and Landon grabbed their tools and made a beeline for the garden's centre, Maeve couldn't help but tease as they drew near.

"So, what's the master plan today?" she asked. "More top-secret 'let's kill the tree' meetings?"

Nyle added, laughing, "Yeah, you two look very suspicious."

Cliff, passing by, added, "Seems like a 'slay together, stay together' kind of deal, huh?"

Despite the teasing, Aaron and Landon managed to make real progress. They pruned away the dead branches and treated the tree with a good combination of nutrients and mulch.

Now, it would be a waiting game.

For the first time, Aaron was keen to see what the next week would bring.

As the day drew to a close, he stood back and admired their efforts, wiping the sweat from his forehead. The tree already appeared noticeably healthier.

Muhammad called them over, rounding them up with a note of pride in his voice. "Good job today, team! Let's keep this up next week!"

As they packed up, Nyle suggested a trip to a barcade in Soho.

"A barcade?" Aaron asked.

Ria, lacing up her shoes, explained, "Yeah, it's a bar with arcade games. It's fun. You should come!"

*

The neon light and a bouncer's looming figure outside the place gave off a nightclub vibe.

Descending the stairs into a basement, the group stepped into a whole other world. Intergalactic-themed graffiti splashed the walls, with planets and spaceships glowing under the lights. The symphony of electronic *beeps* and *boops* from the games blended with the casual chatter around them, setting a lively yet chilled tone.

Nyle leaned in, grinning. "What do you think?"

The lineup of classic arcade games immediately drew Aaron's attention, their screens flickering with flashing lights. Among them, one machine stood out. "Is that Pac-Man over there?"

Landon, coming up beside him, looked amused. "You good at it?"

"I'm more than good." He left out the part about his main competitor, Aunt Olivia, and how she absolutely thrashed him every time.

"Oh really? Prove it."

"You're on. Loser buys drinks."

"Are you sure?"

"Why? Are you scared you'll lose?"

Nyle burst into laughter, joined by Maeve. "Yeah, Lanny, are you scared?"

Landon ignored them and turned to Aaron. For the second time, Aaron caught a glimpse of a smile, revealing a faint dimple.

"So, what's in it for the winner?" Landon inquired.

"Um...free drinks and bragging rights?"

"Let's include a coffee break when we're in Camden Town."

"I don't like coff—" Aaron stopped short, realising Landon had already pegged him as the likely loser.

"Backing out?" Landon asked.

"Not a chance."

Nyle and Maeve, watching their banter, couldn't contain their laughter. "This is going to be epic," Nyle said, rubbing his hands together in anticipation.

Maeve, with a mischievous twinkle in her eye, leaned closer to Aaron. "Here's a deal, Aaron. If you beat the high score, I'll treat you to a drink. Some guy's been reigning over it for months."

"And why's it just me in the challenge? What about Landon? He'd be a cheap win since he doesn't drink."

Grinning, Maeve led him to the scoreboard, its high scores glowing ominously. At the very top, the name 'Lannysteroo' dominated the list.

Aaron turned to Landon, who now sported a knowing grin.

With newfound determination and nerves, Aaron walked over to the first machine, gearing up for a proper fight.

*

After a string of embarrassing losses in every game they played, Aaron was ready to hole up in his room once he got home, the idea of having made a spectacle of himself in front of everyone unbearable.

"At least you put up a *semi-decent* fight," Landon teased, a smile playing on his lips. "I half expected you to bolt after realising I'm the arcade king around here."

"You could have told me."

"And miss out on the fun? No way."

"That's unfair," Aaron protested, but a reluctant smile tugged at his lips.

"You're the one who challenged me. Accept your defeat with dignity."

With a resigned sigh, Aaron turned to the bar. "Tell me what you want, and let's get it over with."

"Just a sec." Landon held up a finger. "I owe Ria a round at *Dance Dance Revolution*. Catch up with you at the bar in a bit?"

Aaron nodded, trailing behind Landon to where Nyle, Maeve, and Ria were sitting. Ria sprang up and followed Landon to the dance machine.

Aaron stood there, watching them.

"Here, this might cheer you up," Nyle said, sliding a fancy glass towards Aaron filled with a bubbly liquid and a tiny *Mario Kart* star floating on the surface. "It's a 'Power-Up Punch', just what you need after all those losses."

Aaron couldn't deny the name was creative, or that the drink was good. But the taste of defeat filled his mouth with bitterness.

"Hot bloke at eleven o'clock," Maeve piped up enthusiastically.

Nyle swivelled around, drink in hand. "Oh my, I'd love to spend even just seven minutes in heaven with him."

"Tell me about it..." Maeve agreed.

"With my luck, I'm sure he's either straight or taken." Nyle turned to Aaron. "What do you think?"

Aaron glanced over. Sure, the guy was fit, but his attention snagged on the guy next to him, rocking a *Legend of Zelda* T-shirt with a cool map of Hyrule Kingdom. "He's all right, I guess."

"All right? *Just* all right? He's fit." Nyle exclaimed.

"Maybe Aaron's more into that girl at three o'clock," suggested Maeve, nodding in another direction.

Aaron turned to get a peek. The girl was indeed attractive, with her stylish outfit and charming laughter. Yet, he felt no particular pull towards her. "I don't know..."

Maeve's eyes widened in mock shock. "You didn't even check her out properly. Seriously, Aaron, what's your deal?"

"Yeah," Nyle joined in. "Are you really bi, darling? Doesn't seem like you're into *anyone*."

"I am," Aaron replied, annoyed. "Just because I'm bi doesn't mean

I want to jump bones with every person I see."

"Fair," Maeve agreed. "But the fit ones? Hell, yeah!"

Aaron sipped his cocktail. Was there even a difference between sexual attraction and just finding someone good-looking?

"All right, Aaron, solve this mystery for us." Nyle leaned in. "We've got this theory, see? Your heart got smashed to bits by someone, probably the same person who gave you that necklace. Tried the whole love thing, but it went south, and they flew off to Australia, maybe even found someone else. And now, you're dead set on going there, trying to win them back. Am I right?"

Aaron shook his head, pushing the floating *Mario Kart* star down with his straw. "Not even close."

"Oh? So, you were the heartbreaker, then?"

Before Aaron could respond, Maeve chimed in, "You remind me of my ex, Aaron. High standards, always held back, like he was allergic to love or something."

Aaron stirred his drink, his mind drifting. In his family, love had been a twisted thing, a word thrown around to excuse the screams and tears that filled their home. But with Tori and Aunt Olivia, he'd found what love should really be—nurturing, not destructive.

He understood it, at least in theory. But as with sex, Aaron never felt that rush people talked about or found someone who sparked that kind of connection.

"It's not that I'm against love. Right now, I've got other priorities. Finishing community service, getting out of London, heading to Australia. That's my focus."

"You could still have some fun while you're at it, you know," Maeve suggested with a wink. "No strings attached."

Aaron shook his head. "I'm good."

Nyle let out a dramatic sigh. "You're gonna get sick of your own hand eventually."

Aaron scoffed at the comment; that wasn't an issue for him. He rarely found himself in the mood, and when he did, it was more mechanical than anything else.

"Whoa, check out Landon getting smashed by Ria." Maeve pointed to them.

Aaron followed Maeve's gesture to where Landon and Ria were sweating off in a dance battle.

Nyle laughed and patted Aaron on the back. "You should challenge Lanny to *Dance Dance Revolution* next time. It's the one game he can't seem to win."

"Right," Maeve intervened. "He's too busy trying to *score* with Ria than bother scoring in the game."

Nyle chuckled. "Sure, he wins with her, just not on the dance floor."

Aaron sipped loudly, not comfortable with where the conversation was heading.

"You know," Maeve mused, "I wouldn't mind a spin with 'bad boy' Landon Bailey myself. I still prefer the super fit guys, but those tattoos and piercings? So hot. Caught a glimpse of one just under his belly button once. Makes you wonder how far down they go..."

Nyle spluttered on his drink. "Maeve, that's my cousin you're talking about!"

"Can't I appreciate your cousin?"

"You can, but in the privacy of your own room."

"He's also Black, which, you know, adds a few points when it comes to size..." She trailed off with a suggestive smile.

"Wow, Maeve, you disappoint me." Nyle put his hand on his chest and shook his head indignantly. "If Ria were here, she'd have a word with you about perpetuating such baseless stereotypes."

"Well, she's been shagging him for months now. Can't be just for his charm, can it? He's only good for a bit of fun."

At this point, Aaron couldn't hold back. He downed his cocktail and slammed the glass down. "If you spent less time running your mouth and more time observing, you'd realise how incredibly wrong and offensive you are. Besides, who sleeps with whom is none of your fucking business."

The table fell into a stunned silence, the only sounds now the distant *blips* and *beeps* of the arcade games.

"You know," Aaron continued, "Landon's not just this tough guy you all think he is. There's more to him, way more."

No one bothered to look beyond Landon's tough exterior, missing the kindness that didn't always come wrapped in softness. Landon was indeed tough but undeniably kind.

Their late-night conversations, those shared moments of tea and cigarettes, had revealed a different side to him, one that Aaron wished others could see too—the Landon who cared for the cherry tree, who respected people's boundaries, and asked for nothing in return.

"Hey, hun, chill out. Maeve was just saying she would gladly...ugh... fuck him." Nyle placed a hand on Aaron's shoulder. "I forgot that you and Landon are practically inseparable these days."

Their conversation dissolved entirely, fading away like the remnants of a bonfire that had burned out. When Maeve excused herself to the toilet, Nyle jumped in to fill the awkward silence with random chatter.

"So, I've got my eye on this wicked jumper for Christmas..." Nyle said with a hint of excitement.

Aaron, however, barely listened, his gaze fixed on Landon, who'd wrapped up the game with Ria. He watched as Landon retrieved Ria's fallen hair tie, a small act but one that spoke volumes to Aaron. These little things defined him, the way he paid attention to the smallest details. As he'd done the other day when they were strolling through the supermarket aisles and Landon had casually tossed a new box of peppermint tea into their basket.

"...and you've got to try the new Christmas sandwich at Pret..."

Aaron drifted again, this time to a recent lunch with Landon by the Regent Canal. The spicy doner kebab had been too much for Aaron, and Landon had offered to swap it for his milder one without hesitation.

"...this guy at the gym, always smiling at me, he's sending mixed signals..."

Aaron couldn't help but recall the faint dimple on Landon's cheek whenever he smiled. *Really* smiled.

Nyle paused, staring at Aaron. "Earth to Aaron! You hearing any of this?"

Aaron blinked, returning to the present. "Sorry, what were you saying about the gym—"

Sudden raucous laughter from a couple of blokes by the bar interrupted their conversation.

"Oi, check that out!" one of the guys yelled, pointing straight at Nyle.

His mate snickered. "You're in the wrong place, *princess*. Gay district's the other way." His eyes scanned Nyle's outfit with clear mock.

"I can't believe it." The first guy shook his head. "They're everywhere these days, popping up like mushrooms. And now, they're invading our spaces."

A wave of anger washed over Aaron. "Seems to me like you're the ones in the wrong place." He pointed towards the toilets. "Maybe you should hang out there instead."

Nyle tugged at Aaron's arm, trying to calm him down, but Aaron was having none of it.

The larger of the two guys stepped forward, sneering at Aaron. "What's this, then? Scarface to the rescue? Mate, Halloween's been and gone." He gestured rudely at Aaron's scars.

Aaron clenched his fists, ready to strike, but Landon stepped in front of him.

"Got a problem here?"

"Yeah," the guy said, "with the guy behind you."

"Listen up." Landon's tone dropped, a clear warning in his words. "Back off, or you'll regret it. I'm not warning you twice."

"Could say the same to you."

"Sure, but only one of us should worry about not listening," Landon said, now cold as steel.

Maeve called out from the background, "Trust me, you don't want to mess with him. Look at this." She held up her phone, showing a video of Landon taking on a guy much larger than him. Despite the size difference, Landon held his own, landing punch after punch with surprising fury. "Not a pretty sight, is it?"

The bloke gulped, visibly unnerved. After a tense moment, he mumbled something under his breath and walked away.

Aaron turned to Landon, still trying to wrap his head around what had just happened, seeing Landon in such an intimidating mode new to him. Was this the reason for the 'psycho' nickname? "Hey, I didn't need you to step in. I could've handled them."

"Sure, you could," Landon replied.

"I was about to punch that guy."

Landon closed the distance between them, his Docs inches from Aaron's trainers. "And then what? Would it have changed anything?"

As Aaron's anger cooled, confusion crept in. He'd expect this kind of concern from Aunt Olivia, but Landon? "Well, it would've given him a lesson, like you did with that bloke in the video."

Landon's expression softened. "That…that was a different story, one I don't want to repeat. Do you think hitting that guy would've taught him anything?"

"Well, it might make him think twice before shooting his mouth off next time."

"Maybe," Landon conceded, more softly now. "But you can't beat up all the dickheads that bother you. There's too many."

"So, you're telling me to just take it? To let them get away with it?"

"No." Landon shook his head gently. "It's not about letting anyone off but choosing your battles wisely. Some people aren't worth your time or energy. Save your strength for the fights that really matter."

Aaron's thoughts drifted back to the heated argument he'd overheard between Nyle and Luzanne about the accusation that Landon had hit their ex-housemate, who also happened to be Luzanne's ex. Had Landon intervened on behalf of Luzanne back then? He'd mentioned that their ex-housemate was a pathological liar with a gambling habit, maybe even using Luzanne's money. Had Landon stuck to his 'choose your battles' philosophy in that situation too?

"What did that wanker say anyway?" Landon asked.

"Oh, just some rubbish about Nyle's clothes."

"And to you?"

Aaron paused, then pointed to the scars on his face. "Nothing new. Another comment about these."

Landon studied the scars briefly, his face giving nothing away. Then, with a slight nod, he headed towards the exit, a pack of cigarettes in his hand. Aaron watched him go. Was this his cue to follow him?

"Hey," Nyle called out. "Sorry about all that mess."

Aaron turned to face him. "You don't have to apologise. But seriously—" He looked at Nyle's bold outfit. "—ever thought about toning it down? The clothes and stuff?"

Nyle's eyes popped, clearly taken aback by Aaron's words, seemingly more so than by the earlier confrontation. "What, this?" He gestured at himself. "This is who I am, Aaron. I'm not hiding it."

"Yeah, but—"

"No, listen. It took me ages to get here. Wearing boring tees and jeans? Been there, done that. But it was like slapping concealer on a zit—pointless." Behind him, Maeve agreed. "This is me being true to myself. Can't and won't change for others. Didn't do it for my parents; won't do it for anyone."

"But you'll keep getting crap for it, won't you?"

"I don't care," Nyle continued. "The thing is, I wasn't born to fit in. I was born to stand out." He laughed. "Plus, if I tone it down, what about those who need to see someone like me shining?"

Aaron studied Nyle with a newfound respect. He'd never considered the deeper meaning behind Nyle's fashion choices. "You're braver than I gave you credit for."

Nyle flashed a playful wink. "So, does this mean you'll finally sleep with me?"

"Err...not a chance."

With a dramatic sigh, Nyle turned to Maeve. "Well, your loss," he quipped as they sauntered off.

Still feeling on edge, Aaron stepped outside. There, in a dimly lit corner, he found Landon against the wall, two cigarettes in hand. Without a word, Landon offered one to Aaron, who gratefully took it.

Side by side, they leaned against the cool brick, smoking in sync. The rhythmic puffs of smoke helped calm Aaron, though his hands still shook slightly.

"Hey," he said, breaking the silence. "Thanks for stepping in back there."

Landon glanced over, his features softening under the neon light. "Didn't do it for *thanks*. No one should have to put up with that sort of crap, especially not for how they look."

Landon's voice held something that hinted at more than just general empathy. This wasn't the first time Aaron felt like Landon spoke from personal experience.

"Sounds like you've been through it yourself," Aaron said.

Landon took a drag, his eyes narrowing. "I've had my fair shares of labels growing up. I was the poor kid, the Black kid, the foster kid. Even got a pretty creative nickname at this posh, mostly white boarding school. 'Hovis Best of Both'." He gestured to himself. "You know, 'cause I'm half white, half Black."

"They bullied you for that?"

"Yeah, it's kind of ironic, isn't it? I was always with white families, so when I went to that school, I didn't even think about being 'not white enough' or 'not Black enough' until they pointed it out. Perspective, right?" Landon looked straight at him, a hint of irony in his tone. "Green eyes didn't help either. They made me stick out even more."

Aaron studied those eyes, finding them captivating rather than odd, even if their exact shade eluded him. "What do you mean?"

Landon shrugged. "Made me a curiosity, I guess. Some were intrigued, others not so much."

Aaron nodded, the feeling of being an outsider, a curiosity, all too familiar.

"Did they make it tough for you at school too?" Landon asked.

"Not exactly." Aaron touched one of the scars on his face. "But after the accident, I wasn't just Aaron anymore; I was 'the scarred guy'. It's weird how one thing can become your entire identity to others."

"Because people tend to focus on what's different, not what's the same. Makes them uncomfortable, I suppose. But it's their problem, not ours."

"Sometimes, I wish my scars weren't so obvious. It's like I'm walking around with a sign saying *Hey, look at me. I'm fucked up.*"

Landon flicked his cigarette, ashes falling near Aaron's shoes. "Don't give those scars too much credit. There's something fucked up about you, scars or no scars."

"Cheers," Aaron replied dryly.

"I see survival marks. You shouldn't be ashamed of them."

Aaron mumbled something, not too much convinced. "It's hard not to feel defined by them. They're always there, always a reminder."

"True, but they don't write your whole story."

"It's not a great story anyway."

Landon's eyes met his. "You're interesting, Aaron. More than you realise."

"I don't think I'm interesting."

"And I think you don't quite understand what it means to be *interesting*," Landon said with a faint smile. He crushed his cigarette underfoot and headed back inside.

Aaron stood there, pondering Landon's words.

He'd been called interesting before, but he'd never paid much attention. Coming from Landon, it struck a different chord.

Was it a simple observation or something more? And why did he care?

Chapter Fifteen

Lost Boys

[Now playing » Kids In The Dark—All Time Low]

Aaron was still mulling over what Landon said last night: 'interesting'.

He'd never seen himself that way. His scars had made him stick out, attracting stares everywhere he went. But all he ever wanted was to blend in, to get lost in his music and be left alone.

Sitting behind the counter in the usual quiet at RPM, Aaron idly sketched koalas in the margins of a Nordic folklore book. Fell hadn't shown up *yet*, despite it being close to their regular lunchtime.

Aaron's thoughts drifted to Landon, who had endured years of bullying for just being himself, and to Nyle, who chose to embrace his uniqueness with open arms. Their courage and authenticity made Aaron question his own approach to life. Maybe there was something to be said for owning who he was now, scars and all.

Taking a break from his drawing, Aaron pressed his phone to his ear, "Something Just Like This" playing in the background.

"Hey, Tori, it's me," he said softly. "I want to let you know that I'm doing okay. RPM's not bad. I kinda like it here. Fell reminds me of Auntie Olivia, you know? He's really cool, and he made me appreciate '80s and '90s rock music. And the group I've been assigned to for my community service? They're all right, especially one guy."

He paused, his words trailing off. "I'm still waiting to hear back from Tom about the job at the wildlife park, but as soon as I do, I'll buy a new ticket. I can't wait to leave everything behind and start fresh."

Ending the call, Aaron stared at Tori's name on the screen, as if reading it aloud or echoing the sound of her name in his mind could somehow bridge the distance between them. *Just a few more months*, he silently promised himself, then he would spread his wings and fly away. He would finally touch down in the places he and Tori had fantasised about during their childhood, those sleepless nights they'd spent weaving dreams until their eyes grew heavy with sleep.

"Fell around?" Landon asked as he stepped into the shop.

Aaron looked up, startled, but quickly recovered. "Not yet," he replied sarcastically.

Landon wandered around the album aisles before coming over to the counter. His eyes landed on the open book. "That's pretty neat," he remarked, nodding towards the koala sketch.

A flush of warmth rushed to Aaron's face. His hand trembled slightly, causing the pencil to jitter across the page. "It's just a silly doodle. I'm a bit rusty."

Landon leaned in, his index finger tracing the lines of the koala with gentle precision. "This is good. Ever thought about doing something more with it?"

"With drawing?" Aaron said, taken aback. "Nah, it's just a hobby. Nothing serious."

"Blasphemy. I'm trying to make a career out of it."

"I mean, what could I possibly do with it?"

Landon paused thoughtfully, then spoke again. "Why not start by putting them online? Maybe create a portfolio."

Aaron scoffed lightly. "Post them? They're not that good."

"They are, trust me," Landon insisted, his tone sincere.

Aaron mulled it over. His sketches had always been for him alone, a private escape. He hadn't drawn much lately either.

Then, Landon reached over and grabbed the pencil. He added a cactus beside the koala. "There, a touch of a prickly personality," he said with a chuckle, his dimple making a brief appearance.

Warmth bubbled up in Aaron's chest. It was a simple addition, but Landon's touch had turned it into something more, something shared.

"Lunch?" Landon asked, locking eyes with Aaron.

They stood close together, close enough for Aaron to catch the faint scent of smoke and coconut that clung to Landon. Though unexpected, instead of pulling away, Aaron found himself leaning in, almost instinctively, nodding in response to the invitation.

Just as they were about to step out, Fell burst into the shop.

"At last," Landon quipped, one foot paused mid-step between the shop interior and the pavement.

"Sorry, got caught up," Fell panted slightly, fiddling with his jacket. "Had a bit of a morning with someone I met last night. You guys off to lunch? Could definitely use a break."

Aaron laughed, full of amusement and disbelief. "You just got here..."

But Fell was already leading the way to the market. As they walked, he launched into a story about his latest flings. Aaron hung back, half listening. He treated Fell's tales like background noise, like a TV show playing that he wasn't really watching.

He was surprised Landon let him talk, even though it was clear from his apathetic grunts that he didn't appreciate the topic either. Nevertheless, he didn't interrupt him. Probably, Fell would offer him lunch as he did every time.

As they neared Camden Lock, the delicious smells of street food started wafting over, and suddenly, Landon got yanked aside by a dishevelled guy with dark circles under his eyes. A beggar maybe? Aaron was about to step in, but it was obvious they knew each other by the way Landon tensed up, facing the guy.

"Ian," Landon said, his tone dripping with annoyance. "What did I say about showing up here?"

"I know. But please, I'm desperate," Ian pleaded, reaching out to grab Landon's arm again, but Landon quickly raised his hand to block him.

"Don't touch me," Landon snapped furiously.

"Sorry, I—"

"No. We're done talking. Don't bother. I'm not changing my mind."

"How can you be so heartless? Don't you care at all?"

"You should know by now that I don't care about anything or anyone."

"Landon," Fell said, looking concerned, "Everything all right? Who's this?"

"He's nobody," Landon answered curtly, not taking his eyes off Ian.

Ian persisted. "Please don't push me away. You know I need you."

"You only need yourself," Landon said, then turned and strode off towards the food stalls, not looking back.

Aaron and Fell shared a confused glance before following him into the crowd.

"Isn't that the bloke from a few months back?" Fell asked, catching up to Landon. "The one who hung around outside the tattoo shop and tailed you to the station?"

"Clearly, he didn't take the hint that I want nothing to do with him."

"He's after money, isn't he? It's always the same with family..."

Aaron's ears perked up at the mention of family.

"He's not family," Landon quickly clarified. "Just because we were fostered by the same people doesn't make us *brothers*."

"People get desperate, don't they? Maybe in his eyes, you're close enough to a brother to hit up for some quids."

Landon grunted, ending the conversation abruptly. He picked up his pace, navigating the busy street with ease. Despite the surrounding chaos, Aaron was able to hear the stomp of his boots on the asphalt.

*

Ten minutes later, they sat by the canal digging into lunch.

"I was just thinking. It's been ages since I've been to a gig," Fell said, munching on his spicy cheeseburger. "What about you lot? What was the last concert you went to?"

Landon finished his bite, took a swig of his soda, and mentioned an obscure band name. Fell nodded appreciatively, patting his chest. His gaze then shifted to Aaron, who hesitated, unsure of what to say. He could've made up something, but he didn't want to risk looking foolish in front of two music buffs.

Fell's eyes widened in mock shock, his hand covered in sauce. "You're joking, right? No biscuits, no concerts... Where are you even from?"

Before Aaron could respond, Landon cut in, grabbing a handful of halloumi sticks. "I'll tell you where he's from," he said with a playful edge.

Aaron trembled, not sure where Landon was going with this.

Landon pointed to the sky. "He's from up there. You know, like in *Roswell*, when Max tells Liz he's an alien?"

Fell looked confused. "Never heard of it."

"How do you not know *Roswell*? It's a cult show!"

Aaron joined in the banter. "And for the record, I'm not an alien."

Landon shot back, "Sure, and now that you've said that, I totally believe you."

"Watch out," Aaron quipped. "I might shapeshift any second, knock you off, and conquer the world."

Fell, finishing his meal, tossed the wrapper in the bin. "Let's hit a live music spot tonight after work."

"Sounds good," Landon agreed with enthusiasm.

"Cool," Aaron said, curious about what the evening would bring.

"Lanny, why don't you invite Ria along?" Fell suggested casually.

Landon nodded, pulling out his phone.

Aaron couldn't quite wrap his head around their relationship. Nyle and Maeve had dropped hints that it might be a 'friends with benefits' deal, but that didn't seem to match up with what he'd observed. Sure, not everyone was like him, and for many, sex was a big deal, but Landon and Ria? They didn't seem the type for that sort of arrangement.

Aaron shook his head, attempting to shut off his thoughts as he and Fell walked back to the shop. Landon had already headed into the tattoo studio next door. Whatever was going on between him and Ria, it really wasn't Aaron's business. Then, why was he so caught up in thinking about it?

*

A wave of warm air, heavy with the tang of sweat and beer hit Aaron as they stepped into a small music venue that evening. The crowd's buzz blended with the vocals of an acoustic guitar–backed singer, making it hard to pick out the song.

Ria, already there, waved them over to a table right at the front. Somehow, she'd managed to snag one of the best spots in the house.

"Check out these front-row seats!" Ria beamed, clearing a pile of bags and coats off the chairs.

"You're a legend," Fell replied, sliding into a seat next to her.

Aaron quietly took the seat against the wall, leaving the more accessible one for Landon. He knew Landon preferred the outer seats and wasn't in the mood to argue, especially after spending all day listening to Fell's love life dramas.

"I'll grab the drinks," Fell announced, heading off towards the bar.

That left Aaron with Landon and Ria.

She turned to him as she leaned forward, her elbows on the table and her face resting in her hands. "So, Aaron, how's the shop treating you?" she asked, her high cheekbones more pronounced in her pose.

"Good," Aaron answered shortly, not feeling like going into details. He started fiddling with a splinter sticking out of the table. From the very first moment he met Ria, something about her put him on edge. It could have been her constant chirpiness or the way her voice sounded too smooth, unnerving to him. Her warmth and attention seemed like foreign concepts, so unlike the stares and whispers he was more accustomed to.

Ria didn't press him further. She turned to Landon instead, striking up a conversation about tattoos and some TV show Aaron hadn't seen yet.

Fell returned, balancing a round of drinks. Aaron grabbed his beer and took a hefty swig, trying to shake off his unease. His attention drifted to the stage, where a singer had started up a new song. He almost chuckled when he recognized the track—"Jumper." Quite apt for the night.

As the music filled the room and chatter picked up around him, Aaron zoned out, playing with his beer label. It was only when Landon pointed out the little paper fragments scattered on the table that he realised what he was doing.

"People actually get paid to design these, you know," Landon remarked.

"Then maybe they should make them tougher," Aaron quipped, trying to deflect.

"You seem tense. Everything all right?"

That took Aaron aback. He hadn't expected Landon to pick up on his unease. Was he that obvious, or was it Landon perceptiveness?

Fell gestured towards the stage. "What do you think, Aaron? Enjoying the music?"

"Yeah, it's not bad," he replied, quickly rubbing his hands on his jeans to get rid of the sticky residue. He had to admit, the live music made for a nice change of pace, and the artist was genuinely good.

But as the night wore on, Aaron became less absorbed in the music and more in watching Landon and Ria, scrutinising their every interaction for clues. He couldn't figure out what their deal was.

Their lack of physical contact struck him most; nothing hinted at anything more than friendship between them. In contrast, Fell constantly found reasons to get close to Ria—a pat on the back, brushing past her to hand her a drink, leaning in to talk over the music. To Aaron,

Fell seemed more connected with her than Landon, who kept shooting wary glances Aaron's way.

After the last notes of the performance had died down, the group found themselves on the pavement next to the canal.

Fell said his goodbyes quickly, mentioning he'd head off in the direction of Camden Town station. Meanwhile, Ria had her Uber waiting at the kerb. After a brief farewell and Landon's reminder for her to text once she was home, she departed.

Then, it was just Aaron and Landon.

Landon peered first at the water, then turned to Aaron. "How about a stroll along Regent's Canal?" he suggested. "We can catch the northern line from King's Cross."

Aaron, kicking a bottle cap ahead of him, nodded. The idea of a leisurely walk in the open air, away from the stuffiness of the Tube, appealed.

"Fancy grabbing a quick bite?" Landon gestured towards a nearby corner shop.

"Sounds good," Aaron agreed, following him. They emerged shortly after with a bag of cheese tortilla chips and two cans of cola.

They crossed the bridge over the lock, then descended to the waterside path. At this late hour, the area was almost deserted, offering a calm respite from the day's hustle and bustle.

They ambled past a group of tipsy girls perched on a wall, and as they continued along the canal path, the area became quieter, with just the odd passerby.

For a while, they walked in comfortable silence until Landon broke it.

"So, what did you think?" he asked, offering the open bag of crisps to Aaron.

Grabbing a handful, Aaron tasted a few. "It was good, actually. Live music's got a different feel to it, doesn't it?"

"What's your kind of music then?"

"I'm not tied down to one genre, really. I'm pretty open to all sorts. The only exception is Nyle's electronic stuff." Aaron crunched on more crisps and washed them down with a swig of soda. "Can't count the times I've wanted to chuck his speaker out the window."

"Be my guest." Landon chuckled, the corners of his mouth lifting in amusement. "Still, that's nothing compared to the sappy love songs he plays on repeat after every heartbreak."

"Never paid much attention to those. Some can be quite moving though."

"Yeah, they do have a way of hitting you right in the feels."

Aaron nodded, understanding all too well. Melancholic tunes had been his go-to in tough times, a balm when everything else felt too heavy. "You reckon?"

"Definitely," Landon affirmed. He paused and sat down by the canal, crossing his legs.

Aaron settled beside him. "It's strange, isn't it? How we listen to sad songs when we're feeling down?"

"Yeah, but it makes sense when you think about it." Landon's gaze wandered to the grand, column-lined villa across the canal. "Music's like a friend for tough times. When you're feeling low, you want something that resonates with that, something that gets it. Sometimes, it's hard to express how rubbish you're feeling. But a song can find those words for you."

Aaron nodded in agreement, finishing off the last of the crisps. "So why tattoo? Ever thought about doing something with music? You know, like working at RPM with Fell?"

Landon sighed, turning back to Aaron. "I did consider it, but drawing's always been my thing. I like turning what's in my head into something tangible."

"I used to draw a lot when I was a kid," Aaron admitted. "I had loads of sketches, made my own little comics even." He paused, the memory of his mother discarding his artwork resurfacing with a sting of bitterness. "But then I got into other stuff and left it behind."

"You should pick it up again, maybe even turn one of your drawings into a tattoo."

"Maybe. I don't know." Aaron scratched his head. "Speaking of tattoos, you have a lot of them, especially on your arms. Did you design those yourself?"

Landon nodded, lightly touching his arm. "Most of them."

"Mind if I take a closer look?"

Landon rubbed his arm. "They're not the best, just some early ideas."

Aaron suspected they were more impressive than Landon let on, but he didn't push it. "Which one are you proudest of?"

After a pause, Landon pointed to the small bone tattoo on his middle finger.

Aaron laughed. "What's that for, flipping people off?"

"Exactly. And, you know, giving death the finger."

Aaron mumbled sceptically. If only it were that simple to ward off death.

"Ever thought about getting one?" Landon asked.

Aaron touched his chest, over his scars. "I like them on others but not for myself. They're too permanent."

"Nothing's permanent. Tattoos leave when we do."

"Cheery thought."

"Just being honest. But I get your point," Landon said, then scratched behind his ear over a tiny star tattoo.

"Does that one mean something special?"

Landon stopped scratching. "Not every tattoo has to mean something."

"But for you, I bet they do. That star behind your ear, for instance."

Landon hesitated, then said softly, "It's not just any star. It's the North Star."

"Why behind the ear?"

Landon half-smiled. "It's like a talking cricket."

As always, Landon had to be cryptic. Aaron leaned back and tilted his head to the night sky. A small dot shone easily among the clouds.

"Sirius." He pointed at the star.

Landon squinted up. "Isn't it Venus?"

"No, it's common to mix them up. But it's Sirius."

Landon turned to him. "Are you messing with me?"

"I just know more than you."

"So, you're really into this astronomy stuff, with the Southern Lights and all?"

"Well, you have no idea what a bored kid with lots of time and books can do. After reading *Peter Pan*, I wanted to find Neverland."

"The home of the lost boys."

"Yes."

"And did you find it?"

Aaron bit his cheek and gazed once again at the sky. "If I had, I wouldn't be here."

The sound of a can being crushed and the crinkle of the tortilla chips bag answered him.

Then, Landon responded with, "But you did find another lost boy," before getting up and tossing the trash in a nearby bin.

As they ambled side by side along the canal, Aaron enjoyed the comforting warmth from Landon close by. They didn't touch, but now and then, their shoulders brushed against each other.

Each time it happened, it sent a small, electric thrill through Aaron, like tiny sparks in the crisp night air that made the chilly breeze bearable.

Though subtle, those brushes stirred a closeness within Aaron he didn't even know he yearned for. Without even realising it, he found himself inching a little closer to Landon with every step they took together.

Chapter Sixteen

Just Another Day on the Calendar

[Now playing » Deep End—Ruelle]

Aaron's birthdays had never been a big deal. Just another day on the calendar.

His parents didn't see the point in celebrating—no parties, no gifts, not even a slice of cake or candles to blow out. The only exception was the secret blueberry muffin from the supermarket he and Tori would sneakily share, their own little birthday tradition.

But when he moved in with Aunt Olivia three years ago, it all changed.

"Birthdays are for celebrating, Aarie." she'd say every year, making sure he woke up to the smell of her special pancakes and a carrot cake in the oven. A gift always waited for him too.

"I don't care about birthdays," Aaron would tell her. But on a

mission to make every birthday count, Aunt Olivia wouldn't have any of that.

Then came Cliff, who added another layer to the celebrations. Suddenly, they were about loud music, belly laughs, and maybe too much to drink. Aaron's eighteenth had been a blast, the first time he bought his own booze.

But this year, Aaron stepped back into the background.

Entering the kitchen, he found no special breakfast, no carrot cake, no muffins, no Cliff. His nineteenth birthday was like any other regular day—uncelebrated by anyone, including himself.

*

That Thursday at RPM felt heavier than usual, not because of a rush of customers—few and far between—but because of his own restless, sleep-deprived mind. The weather didn't help either, raining nonstop since morning.

Aaron skipped the usual lunch with Landon and Fell. Instead, he made a quick dash to the supermarket, grabbed a sandwich, a blueberry muffin, and spent the rest of his break holed up in the shop, zoning out to Netflix.

Fell must have sensed something was off because he blasted "What's Up?" by 4 Non Blondes in the afternoon, trying to cheer Aaron up. It worked, sort of, but the lift in spirits was short-lived.

As the shift ended, Aaron rubbed his eyes, still feeling the sting of sleeplessness. He considered asking Fell and Landon out for drinks, but Ria showed up, Landon tagging along behind her. It struck him then. It wasn't just any day—it was Thursday.

"Where are you two off to?" Fell asked, leaning against a shelf.

"I'm dragging Landon to a veggie burger place," Ria replied.

Fell made a face. "Vegetarian and burger shouldn't be in the same sentence."

Ria laughed and dived into one of her classic debates with Fell, who wasn't one to back down easily. After their back and forth ended without any clear winner, Ria waved a quick goodbye and turned to leave.

Landon, about to follow her, paused abruptly on the threshold. Following his gaze, Aaron noticed the same dishevelled guy from a few days before standing on the pavement across the street.

"Is he also invited to your date?" Fell joked.

Landon gave a grunted sigh. Ignoring Ian, who had moved towards him, he hurried out of the shop with Ria.

Aaron watched them leave, then focused back on Ian, now fading into the crowd. Something about the guy gave him the creeps. "What's his deal with Landon, you reckon?"

"Who knows?" Fell said, packing up, ready to leave as well. "Must be desperate for cash."

Aaron seized the moment. "Hey, fancy a drink at the pub?"

"Tempting, but I've got a date tonight."

"Oh, good luck," Aaron replied, trying to mask his disappointment. "Catch you tomorrow then."

He walked for a while around the area, ending up at Camden Lock. He sat by the canal and scrolled through his phone, realising he didn't have any friends to call; the only one he got hated his guts. On a whim, he texted Nyle, who was often free on Thursdays after the shift at the museum. It didn't take long for him to send a positive reply.

*

"**...a**nd then he left with his girlfriend." Nyle sighed, nursing his second beer. Throughout the evening, he'd fixated on his unrequited crush on a straight colleague. "I don't understand why I always fall for the wrong guys."

"Maybe you're unknowingly sabotaging yourself."

"You're starting to sound like a therapist."

Aaron grimaced. He never liked the therapy sessions Aunt Olivia convinced him to have after the accident. He'd found them useless.

Despite Nyle's romantic troubles, time flew by. Before Aaron knew it, his birthday was close to ending, almost forgotten once again.

His phone suddenly buzzed on the wooden table, startling them both.

He'd been anticipating a call or message from Aunt Olivia that morning, but it hadn't arrived. Aaron figured she must have miscalculated the time difference again, thinking it was now morning in Australia.

As the unanswered call ended, a text message popped up on his screen, clearly visible to Nyle—a big 'Happy Birthday' message, filled with celebratory emojis.

Nyle stared at him, surprised. "Honey, it's your birthday, and you didn't think to mention it? I could've baked you a cake or thrown you a party!"

Aaron shook his head. "Nah, I don't celebrate."

"You can't be serious!"

"Just another year in this fucked up world. There's absolutely nothing worth marking."

"Maybe you feel that way because you've never done it with the right people. Let me throw you a nice party this weekend. Fell can bring beers, Ria and Landon can make cocktails, and—"

"Nyle, please, don't." Aaron's response was sharper than he intended, but it did the trick.

"All right, all right," Nyle conceded, raising his hands in surrender. "But I'm getting you another beer, birthday boy!"

*

The few beers soon turned into five.

Neither Aaron nor Nyle were heavy drinkers, and by the third beer, Nyle's words started to blur into a tipsy ramble.

Getting home turned into its own adventure. They somehow managed to catch the right Tube line but in the wrong direction. It took Aaron five stops to realise it.

They scrambled off, only to find they'd missed the last train back.

"Let's get a cab," Nyle suggested, surprisingly lucid. Luckily, they didn't have to shiver in the cold too long before their car pulled up.

During the ride, Nyle shared the trip status with Landon and launched into a loud rumble about potentially dangerous rides. That earned them amused smiles from their driver, who happily chatted away with Nyle.

Aaron, though, stayed quiet the whole time, watching the city lights blur past the window.

When they finally arrived home, Aaron only wanted to crash in his bed and forget about the day. But he pushed the door open to Landon, waiting in the shadows of the corridor, arms crossed, with an expression Aaron couldn't quite read.

Landon zeroed in on Nyle. "Are you drunk?"

"No, no," Nyle slurred. "I know my limits."

"Knowing them and respecting them are two different things."

"I'm totally fine," Nyle insisted, though his rushed trip to the bathroom suggested otherwise.

Turning his attention to Aaron, Landon's eyes flashed with irritation. "Why'd you let him drink so much?"

Feeling somewhat foggy himself, Aaron retorted, "Let him? Nyle's a grown-up. He makes his own choices."

"But making sensible choices isn't easy when you're not in your right mind."

"In fact, he decided to get drunk when he was still sober."

"I'm talking about the consequences."

"So, what? You never drink because you're afraid of losing control?"

Landon grumbled, "Minus two."

Despite the haze of alcohol, Aaron remembered that odd countdown. "Why so tense? This is stupid."

"And I can't stand stupidity. The last time Nyle got wasted, we ended up doing community service."

"I heard that was on you."

Landon's eyes widened. "Nyle told you that?"

Just then, Nyle reemerged. "Relax, Lanny. We were just having a few drinks for Aaron's birthday."

"Birthday?" Landon looked even more confused.

"Yeah, shocking, isn't it? He didn't tell anyone. Says it's just another year down the drain."

"He's not wrong."

Nyle made a face. "You guys are such downers. No wonder you're friends."

"We're not friends," Landon stated bluntly, causing an odd twinge in Aaron's stomach. He chalked it up to the alcohol.

"Good night," Landon bid them, heading up the stairs.

"Hey, Lanny, wait. Help me to my room. I can't stand."

Landon paused, scrutinising Nyle's hunched form at the base of the stairs. "That sounds like a you problem."

"Oh, come on, don't *meme* me."

"Get Aaron to help you," Landon said, his tone as flat as his gaze.

Landon disappeared upstairs, the only sound the creak of his steps.

"All right, let's get you up there," Aaron offered, wrapping an arm around Nyle's waist for support. They made their way, with Nyle stumbling and Aaron trying to keep them both steady. At Nyle's door, Aaron finally released his grip.

"You can make it to your bed from here, right?"

But before Aaron could turn to leave, Nyle grabbed his arm, pulling him into the room. Aaron, caught off-guard, bumped into the door frame. Nyle was right there, too close, pinning him against the wood.

"Whoa, what's happening here?" Aaron asked.

"Shh." Nyle pressed a finger to his lips. "Your lips...they're so soft... But wait, I gotta tell you something."

Feeling trapped and uncomfortable, Aaron attempted to create some space. "Nyle, maybe we should talk about this tomorrow, yeah?"

Nyle paused, then took a step back, giving Aaron some breathing room. "No, it has to be now. I might not have the guts later."

"What are you talking about?"

"Just...promise me you won't tell anyone."

"Nyle, you're freaking me out. What's going on?"

Nyle took a deep breath. "It's about Landon."

"What about him?"

"Well, the whole community service thing... It wasn't Landon's fault. He got dragged into it because of me."

Aaron leaned against the door frame, trying to make sense of this new piece of information.

"Landon, he...he took the fall for something stupid I did when I was plastered. He wanted to keep me out of trouble. With his jail record and all, I didn't want to make it worse for him, but I did. So, end of the story, we both got community service."

Aaron began to understand, piecing together Landon's earlier mood. "Okay, but what did you do?"

Nyle grimaced. "Smashed my ex's car windows, then egged his house."

It was hard not to burst out laughing. "And they sentenced you for that?"

"Yeah, vandalism," Nyle said with a half-hearted shrug. "Landon tried to cover for me, but it didn't work out. So now, a few more months of community service for both of us."

Aaron groaned, massaging his forehead. His headache, which had been nagging at him for a while, now felt like it was splitting his head in two. The only silver lining was that he probably wouldn't struggle to fall asleep. "Right, I'm off to bed. Goodnight."

"Hold up. Crash here tonight?" Nyle suggested.

Aaron scanned the room, which held only one bed. "You mean, like, sleeping together?"

"Yeah, just to sleep, you know? Not like *sleep* sleep."

The idea only made his headache worse. Sharing a bed, even just for sleep, was a step too far for him. "Sorry, Nyle, I can't do that."

"Just a sleepover, nothing more. Ever had one?"

Aaron grabbed the door handle. "No, and I'm not about to start. Goodnight, Nyle."

Halfway up the stairs, his phone buzzed in his pocket. He braced himself for another message or call from Aunt Olivia, but to his surprise, it was Tom.

Just had a word with the folks at the wildlife park. They've agreed to wait for you through the winter season. Happy birthday, little man!

Chapter Seventeen

The Surprise Birthday Party

[Now playing » Dangerous Night—Thirty Seconds To Mars]

The thing about Nyle was, he never quite took 'no' for an answer.

So, when Aaron walked through the door on Friday evening after a shift at RPM, he got ambushed by a flurry of paper streamers.

"Surprise!" Nyle's voice rang out, high-pitched and jubilant.

Aaron stopped dead in his tracks, staring at the spectacle before him. Behind Nyle, all happy and cheery, stood Maeve, Ria, and a few others he didn't recognise.

"Happy birthday!" Nyle exclaimed, ushering Aaron into the living room.

The room burst into a chorus of hellos as Nyle turned up the music, setting the mood.

"You didn't think I'd let your birthday go uncelebrated, did you?" he asked.

"I said there's nothing to celebrate."

"And I said maybe you haven't celebrated with the right people."

"The 'right people' being you and these strangers?"

Nyle invited Aaron to relax and stay put before disappearing upstairs.

Maeve slid over to Aaron, wine glass in hand, a smudge of lipstick on the rim. "Hey, Aaron!" She greeted him playfully. "Why didn't you tell anyone it was your birthday? We could've had a little celebration together on the day, you know."

"I've already told Nyle I don't care about birthdays."

Maeve burst into laughter. "Oh, come on. A birthday is the perfect excuse to go wild!"

"I had other plans."

"What, like a solo TV show marathon in bed?" Leaning in closer, Maeve lowered her voice to a murmur. "We could team up for that…"

Aaron hesitated, not sure how to deflect. "Perhaps another time," he said, more to get away from the conversation than anything else. He excused himself and headed to the kitchen island.

As he stood there, munching on the crisps, a wave of irritation washed over him. Nyle setting up this surprise party was one thing, but Landon and Fell being part of the conspiracy stung. They'd been around him all day and hadn't breathed a word about it. He spotted them in a corner, casually chatting and laughing with Ria. The sight added to his growing annoyance.

"Hey, I'm back." Nyle popped up next to Aaron, his grin as mischievous as ever while hiding something behind his back. "Did you miss me? I've got something nice for you."

Aaron didn't need to be a detective to guess it was a gift. Sure enough, Nyle revealed a flat, rectangular package with a little bow in the corner.

Instead of grabbing it, Aaron froze.

Suddenly, he was back in that bloody hospital room, Tori lying on the bed with a similar package by her side.

The party, the music, the chatter—it all started to swirl and merge into a dizzying blur. Like spinning too fast in an office chair, the world around Aaron turned into a whirlpool of shapes and sounds. A wave of dizziness and breathlessness washed over him as if he still spun out of control.

"Can you...hold on to it for a sec?" Aaron spoke slightly above a whisper, his words a surprise even to himself. He patted his back pocket as if his phone was buzzing. "Need to take this call. Sorry."

"Aaron, wait—" Nyle tried to stop him, but Aaron was already on the move.

He hurried out to the garden, trying to look as composed as possible. But as soon as he was outside, he unloaded the full weight of the unease that had been building up.

He staggered towards the wooden fence at the back, his steps unsteady. Leaning forward, he rested his hands on his knees and tried to catch his breath. The night air should have been refreshing, but it seemed to hardly touch his lungs. He even unzipped his hoodie in a desperate attempt to breathe easier, but it was no use. His chest tightened, each heartbeat echoing painfully.

"Aaron?" Someone called his name, but it sounded distant, unreal.

Clutching the fabric of his jeans, he cursed under his breath. He should have run farther. The garden was close, too close for anyone to follow. But his legs were jelly, barely supporting him.

"Aaron..."

He didn't have to turn around to know it was Landon; the distinctive metallic jingle of the buckled straps around his boots gave him away. Aaron hoped Landon would take one look at him and leave him be, but his determined step told a different story.

Aaron still struggled to breathe when Landon's hand suddenly appeared in front of his face, catching his attention. He looked up, his vision initially blurry until Landon's face came into sharp focus against the night sky.

"Not now," Aaron rasped out.

Ignoring him, Landon firmly gripped Aaron's shoulders and pushed him down. Unsteady as he was, Aaron couldn't resist the force and ended up with his butt on the damp grass. He tried to stand, but Landon's hands were there again, holding him down.

"Fuck you," Aaron spat out, his breath still coming in short bursts.

"Close your eyes and breathe. That's how you stay alive."

"Screw you."

"At least you're still quick with your comebacks. Can't be that bad, then."

Aaron wanted to fire back another insult, but he only managed a frustrated grunt.

"Stay here," Landon commanded, punctuating his words with a pointed finger.

Aaron bit back another sharp retort. He wasn't sure he could move, even if he tried.

"I'll be back in a sec," Landon said. "Just...breathe."

Closing his eyes, Aaron tried to calm himself. It was hard at first, and he coughed a bit, but slowly, he started to improve.

Soon, the sound of Landon's boots approached again.

Aaron opened his eyes to Landon crouching before him, holding a spoonful of dark sauce extended towards his mouth.

"Swallow this," Landon instructed, his expression serious.

"What's that?" Aaron tried to get a whiff of whatever was on the spoon, but Landon swiftly pulled it back.

"Just take it. No questions."

Exhausted and not in the mood to argue, Aaron reluctantly accepted the spoon and downed its contents. Instant regret followed as his throat went on fire.

"What the fuck?" he gasped, tears springing to his eyes from the burn.

"Worcestershire sauce," Landon replied calmly.

"Fuck you."

"You really need to work on your insult game. They're getting a bit repetitive," Landon teased.

"I'll keep that in mind," Aaron said dryly. "As soon as my taste buds stop feeling like they've been set on fire."

Landon made himself more comfortable on the ground, crossing his legs. "Okay, now that the sauce has given you a kick, try to focus on five different things you can see."

Aaron shot him a long, irritated look. "I see a dick."

"Good." Landon barely smiled. "You don't necessarily have to say them aloud. Just find five things to look at and focus on a detail. Now that you've found one, concentrate on another four, then give me a sign when you're done."

Aaron wanted to breathe fire on him, but he played along. First, he settled on Landon's face, particularly the stark silver piercing in his split eyebrow. He probably got that scar from a nasty bump. Maybe the piercing was a slick cover-up.

His gaze, drifting right, paused at the stretched earlobe, large enough to peek through. Next, he glimpsed a rose tattoo peeking out from under Landon's collar, beside it, the words 'Hell Is Other People'. This made Aaron curious about the other tattoos hidden under Landon's clothes. Maeve had mentioned that ink covered Landon's torso, and Aaron wondered about the stories it might tell.

A small skull centred Landon's T-shirt, circled by the words 'We know what we are, but not what we may be'. A bit of Shakespeare, from Hamlet. To his surprise, Aaron hadn't spotted it before.

Landon's usual attire was a lot more low-key compared to Nyle's flashy get-ups. But now Aaron saw something more in his subtle choices, as with the tattoos. They weren't random; they represented a piece of who Landon was. This idea struck a comforting chord in Aaron. It seemed like Landon didn't do anything without a meaningful reason behind it.

Once he'd mentally ticked off the remaining things, Aaron nodded slightly.

"Now, find four things you can touch."

Aaron didn't fully understand Landon's game, but he went along with it anyway, finding the distraction somewhat helpful.

The first thing was easy, the spoon still in his hand. He focused on its cool, smooth metal under his fingertips, its curved shape oddly comforting. The sensation reminded him of his pendant, so he reached up to the familiar shard of glass.

Next, he glided his hand along the teeth of his hoodie's zipper, which was fully undone.

Finally, Aaron extended his hand to a few damp blades of grass. The moisture and the texture grounded him in the reality that he was in a garden, not teetering on the brink of a high-rise building. The sense of vertigo started to ebb away.

With another nod of his head, he indicated he was finished.

"Three things you can hear," Landon prompted.

At this stage, Aaron went with it, stopping his attempts to figure out Landon's game.

The most immediate sound was the thumping of his own heartbeat, a rhythmic pulse echoing in his ears, strangely in sync with the faint strains of music coming from inside the house. Aaron concentrated and picked up the melody and lyrics of the song, though he couldn't place the title.

"Done," he said.

"Two things you can smell."

That was the easiest. The scent of Landon's coconut shampoo had initially put him off, but Aaron had grown accustomed to it. That, and the persistent tobacco smell on Landon's clothes, created a unique, if somewhat unusual, fragrance.

Landon didn't wait for any sort of acknowledgement and moved on quickly. "One thing you can taste."

Aaron rolled the flavour around in his mouth, the strong, tangy taste of Worcestershire sauce still there. The lingering burn, surprisingly, helped combat the nausea. The shaking in his arms and legs had lessened, his breathing now steadier.

Taking a deep breath, he was amazed at how much easier it felt. This odd game of Landon's had actually worked.

Landon pulled out a cigarette and glanced at Aaron for an okay before lighting it up.

As the smoke drifted towards him, Aaron exhaled deeply.

It was ironic.

Just moments ago, he'd felt like he couldn't get enough air, almost suffocating. But now, sitting there with Landon's smoke wafting in his face, he breathed properly for the first time since stepping outside—a strange kind of relief.

Landon blew out another puff of smoke. "Just saved you months of therapy."

Aaron, drawing his knees to his chest with a puzzled look.

"That thing you just did, it's a technique my therapist showed me for panic attacks. Helps you focus on your senses to get control of your body back," Landon explained.

"You're seeing a therapist?"

"Yeah, a session every other Thursday evening," Landon replied, as he blew out more smoke.

"Don't you go out with Ria on Thursdays?"

Landon blew another stream of smoke towards Aaron. "Ria and I are part of the same...club. We meet on Thursdays. And since my therapist's office is nearby, I usually have my sessions right after."

"So, you and Ria..."

"What about me and Ria?"

"You're not...dating?"

Landon shook his head, almost laughing. "Where did you get that idea from?"

"It's what everyone seems to think," Aaron admitted.

"Classic heteronormativity. Just because a man and a woman hang out, doesn't mean they're sleeping together."

"So, you're not...friends with benefits or anything?"

"Definitely not," Landon confirmed with a smile. "I'm gay."

That revelation took Aaron by surprise. Not because it mattered to him—people's sexual orientations weren't his business—but because everyone seemed so sure Landon was involved with Ria. "Is it—are you not out?"

Landon waved his hand dismissively. "It's not some big secret or anything."

"But how has Nyle not picked up on this?"

Landon chuckled. "He's too wrapped up in his own rainbow world to notice there are different shades of gay, I suppose. Or maybe I just don't fit his idea of what being gay looks like. Who knows?"

He snuffed out his cigarette in a paper cup and stood up. "By the way, about that therapy thing." He pulled out his phone. "I can give you my therapist's contact if you want. Helped me a lot; might do the same for you."

Aaron rose swiftly, brushing off the idea. "Nah, I'll pass."

Landon looked at him squarely. "At least give it a try."

"Been there, done that. Didn't work for me."

"Maybe you didn't find the right one."

Aaron scoffed. "They're all the same, really. What do they do? Wait for you to sit there, spill all your problems, and then magically pretend to fix everything?"

"It's not about fixing. It's about understanding and finding your own way to deal with them."

"Yeah, right."

"Look, therapy is not for the weak. It takes courage to face what's troubling you. And from what I see, you've got a fair bit weighing on your shoulders. It helps to talk to someone."

Aaron hesitated, Landon's words hitting a nerve. "You're weird. Don't trust anyone, yet you spill your deepest secrets to a stranger."

"Well, that's the whole point. Sometimes it's easier to talk to someone you don't know. A friend can only help so much, while a therapist does that for a living. Lottie's great. I wouldn't recommend her otherwise." Landon tapped something on the screen, and then Aaron's phone buzzed.

"What's this?" He checked the message and read the contact details Landon had sent through: Charlotte Starford.

"That's my therapist's number. Think about it," Landon said, calm but firm.

"I won't. I don't need a therapist."

"The way you reacted earlier says otherwise."

Aaron ran a hand through his messy hair, twirling a strand around his finger. He pulled his hood up and swivelled to look at the summer house. Part of him wished he could pick the lock, sneak in there, and hide.

"I shouldn't have let you see me like that," he said, almost to himself.

"Hey, no need to be embarrassed. It hasn't changed what I think of you. We all have our moments, don't we?"

Aaron didn't feel entirely reassured, but he was grateful for Landon's words. He fiddled with his pendant, taking a deep breath. Then, as if releasing a hidden truth, he quietly confessed, "I'm not into gifts."

The soft rustling of grass signalled Landon's movement, but Aaron's hood limited his view, shadowing his face.

"All right, no Christmas presents for you, then."

Aaron turned partially towards Landon. And even like this, even in the fading light, he felt oddly exposed, like the koala doodle Landon had glimpsed the other day. It was as though Landon was studying the sketch again, seeing beyond the simple lines to the deeper emotions it held. In the silence, Aaron felt vulnerable yet understood under Landon's observant eye.

"Aren't you going to ask me why?"

"No. But if you ever want to talk about it, know that I'm here to listen."

Aaron managed a nod, his mind still a jumble. The whole episode, from Nyle's gift to his near breakdown, was too complicated to explain.

"Thanks," he muttered, eyes drifting to their feet. He hoped Landon understood that his gratitude wasn't just for offering a listening ear, but for being there, helping him ride out the storm of his panic attack. He'd remember that little game from now on.

"Do you want to go back inside? It's getting cold," Landon suggested.

"Okay." Aaron moved towards the glow of the living room.

"Wait." Landon stepped in Aaron's path, causing him to stop so abruptly he nearly walked right into him.

He was close enough to feel Landon's sturdy presence—a comforting barrier that seemed to promise Aaron wouldn't have fallen even if they had bumped into each other. It struck him then how Landon had become a sort of safe haven for him, a strange and comforting thought. If Aaron had asked to stay there, outside, Landon would have shielded him from anyone else's intrusion.

When had he started thinking of a person instead of a place as a safe refuge?

Just as Aaron regained his balance, Landon reached out and slowly pulled back his hood, exposing Aaron's face, now open to the cool night air. But instead of the chill, Aaron basked in the warmth from Landon's hands, a warmth that stayed even after Landon had let go.

"There, that's better," Landon said with a small smile. He turned, gesturing for Aaron to follow him back inside.

As soon as they stepped into the living room, Nyle bounced over with a pair of balloons. "Hey, you've been missing out! The party's out here, not in the garden!" He offered them each a balloon. "Fancy a laugh?"

Landon declined flatly, but Aaron accepted.

"These got nitro in them?" he asked.

Nyle's grin widened as he nodded. To demonstrate, he inhaled from his balloon in quick bursts. Within seconds, he was lost in a fit of giggles. "Give it a go. It's brilliant!"

Aaron didn't need much convincing. He took a deep breath from the balloon, the vapour filling his lungs. The world around him seemed to warp and stretch, like a shadow lengthening at twilight. His senses became more acute; the music and lights intensified, and his laughter sounded foreign to him, as if echoing from the depths of a long, dark tunnel.

Over the noise, Nyle, still giggling, shouted, "Isn't this song great?"

Aaron nodded, recognising "My Universe" by BTS and Coldplay. Caught up, he sang along, even attempting the Korean parts.

Landon shook his head. "Since when do you speak Korean?"

"Always full of surprises, aren't I?" Aaron answered, but the effects of the gas had worn off, bringing him back down to earth.

Landon's smile was subtle, almost hidden, but Aaron caught it—a faint uplift at the corners of his mouth. A shadow of it lingered in Landon's eyes, which held a depth hinting at past troubles, but that fleeting smile caught Aaron's attention, holding his gaze.

"You're smiling. I made you laugh," he observed.

"I'm not laughing," Landon replied, but his tone betrayed a touch of amusement.

"Ah, must be a trick of the light, then."

"Or the gas is causing you to have hallucinations."

"Did you know you get dimples when you smile?"

"No," Landon responded with a hint of caution, the amusement still lingering.

Aaron gestured to his own cheek. "Right here."

"I'm not laughing," Landon insisted.

"Oh, I forgot. Black isn't just your colour choice, it's a lifestyle. Laughing might ruin your image."

Landon huffed softly, a sound Aaron had come to recognise as a crack in his usually impassive demeanour. Then Landon made his way towards the kitchen, where Ria signalled to him. With nothing else to do, Aaron followed.

"Hey, Birthday Boy! Enjoying yourself?" She smiled at him.

Landon said, "He's had his fair share of fun for one day."

Ria laughed softly, pushing a strand of hair behind her ear. "Fancy a special birthday cocktail? What's your poison?"

"I'll leave it to the expert," Aaron replied, gesturing towards her.

Ria and Landon shared a glance that Aaron couldn't quite read. Knowing now that their relationship was purely platonic, he felt more at ease around them.

"I'll whip something up," Landon offered, moving to gather various bottles and a shaker.

"Should I be worried?" Aaron asked jokingly.

"Trust me, Landon's a wizard with cocktails."

Aaron watched him at work, captivated by the precise way he

prepared the drink. He could have watched him for hours, but soon Ria handed him the finished cocktail, a blend of soft gradients, topped with a fruit garnish. It smelled predominantly like strawberry, and the first sip, sweet and spicy, left a refreshing aftertaste.

"Well, what do you think?" Ria asked eagerly.

The drink was, quite simply, amazing. Aaron didn't say as much, but his request for a second, then a third, and even a fourth cocktail said it all. He couldn't pinpoint what made the drink so good; he only knew he couldn't get enough of it.

As the night went on, with more rounds of drinks and ever-wilder chats, Aaron started to think that maybe, just maybe, he was actually having a good time at a party. The alcohol seemed to be doing its job because his thoughts had gotten more out there.

Every now and then, he would find Landon, and each time, he'd remember how warm Landon's hands had felt earlier. He imagined the firmness of Landon's hold, a grounding presence in the whirlwind of the party.

Watching Landon take a sip, an absurd thought occurred to Aaron. What would it be like to taste that drink but from Landon's lips?

Aaron shivered, surprised and shocked by where his imagination had wandered. He shook his head to clear it, but the idea lingered.

For the first time ever, Aaron wanted to kiss someone. And not just anyone. He wanted to kiss Landon.

Chapter Eighteen

Scars & Tattoos

[Now playing » Safe & Sound—Taylor Swift]

The flashing party lights kept throwing new shades over Landon, making Aaron blink a few times.

He noticed things he hadn't before: a tiny mole under Landon's right eye, that stubborn lock of hair that always fell on his forehead, how he would fiddle with his lip piercing, and those long fingers with neat nails.

When Landon reached up to grab more cocktail glasses, his T-shirt lifted a bit, revealing a peek of a tattoo on his hip. Usually, Aaron wouldn't pay much attention, but tonight, he found himself drawn to it.

The bit of text disappeared under the waistband of Landon's jeans, and Aaron couldn't help but wonder about the words inked there and the path the tattoo might trace on Landon's body.

He imagined how it would feel to touch it, to feel Landon's warm skin under his fingertips, or to have Landon's body pressed against his, those skilled hands roaming on him, so precise and so gentle, much as they'd been when Landon had traced over his doodle.

Aaron realised he'd been staring longer than he should have when Landon glanced up, catching his eye with a curious look. Heat rushed to his face, and he quickly averted his gaze, pretending interest in something else.

He'd never experienced such a strong, physical attraction with anyone else before. He'd never craved someone's touch like this. What was going on?

A bit dazed, Aaron navigated through the small crowd, making his way towards the corridor. He tried to rationalise it, blaming the cocktails. Perhaps they'd been mixed with something stronger than he was used to, or maybe he could blame the sugar rush.

Just as he neared his room, a hand with sharp nails gripped on his arm.

"Hey, Aaron," Maeve said. "You all right?"

Right then, facing Maeve and her inviting look, a wild idea popped into Aaron's head.

"Hey," he said, "about that offer earlier… Still on?"

Maeve gave him a quick once-over, then her lips curled into a cheeky smile. "Totally!"

Aaron grabbed her hand and led her to his room. He was curious, maybe even a little desperate, to figure out if something was changing in him, if maybe he was just a late bloomer.

The door had barely clicked shut when Maeve pounced, pushing him back onto the bed. In a flash, she was on top of him, their faces so close he could count her lush eyelashes.

They kissed, and Aaron shut his eyes, telling himself it would be different this time, that he'd finally feel something more. But all he sensed was the taste of wine and Maeve's sticky lipstick.

Despite her enthusiasm, the kiss was hollow, like all the others he'd had. He tried, *really* tried, to get into it, to see if it was a matter of technique. But nope, his body and mind were still like two strangers, not knowing how to connect.

Maeve's hands, with her pointy nails, tugged at his hair, nothing like Landon's gentle touch. It yanked Aaron out of the moment.

She stopped and pulled back to sit next to him. "This isn't working, is it?"

Aaron shook his head, lost for words as disappointment and confusion washed over him. "I'm sorry, it's—"

"—not you, it's me?" Maeve tilted her head. "Are you in denial about being gay?"

Aaron snorted in disbelief. "What?"

Maeve shrugged. "I just thought you were picky. But Nyle, he's got a different theory. He reckons you're not into anyone because you've only had, as he puts it, 'boring straight sex.' So, he's convinced you might be a repressed gay."

Aaron sat there, speechless, genuinely confused. Sure, he'd only had penetrative sex with girls, but as Ria had said, sex wasn't just about that. "I'm not— I don't know. I don't think so?"

Maeve patted his knee. "Hey, it's cool; no shame in any of it. I once dated a guy who thought he was bi. Turned out, he was gay and figuring stuff out with me. Take your time." She stood up, making a playful 'call me' gesture. "If you ever figure things out, you know where to find me."

Aaron stayed put for a while, his mind spinning like a tumble dryer full of clothes. He didn't feel the same pull towards Maeve, so what the hell was happening with Landon? Was his attraction to Landon just a random twist? Or was Aaron actually gay and not some kind of unusual bisexual?

He carried these questions with him as he returned to the party, his gaze drifting over the guys in the living area, almost as if he was searching for answers. He decided to test his reactions then and there.

First up in his line of sight was Nyle. Sure, he was good-looking. Aaron had seen enough of him shirtless around the house and on Instagram. But it was challenging to separate Nyle's loud personality from his appearance. Just looking at him now was a sensory overload, drowning any potential physical attraction Aaron might've felt. His thoughts succinctly summed it up: *overwhelming.*

Aaron moved on to Fell. He didn't have Nyle's striking looks, but he possessed a certain charm. Aaron respected him for his random pearls of wisdom, the nerdy T-shirts he wore, which always caught Aaron's attention, and his extensive music knowledge. But despite all these, Aaron felt nothing. *Interesting, but not captivating.*

His focus wandered to some of Nyle's friends. One reminded him of Cliff, and that was enough for Aaron to move on without a second thought.

Another guy was clearly fit, his physique finely chiselled from what must have been many hours spent at the gym. This could be the 'gym guy' Nyle always mentioned. Aaron had to admit, he was undeniably handsome, and he wondered what kind of workout routine could sculpt a body like his. Yet, he couldn't see himself with him, not in the way Nyle often rumbled about. *Easy pass.*

Aaron considered Jean—tall, nice face, decent nose, and all that jazz. But their brief chit-chat in the kitchen—something about his disdain for beans on toast and how the Brits had *butchered* French cuisine—was more than enough for Aaron. He couldn't see what Nyle found so irresistible, constantly raving about Jean's 'sexy' accent, supposedly a major turn-on. Aaron could barely handle Jean in English. The idea of listening to him in French would be nothing short of torture.

But when he caught sight of Landon in the kitchen, it all changed.

Landon casually leaned on the counter, absorbed in his phone. Even in such a simple, unguarded moment, Aaron found him irresistibly attractive.

Warmth spread from his chest and gradually intensified, pooling between his legs.

Okay, clear now—this wasn't about being attracted to men; this was specific to Landon.

To cool himself down, Aaron grabbed a beer from the kitchen island. With clumsy hands, he tried to open it using the countertop edge as leverage. It took a few tries, but when he finally popped the cap off most of the beer splashed over him.

"Shit," he muttered at his now damp T-shirt.

The fabric clung uncomfortably to his stomach, dangerously close to the scars he kept hidden. He couldn't shake the worry that the wet, light-coloured fabric might turn transparent and expose those old, carefully concealed, loathed wounds.

"Hey," Landon said. "You've got that look on your face again."

"What look?" Aaron asked, trying to sound indifferent.

"The 'fight or flight' one, though you seem more in 'flight' mode right now."

"Maybe that's exactly what's happening," Aaron retorted with an edge of annoyance.

Landon set his phone aside and gestured outside the window. "Come on. I know a place where you can relax."

Curious, Aaron followed him out into the garden. They stopped in front of the summer house, the one Nyle had declared off-limits.

Landon undid the padlock and pushed the door open, letting it hang ajar—an unmistakable invitation for Aaron to enter.

Aaron, however, hesitated.

"I'm not going to leave it open forever," Landon said. "You coming or not?"

Stepping in after Landon's nudge, Aaron took a quick look around.

The compact room had a cosy vibe, an almost magical feel, thanks to fairy lights twinkling from the ceiling. All sorts of stuff cluttered the small desk in the corner: a laptop left open, a microphone, an old pair of headphones that looked like they'd had a fight with themselves, a half-empty bag of crisps, cans of soda, and scattered pens and pencils.

A notebook, opened and full of drawings, lay in the middle of it all. The chair in front of the desk doubled as a wardrobe, a couple of hoodies chucked over it, with a futon spread out next to it.

"What is this place?" Aaron had walked into a part of Landon's life he hadn't seen before.

"Lottie told me it's good to have a place to decompress," Landon answered, his fingers tracing the North Star tattoo behind his ear.

Lottie. Star. Charlotte. Starford. The therapist. The talking cricket.

"So, this is where you come to 'decompress'?" Aaron asked.

"Yeah, sort of. Always wanted a treehouse as a kid. This summer house is the grown-up version, I guess."

Realising Landon had let him into his personal refuge, Aaron's face grew hot. He was pretty sure he was blushing, and Landon's knowing look didn't help at all.

"Please, take a seat," Landon said, putting on the poshest accent ever, as he gestured towards the futon.

Before Aaron could even sit, a hoodie came flying at him. Catching it, he looked at Landon, puzzled. "What's this for?"

"You're drenched in beer," Landon pointed out matter-of-factly.

Oh, right. He needed to change. But the thought of changing in front of Landon made him hesitate. No one, apart from Aunt Olivia, had ever seen his scars.

When Landon took the clue and turned to face the wall, Aaron released a relieved breath. That small gesture, giving him space, meant more than Landon probably realised.

With shaky hands, Aaron pulled off his wet clothes. The fresh hoodie was a couple of sizes too big, but it enveloped him like a comfort blanket. It also smelled of Landon.

"Okay, you can look now," Aaron said, settling on the futon.

Landon sat beside him, close but not too close. He was the total opposite of Nyle in that sense.

Aaron played with the hoodie's sleeve hem as he took in the room. He then settled on Landon. "You've never asked about my scars."

Landon met his eyes. "Why? Did you want me to?"

"No, just...wondering."

"I've always believed in respecting personal boundaries."

"Thank you."

"For what? Being decent? You're not the only one running from something, Aaron. And you're certainly not the only one who brought their demons along for the ride."

Aaron gripped the sleeves of the hoodie, the ribbed fabric pressing into his skin. "How can I forget the past when it's written on my body?"

"You can draw over it."

"That's impossible if the canvas is ruined."

"You forget that I work with tattoos. I've seen all kinds of canvases. Trust me, it's possible."

Aaron shook his head slightly. "Not on me."

In the following silence, Landon's eyes seemed to try to look right through the hoodie.

"Want to see them and judge for yourself?" Aaron asked, surprising even himself.

"Only if you're comfortable with it," Landon replied softly.

Aaron had always kept his scars hidden, fearing how others might react. But with Landon, there was this sense of safety, an unspoken understanding.

Drawing a deep breath, Aaron stripped off the hoodie much as he'd rip off a plaster from a wound in need of air. Under the soft, twinkling glow of the fairy lights, his torso lay bare, a crisscross of scars etching a map into his skin.

Landon observed quietly, his eyes moving thoughtfully over each mark. Aaron braced himself, but there he saw no sign of disgust or pity in Landon's expression, only quiet focus.

For Aaron, revealing his scars, something he thought would feel raw and painful, turned out to be oddly relieving, like soothing an ache that had been hidden for too long.

Landon's hand hovered near Aaron's chest, following a scar running across it.

"Car crash three years ago," Aaron explained quietly. "This big one's from the seatbelt. The others"—he gestured to the rest—"came from the windows in the crash. It was pretty bad. My family...they were there, too, and I was the only one who came out of it."

Landon reached out to the pendant—a memento from that fateful day. Aaron didn't say it out loud, but as Landon studied the shard of glass, he could tell Landon had put the pieces together.

"I was right," Landon said. "Marks of survival."

"Survived, yeah, but it's not as if I'm some hero. Just got through, that's all."

"Survival's not about being a hero." Landon held his gaze, a flicker of something similar to anger or pain briefly crossing his face. Who knew what kind of battles Landon himself was fighting?

Then, Landon rolled up his sleeve, revealing an intricate tapestry of tattoos.

Aaron studied the detailed artwork—florals, skulls, sentences, and cryptic symbols, all beautifully executed. The level of craftsmanship took him aback. Despite Landon's earlier claims of amateur work, these tattoos were clearly the work of a skilled artist. It seemed Landon held himself to high standards, especially when it came to his work.

But Aaron noticed something else amidst the ink: thin, raised scars, running in parallel lines. Different from his own but unmistakably similar in their meaning.

"Marks of survival," he murmured, echoing Landon's words.

"Not everyone sees them that way."

"Why?" Aaron wasn't entirely sure what he was asking.

Landon laughed, short and dry, then pulled his sleeve back down. "I think that's enough 'show and tell' for one night."

But Aaron continued to stare at Landon's arm, almost certain the other one had similar stories to tell. "You don't strike me as someone who makes decisions lightly. If you really wanted to...you know, end things, you wouldn't be here now."

Landon laughed more loudly this time, though it lacked mirth. He crossed his arms, fingers idly tracing the scars underneath the fabric. "I used to believe I could manage pain, that controlling it somehow made me stronger. Turns out I'd lost control way before I even realised."

Aaron flashed back to the excruciating pain he'd endured upon waking in a hospital bed, his body wrapped in bandages and heart gripped by panic; there hadn't been a part of him that didn't ache.

For him, pain had been a terrifying reminder of loss, fragility, and death. Landon, though, used pain to remind himself he was still alive.

The difference in their perspectives was stark.

"I used to be ashamed of my scars," Landon continued. "They reminded me of everything I was trying to run away from."

"Is that why you covered them with tattoos?"

Landon shook his head. "It's not about covering them up. It's... transformation, you know? I turned them into something else, something new."

"But they're still there."

"Yeah, they are. But now they're part of a story I decided to tell. These tattoos...they're my chosen scars."

Their eyes met, holding a whole conversation in the brief silence.

Aaron felt a sense of admiration and envy. Landon had managed to turn his scars into art, into stories inked on skin. He'd turned them into blossoms sprouting from seeds he chose to cultivate rather than hide away in regret.

It was a powerful way of dealing with the past, of making something beautiful out of something painful.

Landon's words hit him. He *was* a rabbit. And it dawned on Aaron that no matter how much he kept running, trying to find himself, there was no sure bet he'd land somewhere new. Because, in the end, wherever he went, there he'd be.

Perhaps, like Landon, he could learn to embrace his scars, to find beauty in the broken places.

Caught in the intensity of his thoughts, Aaron soon broke away, shifting his gaze to the safety of the wooden ceiling above. It was one thing to watch Landon, but being seen and understood in return was something else entirely.

"How about a film?" Landon grabbed his laptop and the half-empty bag of crisps from the desk.

Aaron nodded in response, snapping back to the present; he'd forgotten he was still half-naked. Quickly, he pulled the hoodie back on as Landon fiddled with the laptop.

"There we go," Landon announced with satisfaction. "This one's a holiday classic."

Aaron peered at the screen. "*Die Hard*? Really? Since when is that a holiday film?"

"You mean you haven't seen it? It's set on Christmas Eve, the main character's wife is called Holly, and there's even one of the bad guys in a Santa hat. Plus, plenty of Christmas music in the background. It's practically wrapped in tinsel."

"That's a bit of a stretch, isn't it?"

"Trust me, by the end, you'll agree it's a Christmas film," Landon assured him with a confident grin.

As Landon hit Play, the audio of the movie filled the small room.

Aaron lost himself into the cosiness, wrapped up in the warmth of the hoodie and comforted by Landon's presence beside him. It was an oddly soothing way to spend the evening, a stark contrast to the party chaos outside.

As the movie neared its end, Landon had nodded off, arms folded, with the laptop still perched on his legs. Aaron stifled a yawn, his attention drifting to Landon's face, peaceful in sleep but with a hint of restlessness beneath his closed eyelids. He wondered if Landon was dreaming or, like him, haunted by nightmares.

Then, abruptly, one of Landon's eyes flickered open. "I've already told you—staring's rude," he said, more playful than annoyed.

Caught off-guard, Aaron blurted out without thinking, "You're beautiful."

Landon twitched his eyebrow. "And you're still tipsy."

"Maybe, but that doesn't make it less true."

Shaking his head, Landon chuckled softly. He removed his piercings, set them aside on the desk, together with the laptop, and reached down to pull a blanket from beneath their legs on the futon. With a thoughtful gesture, he spread it over them both, silently inviting Aaron to lie down next to him.

As Aaron moved closer, careful not to invade Landon's space, their hands brushed briefly. "Sorry—" he began, but Landon interrupted, gently intertwining their fingers.

A smile broke through Aaron's initial surprise. He hadn't done much hand-holding, but this…was different, special. It was as if they were silently saying *We're in this together*—a sort of unspoken deal to stick by each other.

Aaron closed his eyes, letting a sense of peace envelop him.

He'd never felt truly safe anywhere or with anyone before. But here he was, open and vulnerable, not in some distant, secluded place, but in a small summer house no bigger than a shed, in someone else's garden, under fairy lights twinkling like far-off stars.

It dawned on him that it wasn't the place offering this feeling of safety; it was Landon.

Landon, who had seemed like a walking contradiction when they first met, now offered comfort with his steady presence. Their hands clasped together gently yet firmly, reminding Aaron of the art of holding sand—not grasping it too tightly, but allowing it to lie comfortably in one's palm.

And that's exactly what Landon was doing with him now.

He was offering parts of himself, grain by grain, so Aaron let them rest on his skin.

♫ Intimacy

[Now playing » Podcast, Ep. 20—Intimacy—Don't Listen To Me]

What does 'intimacy' mean?

I once read something in *The Seven Husbands of Evelyn Hugo* that made a lot of sense to me.

It said something like—intimacy isn't just about physical closeness; it's about emotional nakedness.

It's when you can show your real self to someone, and they accept you, making you feel safe.

For the longest time, the whole concept seemed alien to me.

The idea of opening up, of letting someone peel back the layers of self-defence I had carefully constructed over the years, was unimaginable. Or maybe it was the fear of being seen for who I really am and being rejected.

But, you know, there's something liberating in finding a person who can handle your deepest, darkest secrets without batting an eye.

And once you start, it's hard to stop. It's like taking a sip of the most intoxicating sweet drink and not being able to put it down.

I think I might be addicted.

[♫ Closing » Neptune—Sleeping At Last]

Chapter Nineteen

Soft Awakenings

[Now playing » Neptune—Sleeping at Last]

Aaron woke up gradually, sense by sense.

First came his hearing, teased by the noises of the world outside: the neighbour's dog barking, the rumble of a rubbish lorry, seagulls crying overhead, and the occasional sound of car doors closing.

Then, as he lifted his eyelids, the sight of Landon's sleeping face greeted him. The morning light seeped through the window, sanding him down, bathing Landon's skin in an ethereal bluish glow; the twinkling fairy lights must have switched off at some point during the night.

Yawning, Aaron seized the opportunity to admire Landon. He studied his features more closely than he ever had before—the gentle arch of his eyebrows, the small mole below his eye, the light stubble dusting his cheeks and chin, and the curve of his slightly parted, chapped lips.

Without his piercings, Landon looked so soft.

Even softer was the touch between their hands still together on the sheets, resting atop each other.

It surprised Aaron how at ease he felt, even after sharing a bed. He wasn't accustomed to it, yet here he was, finding comfort in the warmth and presence of another person beside him.

"Staring," came a groggy mumble.

Aaron jolted. "Your eyes are closed!"

"That's what makes it creepy," Landon grumbled, rubbing his eyes. The contrast between his grumpy tone and sleepy appearance made Aaron chuckle. "What's so fascinating anyway?"

"You look cute when you sleep."

"You're digging your own grave."

"Right." Aaron didn't take him seriously.

Landon pointed at his desk. "Next time you wake up, you'll have that pencil in your brain."

"If I wake up, then you didn't do it right."

Landon kept his face blank, but Aaron spotted a quick flicker of annoyance there. He found it oddly satisfying to chip away at Landon's tough shell, even if just a little, and getting past his exterior seemed no different than finding his way through the complex maze of the Barbican Centre.

Maybe that was why he liked it. Each turn and twist brought him closer to the heart of it, where the most guarded secrets lay hidden.

There was only one problem. Aaron's own barriers were crumbling too.

Last night was a turning point. They'd both let down their walls, sharing more than just physical space. In that quiet room, a weight had lifted off Aaron's shoulders as he found a sense of safety with Landon he hadn't expected.

He'd known from the start that Landon wasn't an easy nut to crack. Not because of the tough-guy act; one look in his eyes, and Aaron could tell life hadn't been kind to him either. Others saw Landon as someone to avoid, but they never asked what he was avoiding. Finding scars under his tattoos only confirmed to Aaron that the world had hurt Landon long before he started pushing it away.

Landon withdrew his hand abruptly and propped himself up against the wall. He blinked, looking around as if to reorient himself. Clearing his throat, he nodded towards the door. Maybe a hint to get moving. Maybe a less-than-subtle 'fuck off'.

"Breakfast, work," he mumbled in a thick voice.

Aaron stood up on wobbly legs but managed to reach the door. As he stepped out, he nearly tripped when Kat zipped right in front of him. She meowed her way inside the summer house, probably to find Landon, while Aaron took off in the opposite direction, making a beeline for the kitchen.

There, he found Nyle wrestling with coffee stains on his T-shirt, the crime scene of a recent spill evident with the abandoned, still-steaming mug sitting on the windowsill.

"Morning," Nyle greeted with forced cheeriness. "Or should I say...good night?"

Aaron chose to ignore the jab, focusing instead on getting the kettle going. But Nyle wasn't finished. With a not-so-subtle cough, he gestured towards the garden.

"So, came out of Lanny's summer house, didn't you?"

Aaron kept his cool, rummaging for a peppermint tea bag. "Yeah, so?"

"Never thought I'd have to ask you this, but...did you sleep with Landon?"

The tea bag crinkled in Aaron's tightening grip. "Why does it always have to be about sex?"

"Well, Landon isn't exactly the 'sharing is caring' guy...or are you saying you two just held hands all night?"

A flush crept up Aaron's neck. From the cheeky grin on Nyle's face, it was evident that his embarrassment hadn't gone unnoticed.

"Was everything you said before just crap?" Nyle pressed, his persistence bordering on annoying.

"What are you talking about?"

"Well, you've been coy about your sexuality, hinted you're not interested in people or sex. But then, Maeve ends up in your bed, and this morning, you're sneaking out of Landon's."

The kettle clicked off, and a sudden, echoing silence filled the room, punctuated only by the hiss of steam. To Aaron, the rising mist from the kettle might as well have been a manifestation of his simmering frustration.

"First off, what I do or don't do is none of your fucking business," Aaron snapped. "And for the record, nothing happened with Maeve or Landon."

"Maeve said you two made out, but you weren't into it."

"Maeve should keep her mouth shut."

Nyle leaned in closer. "So, what's the deal, then? Did Lanny finally flip a switch for you? And here I was, thinking he had a thing for Ria. Looks like gayness runs in the family."

Aaron sighed, pouring the boiling water into his mug. The cheery unicorn design on it seemed to mock his swiftly souring mood. "Can't figure out for the life of me why you're so fascinated with other people's lives. And I'm not gay. Things aren't always as black and white as you think."

"Cut the philosophy, my dear. You're fucking a guy. Sounds pretty gay to me."

Aaron opened his mouth to argue, then closed it because he knew it was pointless. Nyle had already made up his mind; his expression practically screamed, *I knew it.*

"I must say, I'm a bit miffed you didn't fall for the *obviously* better-looking cousin." Nyle gestured to himself with exaggerated pride. "But watching you two lately, the signs have all been there, right?"

Aaron lifted the mug, letting the soothing mint scent envelop him. "What 'signs' are you babbling about exactly?"

"Oh, come on, I haven't seen that much tension since my last yoga class. And trust me, those poses can be *intense*," Nyle said with a cheeky grin. "Figured it was just a matter of time before you two had a proper go at each other, eh?"

Dismissing the conversation with a scoff, Aaron headed towards his room, eager to escape the conversation. But as he passed the kitchen island, Landon was standing there.

"Speak of the devil," Nyle said with a chuckle.

"What have I done now?" Landon asked, stepping past Nyle to the coffee machine.

"*Him*, apparently." Nyle gestured towards Aaron, but his confidence quickly diminished under Landon's unimpressed look, crumbling into mumbles. Fidgeting with his T-shirt, Nyle said, "I...uh, need a shower."

As the coffee machine hummed to life, Nyle hastily retreated, leaving an uncomfortable silence in his wake.

Aaron and Landon exchanged no words, but the air was thick with things left unsaid, a stark contrast to the light-heartedness of just moments ago. Kat's loud meow did little to cut the tension.

Landon crouched down to feed her, his fingers gently stroking her fur. Aaron leaned against the counter and watched them.

As he swirled the spoon, stirring his tea, something stirred inside him too. He wished for that same gentle touch, leaving him as perplexed as he had been the night before.

He couldn't blame alcohol now; he was completely sober, yet the feelings persisted—his unique desire for closeness with Landon and Landon alone.

And it was confusing, it was strange, it was exciting.

What was going on with him? Was it even possible to be attracted to only one person? Could that be a thing? Or, as Nyle had suggested, was he just a gay guy who didn't know better?

Aaron had never dug deep into his sexuality. His mild interest in both guys and girls had rushed him to identify as bisexual, maybe a bit pushed by his peers to pick a label. After that, he didn't give it much thought, like handing over an exam paper and forgetting about it.

But after the car accident, even that mild interest had dwindled. His head was a mess, and sex was the very last thing on his mind.

Deep down, though, Aaron had always known the 'bi' label wasn't quite right for him. But he didn't stress about it because he still felt attraction. It was just that sex wasn't a priority, and that was okay with him. He'd never fallen for anyone, never craved more, never even known what he was missing out on.

But then came Landon.

For the first time, Aaron felt a strong, undeniable pull rather than a tug, a connection he wanted to explore.

It was like finally spotting a number in those pesky Ishihara colour plates. Landon stood out to him, bold and clear, against the muted canvas of his past experiences.

Clutching his mug tighter, Aaron walked down the corridor, keeping his distance from Landon. He reminded himself that he didn't have time for distractions. In just a month, his community service would be up, and he'd be on his way to Australia, leaving everything behind, including Landon and the confusing feelings he stirred.

Inside the summer house, their world had felt smaller, more intimate. But stepping back into reality, Aaron was reminded that even in dreams, one eventually must wake up.

*

At the retirement centre, everybody seemed to know what had happened between Aaron and Landon, even though Aaron himself wasn't quite sure.

Nyle kept winking at them whenever he passed by. Maeve whispered to anyone while glancing their way. Ria radiated happiness and was all smiley as if it was the best day of her life. And Cliff...Cliff was unusually hostile.

Strangely enough, the entire group decided to join Aaron and Landon in their effort to revive the tree.

Aaron knew that their sudden enthusiasm was less about the tree and more an excuse to keep a close eye on them and fuel the gossip. Muhammad was very excited by the turn of events. Sarah didn't say anything and let them carry on as long as they made improvements to the garden.

Despite the additional help, working that day turned out to be more challenging than Aaron had anticipated, especially because of how on edge he felt around Landon. Every time their eyes met, Aaron quickly looked away. Even the slightest touch from Landon, whether accidental or intentional, sent a shiver down his spine, making his hairs stand on end.

Aaron had told himself he didn't have time for distractions, yet there he was, increasingly distracted by Landon's mere presence.

It didn't help that Cliff was being particularly troublesome too.

Aaron's tools seemed to have a way of mysteriously moving on their own, and he was certain he caught Cliff smiling smugly every time he had to hunt them down again.

Cliff's idea of 'helping with the tree' turned out to be about deliberately sabotaging their plan. The last straw came when Cliff 'accidentally' loosened a branch, causing it to swing too close to Aaron's head.

"For fuck's sake, Cliff!" he snapped.

"Are you having fun, Aaron?"

Aaron glared back at him. "Oh yeah, a total blast."

"You seem to be fitting in just fine," Cliff's replied, laced with bitter sarcasm.

Aaron paused, hands buried in mulch, unsure how to respond. But then he chose to brush it off; he had more pressing things on his mind.

The tension with Landon was becoming a real thing. And it wasn't the kind Nyle joked about. Or was it? Aaron couldn't tell.

He kept wondering if Landon felt the same way, if their night together meant something to him, if Landon also wanted to be close.

Shaking his head, Aaron tried to concentrate on the tree, but it was a lost cause.

With Cliff's games and his own jumbled thoughts about Landon, Aaron was more of a mess than help.

A part of him wanted to explore this unexpected attraction, to see where things with Landon could go before his time was up. But with his own confusion a barrier, did he even know what he really wanted?

As lunchtime rolled around, Aaron still wrestled with the same unsettling thoughts.

Phone in hand, he slipped away to a secluded spot at the back of the building. He needed answers.

With curiosity and hesitation, Aaron started his first real search: *Why don't I feel attracted to people?* The results were all over the place, talking about introversion and mental health, but nothing clicked.

Trying a different angle, he typed in: *Not sexually attracted to anyone. Is it normal?* That led him to a Reddit thread full of people sharing their experiences, including talks about asexuality. He'd heard about asexuality, but he'd never considered it might apply to him. Aaron wasn't repulsed by sex; it just wasn't a big deal for him.

As he continued to read, he stumbled upon terms like 'graysexuality' and 'demisexuality'. He even found information about romantic versus sexual attraction, which opened up a can of worms. Could he be bisexual in a romantic sense but somewhere on the asexual spectrum sexually?

This was all new territory. It was too much. The more he read, the more his head spun.

Feeling more muddled than ever, Aaron pocketed his phone. He needed to talk to someone, but who?

He glanced towards the group in the distance.

Nyle was out of the question; he had already pigeonholed him as gay. Maeve was a no-go after their last weird encounter. Cliff wasn't his friend anymore and clearly didn't understand him.

That left Landon and Ria.

But talking to Landon about this seemed premature. He didn't want to dump all this confusion on him, especially since Landon was part of what confused him in the first place.

That brought him to Ria. She was majoring in sex and gender studies and always up for these discussions. She'd probably be more helpful than some random forums online.

So, Ria it was, despite the slight awkwardness he felt around her and still not fully getting her friendship with Landon.

Chapter Twenty

Revelations

[Now playing » Do I Wanna Know?—Arctic Monkeys]

"Hey, Ria, can we talk for a minute?" Aaron caught up with her after their shift.

As the rest of their group moved ahead towards the pub, Aaron guided Ria to a more secluded spot behind the building. They leaned against a wall near some bins, out of earshot.

"So, what's going on?" Ria asked, her full attention on him, her smile warm as always.

Aaron let out a long, unsure breath. He absentmindedly fiddled with the cord of his hoodie—Landon's hoodie—as he struggled to find the right words. "Mind if I smoke?" he asked, reaching into his pocket.

She shook her head, and he quickly lit up a cigarette.

"So," he started, taking a drag, but the rush of nicotine did nothing to calm him down. "Imagine trying to pick your ice cream flavour. Everyone around you seems to have made up their mind, but you...you just don't know. You look at the available flavours, even think they all look good, but you don't get the hype. You try a few, sure, but none of them...wow you."

Ria looked lost but nodded encouragingly.

He took another drag. "It's not that I hate ice cream or anything. It's just...I've never been that into it. But now, out of the blue, there's this one flavour I've slowly started to notice. Haven't actually tried it yet, but I want to. Just this one. I still don't care about the other flavours, but this one...I want it like nothing I've ever wanted before."

Ria tilted her head, tucking a strand of hair behind her ear, her piercings twinkling. "I think I see what you mean," she said softly. "You need something more than just looks or popularity to be attracted to it. It's like you've only started wanting this 'flavour' after you got to know it, right?"

"Exactly!" Aaron laughed at himself, shaking his head. "God, that sounds so stupid, doesn't it?"

Ria chuckled. "No, but please let's ditch the ice cream analogy. We're talking about Landon, aren't we?"

Aaron nodded a bit sheepishly.

"Do you fancy him?"

"I don't know. Maybe? I've never felt this way about anyone before. It's like my sex drive has woken up, and it's all about him, no one else. And it's confusing."

"In what sense?"

"In the sense that I only seem to want to have sex with him. I don't feel like that when looking at other guys. I mean...I'm not freaking out because he's a guy. I've always thought I was bi. But now I'm wondering if maybe I was wrong? Nyle thinks I'm a repressed gay, but it doesn't feel that simple."

Ria rolled her eyes. "Nyle's confidence in his sexuality doesn't make him an expert on everyone else's."

"Yeah, but—"

"Listen, Aaron, it's okay to feel lost in all this. I've been there my-self," Ria reassured him. "I thought I was straight initially, then questioned if I was gay when I got a crush on my best friend. Eventually, I realised I'm pan. For me, it's about the person, not their gender. It took time to understand that."

Aaron exhaled a cloud of smoke. "Did you ever feel...stupid? For not knowing?"

"All the time. But there's no right or wrong way to discover who you are. It's your journey. Don't let Nyle or anyone else tell you otherwise. Not everyone gets it, and that's okay." Her expression saddened.

"Right," Aaron said. "I've been reading about asexuality, and some of it resonates with me, but then again, I've had sex, and it was fine. But what if my attraction was more about their looks, not really them? I can relate to some aspects of asexuality, but not completely. Is it even a thing to be both bi and...ace?"

Ria nodded. "Definitely. Sexuality is a spectrum. You might feel romantic attraction to multiple genders but only get the sexual attraction part in certain situations, or not at all."

Aaron breathed out slowly. He'd read about that too. "How do you figure out if you like someone romantically or sexually? This sounds so complicated."

Ria's expression brightened. "Well, think of romantic attraction as the desire to be emotionally close to someone, to have that deep, personal connection. It's like wanting to be with someone because you're drawn to who they are, their personality, their essence."

As Aaron pondered, he thought of Landon—his passion for tattoos, his caring nature, his resilience. Aaron felt more than admiration; he wanted to be part of Landon's world.

"Sexual attraction," Ria continued, "is about the physical pull, the craving for intimacy with that person."

"Hmm," Aaron murmured, sorting through his thoughts. "With Landon, it wasn't an instant spark, you know? Didn't exactly warm up to him at first. But then, as I got to know him, the *real* him, everything changed. It's strange. It's not just that I'm into him physically—which, yeah, I am—but there's more to it."

He paused, trying to articulate his tangled feelings. "Feels like I'm safe with him, like he just...understands me. It's not about his looks; it's about who he is that gets to me, you know?"

"Sounds like you might be demisexual, Aaron."

"Demi, huh?" Aaron echoed, remembering what he'd read. "It's when you don't feel sexually attracted to anyone until you get this deep emotional bond with someone, right?"

"Hey," she said softly, placing a reassuring hand on his shoulder, "Labels are just tools to help you figure things out, not box you in. If 'demisexual' feels right, that's great. If not, that's okay too. You don't need a label unless you want one. It's all about what makes you feel comfortable and understood, not about adding stress or pressure."

"Maybe I'm both demisexual and bisexual, then?"

"You know what, Aaron? Don't focus too much on *who* you're attracted to, but more about *how* you're attracted to people. You might be drawn to a guy today and a girl tomorrow, but that doesn't change your identity. Your identity is yours to define."

Aaron nodded, processing this new information.

"I can send you some stuff," Ria said with enthusiasm. "I've got *loads* of resources that could help. Why not drop by one of our Pride social events? It can be helpful to chat with people who've been in similar spots."

"Thanks, that'd be great."

"Just a heads-up, though," Ria added with a slight sigh. "It's easy to fall into the trap of comparing yourself to others. And you know, even within the LGBTQ plus community, not everyone's on the same page about labels and stuff."

"You mean like Nyle?"

Ria hummed. "Yeah, Nyle seems so sure of himself. I kinda envy that simplicity. Would've saved me a lot of confusion and therapy sessions if I was just gay. But the key thing is to be at peace with yourself and to have people around who get you and support you."

Aaron thought of Aunt Olivia, who had been incredibly supportive when he told her he was bi. Maybe even too much when she had him sit through a two-hour presentation on the pros and cons of unprotected sex with both boys and girls.

"So, are you thinking of telling Landon about all this?"

Aaron chuckled nervously. "What, that I'm in the middle of a sexual identity crisis?"

Ria's smile was warm and reassuring. "He likes you, Aaron. Make your move before it's too late."

Chapter Twenty-One

A Bit of Australia

[Now playing » Shot at the Night—The Killers]

The week passed in a blur for Aaron, with Landon a constant distraction in his day.

Besides their commutes, lunches, and planned cigarette breaks between shifts at the tattoo shop and RPM, Landon seemed to be everywhere—behind the kitchen counter after Aaron's morning runs, outside the bathroom in the steamy aftermath of his showers, and in the stillness of the night whenever he needed a breath of fresh air.

It was getting hard to tell if it was all coincidence or if Aaron was becoming super tuned in to Landon's presence. Their lives and routines were meshing together more often than not. And it wasn't just about being in the same place. Landon had taken up residence in Aaron's mind too.

Part of him wondered if he should act on these feelings. But then, the reality check. He'd be off to Australia soon. He'd even rebooked his flight after Tom confirmed a spot for him at the wildlife park. What was the point in diving into something bound to be short-lived?

Yet, with each passing day, the thought of leaving Landon behind felt less like a simple fact and more like a regret. Aaron wrestled with this nagging what-if, unable to shake it, even amidst RPM's festive buzz.

Mariah Carey's "All I Want for Christmas Is You" blasted through the speakers, courtesy of Fell's choice on the turntable. Aaron, knee-deep in vinyl records, shuffled them for probably the umpteenth time that morning; nothing seemed right.

He'd step back, squint at the setup, then dive back in, rearranging the albums.

Fell perched on the counter, feet tapping in time with the music. "Hey, Aaron," he called out. "You've seemed a bit off since lunch. Every-thing all right?"

Aaron didn't respond, only glanced up as he continued arranging the records.

"Is this about you and Landon sleeping together?"

That got Aaron's attention. One of the records slipped from his grasp, clattering to the floor. "Great, so the whole world knows," he mut-tered, more to himself. He picked up the record and clutched it like a shield, still crouching.

Fell stifled a laugh. "Well, it wasn't exactly top secret, you know. Ria and I saw you guys sneak off to the summer house. You never came back."

"Nothing happened," Aaron clarified tightly.

"Hey, no judgement here. Just saying it's nice, you know, if there's something going on between you two."

Aaron straightened up, the record still in his arms. "There is no 'us'," he said firmly.

"Is that because you guys talked it out, or are you not into an 'us'?

"I don't have time for this. It's nothing, really. We didn't do any-thing, only...shared a bed, that's all."

Fell gave him a knowing look. "Yeah, okay. But it's pretty obvious you're both into each other."

"Why would you say that?"

"Seriously, Aaron? Are you trying to be dense, or what?"

Their eyes locked, and in a flash, he was right back under one of Aunt Olivia's stern scowls, the kind that always made him second-guess himself.

"Let me put it simply," Fell continued. "You like *like* Landon, right?"

His feelings for Landon were messier than the album display he was trying to rearrange, something he couldn't shove into neat little boxes labelled 'yes' or 'no'. He picked at the cardboard cover, tiny bits of paper sticking to his skin. "How can you tell when you like *like* someone?"

Fell slid off the counter and stepped closer. He gently took the record from Aaron and placed it back on the shelf. "Well, for starters, you can't stop thinking about them. And every little thing they do seems to matter more than it should." He glanced out the window at the clothing shop across the street. Aaron had a hunch Fell's thoughts had drifted to its owner, the woman who often shared coffee and muffins with him. "And when she—*they're* near you, it's like the fizz and pop of a soft drink, happening inside your stomach."

Aaron wrinkled his nose at the analogy but didn't interrupt. He'd used ice cream while talking with Ria, so he wasn't in a position to judge.

"When you meet the right person, there's this unique connection, an understanding beyond words."

Aunt Olivia's talks about finding 'the right one' surfaced, the idea of a soulmate who could change everything. Aaron had never bought into that crap, and he certainly didn't see Landon as 'the one'. Yet, he couldn't ignore their bond and the unspoken understanding they'd built over time.

"You and Landon, there's clearly something there," Fell pressed on. "And Landon—he's a good chap. He's very passionate about his tattoo job and puts everything into it. Heck, he even convinced me to get this at thirty-two." Fell lifted his jeans leg to show off a small music note in Landon's style. "Just think about it, Aaron. How often do you find someone you click with? When you stumble upon that kind of connection, walking away isn't easy. Does Landon make you feel that way?"

Fell's question echoed in Aaron's head throughout his shift.

Later, when he saw Landon waiting for him outside the shop, his stomach didn't fizz and pop as Fell had described, more like a popcorn machine on overdrive.

Wrapped up against the nose-freezing cold, Landon stood there, peering into his phone, his face barely visible beneath a snug scarf and beanie.

"Hey," Aaron greeted, his breath forming clouds in the frosty air between them.

Landon looked up and offered a muffled, "Hey," back through the scarf. Annoyance flickered across his eyes as he pocketed his phone.

After a moment of silence, Landon's phone started buzzing. He pulled it out, glanced at the screen with irritation and resignation, then quickly silenced it and shoved it back into his pocket.

"Everything okay?"

"Just spam," Landon replied. "Fancy a walk?"

Aaron nodded, welcoming the chance to spend a bit more time with him, even though the temperature had dipped close to zero. The crisp December air hinted at the possibility of a rare snowy Christmas in London.

As they strolled down the windy towpath of Regent's Canal towards King's Cross, they passed several boats moored along the way. One stood out—an old vessel converted into a floating bookshop, bearing the sign *Word on the Water*.

"Want to check it out?" Landon asked, already halfway up the ramp. "Mind your head," he warned as they ducked down the stairs.

Inside, the boat felt like an old pirate ship filled with treasures. But instead of gold, it held books. Owl figurines and vintage typewriters added to the charm.

"Quirky, isn't it?" Landon said, browsing the shelves.

"This place is sick. How'd you find it?"

"Ria's a regular here. She comes for her poetry club." Landon picked up a book and flipped through it before giving it a sniff.

"So, this is where you come for your...victims?"

Landon laughed. "Something like that. They have a great selection, especially the classics." He showed Aaron a well-worn copy of *The Hobbit*.

"A Tolkien fan, huh?" Aaron eyed *The Lord of the Rings* on a shelf nearby and picked it up for a quick scan.

"I hope you've read these, not just watched the films," Landon said in a teasing tone.

Aaron raised his hands. "Guilty."

"Shame on you."

Eventually, they found themselves on the recently vacated sofa by the window, sitting side by side.

Aaron leaned forward to peer out at the canal, its dark water shimmering with the reflections of nearby lights.

He turned to Landon, absorbed in his book. "Spending the evening here?"

Landon snapped the book shut. "Got something else in mind, actually."

Aaron's pulse quickened. "Like what?"

Landon stood. "Follow me."

Back on the canal path, Aaron snuggled deeper into his jacket, his face still at the mercy of the biting wind. It nipped at his nose and cheeks, sharp and relentless.

"What's the plan?" he asked.

"You shall see." Landon's eyebrows hinted at a hidden smile behind his scarf.

Aaron followed, intrigued. But when they arrived at the entrance to the London Zoo, he looked questioningly at Landon, who simply grinned and led the way inside.

They walked past enclosures that resembled mini safaris containing zebras, giraffes, and warthogs—a slice of Africa in London.

Approaching the wallabies, Landon gestured towards them. "Here, a bit of Australia for you."

Aaron observed the hopping creatures, his smile widening.

Landon jokingly added, "See? You don't need to fly across the world for a taste of the wild."

That comment filled Aaron with a warm, happy glow.

Their adventure continued into the Reptile House, then they marvelled at the tigers and lions but laughed hardest at the monkey exhibit, especially when one tried to nick Landon's scarf, almost snagging it.

Landon pretended to be annoyed, but Aaron couldn't stop laughing.

"They don't give a monkey," he joked.

In the bug house, they both tensed up at the sight of spiders looming in the tree branches over their heads. Neither of them was a fan. This might turn into a real problem in Australia.

"Watch out, there's a humongous one above you," Aaron teased.

"Maybe I'll get bitten," Landon replied playfully. "The world could use another mixed-race Spider-Man like Miles Morales."

They joked and laughed at every opportunity. For Aaron, it all felt like a journey back to a childhood he'd never fully experienced, one filled with wonder and freedom. He couldn't remember the last time he'd felt so light and carefree.

At the flamingo enclosure, Aaron even learned something new.

"*Flamingos are born dull grey, and then they turn pink,*" he read aloud.

Landon snapped a photo with the flamingo fact sign in the background and tagged Nyle in it, captioning, *Be a flamingo in a world full of pigeons.*

As the afternoon went on, Aaron became increasingly drawn to Landon's laughter. It was like hearing a melody from the next room, close enough to enjoy but out of reach. He feared getting too close might somehow change the easy-going nature of their day. So, he kept a bit of distance, savouring the experience yet keeping his guard up.

"Well," he said as they headed towards the exit, "that was...enlightening."

Landon's laughter rang out again. "Enlightening, huh? Wonder what's next on the agenda?"

"What do you mean?" he asked, curiosity mingled with confusion. Could this be a...date?

They left the zoo, Landon setting a brisk pace.

Aaron kept up as they passed quaint rows of houses and cosy-looking shops adorned with festive Christmas decorations, their windows aglow with warm light.

As they entered Regent Park, savoury and sweet aromas from food stalls wafted through the air. Landon paused briefly at a churros stand, seemingly tempted, but he continued walking.

"Hold on a sec," Aaron called out. He quickly bought a cup and caught up to Landon.

"I thought you weren't into sweets," Landon said, surprised.

"You're right." Aaron handed over the churros. "For you."

Landon glanced from Aaron to the churros and back. He accepted them with a soft "Cheers," and took a Nutella-filled bite. "You sure you don't want one?"

"Nah, too sugary for me. But seriously, how do you eat all those sweets and not turn into a pudding?"

Landon shrugged. "Actually, Nyle's been nagging me to hit the gym with him. Reckons I'm losing my shape."

Aaron gave Landon a once-over. Sure, he wasn't all muscle and six-pack like Nyle, but that hardly mattered. Even wrapped up in his coat and beanie, braving the cold, there was something quite attractive about Landon.

"You, uh, look more than good to me," Aaron said quietly, then quickly averted his gaze to his shoes before glancing back up. "But hey, if you're up for some exercise, why not join me for a run sometime?"

Landon raised an eyebrow—the pierced one, which Aaron was pretty sure only Landon could arch that way. "At the crack of dawn? Not a chance."

They continued until they reached Primrose Hill. The area buzzed with excitement, with signs pointing towards an art installation mimicking the Northern Lights.

"What the—" Aaron turned to Landon with his eyes wide.

"I know it's not the real thing, but when I heard about this, I thought it'd be nice to bring a bit of Southern Lights to you since you're so excited about it."

Happiness flooded Aaron. Right then, he had an urge to lean in and kiss Landon. But for some reason, he couldn't muster the courage. Kissing others had been a no-brainer, mainly because he didn't care about them. But with Landon, it was different. A wave of fear hit Aaron, holding him back.

They eventually found a spot on the crowded grass and lay down to wait for the show to start.

With the darkness acting as a canvas, lights danced across the sky. Projected through artificial mist, they created a breathtaking illusion of the Northern Lights.

Despite knowing it was fake, Aaron felt as if transported there, to Australia, under the Lights Tori had loved so much. Magical and surreal, the shifting glow swirled like some cosmic dance.

Lying next to Landon, hands clasped on his stomach, Aaron narrowed his eyes as he drifted to some distant beach, imagining the sound of waves. Soon, the smell of the sea mixed with that of fresh grass.

"You like it?" Landon's voice gently pulled him back.

Aaron turned to Landon, now bathed in the kaleidoscopic light. He appeared almost otherworldly as if he were part of the spectacle.

He pictured Landon right there with him in Australia as he had with Tori when they'd messed around with torches under their sheet forts. Aaron started to question if he really needed to jet off to the other side of the world to feel this alive again.

Maybe Landon had a point.

Was chasing dreams as far as the second star to the right even necessary? Perhaps his own version of Neverland was right here, closer than he'd ever imagined.

"It's wonderful." Aaron offered him a small, heartfelt smile, not like those Ria gave out, but he hoped it showed how thankful he was.

Then, almost without thinking, Aaron slowly reached out across the soft grass and brushed his fingertips over Landon's clenched hand.

Landon's hand relaxed, and their fingers slid together effortlessly.

They didn't say anything else, there was no need. They lay there, hand in hand under the artificial Northern Lights, figuring out this unspoken language of theirs—a bit new, a bit clumsy. But that was okay. It only mattered that they were creating it together, learning as they went.

*

They returned home way past midnight.

Landon dumped his shoes, coat, hat, and scarf at the door. Pausing in the corridor, he mimed smoking, nodding towards the garden.

"I'll head to bed," Aaron said quietly. "Today's been...a lot." He left unsaid how his emotions were in overdrive, pulsing in his chest louder than the house's silence.

"All right, goodnight, then," Landon said, already disappearing into the shadowy corridor.

"Wait, Landon..."

The floorboards creaked, and then Landon came back into view. "Yeah?" He leaned awkwardly against the wall.

Aaron edged closer, his feet sliding on the wooden floor. "Thanks for tonight," he murmured, a few inches from Landon. "Haven't had this much fun in ages."

"So, reckon we could do it again?" Landon held his gaze, seeming to shrink the gap between them even further.

Aaron met his eyes, heat prickling behind his collarbone. Landon's breath tickled gently against the frozen tip of his nose. "I'd like that," he managed to say.

"Can I—"

A *Super Mario* ringtone cut Landon off, and Aaron fumbled for his phone. He hesitated when Aunt Olivia's name flashed on the screen.

"Just a sec," he said to Landon. "It's my auntie. I'll be quick."

He drifted towards the entrance, phone to his ear. "Hey, Aunt Olivia! Yeah, everything's good. Just having a late breakfast."

Aaron wove a tale about a day that never happened, his words tumbling out in a hurry, keen to get back to Landon.

But when he spun around, Landon was nowhere to be seen.

Chapter Twenty-Two

Cold Winter

[Now playing » This December—Ricky Montgomery]

Ever since that night out—which Aaron was pretty sure counted as a date—he hadn't hung out with Landon, apart from when they had to.

Something had shifted.

Landon had become more distant, as if he was pulling away. Their usual Tube rides and lunch breaks with Fell had turned into sessions of brief, straight-to-the-point chats. The sleepless nights they used to share were a thing of the past, with Landon now spending more time alone, often retreating to the summer house in the garden.

Aaron found himself with unsmoked cigarettes in his pocket and fewer bags of peppermint tea around the house.

A part of him believed it was all for the best. Distractions were the last thing he needed right now; soon, he'd be in Australia, starting fresh. But the other part stubbornly refused to give up hope.

His mind kept drifting to the Lights show and, more so, to what almost happened—or rather, what didn't happen—when they returned home.

He was pretty sure Landon had been about to kiss him, right before Aunt Olivia's call interrupted them. Aaron couldn't shake the worry that he might have messed things up without meaning to.

Nyle seemed to pick up on the tension and had stopped his usual teasing. Fell, too, had noticed something off between them. He'd tried to ask Aaron about it a couple of times, but Aaron always managed to dodge the question, either cranking up some tunes or pretending to be busy.

Ria was the only one who didn't poke around. She simply winked at Aaron knowingly before disappearing with Landon on their Thursday date night.

On Friday morning, Aaron accidentally ended up overhearing a conversation between Landon and Nyle in the kitchen. He'd just returned from his morning run, and Nyle's voice echoed through the corridor.

Aaron lingered out of sight, not because he wanted to eavesdrop but because he wasn't in the mood to deal with Nyle so early in the day.

But then, hearing his own name, his attention was hooked.

"He's more than just a 'friend with benefits', isn't he? You actually *like* him," Nyle was saying, sounding pretty serious for once.

Landon said something back, too low for Aaron to make out.

"'I burn. I pine. I perish'," Nyle dramatically quoted. "Look, Lanny, as your cousin, I've got to say this. The way you are with Aaron, it's different. You've never opened up like this to anyone. Heck, since you moved here, he's the only one you've brought into your Fortress of Solitude. Not gonna lie, kinda jealous here, but hey, I love you. Just...don't let this slip away, okay?"

"Don't let what slip away?" Landon asked.

"Aaron."

After a choked laugh, Landon retorted, "We both know as soon as he's done serving his sentence, Aaron will fuck off to Sydney...or wherever he plans to go."

"Doesn't matter. Life's all about grabbing those good moments, even if they're short. Enjoy it while you can."

Everything went quiet for a bit, and then Nyle spoke up again, "You hear me?"

"Yeah, I heard you."

"You deserve some happiness."

Right then, a soft, furry thing brushed against Aaron's legs—Kat, purring away in the shadows. Aaron crouched to give her a gentle stroke on the head, her big eye looking up at him.

Maybe Nyle was onto something. Aaron figured perhaps it was time to stop overthinking and live in the moment like his parents never allowed him to.

*

That Saturday, after a quiet—and strangely productive—shift at the retirement centre, Nyle got the gang to check out the Christmas lights on Regent Street. Same as last year, massive angels lit up the street.

Aaron didn't exactly buzz about it, mainly because of the crowds. He struggled to keep up, especially when Nyle turned the whole experience into his own personal photoshoot, nearly getting run over by taxis and buses every two minutes, trying to get his 'perfect shot'.

Meanwhile, Landon stayed in his own little world, hands stuffed in his pockets, wandering and looking at all the Christmassy window displays. He didn't chat with anyone, and even Ria's attempts to cheer him up didn't work.

"Let's check out the Christmas market at Trafalgar Square," Nyle suggested, and pretty much everyone seemed game for it. Well, everyone but Aaron and Landon.

They went along anyway, finding themselves in a packed square with the traditional sad-looking Christmas tree in the middle and a bustling faux-German market.

The food stalls heaved with people, and the aroma of grilled sausages was too good for Aaron to pass up. He got in line with Nyle and Maeve. Cliff joined them shortly after. Landon and Ria, on the other hand, made a beeline for a burger stall not too far away.

As they waited, Nyle and Maeve chit-chatted, catching up on their plans for the holidays.

"This year's gonna be epic. We're all doing Christmas Day together," Nyle said, all pumped up. "Luzanne's off work, and Landon's even agreed to give my gran's turkey recipe a go."

"What about your folks?" Maeve asked. "Still a no-go with them?"

Nyle let loose a muted groan. "Told them *straight* up—if they can't accept me for who I am"—he gestured to himself—"then that's it, no more visits. I won't go back there and pretend to be what I'm not. I don't care if they think I'm embarrassing myself. I'm proud of who I am now."

Maeve looked at him sympathetically. "As you should be. You know, one of my brothers is a huge fan of yours."

"The hot one?"

"Oh, fuck off." Maeve playfully shoved him. "It's little Sammy. He loves your outfits, and he's been asking Mum to get some of them for Christmas."

"He's got good taste, then. He'll turn out fine."

Maeve then turned to Aaron. "And what about you? Any family plans?"

Before Aaron could say anything, Nyle jumped in.

"Aaron's got no family, so he's one of us."

Cliff gave Aaron a 'what the hell is he talking about' look from behind Nyle.

Maeve patted Aaron's back, apologetically. "You're welcome at my place too. My mum always cooks like there's no tomorrow, and with seven of us, who can blame her?"

Nyle chuckled. "Bet it's pretty cool having six brothers, huh? They seem super protective of you."

"You have no idea. They can be a pain in the ass though. They'd give Aaron the third degree if he popped over."

Nyle wrapped an arm around Aaron, pulling him in close. "Nah, Aaron's part of our crew. Even Kat loves him."

"You must be quite the special guy, Aaron."

Maeve's comment had him feeling anything but. As she and Nyle kept on talking, Aaron zoned out, his attention drawn to the food stall. The sizzling sausages almost hypnotised him with how the heat made the air above the grill crinkle, reminding him of scrunched cling film.

Christmas was around the corner, but Aaron wasn't feeling the holiday cheer. Each year, the festive season left him more alone, a reminder of how disjointed his family had always been, long before the car accident changed everything.

He shivered in a chilly gust as he stood waiting for his food. The cold bit at his nose and ears, his hands and feet turning into blocks of ice. He only started feeling his fingers again when he finally got his hands on his piping hot bratwurst.

Landon and Ria had somehow managed to beat them to it. They'd already finished their burgers and had joined the queue for some hot chocolate. Nyle and Maeve approved the idea and joined them, leaving Aaron and Cliff by themselves.

"So, when did you become an orphan?" Cliff asked, his eyes narrowing.

"I *am* an orphan," Aaron replied.

"What about your aunt? She's still around, isn't she?"

Shit. Aaron flicked his gaze away.

"You haven't told her, have you?" Cliff continued. "And here I was, thinking she kicked you out after finding out what a twat you are. You're just a bag of lies."

Aaron tried to move away, but Cliff grabbed his arm.

"You know," he pressed on, "back when we were at school, with all the chatter about the 'scarred boy' who just transferred, I genuinely wanted to be your mate. I remember seeing you doodling those Marvel heroes in your textbook during class. Your drawings were wicked. And I caught bits of your music taste when you played your tunes in the corridor between classes. I get it now. I thought you were my friend, but I never was yours."

"You don't understand. It was a tough time—"

"Don't bother with the trauma story. I might not understand everything you went through, but I wanted to. I waited for you to open up, but you never did. I even overlooked all those lies you told. Is this Australia thing even real?"

"Yes, it is."

"And who's Tori, the girl in your voice messages?"

That caught Aaron off-guard. He hadn't talked about Tori with anyone, least of all Cliff. He wasn't about to start now.

Cliff's expression held frustration and something else. "You're the usual selfish prick. You just can't help it, can you?"

"And how exactly am I being selfish?"

"Well, let's see. Befriending Landon like you befriended me in school, only for your own benefit. Smart move, Aaron. Even better, fucking him. That's so *you*. I almost feel sorry for him when he realises how you'll screw him over...in more ways than one."

"Fuck off," Aaron snapped, shoving Cliff.

Ria, hot chocolate in her hand and halfway towards them, picked up her pace at the scuffle.

"Whoever you're chasing in Australia," Cliff added, "I hope they see through you. You don't deserve anyone."

As Cliff stomped off, Ria's eyes met his worriedly, and she mouthed, "Are you okay?"

Aaron wasn't sure himself. He managed a weak smile and glanced away, but inside, he was a mess. Cliff's words stung. Was any of this real, or was he as selfish as Cliff had said?

Not too long after, Nyle joined them, carrying a steaming Christmas mug, and for the first time, Aaron welcomed the distraction of having him around, chatting away about nothing in particular.

"How about giving your aim a go?" Nyle suggested to Aaron, gesturing towards a stall draped in plushies, all hanging like ivy from its roof with tin cans lined up behind them on shelves.

"Even if I was any good, those games are rigged."

Landon chimed in, the first time he'd spoken to Aaron all day. "So, you're saying you're rubbish, then?"

Aaron shot back, "Got another fair game record to break, 'Lannyster zero zero'?"

With a cheeky smile, Landon handed his drink to Ria. "Hold my chocolate."

He marched over to the stall like he meant business. Nyle whipped out his phone to film Landon.

Aaron watched, doubtful, but his scepticism quickly faded when Landon knocked down all the cans with three throws. The smug look Landon tossed him afterwards sent a shiver down Aaron's spine.

The stall guy, equally impressed, told Landon to pick a plushie. Landon chose a tiny one, then strolled back, holding it out. Nyle, jumping up and down, seemed to expect the prize, but Landon sidestepped him and lobbed the toy straight to Aaron.

Aaron caught it just as Nyle's face dropped in disbelief. The tiny bunny plushie, attached to a keyring, held its arms outstretched as if begging for a cuddle.

"See any resemblance?" Landon teased.

"Yeah, hilarious. What am I supposed to do with this, then?"

"Keep it, bin it, set it on fire for all I care. It's your problem now." Landon grabbed his hot chocolate from Ria and wandered off with Nyle, who continued to moan about not getting the plushie.

Aaron examined the little bunny. When he poked its belly, its arms and legs wrapped around his index finger. A smile crept in at the sight of the silly thing before he shoved it into his pocket.

The group approached Nelson's Column, where everyone pretty much ignored the barriers around the lion statues at the base. Some people even chilled out on the steps of the column.

"Who's game for sitting up there?" Maeve asked.

Without a second thought, Aaron hopped the barrier and started climbing the monument. Halfway up, he paused when a pair of combat boots stopped in front of him.

"First one to the top wins," Landon said as he kept moving.

By the time Aaron caught on to the challenge, Landon had already made it to the top, lounging there, looking pleased with himself.

"Beat you to it," Landon said with a cheeky grin.

Aaron settled beside him without making a fuss about losing. He glanced down at the crowd—Nyle, Maeve, Ria, and Cliff had stayed amidst the bustle. They hadn't made any effort to join in, despite throwing the challenge. Or maybe that had been their intention all along.

Aaron leaned back on his hands, gazing up at the black-stained sky, not a star in sight. If he squinted, he could just about make out the shape of the clouds, so dense they blocked any moonlight from seeping through. The artificial lights around them, though, did their best to make up for the lack of natural light.

"Do we really need all this extra energy wastage just for Christmas?" Aaron wondered out loud.

Landon, blowing a puff of smoke, shot him a playful look. "What, you allergic to Christmas too?"

"Maybe. It's never been my favourite holiday."

"Is that why you don't like presents?"

Aaron turned to face Landon. "Actually, I barely even got any Christmas presents. My parents didn't buy into all the commercial hype. They reckoned you shouldn't need a special day to spend time with family, said Christmas was the worst time for it."

Landon seemed to mull over something, then said, "They weren't entirely wrong. Twelve families and very few decent Christmases to remember..." He bit his lip, playing with his piercing as if he wanted to say more before stopping himself.

Sensing something wrong, Aaron asked, "Did you get many presents at least?"

"Oh yeah, loads of them."

"That doesn't sound too bad, does it?"

Landon gave a half shrug. "You'd be surprised. Some people think a pile of gifts can make up for a lot of things."

He said it in such a flat way, his eyes distant, that Aaron got the hint there was more to it. But he didn't pry. He suddenly felt daft for his remark. Foster care must've been tough for Landon—always moving—

with things probably staying the same in his own family.

Sad, frustrating, a never-ending cycle of misery.

"Well, I only had one family," Aaron replied, "and trust me, it wasn't all sunshine and rainbows there either."

"Strict parents?"

A soft murmur slipped out of Aaron at 'strict', an understatement. "More like authoritarian. They had to control everything, had a say in every little thing I did."

"Is that why you learned to lie?"

That hit a nerve. Aaron pulled his coat tighter at a sudden chill. Lying to Aunt Olivia with Landon around had been a misstep, and it had come back to bite.

"Why do you keep lying to your aunt?"

Aaron had seen the question coming, but it still threw him off. "I was too embarrassed to tell her the truth. If the police hadn't caught me that night, I'd be in Australia now. So, it's kinda...half true?"

Landon looked sceptical.

"I didn't want to burden her more. After the accident, she was great to me, and I'm...well, not a good nephew."

"You're not a bad person, Aaron."

"I am. I'm a selfish little prick."

"Aren't we all? But maybe your aunt deserves to know the truth. Does she even know you're planning to move there permanently?"

"Nah, and it's better that way. She won't miss me."

"You're too harsh on yourself."

"That's a bit rich coming from you. Why do you put on this bad-boy front?"

"I'm not acting. People see what's easy for them," Landon replied defensively.

"But it seems like you're okay with them thinking that. Why didn't you tell Luzanne the real story? About her ex and why you and Nyle ended up doing community service?"

"Wouldn't have changed anything."

"It might have."

"Wouldn't have changed anything for *her*," Landon corrected. "She already had it in for me. She wouldn't have believed me."

"Did you try?"

"No, and I didn't need to."

Aaron dug his nails into his palms, feeling the crescent shapes imprinting into his skin. "Do you get a kick out of people seeing you a certain way, or are you scared to show you actually care?"

"And what about you? Running off to the other side of the hemisphere to dodge your issues. But here's the thing. If you keep running with all that baggage, it's gonna weigh you down, ready or not."

"I'm not running," Aaron said firmly. "I made a promise, remember?"

"To who? A ghost named Tori?"

Aaron shivered. For the second time that day, someone other than Aunt Olivia had said Tori's name. He wrapped his arms around himself.

"Sorry, I didn't mean to—"

"Tori was my sister."

Landon opened his mouth, but no sound came out.

Stopping his self-hug, Aaron looked straight into his eyes. "The whole Australia trip was her thing. She was mad about it, had this notebook full of places she wanted to see, the Lights, the koalas..." He smiled at the memory of her always sharing a fun fact about the cute, cuddly animals. "Did you know koalas smell like eucalyptus? Or that they sleep, like, twenty hours a day?"

"No, but now that I do, I can say you've made my day," Landon replied, not flippantly.

"She was so close to making it to Sydney, but then..." Aaron reached for the pendant, the rough texture grating under his fingertips.

"The accident?"

"Yes." Aaron's voice caught in his throat.

"So, the messages you've been leaving..."

"I know, I know, it's stupid. Tori will never hear them, but it helps me if I feel like I can still talk to her."

Landon shook his head gently. "No, it's not stupid. It's actually...

nice. But at some point, you need to move on."

"That's what I'm trying to do."

"Just putting one foot in front of the other isn't enough to move forward. You need to move on in here too," Landon said, tapping his temple.

"What, you reckon I should call that Lottie therapist you mentioned?"

"I gave you her number. But in the end, it's up to you. Like everything else."

Aaron flashed a half-smile and glanced down. Nyle and Maeve hadn't been subtle with all their sneaking looks up at them. "We should probably head back."

He was about to climb down when Landon reached out to stop him.

"Wait. You've shared a lot. Fair's fair. Ask me something."

Caught unawares, Aaron's pulse quickened, a jumble of emotions shaking him. He sifted through a million things he wanted to ask, finally settling on one, his voice wavering.

"So...uh, what's your favourite song?"

Landon's eyes went wide. "Seriously? Is that what you're asking?"

"Hey, it's a question, isn't it?"

Landon laughed, shaking his head. "All right, here, let me show you." He pulled out his phone and handed Aaron an earbud. "There's this song I've been listening to...kinda makes me think of you."

Aaron put in the earbud and burst into laughter as he listened, particularly at the chorus. Glancing at the phone screen, he read the title, "Favorite Liar" by The Wrecks.

The world faded away, leaving Aaron and Landon in their little bubble. With Landon so close, the cold didn't seem that bad after all.

They were almost touching, Landon's warmth nearly chasing away the chill on Aaron's cheeks. Yet, this tiny space remaining between them felt massive.

It seemed as if Landon was waiting for him to close that gap.

Aaron almost did, leaning in, heart racing. But then he hesitated.

His previous kisses had always been nothing special. Would kissing Landon be any different?

"We should go before I freeze into an ice lolly," Aaron finally said, breaking the spell.

"Right," Landon agreed, drawing back, and suddenly the night air became even chillier.

As Aaron made his way down, he glanced at Big Ben, glowing in the night, a silent witness to their almost-kiss.

It could've been a disaster.

It could have been the best kiss ever.

Chapter Twenty-Three

The Worst Best Kiss

[Now playing » Apocalypse—Cigarettes After Sex]

Aaron traced over Tori's image on his phone screen. In the photo, her eyes sparkled with a hint of irritation, contrasting starkly with his own image, caught mid-laughter.

He was glad he'd never deleted it.

Tori always made a fuss about being 'unphotogenic', begging him to stop snapping her at random. Of course, for Aaron, that was more reason to do it. He loved sneaking in candid shots when she least expected it.

Their little game had led to a lot of photos and videos—all he had left to remember her by. It was getting harder each day to picture the little details of her face or to recall the exact sound of her voice.

He lingered on the image before flicking over to his recent calls.

Holding the phone to his ear, Aaron waited for the song to finish, then started to speak.

"Hey, it's me again. Just wanted to say I hope you're doing all right, wherever you are, and that you've found your happy thought."

He glanced out the window at the quiet Christmas day, the streets empty, everyone holed up inside for festive dinners. "Guess what? I'm about to have Christmas dinner with Nyle, Landon, Luzanne, and her boyfriend. It's weird. Never thought I'd be spending Christmas like this, but here I am with people I never expected to get along with. You're the only one missing. Merry Christmas, Tori."

As Aaron disconnected, the floorboards outside his room squeaked. Turning, he spotted Landon leaning in the doorway, arms crossed, one foot over the other. Thanks to Nyle's nagging, he'd finally succumbed to the festive spirit, rocking a Darth Vader Christmas jumper. Not exactly what Nyle had in mind, but this was Landon's nod to the holiday while sticking to his usual dark style. The socks, though, adorned with baubles and mistletoe patterns, were on theme.

Aaron wore the Christmas Pokémon jumper from Aunt Olivia, the one with Pikachu making a snowman.

"So, did you wish Tori a Merry Christmas?" Landon asked.

Aaron grunted, shoving his hands in his pockets. "It doesn't seem right, you know? She shouldn't be gone."

"It isn't something you can control."

"But maybe I could've, should've…"

"Even if that's true, it's too late now. Replaying the past doesn't change a thing. I know something about that."

Aaron gave Landon a long look, understanding in his eyes and the same emptiness Aaron had noticed from the start, the one that, sadly, also filled his own. "Ever wish you had a normal, happy family?"

"Would be nice, wouldn't it? But I figured out pretty quick that wishing doesn't get you far. It's about what you can do, not what you can't."

"So, we're talking about changing the future here?"

"More like right now, the present."

Aaron kept staring at him. The present felt unreal, warm, and smelled like roast turkey.

"Guys," Nyle's voice cut in from down the corridor. "This is not the time for a quickie. Dinner's ready!"

*

Christmas dinner turned out surprisingly nice—loads of food, French wine, Nyle explaining every tradition they had to follow, plus an absurd number of Christmas crackers for only the five of them.

Nyle and Jean had a heated discussion about food, particularly about the turkey. They debated whether it was authentic enough and why it was even a tradition. According to Jean, the French way of cooking it was supposedly superior. God, he was so annoying. To Aaron, food was just food.

When they'd finished dessert—and they'd been eating for hours—Aaron leaned back, patting his belly. He was stuffed, but in a good way. He couldn't even recall the last time he'd had such a feast.

"Looks like dinner was a hit!" Nyle said, sitting across from him with a stack of paper crowns on his head. He'd jokingly called himself the 'king of Christmas', but he looked ridiculous. His jumper, flashing like a Christmas tree, didn't help much either.

"Everything was spot on," Aaron replied.

"I knew it would be," Nyle boasted, tilting his head and almost losing a crown. "Used grandma's recipes—she was the best cook."

"How many Christmas meals have you had?" Landon asked Aaron from his end of the table. Unlike Nyle, his single crown added a touch of majesty.

"Uh, well, I never did a proper one with my family."

"See," Landon said to Nyle. "Don't read too much into the praise from someone with no basis for comparison."

"Hey," Nyle shot back, "Luz liked it too! Right, darling?"

Luz, finishing her mince pie with a full mouth, replied, "They're amazing. Taste like grandma's, maybe even better!"

Nyle sent a smug look to Landon as if to say, *Told you so.*

"Luzanne can think what she likes," Landon said. "I never knew what grandma's mince pies tasted like anyway."

The mood tensed up in a flash, so fragile a mere breath could shatter it.

"Why do you always make me feel like rubbish just because I stayed with the family, and you were fostered?" Luzanne snapped, her voice sharp. "Mum didn't pretend to be your aunt for the first five years of your life. She even took you in for a bit, but as always, you messed it up."

"That woman isn't our mother just because we came from her womb. To me, she's just someone who gave birth to me. You're kidding yourself if you think otherwise."

"So, I'm kidding myself thinking you're my brother?"

"I'm not your brother."

"No, you're not. A brother would care about his sister. You love making me miserable." With that, Luzanne stood abruptly, slamming her hands on the table, poised to storm out.

Aaron was about to leave as well, but Luzanne's piercing look stopped him. The resemblance to Landon, especially her eyes, was uncanny; they were unmistakably siblings.

"Don't leave, Aaron," she said. "Better to know who you're dealing with before it's too late."

"And who's that?" he asked.

"A resentful cynic. Don't expect Landon to care about anyone. He's incapable of love."

Aaron should've kept quiet, being the outsider in the house. But he was tired of the constant jabs at Landon, especially from his own sister.

"I'm not looking for anything from him. Like I've never expected anything from anyone. But I'm up for whatever he's willing to offer."

Luzanne's face was a picture of brewing anger. With a huff, she headed for the stairs. "Well, good luck with that."

Her stomping ended with her bedroom door slamming.

Aaron raised his wine glass and finished the last sip. "See, told you," he said, glancing at Landon. "Christmas is the worst time for family gatherings."

Nyle discarded his paper crowns and shook his head in disbelief. "You two...a perfect match, but not in a good way." He got up, followed by a concerned Jean.

Landon gulped down his wine, then gestured towards the garden. But Aaron had another idea.

"How about a walk?" he suggested.

"Where to?"

"Just come with me. You'll see."

*

London's heartbeat seemed to pause on Christmas Day, the usually bustling streets now still.

Aaron and Landon's footsteps echoed in the unusual silence, with only the occasional pigeon for company, pecking at a forgotten sandwich by the Thames. It was like a scene out of some apocalyptic movie, the perfect atmosphere as they stopped in front of an imposing iron gate, crowned by a once-vivid sign, now faded by time: *Riverdreams Wonderland.* Beyond the gate, the faint outlines of long-forgotten rides beckoned.

Landon's brow furrowed. "What the— a theme park?"

"Even better," Aaron said, nudging the rusted gate open with his foot. The creak broke the night's stillness. "An abandoned theme park."

They navigated paths overcome by nature, littered with memories and decay. Passing through a graffiti-laden tunnel, they emerged to a haunting scene of forsaken rides, like prehistoric behemoths frozen in time. The whistle of the wind made even the once-loved roller coaster seem threatening.

"This place gives me the creeps," Landon remarked.

"I find it fascinating."

"Why'd you bring me here?"

Aaron kicked a bottle cap along the path, his gaze fixed on the ground. "At the bonfire night, you mentioned this was the one place you always wanted to visit but never got the chance."

Landon chuckled, seeming surprised. "I meant when it was buzzing. This is a ghost town."

"Frightened, aren't we?" Aaron nudged him.

"Why would an old, lifeless place like this frighten me?"

"Some places can be scary."

"I reckon it's the memories, not the places that are scary."

Aaron pointed to a run-down building topped with a skeletal figure. "What about the haunted house, then?"

"You think that'd spook me?"

"Only one way to find out."

They approached the building, its entrance covered in thick cobwebs. Aaron brushed them off and shoved the old wooden door open, its hinges protesting. Inside, a semi-dark passage greeted them, filled with a musty, damp smell, like laundry that hadn't dried properly. Faint shafts of light seeped through the cracks in the walls and ceiling, casting eerie shadows that danced along the corridor.

They turned on their phone's torches, the light revealing faded spots on the walls where pictures used to hang.

Leading the way, Aaron stepped over rubbish and leaves until he reached a staircase. As he made to climb it, the sound of a kicked can behind him startled him.

"It's just me," Landon said, flashing the light in Aaron's face. "So much for not getting scared."

"I'm not."

"Liar."

Shaking off the comment, Aaron started up the creaky stairs, carefully avoiding weeds and mushrooms sprouting in the damp corners.

"Reckon if we eat one of these, we'll end up in Wonderland like Alice?" Aaron joked.

"We'd more likely end up in A & E," Landon commented dryly.

Reaching the top, they shone their phones around the room, though a large, glassless window let in a faint glow from outside. It was pretty much an empty room, save for a baby grand piano against the wall.

Aaron headed straight for it, stirring up a cloud of tiny insects in his wake. Pocketing his nearly dying phone, he poised his hands over the dusty keys.

"Do you play?" Landon marvelled, standing beside him.

"They used to call me 'Mozart'."

As Aaron hit the keys, the air filled with the jarring sounds of 'Rudolph the Red-Nosed Reindeer', though terribly off-key. It didn't help that it would have been equally terrible, even in tune.

"You're awful," Landon said as a gust of wind howled through the room. "Mozart must be turning in his grave. Who called you that?"

"My sister." Aaron laughed, stopping to brush his dirty fingers on his jeans. "She had the talent. I'm rubbish at music. What about you?"

"Same. I'm better off listening."

Aaron smiled and shoved his hands into his fleeced coat pockets. Despite being inside, it was as freezing as outside, his breath visible in the air.

"Shall we get going? Doesn't seem like there's much more to see," he suggested.

Landon nodded, taking the lead this time, his phone lighting their path as they moved from one empty room to another. They occasionally tripped over cans and food wrappers or disturbed a rat's hiding place but found nothing truly frightening.

As they reached the ground floor, the beam from Landon's phone disappeared, plunging them into the moonlit narrow corridor.

"Shit, the battery's gone," Landon said.

Aaron kept calm. They weren't too far from the exit, and it wasn't that dark. But he found his closeness to Landon in that confined space unsettling.

"Afraid of the dark?" Landon teased with a tremor.

"Not at all," Aaron replied, though he didn't sound too convincing.

"Afraid of what you can't see, are you?" Landon's hand went to his coat collar and tugged it. He shuffled on the spot, his feet seemingly glued to the floor, avoiding any steps deeper into the shadowy corridor.

That's when it hit Aaron. Landon was afraid of the dark. The lights, always left on in the summer house until dawn, weren't aesthetic but to keep the darkness away.

"Well, it works both ways. You can't see others, and they can't see you," Aaron said, trying to reassure him. "And here's a fun fact about people who are colour-blind. They see better in the dark."

"Bullshit."

But there, in the dim corridor, it seemed Landon could truly see him, more than anyone ever had.

Aaron paused, observing Landon's silhouette, illuminated by the soft glow from the distant doorway and the light seeping through the cracks. The silence stretched on until Landon's fingers brushed down Aaron's arm to rest on his wrist.

"Your heart's racing," Landon noted, the weight of his touch palpable against the throbbing pulse. "Is it the dark you fear, or is it...me?"

"Neither." Aaron's voice shook a little. "You've never scared me. You're not the psycho people say you are. But you seem to like that idea, or maybe you *want* it."

Landon chuckled softly, his breath fogging in the space between them. They were so close Aaron could hear Landon's breathing.

Switching it around, Aaron pressed his thumb to Landon's wrist, the pulse frantic, just like his. "Your heart's going fast too. What are you afraid of?"

Landon looked away for a second, then met Aaron's scrutiny again. "Can I?"

"Can you what? Kill me and hide my body in these ruins?"

"Kiss you."

"Oh." Aaron glanced quickly at Landon's lips, then back to his eyes. He seemed all over the place—nervous, excited, unsure.

"I only accept binary answers." Landon leaned in, the gap between their mouths narrowing. "Can I kiss you? Yes or no?"

For a brief, heart-stopping moment, Aaron worried that a kiss with Landon could ruin everything between them, especially if it was as lacklustre as his past experiences had been. But as he gazed into Landon's eyes, he realised he had never longed to kiss someone as deeply as he wanted to kiss Landon now.

"Yes," Aaron breathed out, his anxiety and anticipation evident.

That seemed to be all Landon needed; he cradled Aaron's face and brought their lips together.

The kiss, unlike what Aaron had braced for, was soft, almost tentative, lasting perhaps five, ten, fifteen seconds.

Yet, it was enough to jolt every nerve awake, to spark something he thought was long dormant, much like the derelict rides around them. Inside him, a series of tiny lights flickered to life, echoing those in the summer house.

As they drew apart, Aaron's heart pounded wildly. Their foreheads touched and their breaths mingled, melting the visible cold that hung in the air between them.

Aaron sighed, not from disappointment but from wonder at what other sparks Landon might ignite in him.

So, he leaned in and captured Landon's lips once again.

If their first kiss was a light brush, this one was all-consuming, an eager clash of noses and teeth and lips and tongues.

Despite their initial clumsiness, they soon found a rhythm, harmonising their movements.

For Aaron, it was revelatory, answering questions he didn't even know he had.

In the midst of Landon's kiss, he finally got what *desire* really meant. It was there, under Landon's tongue, in the way their mouths pressed and gasped for air, in the fingers entwined in his hair, and in the gentle nip of Landon's teeth on his lower lip.

And it wasn't fair.

Kissing someone wasn't supposed to make him feel both thrown off balance and grounded. Like sliding too fast down a very high slide but trusting the landing. He wasn't prepared for this.

He'd expected a bit of excitement, a teaser for what might come next, a warm-up. His mind and body had always run on separate tracks, never meeting. But now, they merged.

It didn't matter that the kiss was messy, that their noses bumped yet again, that he kept his hands awkwardly stuffed in his pockets because he wasn't sure what to do with them, or that Landon's stubble and the edge of his metal piercing scratched against Aaron's chin.

What made the kiss special was its unique taste—a blend of sleepless nights over tea and cigarettes, the songs they shared on Tube rides, deep chats by Regent's Canal, the stories behind each scar and tattoo, and soft awakenings in the summer house.

That kiss tasted like a safe place; it tasted of Neverland.

And it was the worst; it was the best.

It was too much. It wasn't enough.

Pulling back slightly for a breath, Aaron found Landon already waiting for him. The real world started to creep back in. The musty smell of the old building and the sharp chill of December air reminded him of where they were.

Undoubtedly, a ghostly house in an abandoned theme park was the strangest and most unsuitable place to let go and feel safe. Once again, in a surreal present. Once again, somewhere he shouldn't have belonged.

But then, Landon's lips met his again, as naturally as if they were made to fit together, like a key turning in a lock, opening the door to a home Aaron never had but had always longed for.

"Merry Christmas, Aaron," Landon whispered against his lips.

"Merry Christmas, Landon."

Chapter Twenty-Four

Landon's Rules

[Now playing » sex—EDEN]

That kiss with Landon replayed in Aaron's mind all night, like a catchy song he couldn't get out of his head.

Unlike his previous forgettable kisses, this one left him craving more.

He hadn't thought a kiss would change much. He was still dead set on leaving once his community service was done, no intentions of coming back. Especially now that he'd secured a ticket and a job.

But the truth was that something *had* changed within him after that kiss.

A voice kept whispering that things were different now. But how different could they really be?

Aunt Olivia used to say the best things in life came when you least expect them. It made sense now. He hadn't been looking for someone like Landon, but somehow, Landon had become one of the best surprises in his life.

Come morning, with a yawn, Aaron wandered into the kitchen. There was Landon, just as sleepy, fumbling with the coffee machine, pouring beans into the grinder, but as he looked up at Aaron, he spilled a few.

"Shit..." Landon muttered, quickly sweeping them up before Kat could pounce.

Awkward tension thickened the air as if their shared kiss had become an inconvenient third wheel.

"Tea?" Landon said, finally breaking the silence, reaching for some mugs.

"Actually, how about a cappuccino this time?"

"Really? Thought you weren't a fan of coffee."

"Well, seems there's a lot I thought I didn't like, but...you know."

Landon didn't say anything and grabbed the milk from the fridge. As he was about to froth it, Aaron, wanting to ease the tension, stepped in to give it a try. His first attempt was noisy and clumsy, and the steamer whistled loudly. Landon leaned in to guide him, and their fingers brushed fleetingly, sending a shiver down Aaron's spine.

Aaron flinched but managed to finish making the cappuccinos as well as he could.

Taking a deep breath, he faced Landon. "About yesterday..."

"What about yesterday?" Landon said, sniffing his cup.

"You kissed me."

"Yeah, I was there. And if I remember correctly, you kissed me back."

Aaron tried his cappuccino and winced as it burned his tongue. He tried to hide his reaction, but Landon chuckled and shook his head, enjoying another sip of his drink.

Holding Landon's gaze, Aaron watched the steam gently curl away from those lips, a familiar pull of longing inside him. He set down his cup and closed the small gap between them.

"Can I kiss you?" he echoed Landon's question from the night before.

Landon swirled his cup, his focus locked on Aaron. "I don't know. Can you?" He kept his tone light but laced with an inviting challenge.

Accepting it, Aaron took the cup from Landon's hand and placed it on the counter. He tiptoed slightly, reaching up to frame Landon's face, his heart thumping. But just as his fingers were about to touch Landon's cheeks, Landon caught his wrists in a gentle but firm hold.

Their eyes met, intense and searching as if Landon was asking a silent question, both a check and an invitation.

Landon inched closer, his breath ghosting over Aaron's lips as he murmured, "Go on. You can kiss me now."

That was all Aaron needed. He pressed his lips to Landon's, and in an instant, they became a blend of mingled flavours—coffee and toothpaste—and panted breaths and accelerated heartbeats.

This time, their kiss was less of a mess and more intense, more urgent, as Landon's tongue moved eagerly with Aaron's.

As they continued, Aaron found himself backing up until he was against the kitchen island, his fingers intertwining with Landon's on the cool countertop.

When they finally parted to catch their breath, Aaron felt as worn out and invigorated as after finishing one of his usual morning runs. A surge of dopamine flooded his system, but he was still keen to head out again, just for the thrill of it.

Landon leaned in close to Aaron's ear and whispered, "How about we move this upstairs to my room?"

"Your room?" Aaron tried to make sense of the suggestion while Landon's lips began a gentle exploration down his neck.

"If you're not feeling it, it's totally fine. We can just—"

"No, no, I'm in!" Aaron rushed out, maybe a little too enthusiastically. "I mean, yes, I'd like that."

"All right," Landon said softly, nipping just above Aaron's collarbone.

He got lost in the sensation of Landon's warm breath tickling against his skin until rapidly incoming footsteps interrupted them.

Aaron groaned, frustrated, which only made Landon smile a little as he quickly stepped back.

"Morniiiiing," Nyle announced with a cheeky grin.

Aaron turned to the counter in a rush, grabbed his cappuccino, and took a big sip.

"So," Nyle said, approaching with a mischievous look. "Don't we already have enough *bananas* around here?"

Aaron almost spit out his coffee.

Landon, cool as ever, finished his. He casually took Aaron by the arm and led him out of the kitchen. Behind them, Nyle continued chuckling and making playful comments.

They jogged up the stairs and reached the top floor in record time. As Aaron stood in front of Landon's door, the once intimidating *Fuck Off* warning on it suddenly seemed less daunting.

Landon pushed the door open, and Aaron paused at the threshold, taking in the sight—walls plastered with papers, photos, and drawings, shelves crammed with books, a desk positioned near the window with a view of the garden, and a double bed that looked inviting.

Aaron entered and slowly stepped to the centre of the room, scanning the walls. He recognised Landon's designs for tattoos next to snapshots of Landon with friends, including Ria, Nyle, and Fell, as well as various quotes. One in particular grabbed his attention. "Imagination is the only weapon in the war against reality" by Lewis Carroll.

But what struck Aaron even more, once he raised his head, was the starry ceiling.

"You painted this?" he asked, taking in the countless bright dots against the dark background. "It's wicked!"

Landon hummed in agreement, coming to stand beside him.

"I always wanted to do something like this in my room," Aaron said, still looking up. "But, you know, told you my parents were strict. They never allowed me to. I used to sneak posters up but had to rip them down before school."

Landon's eyes darkened as he looked at him. "I get it. Never had my own space as a kid. I was always moving."

"Well, you've definitely compensated for it now. This room's like a masterpiece. Should be on display at the Tate Modern or something." He turned back to the ceiling. "Are the stars glow-in-the-dark?"

"I didn't bring you up here for a room tour, you know."

"No?"

Landon caught Aaron's chin between his thumb and index finger, focusing his attention. He edged his face closer, letting Aaron feel his breath but stopped short of a kiss.

"If we keep this up"—Landon motioned between them—"there are some rules. Are you okay with that?"

"What sort of rules?"

Landon sighed, his hold firm. "First off, this is just for fun, a distraction. Handy since you're staying here."

Aaron's heart sank at those words. He had thought their connection was something more than that. The kiss they'd shared didn't seem to imply a casual fling. Yet, he masked his disappointment, understanding the difference in their emotional landscapes. Landon was openly gay and not on the asexual spectrum like him. It wasn't fair to expect Landon to feel the same emotional intensity Aaron was experiencing.

"I'm not here for long, though," Aaron managed to say, though it came out strained as he fought the lump forming in his throat.

"Exactly my point. So, shouldn't be a problem for you, right?" Landon waited for Aaron's nod before carrying on. "Rule number two. We gotta be honest with each other. If something's not sitting right with you, I wanna know. 'Yes' means 'yes', and 'no' means 'no'. Consent isn't a one-time deal. You good with being straight-up about that?"

Aaron blinked. This sounded more like a caring ask than a rule. "Yeah, but that goes both ways, right? If I ever do something you're not comfortable with—"

"That's rule three," Landon cut in, his finger shaking slightly under Aaron's chin. "You can't touch me until I give you the green light."

Aaron hadn't expected that, but it made him think about how he always felt jumpy when someone touched him, especially on his scars.

But with Landon, it was different; he trusted him. The tremble in Landon's grip and how he kept toying with his lip piercing told Aaron these rules must have their reasons. So, instead of asking why, he simply said, "Okay."

"Okay? You're not going to question it?"

"I won't," Aaron answered. "I'm usually not great with rules, but I understand these are important to you. So, I'll respect them. How did, um...others react to your rules?"

"I'm not sure." Landon let go and turned towards the window. "Not many have respected the third one, to be honest."

Aaron opened his mouth to speak several times, but the words wouldn't come.

"Yes or no?" Landon asked, turning to face him.

"Yes," Aaron whispered.

Landon closed the distance between them with a hungry kiss, nudging Aaron towards the edge of the bed. In a fluid motion, he removed his jumper, unveiling the tapestry of tattoos covering his torso, a blend of floral patterns, skulls, daggers, and words.

Aaron had pictured him just this way, a real piece of art.

The tattoo on Landon's chest, drew him immediately, the only one clashing with the others, right over his heart—an ECG line interrupted by a semicolon. Its meaning piqued his curiosity, but then something else grabbed his attention—a glint of metal in Landon's nipple.

"Did that hurt?" Aaron asked, pointing at the piercing.

Landon looked down, then at Aaron with a half-smile. "Oh, the piercing? Yeah, it was pretty painful. But that was ages ago. I hardly notice it now."

"I like it. Suits you."

Landon didn't add anything, and the lengthening silence pointed to his turn. Aaron hesitated, his hand gripping the hem of his T-shirt.

"You don't have to take it off if you're not comfortable."

Thinking of that time in the summer house, when Landon had been so considerate after seeing him shirtless, was enough to help Aaron make up his mind. He peeled off his T-shirt and let it drop to the floor.

Landon paused, his gaze sweeping over Aaron, taking in every detail. The intensity and burning desire there set Aaron alight as Landon's eyes traced every part of him, not just his skin but also the scars and the stories beneath them.

It made Aaron feel vulnerable. It made Aaron feel strong.

Then they were back at it, moving onto the bed as one. Aaron sank into the soft mattress, Landon's weight on top of him as their lips sought each other again; their chests brushed together.

Kissing was different skin against skin.

When Landon's cool fingers slipped under the waistband of Aaron's joggers, a shiver ran through his spine.

"You still okay?" Landon murmured, his lips close to Aaron's.

Aaron nodded. "I'll tell you to stop if I want you to stop."

That earned a faint smile from Landon, his mouth grazing against Aaron's cheekbone, causing another shiver. Much as he did with tattoos, Landon turned into an artist with his lips, riding each wave of gooseflesh from Aaron's chin down to his neck. He continued across the scars on his abdomen, each kiss as soft as a brushstroke, smoothing away the rough edges of the memory tied to those nasty marks.

Bit by bit, Aaron let go of all of his layers, lying there bare under Landon.

"Any preference?" Landon asked with the same casualness one might use when choosing from a restaurant menu.

"Uh...I don't know. I mean, I've been with a guy, but we never—" A warm flush crept down his nape. "You know...went all the way."

Landon rolled his eyes. Maybe he was annoyed by Aaron's inexperience.

"Didn't Ria lecture you on this already? Penetration isn't the be-all, end-all of sex."

"No, yeah, I know that, but—"

"There's no but," Landon cut in. "I wasn't planning on that today. There's plenty of other stuff we can do. Just asking where you want to start."

"What did you have in mind? And have you..."

"Yes." Landon's response was swift.

"And was it— How..." Aaron stumbled over his words, unsure of what exactly he was trying to ask. And why was it suddenly so difficult to string together a coherent sentence?

"It can be good, but it's okay if you're not up for it."

Aaron scratched his chest as if that gesture alone could calm his pounding heart and all the emotions and thoughts bubbling up inside him, ready to burst out.

He wanted *this*. He wanted Landon.

"I think I'd like to try," he said finally. "With you. Sometime. Would you?"

Landon gazed at him for the longest moment. "Yes. With you. Sometime."

They kissed again. Landon's hands roamed over Aaron, mapping him out. As they moved lower, Aaron's thoughts briefly flickered to a similar time with someone else, one that hadn't been so great. But this was different.

This time, Aaron responded, craving Landon's touch. He now understood what his mates had been on about—that urge to be close, to feel that rush of pleasure. He wanted it like never before.

Despite a tingling itch to touch Landon, Aaron kept his hands to himself. He found a spot on the headboard to rest them, his fingers discovering a small dent in the wood.

Landon kissed him softly, then guided Aaron's hands to his shoulders. "It's okay. You can touch me here."

Aaron allowed his fingers to glide over Landon's warm skin, tracing the tattooed outlines of rose petals and leaves. He wanted to dive further but stayed within the boundaries.

Landon moved lower, his lips pausing just below Aaron's navel, a single nod from Aaron all the confirmation he needed to continue.

Aaron closed his eyes and let Landon pin him down, pulling him apart and holding him together all at once. He gripped Landon's shoulders, trembling as though chilled, yet sweat beaded on his skin as if he were aflame. Landon's warmth enveloped him, and he lost himself in the scent of coffee, coconut, smoke, and clean sheets.

He couldn't contain the strangled noise that escaped his lips, his fingers brushing against Landon's neck in search of better purchase.

But suddenly, the warmth vanished.

Blinking in confusion, Aaron found Landon now sitting at the edge of the bed, staring out the window. He shifted closer to him, still unsure, and reached out towards Landon's shoulder tentatively. "Landon…"

"No," Landon cut in firmly.

Aaron pulled away, folding his hands in his lap. He kept his eyes fixed on Landon, still staring outside the window, lost in his own world. Aaron had never been great at picking up on subtle changes in skin tones, but he was certain Landon's face right now was the same unsettling shade of his waking nightmares.

He tried again, softer this time, "Landon…" wanting to reconnect the dots that seemed to have scattered when, just a second ago, there'd been no space at all between them.

But Landon was unresponsive, his fingers clenched so tight on his trousers, wrinkling the fabric. Then he sprang up, snatched his phone, and stormed off into the bathroom, the door banging shut behind him.

Aaron sat there, listening to the sound of running water, feeling a million miles away from Landon. He got dressed and settled on the desk, staring out at the grey clouds. What had set Landon off like that?

After what seemed ages, the bathroom door opened, and Landon came back into the room.

"You're still here?" he blurted out, water dripping off his hair and chin. He was still shirtless, and though he seemed more relaxed, the anger on his face wasn't a welcome change.

"Where was I supposed to go?"

"To your room, outside, anywhere but here," Landon snapped, irritation oozing from every word as he grabbed his jumper off the floor and jerked it on.

"You invited me in."

"And now I'm telling you to leave."

Aaron stood his ground, locking eyes with Landon. "Did I do something wrong?"

That seemed to wind Landon up even more. "You're missing the whole point of rule one. We have a bit of fun, and then you leave. End of."

"Not until you tell me what's wrong."

"Nothing's wrong."

"Landon..." Aaron pleaded, his frustration growing. "How am I supposed to avoid messing up again if you don't tell me what I did wrong?"

"You can't," Landon shot back. Aaron was about to argue, but Landon was quicker. "You can't because it's not your fault."

Those words hit Aaron hard, like a punch in the gut. "Look, we don't have to do anything at all. I know I said yes, but I won't die if we don't have sex."

Landon went quiet, then sat on the bed, back against the headboard and legs pulled up. He hid his face in his knees, took a couple of deep breaths, and looked up, resignation clear. "So, that first night, were you being honest about not caring for or enjoying sex?"

Aaron took a deep breath himself. "It's complicated. I'm kind of on the asexual spectrum." He made a vague gesture in the air to draw it but didn't quite do a good job at pinpointing where exactly he fell on that line. "Let's say I only enjoy sex in certain situations." He chose not to get into the nitty-gritty of demisexuality just then. The specific details didn't seem vital for Landon to grasp right now, particularly as they appeared to be on different wavelengths emotionally and sexually.

Landon looked lost. "So, like, were you enjoying this, or..."

"No, yeah, I was. A lot."

"As much as you enjoy running, or music, or getting lost in a good series?"

Aaron smiled. "More, I'd say. What about you? Were *you* enjoying it?"

Landon mumbled a soft, "Yes" and rubbed his cheek against his trousers. "It's only that..." His eyes darkened, and he searched for something out the window, past Aaron.

Aaron sat next to him on the bed, cross-legged, careful not to touch him. "You know when Nyle tried hitting on me when we first met?"

Landon paused, then nodded.

"I'm not great with unexpected touching either. But you...you're different. I feel safe with you. I know you won't cross any lines, and I won't either. I won't take anything you're not ready to give."

Landon stretched out his legs and lay back on the bed with a little pat to the space next to him as an invitation. Aaron took the hint and joined him as they had on Primrose Hill, resting his hands on his belly. Together, they gazed up at the starred ceiling.

"Tori always said that to see the most stars, you've got to head to some remote spot in the middle of nowhere."

"Point Nemo?"

"Maybe."

"I've always wondered what's so captivating about stars."

"Well, you must find them intriguing, too, or you wouldn't have painted them."

"They are," Landon said, turning towards him. "Most of the stars we see don't even exist anymore, but their light's still reaching us. It's like wandering through a graveyard, in a way. Fascinating, isn't it?"

"Sounds like you're into creepy stuff, despite your fear of the dark."

"I'm not afraid of the dark. I'm afraid of what I can't see."

Aaron turned to face him. "Just because you can't see something doesn't mean you should be afraid. Trust someone who's colour-blind."

"Trust you?" Landon scoffed.

"I've always used lies as a shield against my parents or out of habit. But I don't need that with you. I trust you."

"Guess you are a bit daft after all."

"I trust you, Landon. Otherwise, I wouldn't be here with you, in your bed."

Landon's gaze dropped, and he reached out to touch Aaron's face. His fingers followed the contours of Aaron's cheek, nose, and lips as if he were reading a story written in Braille. "You really are something, Aaron Walsh."

Something shifted in Landon's eyes, a softening of the storm, though Aaron wondered if it had only retreated deeper within him.

As Landon's fingers paused on his lips, Aaron pressed a gentle kiss to them. A surprised expression flashed across Landon's face—priceless—prompting a smile from Aaron. However, it was short-lived as Landon leaned in and stole that smile right off Aaron's face with a kiss.

"How about we watch a film or something?" Aaron suggested, their lips barely parting.

Hand in hand, they made their way downstairs. They stopped by the summer house to grab the laptop and then scouted the kitchen for some snacks. There, they discovered a note from Nyle attached to a solitary banana.

Gone out. Back late. VERY late. Do precisely what I'd do if I were home alone with a bloke.

"Is he really your cousin?" Aaron asked.

"Unfortunately," Landon replied, crumpling the paper and tossing it in the bin.

Before heading back up, Aaron checked his phone. He'd left it by the fruit bowl since that morning without much thought. To his surprise, notifications swamped his screen—loads of missed calls and messages from Aunt Olivia.

Odd, especially since they'd exchanged Christmas wishes the day before, and he'd promised to call her on New Year's Eve.

As he opened the messages from his aunt, his heart sank.

I've found out from your friend Cliff that not only have you never planned to travel to Australia together, but you're also still in London because they caught you with weed at a party! What on earth's been going through your head?

I've been trying to call you all day. Why aren't you picking up? Please, let me know you're safe.

I don't even want to know why you've been feeding me

all these lies.

I know the rough patch you've been through, and I understand how tough it's been for you to pick yourself up since the accident.

But you need to know that it pains me to think you felt you couldn't confide in me. You know I care for you deeply, see you as a son, and it's heartbreaking to think you didn't feel safe enough here with me.

Remember, I'm here for you, Aarie. I always will be. Please, come back home.

"Everything all right?" Landon asked.
"Everything's fine," he lied.

Chapter Twenty-Five

Monsters Under the Bed

[Now playing » Monsters—Seafret]

Aaron had been hoping to dodge a confrontation with Aunt Olivia for as long as he could. But it looked like he didn't have much choice now.

When his phone lit up again on the bedside table the next morning, he flipped it over, face down. Muffling a groan in the pillow, he lay still, waiting for the buzzing to cease. What could he possibly say to her? The truth was out in the open, and continuing to lie wasn't an option. He was fucked.

He knew Cliff wouldn't keep quiet once he realised Aunt Olivia was oblivious to the whole situation. But doing it at Christmas? That was a low blow.

"Aren't you going to take that?" Landon asked, still lying in bed next to him. "It's been going off since last night. Could be important."

"I'll call her back later."

"Need more time to come up with a believable story? Why not be honest with her?"

Aaron lifted his head from the pillow. "What's the point? I'll be gone soon."

"She deserves to know, Aaron."

"No, she doesn't. It's better off this way."

"For her or for *you*?"

Aaron sighed, turning to the starred ceiling. "I want a fresh start. A clean slate."

"Do you really think you'll find that in Australia?"

"I made a promise."

"I get that, but is it the right move for you?"

"What other choice do I have? There's nothing left for me here anymore."

Landon's hand brushed across Aaron's chest, pausing at the glass pendant tucked under the hoodie. "Maybe you're so focused on what's ahead, you can't see what you're leaving behind."

Aaron covered Landon's hand with his own. He opened his mouth to argue, but words failed him. Since Tori had gone, he'd been pushing relentlessly forward, afraid that stopping even for a second might mean he couldn't start again.

"You're a liar and a rabbit." Landon's thumb grazed over the scars on his cheek. "But you don't have to be, not if you don't want to."

Their lips met in a fleeting kiss, soft and velvety and sweet, like the foam of yesterday's cappuccino.

"You're also a thief," Landon whispered, his tone more amused than annoyed. "You've nicked my hoodie."

"I grabbed the first thing I could find." Aaron defended himself quickly. So much for not being a liar. "I could take it off if you want it back."

"Keep it. Looks good on you."

"You sure you want me to keep it?" Aaron teased, the weight of the conversation lifted as they tangled in the sheets.

But it wasn't just Aunt Olivia weighing on Aaron's mind.

*

Over the next few days, it became a regular thing for Aaron and Landon to share a bed.

Yet, whenever they tried to have sex, they'd hit a bump. Aaron was careful, strictly following the rules, touching only where and when Landon indicated. But despite his caution, it seemed as though he always ended up doing something wrong.

Landon would abruptly stop, pull away, and go completely silent, looking shaken.

This pattern left Aaron puzzled and concerned. Was there something deeper going on with Landon, something serious he wasn't talking about?

Aaron didn't want to pressure him; he hoped Landon would come around and open up in his own time. But when it happened again that afternoon, Aaron followed Landon into the garden, bringing along two steaming mugs of tea.

Landon sat on the grass, puffing away, staring up at the sky as if trying to find some answers up there.

"Hey," Aaron said, trying to get through him.

Nothing. Landon kept smoking, lost in thought.

"Please, talk to me."

Landon blew out another cloud of smoke, his fingers trembling around the cigarette. Aaron saw through the act. He knew tough exteriors often hid deep fears. And when those fears managed to breach the walls, they showed up like this—tensed shoulders, uneven breaths, and trembling hands.

Aaron wanted to reach out, to lace their fingers together to comfort him, but he was aware that touch might not be welcome right now. So, he sat cross-legged across from him and set the mugs on the ground.

Landon, still in his own world, took another drag. When he lifted the cigarette again, Aaron plucked it from his fingers and took a drag himself.

That was enough to get Landon's attention.

"I can't stand you," he said, looking over. His tone and gaze tried hard to be sharp but came off weaker than anything.

Aaron faced him straight on, blew out the smoke defiantly, and squashed the cigarette out. "How about we skip the act where you pretend you don't like me and just talk? What's eating at you?"

Landon started messing with his lip piercing, a far-off look in his eyes. He seemed to be mulling over something big, his expression serious and pensive. Then, almost as if he'd decided against saying whatever was on his mind, Landon looked away, still fiddling with his piercing. "I don't want to hurt you."

"What are you talking about? You didn't hurt me at all."

"Don't lie. Earlier, when I tried to...you flinched."

He did? Was Landon holding back because he was scared of hurting *him*?

"Landon, listen, it's okay. I would have told you to stop if I didn't like it. Besides, you made the rules clear, remember?"

Landon's eyes met Aaron's again, full of care. The guy was a bundle of contradictions. He kept saying what they had together was nothing, but his actions proved otherwise. The way he worried, the way he let himself be vulnerable with Aaron, it wasn't just nothing.

"How come you're okay with my rules?" Landon said. "You should hate them. Why do you even *trust* me?"

Aaron sniffed his tea. "You know, it's weird. With my parents, it was always 'do this, don't do that', no questions asked. But with you, it's not like that. Your rules...they're about being on the same page, not bossing me around. It feels...safe. I know I can speak up, and you'll listen. That's why I trust you. I'm okay with your rules because they're fair, not controlling."

"You're absolutely insufferable," Landon said, but the corners of his mouth twitched into a small smile, infectious enough to spread to Aaron.

Their hands found each other in the grass, fingers weaving together naturally. Just holding hands felt right. They sat there in the quiet of the afternoon, drifting away, letting the silence speak for them. Sometimes, words weren't necessary. But Aaron had this nagging feeling in the back of his mind, a reminder that calm often comes before a storm.

And sure enough, the next morning brought its own chaos.

It wasn't Aaron's phone buzzing non-stop on the bedside table this time. It was Landon's.

Landon groaned and reached through the sheets to grab it. His face fell as soon as he saw the screen.

"Everything okay?" Aaron asked, sitting up.

Landon didn't answer. He stared at his phone, his face full of shock and disbelief.

"Landon…"

"It's far from okay," Landon's said, his voice flat as he extended his arm, showing Aaron the screen.

Aaron, still groggy from sleep, blinked and focused on the phone, displaying an article.

> *Familial Betrayal and Tragedy: Teenage Life Cut Short Days Before Christmas*
>
> *In a harrowing turn of events just days before Christmas, eighteen-year-old Ian Thompson tragically ended his life…*

Aaron recognised the guy in the photo. "He's the one who hassled you in Camden Town, right? Your foster brother?"

Landon nodded, putting the phone down. He took several deep breaths, the kind he'd taught Aaron to take during panic attacks, and then buried his face in his hands.

"Hey…" Aaron squeezed Landon's shoulder reassuringly.

Landon shook his head, looking up. "Can't right now. Need some space."

With that, Landon got out of bed and threw on some clothes.

As soon as Landon left the room, Aaron grabbed his phone and searched for more information. What he found didn't make things any better.

Chapter Twenty-Six

Sharp Shards

[Now playing » Blurry—Puddle Of Mudd]

In a deeply moving post on his Instagram, eighteen-year-old Ian Thompson has shared his feelings of despair and betrayal. Thompson has accused his former foster father, prominent criminal solicitor David Green, of sexually abusing him. Green had been Thompson's foster parent for two years, starting when Thompson was just thirteen.

Thompson often took to social media to speak about his experiences in the foster care system and the challenges he faced. Sadly, his open discussions attracted negative comments, with people accusing him of making up stories for attention.

The situation tragically worsened when Thompson's own biological family refused to support his legal case against Green. Their lack of support, especially during a time like the festive season, which traditionally emphasises family unity, left Thompson feeling even more isolated and hopeless.

Even though Aaron had only seen the guy once in passing, he felt a gut punch of empathy. The thought that Landon might've gone through the same abuse was even more gut-wrenching.

Aaron started piecing things together—Landon's tough exterior, his touch aversion, his issues with sex, his need for consent, his habit of sitting with his back against the wall...

He hoped he was wrong.

After staying in Landon's room for a few more minutes, Aaron got out of bed, not to follow Landon but because he needed a drink.

In the kitchen, he found Nyle and Luzanne huddled at the table, talking in hushed tones. As soon as they saw him, their expressions said it all.

"You knew about this?" Nyle's voice was tight.

Aaron shook his head. "Did Landon..."

Nyle managed a strained noise, glancing over at Luzanne, who dipped her chin in silence. "Landon was in the same foster home as that kid for a period," he said. "We all thought he hit the jackpot, as the Greens are loaded and living in this swanky house in Chelsea and all. But it was while he was with them that he started acting out, getting into fights, breaking stuff. And shortly after, he ended up in jail."

"I bet Landon went through the same hell in that house," Luzanne spoke up. "I used to be jealous of him, what with the posh school, all those gifts, and fancy stuff he got from the Greens. I didn't see what was really happening."

"How were we supposed to know?" Nyle said, jumping in. "Landon's always been tough, always kept to himself. He never talks about stuff, never opens up."

"We should've picked up on something," Luzanne said, fiddling with her hair. "We're meant to be his *real* family."

"But are we?"

Luzanne looked out the window at the summer house. "Why didn't he say anything? We could've helped him, brought him back to us..."

"Some things are too hard to talk about," Aaron said softly, still trying to process everything.

Nyle turned to him. "He didn't open up to you either?"

Aaron sighed heavily, shaking his head. "I kinda suspected something, but..."

Nyle rubbed his chin. "I bet Ian wanted Landon on his side for the case against Green. When that didn't happen...well, it was too much for him. Poor soul."

Aaron's thoughts raced back to the brief confrontation he'd witnessed between Ian and Landon. Things clicked together—Ian's desperation, Landon's tattoos hiding his scars... It made him sick to his stomach.

"He's holed up in the summer house." Nyle gestured outside the window. "He won't talk to us, but maybe you can get through to him."

Luzanne snorted. "Right, so he trusts the random dude he's shagging more than his own family?"

That hit Aaron like a slap. She had a point though. But it still stung. What were he and Landon to each other anyway?

"Come on, Luz. That's harsh," Nyle admonished. "You should be happy he has someone he can rely on."

"But it could've been us, couldn't it?" Luzanne said bitterly. "Instead, he always looked at us like we were rubbish. I know he's been through a lot, but it's not my fault I got to stay with our family while he was put in foster care. That doesn't give him the right to hate me or go around beating up my boyfriends."

Nyle stared at her. "Wait, are you talking about Rob? The guy was a total liar, gambling away your cash. Landon was right to push him away."

Luzanne's eyes widened. "Wait, what? That can't be true."

"Hard to take in, I know. We didn't tell you because Landon didn't want to upset you more. But yeah, your ex was basically a leech."

"And Landon couldn't just talk to me? Does he get a thrill out of being an asshole, or is he just crap at dealing with people?"

"He didn't exactly have the easiest childhood," Nyle reminded her.

"I get that, but it's no excuse for him to be so bloody harsh all the time," Luzanne shot back. "Would it kill him to be nice for once?"

Despite everything, Aaron had to smile. "Landon's not one to wear his heart on his sleeve, but he's actually pretty kind."

Luzanne squinted at him as though he'd lost his mind.

"Kindness isn't about being sweet," Aaron explained. "It's about caring and doing stuff that shows it. Landon's way of caring is, well...different. But he's always putting others first. Like, he's the one who took the fall for Nyle."

Nyle tried to shush him with the sole force of his stare, but Aaron pressed on.

"Nyle did something stupid, and Landon took the blame for it. That's the real reason they're both on community service now."

Luzanne turned to Nyle, who nodded and added, "He made me swear not to tell you 'cause he figured you already hated him and wouldn't have believed a word he said."

"That's not kindness," she stated. "That's selfishness and—"

"How can you not see?" Aaron cut off whatever mean stuff she was going to say. "He's always doing things for nothing in return. He rescued Kat, didn't he? And he practically gave me the job with Fell...and cared for that bloody tree at the retirement centre when everyone thought he was killing it."

"Oh my God," Luzanne cried, shocked. "I just thought... I think I got it all wrong..."

"You still have a chance to get to know him better," Nyle intervened, "if you're willing to try. For *real* this time. We need to be there for him and act like a proper family now. And I swear I'll see that bastard get what he deserves." All fired up, he headed down the corridor.

"Where are you going?" Luzanne called after him, with Aaron trailing behind.

"I'm off to give that scum a piece of my mind," Nyle declared, hastily shoving on his shoes and coat. "Ria's already protesting in front of his house."

"Don't be an idiot." Luzanne tried to grab his arm, but he shrugged her off. "The only protest you've ever been to is Pride, and trust me, this one won't be all rainbows and glitter."

"I'm dead serious," he said, hand on the door, ready to bolt.

Luzanne blocked his way. "Nyle, please, don't make things worse. Don't wanna lose another brother."

"You won't. Just let me be. I owe him this." He pushed past her and disappeared into the night.

"I'll handle it," Aaron assured her, quickly grabbing his coat and stepping into his trainers. "I'll bring him back. Don't worry."

Luzanne let out a doubtful groan but didn't stop him.

*

Convincing Nyle to ditch his plan for revenge was tough, and showing up at the Greens' place, in the middle of a protest, didn't help.

The scene was intense, with people everywhere waving signs and shouting for justice. Aaron spotted Ria at the front, leading the charge with a megaphone in hand. Some of the more fired-up protestors chucked stones at the house windows as others spray-painted the Porsche in the drive.

Naturally, Nyle headed straight for the ones causing the most ruckus, but Aaron grabbed the end of his coat and yanked him back.

"We should leave before the police get here," he advised. "You don't want to get caught vandalising again, do you?"

"I don't give a shit. I'd happily land in jail for Lanny."

Aaron tried to make him see sense. "Think about it—would Landon want you locked up? After everything he's done to keep you out of it in the first place?"

"Landon doesn't have a say in this."

"Actually, if anyone has a say, it's him. He wouldn't be happy to know you're here."

"Landon's never fucking cared about himself, otherwise he would've reported Green with Ian. I'm doing this for him."

"The best thing you can do for Landon is be there for him," Aaron insisted. "Let him make the call on what happens next."

Nyle held Aaron's gaze, then sighed and relaxed his posture. "All right, but since we're here, let's have some fun."

Aaron watched Nyle grab a couple of spray cans off the ground and give them a good shake. When he handed one to him and nodded towards the Porsche with a cheeky grin, the temptation was too much.

So, there they were, tagging the car with all sorts of insults.

Aaron wouldn't say it out loud, but every spray of paint brought out something weirdly satisfying. But their fun didn't last long. The police turned up, and the whole crowd started scattering.

Aaron was ready to run as he had any other time. But instead of bolting on his own, he grabbed Nyle by the arm, ensuring they both left together.

Back home, as soon as the door opened, Luzanne wrapped Nyle in a tight hug. "Please tell me you didn't do anything stupid."

"I didn't do anything stupid," Nyle repeated, amused.

Luzanne stepped back, her scepticism clear, then turned to Aaron for the real story.

"Well, at least we didn't get caught," Aaron added.

"You didn't get caught doing what?" Landon's voice cut through the room, surprising everyone. He emerged from the corridor shadows, looking annoyed and exhausted. He stopped, facing Nyle, his expression more weary than furious.

"That creep deserves to be behind bars for what he did to you," Nyle said.

"When exactly did I ask you or Ria to start a crusade for me? Because I'm pretty sure I never did."

Landon's cold response sent a chill through Aaron.

"Actually, it was my idea to join the protest," he said, trying to ease the tension.

Landon's eyes flicked to Aaron, sparking with an intensity that almost pulverised him on the spot.

"Lanny, it was all for you," Nyle admitted.

"You're mistaking me for someone who needs help. Even worse, revenge. For me, that chapter's closed."

"Ian was all alone, but you have *us*," Nyle persisted. "We're your family; we're here for you."

"It's too late," Landon said quietly before disappearing outside again.

Nyle and Luzanne shared looks of sadness and disbelief.

Aaron wondered how Landon could just brush it all off like that? Without thinking, he followed him out and barged into the summer house after him.

"I didn't ask you to come in," Landon said coldly.

"I couldn't care less."

In a flash, Landon grabbed Aaron by the collar and pinned him against the wall. "You're playing with fire," he warned.

"I've been burned before. Doesn't scare me," Aaron replied defiantly, holding up his scarred hands.

Landon's eyes darted between Aaron's hands and face. "You're really something, aren't you?" His grip on Aaron's collar tightened as if he was about to chuck him out. But then Landon dropped his head in the crook of Aaron's neck, resting it there.

He wasn't pushing him away; he was holding him in place.

They stayed like that, wrapped up in a silent hug. Aaron hovered his hands near Landon's waist, unsure whether to pull him closer.

In the end, Landon broke the tension. He leaned in and kissed Aaron slowly, desperately. The kiss did little to calm the storm inside Aaron.

"If you ever want to talk," he said, "I'm here."

"I don't want to talk. And I definitely don't need you or Nyle or Ria playing the heroes."

"I already told you it was my idea."

"When are you going to stop with the lies?" Landon stroked his thumb over Aaron's cheek. "Still, I guess I should thank you for looking out for Nyle."

"Don't get used to it. I did try to tell him it was a bad idea, but you know Nyle…"

Landon grumbled in annoyance.

"I also told him you should be the one to decide what to do."

"I don't want to do anything."

"Why not?" Aaron couldn't hide his frustration.

"Because it's pointless." Landon slumped, resigned, onto the futon and drew his knees up to his chest. He stared blankly at his socks.

Exasperation bubbled up inside Aaron as he watched Landon giving up so easily. He couldn't understand why Landon wouldn't fight back when Aaron was ready to go to war for him. His little adventure with Nyle felt trivial compared to what he really wanted to do.

Still leaning against the door, Aaron observed Landon in silence. After a while, he sat next to him on the futon, leaving space between them.

"Don't you think he should pay for what he did to you, to Ian…and God knows who else?" Aaron said, struggling to keep his emotions in check.

Landon didn't respond. He kept staring at his candy-cane patterned socks.

"Landon…"

"You're wasting your time," Landon snapped, turning to face Aaron, his eyes burning with bitterness. "You can't save me from something that's not even a threat anymore."

Aaron wasn't buying it. "Now who's lying to themselves?"

In response, Landon yanked up his jumper sleeve, revealing his tattooed arm. He grabbed Aaron's hand and pressed a finger against one of the scars under the ink.

"See? Just like I said," Landon insisted. "This doesn't hurt anymore. You think it does because that's how you want to see it, but nothing can touch me now. You can't break what's already broken."

Aaron jerked his hand away as if he'd touched something electrified. "You can't let him keep controlling you. By staying quiet, you're letting him win."

"You sound like Ian now. Can't you see? It's all for nothing."

"What are you afraid of? Or is it shame? It should be him feeling that, not you. Don't let him keep living it up while you suffer in silence."

"Revenge is a mug's game."

"It's not about revenge. It's about justice."

"Justice?" Landon let out a hollow laugh, as jarring as the notes from the decrepit piano in the haunted house. "Justice doesn't exist for people like *me*."

"People like *you*?"

"Foster kid, criminal, ex-convict, gay, Black... Take your pick. There's plenty of choice."

"But that's not fair," Aaron argued. "He needs to face the consequences for what he's done. You need to testify against him."

Landon shook his head. "It wouldn't change a thing. I'm almost ten years too late. Plus, the ones with the money and the status always come out on top. David's the white, respected solicitor with the perfect family, living in Chelsea. My testimony, in all likelihood, wouldn't even be believed. Trust me, I know a thing or two about this."

That hit Aaron. "Wait, you once said...something about people being too thick to see the truth even when it's right in front of them. You told someone about it, didn't you?"

"That's the thing about you. You pay attention to what I say." Landon shot him a look, half annoyed, half impressed. "Yeah, I told my foster mum and the guy who managed my foster placements. Both didn't believe me. Said I was a nobody looking for a quick quid. After that, I figured I was on my own."

"But it's different now," Aaron insisted. "I believe you. We all do. And after what happened to Ian, maybe there's a shot. You could find others, team up, and—"

"Stop. Just...stop. You don't get it, do you? Your whole privileged white lens is blinding you."

"Don't pull the race card on me. I've had no privileges, you know that."

"I don't know shit about you, Aaron Walsh, do I? You're always lying, always planning to run away."

"And aren't you running from your own problems right now?"

"It's not the same."

"I think it is," Aaron shot back. "You're just avoiding dealing with it."

"There's nothing to deal with."

"I bet your therapist would say otherwise."

"And what about yours?" Landon said sarcastically. "Oh, right, you don't have one because you don't have any issues."

"Don't change the subject."

Their words hung heavy in the air, creating a palpable tension. Despite sitting so close, they might as well have been time zones apart.

Aaron softened his tone slightly. "Before, you were on your own. But now, you have Nyle, Luzanne, Ria...me."

"I don't need you," Landon said flatly.

"I know," Aaron replied, his voice hardening. "But I'm here for you."

"Until when?"

His question caught Aaron off-guard. "Until when...what?"

"How long are you going to *stay*?"

"I, um..."

Landon rose swiftly, towering over Aaron. "You're a hypocrite. You say I should face up to things, but you're avoiding your own problems. Can't even deal with your aunt."

"I told you; it's for the best," Aaron replied, standing to match Landon's height.

"Right, running away is always the easy option."

"I'm not running. I'm keeping a promise."

"Excuses," Landon scoffed, folding his arms. "You're so used to finding reasons to leave, you've forgotten to look for reasons to stay."

Aaron gaped, unable to retort.

"If going to Australia is really what you want, then, go and never come back. But if you're doing all this just to please a ghost, maybe you're not the one to give me advice about dealing with my trauma when you're still haunted by your own."

Aaron struggled for breath. The truth was a concept much harder to swallow than a lie.

"Maybe you should go back home," Landon said, opening the door.

"I don't have a home."

"Minus three. Game over, Aaron."

Aaron remembered the first time Landon mentioned that strange countdown. He'd asked back then what it meant to lose all his 'lives'. Now, the answer was painfully clear to him.

"So, is this it? We're done?" he asked, barely above a whisper.

"There was never an 'us'. It's always been you and the ghost of your sister."

With that, Landon pushed him out and slammed the door.

Despite the finality of the gesture, Aaron told himself Landon hadn't pushed him away. Instead, he, Aaron, would be taking charge, closing a chapter. Landon had only been a detour. Aaron's real destination, his true purpose, was still out there, waiting for him halfway across the world.

Chapter Twenty-Seven

Broken Pieces

[Now playing » Midnight—Coldplay]

Aaron knew he owed Aunt Olivia an explanation. She'd been nothing but kind since he first arrived at her place three years ago. Despite all the lies and the trouble he'd caused, she never once made him feel like he was in the wrong.

She welcomed him, same as ever, with open arms and led him to the living room. They sat on the sofa, their go-to spot for heart-to-hearts, each cradling a steaming mug.

"Auntie Olivia," Aaron started shakily, "I'm sorry for all this mess. It's just that...I was trying to..." He brought the tea to his nose, hoping the mint would chill him out. But no luck. His fingers did a clanky tapping on the handle. Even one of Nyle's quirky mugs wouldn't have cut the tension this time. "I don't know where to start."

"Perhaps start with your plans to move to Australia and never come back," Aunt Olivia suggested flatly.

"Look, I didn't—"

"No, Aaron," she cut in sharply, her fingernails scraping the ceramic mug. "Do you really think you're the only one hurting, struggling to get past this? I lost my sister and niece in that crash, too, remember?"

Aaron's throat scratched like sandpaper as he gulped, eyes fixed on the coffee table.

"I know exactly what it feels like," Olivia pressed on. "Every morning, I wake up hoping it's just a nightmare. But it's real, and we both have to face it. Now, why were you planning to move to Australia without telling me?"

"I still *want* to go to Australia," he corrected softly.

"Because that's what Tori dreamed of?"

He stayed silent, avoiding her gaze.

"Have you opened the book Tori left you?"

Aaron flinched. "It's just a kid's book."

"It's more than that, and you know it. Tori made me promise, with her last breath, that you'd have it."

"I don't need to open it. I know what it says."

"Or maybe it's too hard because it reminds you of her."

"Everything does," he admitted, finally looking up. He was sure his eyes were glossy, on the verge of tears. Something he hadn't done in years, not even on the day of Tori's funeral, which he'd been unable to attend.

"Aarie..." Aunt Olivia stretched out her hand on the cushion to touch his. "What happened is unfair, but Tori would want you to live fully, to find happiness."

"I'll find that in Sydney," he whispered.

"Do you truly believe that?"

Aaron faltered. Like Landon, Aunt Olivia questioned his decision, one he'd been mulling over for ages about the promise he'd made to Tori. Why couldn't they get that?

"You never talk about the crash or losing Tori, but maybe it's time you did. If it's not with me, maybe a friend or...a therapist?"

Aaron felt the urge to roll his eyes. The only useful thing he'd picked up from those therapy sessions Aunt Olivia had insisted on after the car crash was about how scents trigger memories. That was why he'd started sniffing mint. It took him back to Tori. She always loved peppermint tea and would insist on him drinking it whenever he was sick, though he never liked it.

"There's nothing to talk about." His words echoed Landon's when Aaron had tried to get him to open up. Funny how he was pushing Landon to do the very thing he was avoiding.

"Talking helped me," Aunt Olivia insisted.

"What's the point? Tori's gone." Aaron pulled his hand away and fiddled with his pendant, a constant reminder of his survival. But at what price? "Chatting about it won't bring her back."

"No, it won't," Aunt Olivia agreed softly. "But you can't live in her shadow forever. You need to find a way through your grief."

"I am through it. I'm moving on."

"It looks more like you're stuck."

"I won't be for long. As soon as my community service is done, I'm off. Starting fresh."

He sniffed the tea and made a face; the smell wasn't right. "Is this a new brand or something?"

"Don't change the subject, Aaron. And why keep me in the dark? It wasn't fun finding out what happened from Cliff. And that you were only a few miles away? Why didn't you tell me the truth?"

"I'm sorry. I was...ashamed." He set down his tea and covered his face with his hands.

"I can understand that. And I know people can do a lot of stupid things. I've done plenty myself and would never judge you. If you'd told me, I would've been there to help."

Aaron looked up, meeting Aunt Olivia's gaze. "I don't need help."

"That's exactly what someone who needs help would say," she pointed out. "I'm here for you. I wish I'd known earlier what you and Tori were dealing with at home."

"How could you? I didn't know myself. Mum and Dad were good at playing the 'happy family'." He snorted. "They dragged Tori and me into their mess just because they were too stubborn to admit they weren't right together. All their nonsense rules, the fights, the spiteful games, and using us as pawns..."

"Yeah, they definitely brought out the worst in each other," Aunt Olivia agreed. "But they did love you both."

"Maybe, but it wasn't the kind of love that did us any good."

Aunt Olivia sighed. "I never liked your dad, to be honest. When he and Joanne got together, he charmed everyone. He was so polite, so generous with gifts, not just to your mum but to all of us. He was a smooth talker, hard to argue with. And those love letters he wrote to her were like something out of a romantic movie. I guess that's why she fell for it."

Aaron scoffed. His memories were of them shouting, always bickering, even when they weren't yelling. They'd constantly moan about any silly thing around the house or complain about him and Tori. Any slip-up. and "Oh, because it's your son," as if being related was an insult.

He loathed living in that toxic atmosphere. Throughout his childhood, Aaron wished they'd split up so he could escape the constant tension. He'd even thrown himself into every school activity to stay out of the house as much as possible.

Yet, after they were gone, he didn't feel any relief. He missed them. Not the anger and the arguments, but his parents. The good times, rare as they were, played back in his mind, tinged with sadness for what might have been and what was lost forever.

"I wish I'd done more," Olivia continued. "I didn't realise it was that bad. Sure, I saw them argue now and then, but that's normal for couples, right? And when you have kids, you always think you're doing what's best for them." She set her mug down and gripped her knees. "But looking back, I'm not sure they made the right choices."

"They should've divorced."

"Yeah, they should have. Maybe things would've been different for you. Maybe you wouldn't have..." Her voice trailed off.

Aaron flashed back to the fateful day of the accident, freezing him in his tracks.

It had started with a trivial but familiar squabble in the backseat of their car. *"I want to sit on this side,"* Aaron had insisted.

"But I always sit there," Tori protested, tinged with annoyance. Eventually, though, she sighed and gave in. *"Fine, take it."*

As they settled into the car ride, Tori kept her eyes glued to her phone until she squawked excitedly, *"Oh my God, I've been offered a scholarship in Sydney!"*

Their parents exchanged a glance that spoke volumes. Aaron could sense the tension beginning to simmer.

"Sydney?" Mum sounded worried. *"That's an entire continent away, Tori. It seems so...drastic."*

"But this is my dream, Mum. This is a once-in-a-lifetime opportunity. I've always wanted to do something like this, and now I have the chance!" Her enthusiasm was undeterred. *"And that's not all. Tom has connections in Sydney. I can work with koalas, get hands-on experience... It's everything I've ever wanted."*

Mum's voice rose in volume. *"We need to think about this, Tori. It's a big decision."*

"There's nothing to think about. This is what I want. Why can't you get that?"

Dad spoke up, sounding all serious. *"You're too young to know what you want. We're your parents. We know what's best for you."*

Tori pounded her fist lightly on the seat. *"No, you don't. I'm eighteen now. I make my own choices. And guess what? I've found a student year program in Sydney for Aaron too,"* she said, turning to him.

Aaron recalled his father's hands tightening on the steering wheel.

"What? Now you're dragging your little brother into this too?"

"I'm not little," he'd protested. *"And it'd be sick to do a year abroad."*

But that's when everything went haywire with Mum and Dad arguing, voices getting louder. Tori tried to stand her ground, Aaron's stomach doing somersaults.

Suddenly, Dad turned around to give Tori a piece of his mind, completely forgetting about the road. *"You're not going anywhere!"* he'd shouted.

That was the last thing Aaron remembered before the screech of tires filled the air and a deafening crash silenced everything. The aftermath was a blur—Mum yelling Dad's name in panic, Tori grabbing Aaron's hand as the world turned upside down and a rain of glass poured over him.

Tori kept squeezing his hand till the very end, even though she sounded tired. *"It's going to be okay, Aarie."* She didn't let go, even as a jagged piece of glass lodged between their interlocked palms. *"Hold on to a happy thought, and we'll fly away to Neverland, okay? Don't let go."*

"Aarie," Aunt Olivia's voice cut through his thoughts like a beacon, her touch on his back grounding him.

Aaron realised he was shaking all over.

"Just breathe, Aaron. You're here with me." Aunt Olivia's hand moved in soothing circles on his back. "You're safe. Everything's okay now."

He took deep, uneven breaths. Then, just as Landon had taught him, he mentally ticked off the first five items in the room that he could see, felt four different textures under his fingertips, and listened to the sounds drifting in through the open window. When it came to smells, though, Aaron skipped the tea and instead buried his nose in his oversized hoodie and the scents of coconut, a hint of smoke, and something that reminded him of Landon's skin.

It was familiar and comforting. But then, memories of their last fight stirred up a nasty knot in his stomach, making him long for the sharp tang of Worcestershire sauce to kill the nausea.

After a bit, Aaron managed to catch his breath and blurted out, "Everything's a fucking disaster." He turned abruptly to Aunt Olivia with a choked sob. If only he'd sat on the other side of the car, maybe Tori would still be here. "It's not fair... I shouldn't be the only one left."

"Don't spout such nonsense," Aunt Olivia scolded him. "You're deserving of every good thing in life. But you need to live it. Running away from everything isn't going to help. If you let your past eat up your present, you're throwing away any chance of happiness in the future."

"I'll find happiness in Sydney."

"Stubborn as your mother, you are."

"Only the finest traits," he replied dryly.

"Think about it, Aaron. Tomorrow's the end of the year, with a new beginning around the corner. Don't trip up before you even start."

"That's just it, isn't it? Starting anew."

With a huff of frustration, she added, "At least consider what Tori left you. It might help."

But Aaron was done with the conversation. He got up and retreated to his old room.

*

Aaron spent the day in a bit of a daze, feeling none of the buzz about New Year's Eve. Aunt Olivia didn't push him to talk or anything; she just let him be. So, he holed up in his bedroom, binge-watching movies and feeling pretty down.

Nyle had been texting him non-stop since he'd left, trying to convince Aaron to come back or at least join them to celebrate, making it sound like a must-do family thing. But after the argument with Landon, Aaron couldn't see himself returning there.

"If going to Australia is really what you want, then go and never come back. But if you're doing all this just to please a ghost, maybe you're not the one to give me advice about dealing with my trauma when you're still haunted by your own."

Aaron tried to shove those thoughts to the back of his mind. His emotions were all over the place, and even his Spotify playlist seemed to be against him, playing songs like "Misguided Ghost" by Paramore. And *Peter Pan* sat on his shelf, staring at him like a ghost.

Was he messing up his present and future by running from his past? Was he aimlessly running, like that song was saying? Had he been so focused on leaving that he'd forgotten any reason to stay?

Memories of the past few months with Landon, Nyle, and the others played in his head like scenes from a movie. It was wild how much had happened in such a short time. He never thought he'd make such connections after Tori's death.

When "Peter Pan Was Right" by Anson Seabra started playing next, Aaron had had enough. He got up and left the house.

He ran through the busy streets, not thinking about where he was going. Somehow, he ended up by the Thames, right by the Greenwich Meridian marker. It was as if his legs had known where to take him.

Exhausted, Aaron plopped down on the asphalt next to the sign, his back against the cold metal pole. He exhaled, his breath fogging up in the chilly air. A weight of sadness pressed down on his chest.

The Thames stretched out in front of him, its dark waters reflecting the glittering lights from Canary Wharf. Fireworks burst in the sky here and there, each explosion followed by a wave of cheers.

Aaron fished out his phone, the digits 00:00 glowing on the screen.

Another year had begun. Another missed start.

All around him, people were celebrating—laughing, popping champagne. He could see folks having a great time through the windows of nearby buildings.

But there he sat, alone by the river, raising a toast to demons and ghosts.

He tried to call Tori, but of course, the network was jammed. Nyle's messages, though, kept coming through, urging him to join their New Year's gathering. But it was too late for that now.

Curiosity got the better of him, and he read through Nyle's latest Instagram stories. His heart sank when he saw Landon in one of them, sitting by the window, looking distant and lost in thought, cigarette in hand. He seemed out of place amid the party buzz, but his vibe was the only one Aaron could connect with right now.

Sitting there, wrapped in Landon's oversized hoodie, Aaron imagined he was in his arms. His skin warmed with the memory of him.

He missed Landon. He wondered if Landon was missing him too.

Glancing at the *Here 24,859* sign, Aaron pondered. Maybe the distance needed to sort himself out and grab hold of a bit of happiness was way shorter than that.

Had Tori been trying to tell him something with that *Peter Pan* book? Why else would he be so scared to open it?

Aaron almost replied to one of Nyle's messages, almost said he'd show up. But then he pulled out the rabbit keyring with the keys to the house they all shared. He knew he couldn't just waltz back in there, not yet. Not until he sorted out the things that had been haunting him. Landon's words echoed in his mind, and deep down, Aaron knew they were true.

"You're a liar and a rabbit," Landon had said, so close to him. Aaron could still feel the ghost of Landon's thumb on his cheek. *"But you don't have to be, not if you don't want to."*

Holding the little plushie in the fading light of the fireworks, Aaron stood up. Could he really change? Stop being the person always running away, always hiding?

He looked one last time at the Meridian sign, then turned and jogged back the way he'd come. It was time to confront his past, his fears, and whatever else was holding him back.

Time to face those ghosts.

♫ Happiness is a harbinger of pain

[Now playing » Ep. 30—Happiness is a harbinger of pain—Don't Listen To Me]

Happiness is a harbinger of pain. But my therapist said that without pain, there can be no happiness. A bloody vicious circle, isn't it?

The good news is that nothing lasts forever. So, pain, too, is fleeting. But no matter how temporary, it doesn't hurt any less.

I should be used to it by now, to instability. My whole life's been about hopping from one place to another. My childhood was a series of houses, families, everything I owned stuffed into bin bags and boxes. Always on the move, never a place to call home, never a family.

After all these years, you'd think I'd have learned. I shouldn't get attached to things that won't last, shouldn't want things I can't have. But I always do. I always fall for it.

Even after being knocked down so many times, I still hope that maybe, just maybe, this time it'll be different. Perhaps I'm starved of affection, the kind I never received as a kid and still crave like a fool.

People think I'm allergic to love, but the truth is, it feels like love's allergic to me. I've given my heart away more times than I can count, only to get it back bruised and battered.

They say it's better to have a heart that's been used than one that's been kept pristine. Maybe they're right, but it doesn't feel that way when every heartbeat reminds you of the breaks.

You know, in ancient times, when they performed human sacrifices, they always held a beating heart. I think it's kind of like that with love. We open up our heart, hoping it'll be treated kindly. But when it's not, the pain feels as real as if your own heart was right there in someone else's hands—exposed, raw, and vulnerable.

And it sucks.

[♫Closing » If You Want Love—NF]

Chapter Twenty-Eight

The Note

[Now playing » If You Want Love—NF]

Aaron stood there, back at Aunt Olivia's, his hand hovering a few inches from the cover of *Peter Pan*. He only needed to stretch a bit more to grab it, but he froze. The memories linked to that book overwhelmed him; Tori had read it to him so often he knew parts of it by heart.

He was so close, though, his fingertips nearly brushing against the spine. Then, a sudden knock on the door made him jump back.

"Unless you've been honing your Jedi skills in the months you've been away, I don't think the book is going to move with the Force," came Aunt Olivia's voice, tinged with humour.

Aaron turned to find her leaning against the doorway, arms crossed, a smug look on her face. He managed a half-smile in response.

"Why not join me for breakfast?" she suggested cheerfully. "A full stomach might help you think more clearly."

Aaron trailed after her without a word. He sat at the table, facing the kitchen, and watched as Aunt Olivia skilfully managed the chaos of breakfast-making—measuring cups, pans, and pancake batter—all in fluid motion. When she opened the cabinet to grab the usual peppermint tea bag, Aaron stopped her.

"Could you make me a cappuccino instead?" he asked, surprising both her and himself with the request.

Aunt Olivia didn't question it. She popped two capsules into the coffee machine and went back to flipping pancakes. Once everything was ready, she joined him at the table, sliding a plate and the steaming cup in front of him.

Aaron inhaled the coffee's aroma, his mind drifting to the memory of the cappuccino Landon had made him after their first kiss.

"When did you start liking coffee?" Olivia asked, pouring maple syrup over her pancakes.

"I don't really like it. It's just the smell."

She wrinkled her forehead and took a bite of her pancakes. "So...*who* is it?"

"Who is who?"

"The person who's got you changing your mind about things."

Aaron hesitated. "There's no one."

"Uh-huh." She didn't seem convinced but kept up her amused gaze. "And what about the hoodie? Not your style."

"Can't a guy change his style?"

"Sure, it's possible. But we both know how stubborn you can be. Change usually needs a reason. Something big, or...*someone* special."

Silence stretched between them as Aaron gripped his coffee mug a little tighter.

"You've met someone, haven't you?"

Aaron quickly took another bite of his breakfast, his eyes firmly on his plate, trying to dodge the incoming questions.

"I'm happy for you, you know."

"Why do you think it's someone?" Aaron asked, still avoiding her gaze.

"You've been wrapped up in that hoodie and miles away in your thoughts since you came back."

Aaron gaped. Had he been so obvious?

"So, what's, uh...their name?"

He sighed and took a long sip of his coffee, wishing he could avoid talking about his love life—or lack thereof. But the weight of her curious gaze was too much hard to ignore.

"It's Landon," he finally answered. "His name is Landon."

Aunt Olivia's face lit up. "And what's he like? Is he a decent guy? Handsome? Any photos?"

Slightly taken aback by her enthusiasm, Aaron pulled out his phone and opened Landon's Instagram profile, filled more with artsy London shots, Kat, and tattoos than personal pictures. Landon rarely showed his face full-on in his few photos. Still, Aaron hoped it might give her a glimpse into who he was.

She leaned in to get a better look. "He's got an edgy vibe. Is he older than you?"

"Just by a few years, he's twenty-two."

"Hmm...and he's a tattoo artist?"

"Yeah, an apprentice for now, but he's super talented." Aaron kept scrolling, pointing at some of Landon's sketches on the screen. "Look at these. He should definitely have his own studio."

She nodded in agreement, then looked up at Aaron with a more serious expression. "Have you slept with him?"

Aaron cheeks started to burn. He barely stifled a nervous laugh. He wasn't sure how to answer, especially since he and Landon's sex life had been far from straightforward.

"I'm not asking out of curiosity or to stick my nose into your business. It's only...I want to understand where you two stand."

"Why does that matter? People hook up all the time."

"But that's not *you*," she replied softly, understanding in her eyes.

Aaron raised an eyebrow, surprised and relieved by how well she could read him. She knew him better than he wanted to admit.

"So, what's going on with you two?"

"Nothing. Or at least, nothing serious. It's over now anyway." He took another sip of his coffee and focused on finishing breakfast.

"It is *serious*," Aunt Olivia countered, pounding her fists on the table. "Even if he doesn't feel the same way, your feelings matter."

He sighed and pulled the hood over his head. Leaning forward, he rested his head on his arms, wishing he could disappear along with all the confusing emotions inside him.

"Have you fallen in love, Aarie?"

"No," he replied, the word muffled against his sleeves and the table. Then he lifted his head. "I don't know. Maybe. If feeling miserable is what love is...then yeah, probably."

Aunt Olivia chuckled. "Considering you're practically living in his hoodie, I have a hard time believing he doesn't feel something for you too."

"I was just a distraction for him. He told me as much. Plus, we both knew it wouldn't last."

"Why not?"

"Because I'm leaving for Sydney in a few months. Tom sorted me a winter job at a wildlife park."

Aunt Olivia let out an exaggerated sigh. "Still on about this, are we?"

"It's the path I've chosen."

"You mean it's the story you keep telling yourself."

Fiddling with the pendant around his neck, Aaron's whispered, "I promised her."

Aunt Olivia rubbed a hand over her face. "Look, Aaron, I want what's best for you. If you truly believe that going to Sydney is the right thing, I won't stop you. But you deserve so much more than what you've had. You deserve a real shot at life, at happiness."

Aaron didn't say anything. Could he really?

"I understand it's hard for you. The nightmares, the 'what-ifs'...but things will get better. I promise. You think leaving is the right choice, but I honestly believe you should stay."

"But I have to—"

"Tori loved you, and you loved her. Your bond was special. No one is ever going to change that. But you're losing yourself in her dream instead of living your own."

"I want to finish what she couldn't."

"That's beautiful. But she wanted you to be happy. Have you forgotten what she last told you?"

A wave of vertigo overtook Aaron. He gripped the table, trying to steady himself. His head pounded, matching the rhythm of Tori's distorted words echoing within.

"*If you ever feel stuck or lost,*" she had told him, "*try to look in here to find your way home.*"

"Of course, I remember. She told me to read that stupid children's book when I felt lost. But I know exactly where I'm going. I've got my plan."

Aunt Olivia shook her head. "No, Tori told you to *look* in that book."

Aaron studied her, confused and shocked. He hadn't thought about Tori's exact words, but now it hit him. It wasn't about *reading* the book; it was about *looking* into it.

With a sudden burst of energy, he released his grip on the table and rushed towards the stairs. He felt dizzy but pushed through, climbing the stairs two at a time.

Rushing into his room, Aaron went straight to the shelf and grabbed his dusty copy of *Peter Pan*. His heart thudded faster as he flipped through the pages, finally stopping at the map of Neverland. There, hidden in the folds, he found a small sticky note.

Neverland isn't a faraway place you can reach. It's a state of mind.

Find your happy thought.

Aaron froze, his fingers trembling on the paper.

"Aarie…" Aunt Olivia tried to touch his shoulder, but he flinched away.

"You knew," he accused her, his voice quivering. "You knew all along."

His eyes stung as he fought back the tears threatening to spill. How could she have kept this from him for so long?

"Of course, I knew," she confirmed, calm and steady, a stark contrast to the tempest raging within him.

"Why didn't you tell me?"

"Because I needed you to find it yourself when you were ready."

Aaron collapsed to the floor, the book open in his lap. He read the words on the sticky note over and over, each time feeling like a fresh wound, until his vision blurred with tears.

Aunt Olivia sat beside him, her arms wrapping around him. She tried to comfort him as best as she could, holding him close as he grappled with the flood of emotions.

"I miss her," he choked out between sobs. "I miss her so much."

Olivia's eyes filled with tears too. "Me too, Aarie. I miss her too."

They sat there for a while, crying together, sharing their grief. Somehow, crying seemed liberating, making him feel a little less heavy.

"I don't want to forget her," he said shakily. "I don't want to stop missing her."

Aunt Olivia wiped his cheek with her thumb. "Remembering and missing her is part of moving forward. You should embrace those memories and think about what it is you miss most about her. Maybe it's something you two shared, something you can find again with someone else."

Aaron's gaze drifted away, considering the possibility.

"Grief's strange," Aunt Olivia added. "Sometimes, it's less about the person and more about the void they left. It's okay to feel that way. But also think about the people who are still here in your life. What makes them special? Why do you keep them around? Maybe you'll see that what you miss about Tori might be something you can find in someone who's still here with you."

Aaron's thoughts drifted to Landon, to the effortless understanding they had. But then, his mind expanded to include the others.

He thought of Nyle, so flamboyant and direct, brave in being himself, always managing to make the world seem less dull with his jokes, playful teasing, and those quirky mugs Aaron had grown to appreciate. And Ria, so passionate about what she believed in, constantly challenging others' opinions. She'd been a huge help in making him feel more comfortable with his sexuality, guiding him to feel accepted, not broken. And Fell—an alternate-universe version of Aunt Olivia, with his wise words and impeccable music taste that always seemed to set the right mood.

Maeve, with her boundless energy, added a certain spice to their group, even though she could be too much sometimes. Lastly, he thought of Cliff, his only friend during school, the one who'd helped him forget about his dull world, even if just for a while.

Each of them had carved out their own special place in his life, turning his world into something richer and more...colourful.

"This changes everything," Aaron murmured, holding the book to his chest.

"It only changes things if you let it." Olivia held out her phone. "There's more you need to know."

Confused, Aaron peered at the screen, his tears still clouding his vision. Unlike Tori's note, this message left no room for misinterpretation: a bank account page in his name with more money than he thought he had. Still, it raised so many questions.

Aaron's gaze shifted from the phone to the note, then to the map of Neverland, and back to Aunt Olivia, silently asking if he'd understood it right.

She nodded, her smile a tiny light in the dim room. "Are you ready to live your life?"

He took a deep, shaky breath. "I'm ready."

Chapter Twenty-Nine

New Year's Resolutions

[Now playing » Those Eyes—New West]

First week of the year, and Aaron was back at RPM.

He hovered around the shop, half expecting to catch a glimpse of Landon, half dreading it. Aaron had geared up for a big confrontation, except it never happened.

Turned out, Landon had lost his job.

The news hit Aaron like a punch to the gut. His first instinct was to reach out, to bridge the gap between them, but he caught himself, phone half raised. Landon had made it crystal clear: it was over between them. So, Aaron stuck to getting regular updates from Nyle, who somehow managed to keep an eye on Landon.

From what Nyle had said, Landon was practically a ghost, drifting from his room to the summer house, barely making appearances even for food. Aaron considered asking Ria for some advice, but she was as reachable as those half-melted snowflakes outside, leaving him on 'Read'. Fell contributed with his take—give Landon some space, then try to patch things up. Maeve added her support into the mix, letting Aaron know she was rooting for them.

Still, Aaron found himself doing a whole lot of nothing about the situation. He wasn't even sure where he and Landon stood now. And on top of that, Tori's note had messed with his head. It had him all over the place, swimming in thoughts and feelings, and he hadn't a clue what he should do next.

Then came Saturday morning. Community service was not done yet.

On the Tube, Aaron tried to lose himself in music, headphones on, blocking out the world. But every song reminded him of Landon. His heart raced at the thought of finally seeing him again.

When he arrived at the retirement centre, his nerves had gotten the best of him—sweaty hands, dry mouth, and hair he might have messed with too much. He continued through the gardens, finally spotting his lively, laughing group. Like a magnet, Landon drew his attention, the south to his north.

He stood apart from everyone else, looking more worn out than in the photos Nyle had sent. The under-eye bags spoke volumes about his latest sleepless night. It hit Aaron that Landon was probably just as restless as he was.

Having Landon around at night had become a comfort blanket for Aaron. His presence had been a real help when nightmares or panic attacks struck. Now, waking up without him made for a harsh jolt back to reality.

He remembered how Landon had shown him that little trick with the notch in the headboard, a way to ground himself. After learning about Landon's past and his struggles with abuse, Aaron understood it even more.

He couldn't shake off how brave Landon had been to let him in so much—into his summer house, his room, his bed, and maybe even into his life. Aaron had to face it, no matter how hard it was to admit: Landon had wormed his way into his mind and heart in a way he'd never thought possible.

"Hey," Nyle approached him, all smiles and enthusiasm, with Maeve not far behind. Together, they bombarded him with a million questions.

Out of the corner of his eye, Aaron caught Ria's stink eye and Cliff's sorry look, which made Aaron want to roll his eyes.

Sarah came over, asking everyone about their holiday breaks, her conversation a welcome distraction. But Aaron had his eyes set on Landon, who didn't seem to notice him at all.

As they picked up their tools, Aaron waited for Landon to say something, but Landon just collected his things and trod off to the cherry tree.

Aaron had hoped that seeing Landon again, maybe catching his eye or hearing his voice, might start to mend the rift that had grown between them. But their silence made things more strained, as if they were drifting even farther apart.

Throughout the first half of their shift, Aaron stole fleeting glances at Landon. Whenever he made a small mistake, he'd catch Landon's sceptical look, but neither of them made any effort to actually come closer or start a conversation.

Aaron felt like he was on tenterhooks. Then it hit him—while he was holding back, waiting for Landon to make a move, Landon seemed to be doing the exact same thing. They'd reached an impasse.

Finally, when lunch break rolled around, Aaron mustered enough courage to try to engage Landon. He spotted him in a quiet corner of the garden, the very same spot when they'd first met. Landon leaned against the conservatory wall, now free of graffiti, with a vape pen in his hand.

"You quit smoking?" Aaron asked as he edged closer, trying to break the ice.

Landon glanced at him and then stared off into the distance. "New Year's resolution," he said sharply. Up close, Landon's under-eye bags were more noticeable than ever.

"Maybe I should give it a try."

Without a word, Landon handed him the vape pen. Their eyes met, and the weight of Landon's intense stare almost crushed him.

They stood there, the only sounds from the pigeons cooing and the faint buzz of traffic in the background.

Aaron wanted to say something, *anything*, but he couldn't find the right words. Landon's coldness worried him; maybe things between them were too broken to fix.

So, he waited, hoping Landon would jump in. He'd been the one to approach, after all. But Landon stared at him for a little longer, then sighed and strode away, leaving Aaron there by himself.

He was about to head back to the others when Cliff came over.

"Heard about Landon. Everything okay?"

"Why the fuck do you care?" Aaron snapped. "Happy now? I'm back with my aunt, and whatever was going on with Landon is done. We're even."

Cliff's face hardened. "I'm not happy, nor sorry. Your aunt needed to know the truth."

"Yeah, I guess you're right. "

"You're just— Wait, what?" Cliff's forehead wrinkled.

"Yeah, you're right. She needed to know." Aaron slid his hands into his jeans pockets and shifted restlessly on the balls of his feet. "Look, Cliff, I'm sorry for all the crap before. I was a mess. I still am, but I'm figuring stuff out."

"Sorry doesn't fix a thing, you know."

"It doesn't. But it's where I can start. I was a prick. You didn't deserve how I treated you. After the crash, when Tori...my sister, died, I was trying to survive, but I never thought about who I was hurting."

Cliff opened his mouth, paused, closed it, then said, "Why didn't you ever tell me that?"

"I couldn't. Talking about her, the accident...it was too much. I didn't want to make it feel real. But it is, and I need to face it."

"You really are a prat." Despite his words, Cliff stepped forward and hugged him.

It was awkward, but Aaron went with it. They'd only hugged once before when Cliff got dumped by his one and only girlfriend.

"For what it's worth," Cliff said, stepping back, "I hope things turn out well for you. With Landon, your aunt, your trip...everything."

"Cheers, Cliff. And I am sorry. Really."

Cliff tilted his head, the air between them starting to clear. "It's okay. Maybe it's time we both moved past all this."

As Cliff left to join the others, a heavy weight lifted from Aaron's chest, not full-on forgiveness but something else. Closure, maybe. And for now, that was enough. He knew he had more to sort out, more apologies to make, but this was a step in the right direction.

At the end of the day, Aaron lingered, half expecting the usual shout to go somewhere. But it never came. With a dull pressure still clinging to him, he headed home.

Aaron was almost halfway to the station when Ria called out to him, stopping him in his tracks. Turning, he faced her, but her usual bright smile had gone. She appeared upset, and Aaron knew it had to do with him.

"Landon's waiting on your next move," she said.

"I know. I do want to sort things out."

"Do you?" Ria's gaze pierced him, as chilly as the friend she was defending. "Landon's been through a lot. If you're not fully in it, then maybe it's time to call it quits, quick and clean. Better than dragging it out and hurting more later."

Aaron clenched his fists as he met Ria's confrontational stare. "Landon doesn't need you to fight his battles. Back off, will you?"

"How about you stop being such a coward and grow up? Or are you really a selfish prick as Cliff says?"

"Get lost, Ria. I'm not in the mood for this." Aaron turned to leave, trying to keep his anger in check.

But Ria wouldn't back down. She followed him, relentless. "What's your deal, Aaron? When you found out about Landon's past, you vanished. Are you one of those who can't handle being with someone who's been abused? Does it make you sick, dealing with something so dirty and contaminated?"

Aaron spun around. Despite her petite frame, Ria stood her ground. Maeve was right—Ria could turn from a cute kitty into a fearsome tiger. "Don't ever talk about Landon like that again. He's not dirty or contaminated. I'd take down anyone who made Landon feel that way, if only to make him feel better."

"So, you do care about him."

"Of course, I do!"

"Then why did you disappear when he needed you the most?"

Aaron bit the inside of his cheek. He knew how it must look, as if he'd bailed on Landon right after finding out about his past. "It's not like that. I want to be there for him, I really do."

"Looks to me like you're running away."

"I'm not," Aaron replied, frustrated. "We needed some space. Landon told me to go."

"Oh, to hell with what Landon told you! He'll never admit it, but he needs you."

"He doesn't need me. He doesn't need anyone." Aaron reached into his pocket and pulled out the stuffed bunny. "Landon's not held back by his past, not like I am. He's incredibly strong, the strongest person I know. And me? I'm like this silly little rabbit, always ready to run. Today, I couldn't even say more than a word to him."

Ria laughed, then moved closer to him. "You're good for him, Aaron."

"I highly doubt that."

"I mean it." She took the bunny from his hands and fiddled with it. "People like me and Landon—we find it hard to trust. We've been hurt badly. So, when we meet someone who understands, who's been through something like we have, it's an instant bond. It makes us feel less...alone." As she poked the bunny's belly, sadness flickered in her eyes. "That first night, at the bonfire, when Nyle touched you...we thought you were one of *us*. But I'm glad you're not."

Aaron caught her deeper meaning. He'd always wondered what bonded her and Landon, two people so different in appearance and attitude. But now, seeing that haunted expression in Ria's eyes, he understood.

"That group you and Landon are part of…" Aaron started, but Ria was quicker.

"It's a support group for survivors of sexual abuse. I haven't been through half of what Landon has, but one bad experience was enough for me."

Aaron's throat tightened. He wished their shared experience had been anything but this.

"Don't worry, I'm in a much better place now," Ria added, her smile coming back. "That's precisely why I believe Landon sees something special in you. He wouldn't have let his guard down otherwise. You feel the same way about him, don't you?"

"Yes." The response tumbled out instinctively, without hesitation.

"You've seen it by now, right? Under all that tough guy act, Landon's a softie. He's the kind of guy who'd step in front of a bus for someone he cares about. Like the time with my ex at the pub… Well, you saw the video." She paused, squeezing the rabbit a little too much. "Landon was there like a shot, told him to back off or else. And when talking didn't work, he made sure my ex got the message to never bother me again. I bet he'd do the same for you."

Aaron looked down. "I don't deserve someone like him."

Ria smacked him upside his head. "You're talking rubbish. You and Landon are both so stubborn. Why is it so hard for you to believe you deserve good things, eh? What's so wrong in seeking happiness? We may be fractured, sure, but that doesn't mean we can't piece ourselves back together. You, me, Landon…we all have a right to be happy."

A wave of memories washed over him—those good times with Landon, the happiness he'd thought gone for good after Tori's death.

Ria was right in a way, but also not quite.

He and Landon were fractured, but they could never piece themselves back together. Fragments of their old selves, they'd been reshaped and cracked too many times to ever return to what they once were. They weren't jigsaw pieces that effortlessly snapped together, more like jagged bits, each trying to align without further damaging the other.

Perhaps their coming together wasn't about perfect alignment but gradually smoothing out those harsh edges, little by little.

"So, what should I do? Show up at his door with handwritten signs like in *Love Actually*?"

"Hold on." Ria fished out her phone. "Let me send you something. It might help you figure things out with Landon." She tapped away and then looked up at him. "Check your messages."

Aaron opened the link she'd sent. "*Don't Listen To Me*," he read out loud. "*My name's Psycho. If we met in real life, you probably wouldn't want to chat or hang out. So, don't bother with my podcast either. It's not for you; it's my way of letting off steam.*"

Ria's grin widened. "Classic Landon, that is."

"Landon?"

"Yeah, 'Psycho'. He took the nickname people threw at him and owned it. He's been making this podcast for a while now."

Aaron remembered seeing Landon's recording setup in the summer house, but hadn't realised what it was for.

"He started it as a kind of self-therapy. But to show his commitment to Lottie, he made it public."

"Do you both see the same therapist?"

"She's brilliant. I'd definitely recommend her if you're considering therapy."

Aaron wrinkled his nose. He'd saved her number ages ago but never had the nerve to call.

"Listen to the episodes from the start," Ria suggested. "They might seem a bit all over the place at first, but there's a clear thread running through them."

Aaron quickly browsed through the episode list. Not too many, and not too long. "Are you sure Landon would be okay with me listening?"

"It's out there for everyone, isn't it?"

"I know, but—"

"Just listen to it, Aaron. Stop overthinking. If anyone needs to hear what Landon has to say, it's you."

Aaron sighed. "Why are you doing this?"

"Because I care about Landon. I've seen something special when you two are together, when you drop your defences. Don't miss out on this chance. There's enough sadness in the world. Grab the happy moments when you can."

Ria handed back the stuffed rabbit and turned to leave. But after a few steps, she paused and faced him.

"You know, rabbits are smarter than people give them credit for. Everyone thinks they're cowards because they run from danger. But that running is their survival strategy—a smart move."

"You into animal documentaries like Landon?"

"He got me into them." Ria glanced at the bunny in his hand. "Still in flight mode?"

Aaron held the plushie closer to his chest, then slipped it into his pocket.

"Not anymore."

Ria's smile was as wide as when they first met. As she disappeared around the corner, Aaron headed towards the station, his mind swirling with thoughts and his heart heavy with unspoken emotions. But instead of going home, he went straight to the Barbican Centre.

The Centre always drew him whenever he felt the need to vanish—his secret getaway in the middle of the city, a place so twisty and confusing no one would ever think to look for him there. And even if they did, they'd probably get lost first.

Hood up and tunes streaming through his earbuds, Aaron found his regular spot on the low wall overlooking the main courtyard and let Landon's voice wash over him.

"Hello, I'm Psycho, your not-so-friendly neighbourhood voice..."

Chapter Thirty

Don't Listen to Me

[Now playing » Daylight—David Kushner]

[♫Now playing » Podcast, Ep. 1—Pilot]

Ever since I was a kid, I've felt like life's personal punching bag. Punch after punch, I've taken them all.

How long can someone keep getting hit before they just …break?

I'm carrying around so much anger and hurt. Honestly, there are days I'm surprised I don't just explode.

So, I went to my therapist. Told her I needed to get rid of all this pain inside.

She said, "If you want to control it, use it. Channel all that dark energy into something, like writing a diary."

Writing a diary? Not my cup of tea. It'd just end up forgotten in some drawer.

So, here I am, doing this podcast instead. And I've gone and made it public. Thought I'd share a bit of my headache with you lot who've got nothing better to do than listen to me waffle on.

I'm hoping to spoil your day a bit, just like mine was when I found out some songs I thought were all about rainbows and sunshine are actually pretty bleak. I've got a whole list of them, but let's start with "Mr. Brightside" by The Killers.

[♫Closing » Mr. Brightside—The Killers]

[♫Now playing » Podcast, Ep. 17—Human]

I've got a laundry list of problems. Mental, physical, legal, financial...you name it, I've probably got it.

But know what's been messing with my head the most lately? A guy.

What can I say? I'm still human, right? Got those basic needs and all that. Thought I could sort myself out like always, or perhaps find some random bloke around.

But it's not working.

Everything has changed since he came into the picture, or maybe I'm the one who's changed.

Feels like I've lost the plot, both in my head and body. Like I'm in this weird, liminal space, and it's left me all over the place.

I've never wanted someone so badly. I mean, sure, I've had my fair share of wanting, but this is different. Usually, it's just about the sex, but this time...I don't think a quick shag is going to get him out of my system.

For the first time in ages, I actually want to be touched.

But not by just anyone.

I want to be touched by *him*.

Didn't see that one coming, did I?

[♫Closing » Never Saw It Coming—The Federal Empire]

[♫Now playing » Podcast, Ep. 22—Rigor Samsa]

I can't stand it.

I can't stand this feeling of being understood by someone because before *him*, no one ever really saw me. Not even my family. So, I'm at a bit of a loss on how to deal with it.

My therapist reckons I'm drawn to him because he's like me. Someone with similar scars, who can understand when I need him close and when I need him to step away. But I don't need that. I've never needed anyone.

Thanks to some late-night googling, I stumbled upon John Koenig's "Dictionary of Obscure Sorrows." That's where I found this word: *rigor samsa.*

That's like a psychological armour built to shield you from all the hurt. And I've been putting mine together for ages, but it's never really been foolproof.

Truth is, I'm not as tough as I thought. That's why I'm so fed up with myself. I'm fed up with him for making me feel this way.

I hate him. I hate that I don't actually hate him.

[♫Closing » Everyone but You—The Front Bottoms]

[♫Now playing » Podcast, Ep. 23—Explosion of Colours]

Most people reckon it's tougher to give than to get. It's seen as a grand, selfless thing, doing something for someone else. But for me, it's way harder to take than to give.

When you're giving, you're the one calling the shots. But when you're on the receiving end, you're handing over the reins, making yourself open to getting hurt. And I can't have that.

As a kid, I got plenty of 'gifts' in exchange for my silence, my compliance. So, now, when someone's nice to me, I get all wary. I'm always thinking, what do they want in return?

But with him, it's a whole different story. He was kind in such a gentle, no-strings-attached way that I couldn't help but take it.

Maybe it was the dreamy vibe tonight, all light and warmth, and soft skin, and those eyes that seemed to get through me. Maybe his colour-blindness really is like a superpower, letting him see past all the superficial stuff.

I wanted to see things differently, too, lying there under the artificial Northern Lights that painted the sky so beautifully. But when I took his hand and focused on us, amidst all those lights, he was the true explosion of colours.

[♫Closing » Heat Waves—Glass Animals]

[♫Now playing » Podcast, Ep. 28—Rules]

I laid it out straight for him—well, maybe not *straight*. This is just going to be about sex, a simple way for us to kill time. I set down some rules, even told him he couldn't touch me until I said he could. My terms, not his.

Any sensible person would've bolted, especially a guy like him, who's already running away from his problems. But he wasn't fazed, not even a bit, didn't even throw a single question. Instead, he had the nerve to say, "Okay." Just "okay" as if I hadn't said anything out of the ordinary, or worse, as if he totally trusted me and my daft rules, which, to be honest, I wish I didn't need in the first place.

[♫Closing » We'll Never Have Sex—Leith Ross]

[♫Now playing » Podcast, Ep. 29—Hellhole]

I'm exhausted. I'm sick of the triggers, sick of having to fight every single emotion, whether it's good or bad.

There's something wrong with my head, and no matter how hard I try, it doesn't change. There's always something—a smell, a word, some off gesture drags me back to that hellhole I can't seem to escape from.

It's like I left that place, but that place never left me.

I want to tell him about it, but then I remember he's not sticking around for long. And then I remind myself, none of this matters anyway. Maybe that's for the best.

[♫ *Closing » Say It Right—Nelly Furtado]*

[♫*Now playing » Podcast, Ep. 30—Loser]*

At the barcade, I've been unbeatable for ages, always smashing the high score. But when it comes to real life, I just can't seem to win.

I knew from the get-go that things with him were a no-go, but I still went for it. And now, here I am, back at square one, empty-handed.

I wish I could be one of his reasons to stay.

[♫ *Closing » Arcade—Duncan Laurence]*

[♫*Now playing » Podcast, Ep. 32—New Year's Resolutions]*

A new year's kicked off.

I don't usually bother with resolutions, knowing I'll probably ditch them, but this time, I feel like giving it a shot. I'm ready for a fresh start, a change, and maybe I have to thank the guy who's been keeping me up at night for that. I don't want to be like him, the scared rabbit, always running from stuff I'd rather not face. So, cheers to him for nudging me towards this change, even if he didn't mean to.

But I have to thank him for something else, too—for his respect, trust, and a sense of safety in just a few months, stuff I've never had before. It wasn't easy for him to offer those things, and it wasn't easy for me to take them either.

I'm not bitter about him leaving. More annoyed with myself for not being able to show him how much he matters to me.

There's this line from V.E. Schwab's book I've been reading, *Vengeful*, that hit home. To put it my own way, it's like how, in life, some people are like matches—they emit a bit of light but no warmth. Others are like furnaces—warm but not bright. And then, once in a blue moon, you come across a bonfire, so brilliant and hot, you're bound to get burned if you get too close.

He's that bonfire.

[♫Closing » Catastrophize—Noah Kahan]

Aaron ran a hand over his chest; his heart pounded as if it were trying to break free. He stood there, frozen for what felt like forever, staring at the podcast cover as the last notes of the closing song faded into silence.

Then, quickly switching screens, he sent Landon a set of coordinates and a time, no explanations given.

He hopped down from the low wall, taking in the stark landscape around him—the relentless brutalist buildings and the tangle of overhead bridges connecting them. He'd lost himself in this concrete maze more times than he could count, often longing for an escape to some other world.

Navigating the twisting tunnels, a clear thought formed in Aaron's mind: he was done with getting lost.

This time, he wanted to be found.

Chapter Thirty-One

Lost and Found

[Now playing » Someone to Stay—Vancouver Sleep Clinic]

Aaron sat on the ground in the quiet foot tunnel, knees up, rhythmically tapping his shoe on the asphalt. He held an unlit cigarette in one hand and phone in the other, glancing between each passerby and the clock on his screen.

Any minute now, Landon should appear.

Part of him worried Landon might not show up. But then, right on time, he turned up, as reliable as ever.

"I've found you," Landon said, nudging Aaron's canvas trainers with his combat boots.

"Isn't that what lost boys do?"

Landon snorted loudly and stepped on Aaron's tapping foot. "What's with all the mystery?" He crouched to Aaron's level, flaunting a map screen. "You've got GPS on your phone. Why not just send me the location?"

"Could have," Aaron replied, pocketing both his phone and cigarette. "But that would've been too easy. I wanted to make sure you really wanted to find me."

Landon snorted again and plopped down next to him. "Seriously though, why here? It's bloody freezing today."

"I needed somewhere good to talk about Tori, somewhere with good memories." Aaron ran his fingers over the cold metal strip in between them, marked *Longitude Zero*. "This place was one of her favourites. Every time we came to London, she'd be so excited to show Aunt Olivia and me around, exploring every spot where the Greenwich Meridian line runs."

Landon peered up at the metal strip running along the wall.

"We'd do this thing," Aaron continued. "She'd stand on one side of the line, and I'd be on the other, just like we're doing now. We'd pretend we were from parallel worlds, daring each other to cross."

"And what if you did?"

"We'd poof into thin air. Can't handle the other world's atmosphere or something."

Landon shuffled a bit. "Well, I guess I better stick to my side, then."

That comment drew a little smile from Aaron, but it was bitter with memories. He took a deep breath and pulled out his necklace, fingers playing with the pointy pendant.

Landon's eyes dropped. "You and Tori. You had something special, didn't you?"

"She was my best friend, the only real one I ever had," Aaron admitted, his voice breaking as a tear traced its path down his cheek. "Tori was…she was always there for me, always trying to cheer me up. Right till the end, she was thinking about me. But I…I got so caught up in my own stuff, and now I'm full of guilt. I should've been a better brother, should've kept my promise to her."

"Like moving to Australia?"

Aaron nodded. "It was Tori's big dream. Mum and Dad, though, were totally against it. I told you, didn't I? They were...suffocating. No parties, no sleepovers, and they even made up allergies to control what Tori and I ate. It was pretty miserable, to be honest. And they were always at each other's throats, every single day."

Landon's eyes widened. "Were they...I mean, was it abusive?"

"Not physically." Aaron gripped the pendant so tightly he was sure the shape would imprint in his palm. "But it was too much. Tori couldn't take it anymore. She had this plan to start fresh in Australia with her boyfriend, and she wanted me to tag along so I wouldn't be stuck here alone. We were looking into options for me to study abroad as well. But then..." He started trembling.

"It's okay. You don't have to—"

"I *need* to." Aaron let go of the pendant and grabbed his knee instead.

He fixed his eyes on a random damp spot on the opposite wall, anything to keep focused as he recounted the day of the accident, Tori's excitement about getting into her dream uni in Sydney, the heated arguments in the car, and how his dad had lost control. "I can't remember much after that. Just the crash, the car flipping, the glass, and ending up on the other side of the road. It was all wrecked. And Mum and Dad...gone, just like that. And the last thing I remember is them arguing. They didn't even leave me with a good last memory."

He dug his nails into the fabric of his jeans. Thinking about them always stirred up anger. And sadness.

"Isn't it fucked up that I miss them but also...don't?" Aaron said, more to himself than Landon. "I feel like I lost them way before the accident."

"No, you're not fucked up for feeling like this," Landon offered. "My mom's a junkie, and my dad might as well be a ghost. It's different, I know, but feeling all over the place about parents, I get that. Family is...complicated, and it's okay to feel sad, angry, relieved, all of it."

Aaron's eyes welled up. "It's just...with Tori gone, too, I feel so lost."

He took a deep, shaky breath, trying to steady himself. Everything was spinning. He pressed one hand harder against the dirty asphalt, but it was only when Landon's pinkie caressed his that he found stability.

"Tori held my hand before it all went dark. She always did that, when Mum and Dad argued, to calm me down. And even though she was hurt, she didn't let go. Told me to hold on to a happy thought, find my own Neverland."

He stared at the wall, the memory blurring like the damp stain. "I woke up in a hospital room with Aunt Olivia by my side. Everything hurt, but I was okay. They said Tori and I were lucky." Tears spilled down his face, salty on his lips. "She seemed all right at first, had surgery, the doctors hopeful. I saw her, alive, talking, even laughing... But then she got worse. A week later, she was gone. Now it's just me and this damn necklace." He clutched the pendant again, its rough edges digging into his skin. "It should've been Tori who made it, not me."

Landon's grip on Aaron's pinkie tightened. "Maybe so, but you can't keep living in the past. Focus on what's in front of you, the here and now."

"But don't you get it?" Aaron turned, his eyes searching Landon's. "I was in her seat that day. What if I—"

"You could drive yourself crazy thinking like that. Going over and over those what-ifs won't change a bloody thing. It happened, and it's awful, but it's done. You can either let it eat you up or let it go. Cry, shout, punch a pillow, whatever you need to do, but you've got to move on."

"That's exactly why I'm telling you all this. I don't want to be haunted for the rest of my life."

"Then don't be. You have to let it out. All of it." Landon glanced around the tunnel. "You know what? Do it now. Scream."

"What? Here?" Aaron took in their surroundings, half in disbelief, but Landon's serious expression told him he wasn't joking.

"We're in London. No one gives a shit if you scream your head off in a tunnel."

"And what do I scream?"

"Anything and everything that's bottled up inside you."

Aaron sniffled, then let go of the necklace and wiped his cheeks. Despite the oddity of the suggestion, he trusted Landon.

Gearing himself up like he was about to make a giant leap, Aaron screamed.

He released all the anger, sadness, and frustration that had been building up inside him. His voice echoed off the tunnel walls, his throat burning and eyes tearing up once again.

"Any better?" Landon asked once the echoes died down.

Nodding, slightly out of breath, Aaron rested the back of his head against the cold, rough tunnel bricks. To his surprise, he did feel a sort of relief wash over him.

"If Tori were here, what would you say to her?"

Aaron closed his eyes, picturing his sister smiling beside him, maybe reminiscing. "I'd tell her I'm an idiot for not opening the book she left me."

"What book?"

"*Peter Pan.* We both loved it, but I only got the message now." Aaron opened his eyes, meeting Landon's gaze. "I thought I had to go far away to find my Neverland. But now, I don't think that's true."

"So, you're not thinking of Australia anymore?"

Aaron shook his head. "You were right. I was so focused on what was ahead I didn't see what I had right here. These last few months with you and Nyle, and the others, I've felt more at home than I ever did anywhere else."

Landon looked down, and Aaron followed his gaze to where their pinkies were entwined above the Prime Meridian line.

"I want to stay here," Aaron said firmly. "I want to stay...with you."

Abruptly, Landon withdrew his hand and moved away. "Don't say things you're not sure about."

"You asked me to be honest, right? Well, here it is. I want to be with you, Landon. I've never been so sure about anything."

"And what exactly do you expect from me?"

Aaron frowned. "Nothing."

"Nobody wants nothing."

"I just want to be around you, that's all."

"In what way?"

Aaron hesitated. "I don't know...in a way that's good for both of us."

"You're not being helpful."

"Hey, it's not like either of us is an expert in relationships, so don't pin it all on me."

"So, you're saying you want a *relationship*?" Landon asked a bit mockingly.

"I...maybe? I think so, yeah." Aaron ran a hand through his greasy hair, feeling cornered under Landon's intense gaze.

"A relationship," Landon repeated, biting his lower lip to play with the lip piercing. "I don't even know if I can do that."

"Me neither, but I'm up for giving it a shot. How about you? What do *you* want?"

Landon paused as if weighing his options. "I stopped wanting things a long time ago. No want, no risk of getting hurt."

"But what if what you want...wants you back?" Aaron asked, hopeful.

Landon gestured towards himself dismissively. "You want this? Look at me. I'm a mess."

"News flash. So am I."

"Yeah but—" Landon kept fiddling with his lip piercing.

"I don't care about your past. If that's what you're afraid of. I don't see you any differently than before."

Landon laughed. "Of course you do. You see me with the wrong colours."

"I'm colour-blind, not blind to who you are. I see you perfectly well, Landon Bailey," Aaron remarked with a firm voice. "I've seen you for what you are from the very beginning. You can fool others, but you can't fool me."

"And what is it that you see?"

"I see someone who's beautiful. And caring. And selfless. And strong. That's why I want to be with you. If you'd let me," he confessed, heart racing. "Do you trust me?"

Landon paused, eyes fixed on his own hands. "It's not about trusting you. It's about me...trusting myself. Even though I have a reminder here." He indicated the letters inked across his knuckles. "Trust. Nobody. Except. Yourself."

"Is that what it means?"

"Thirty-five per cent."

Aaron studied him, puzzled. Was this another one of Landon's video game references?

"Thirty-five per cent of sexual abuse victims are at risk of becoming abusers. I'm scared of losing control, of not being able to stop myself. I couldn't bear it if that happened with you."

"You won't make it happen," Aaron reassured him. "I trust you."

"What if I say yes to this? To *us*?" Landon stopped picking at his lip piercing. "I can't give you that much, can't make you promises, especially not now with all this shit going on." Landon dropped his hand again to the ground, next to Aaron but still on the other side of the line. "I'm going to testify."

Aaron couldn't stop the smile tugging at the corners of his mouth, despite the salty taste of tears. "You're making the right call. I'm proud of you."

"I'm not doing it for Ian or because I feel I have to. It's for me, for my own closure."

"That's brave, you know."

Landon murmured, not entirely convinced, "But going through all this...feels like I'm stuck in the past again. And it sucks, Aaron. I can't give you anything right now, let alone...sex."

"I don't need sex. I don't need anything more."

"You say that now, but what if one day, I think I want sex and then change my mind later on?"

"We'll wait until we're sure. Both of us," Aaron said matter-of-factly.

"What if it's always a no for me?"

Aaron caught the real question behind Landon's words. "Then that's how it is. Look, Landon, the only reason I'd even think about sex is because it's with *you*, but I'm not desperate to do it every second." As he regarded Landon, so soft and beautiful under the faint tunnel lights, a warmth spread through him. "I mean, don't get me wrong, I'd happily do it with you all day, every day, but it's still not a top priority."

Landon seemed to ponder that. "So, where do you stand with asexuality?"

Aaron's cheeks warmed a bit. "I think I might be demi. That seems to fit. I've always struggled to find anyone sexually attractive. I can't do it like Nyle and Maeve, who look at someone and say things like 'they're hot' or 'I want to have sex with them.' It...doesn't work that way for me. I need to, uh...feel an emotional connection first to even think about that." He chuckled nervously; saying it out loud was more awkward than he'd expected.

"And you're cool with my 'friends with benefits' idea?"

"Yeah. Because it's *you*."

Landon scratched behind his ear. "So, how does that work? I won't lie; I don't know much about demisexuality. I did ask Ria and read some stuff, but I'd rather hear it from you."

Aaron shrugged. "Honestly, I'm still figuring it out. This is new territory for me too. Let's say you're the only one I want to have sex with because I feel that connection with you." Landon's obvious confusion made Aaron feel even more awkward. "Sounds weird, I know."

"It's not weird," Landon assured him quickly. "Guess I have a lot of learning to do."

"So, you're okay with it?"

"Are you seriously asking me, someone who might not even be up for sex all the time, if I'm okay with you being demi?" Landon seemed amused.

"Yeah, of course. It's as important that you're okay with me as I am with you."

A hint of a smile appeared on Landon's face, showing off the dimple Aaron adored so much. "I'm okay with it. Are you?"

"Yeah, only wanted you to know where I stand. No pressure."

"It might still be a bit of a challenge though."

Ria's words about doing the work to save the cherry tree at the retirement centre came back to Aaron. "Only because something takes effort doesn't mean it's not worth it. We'll figure it out. Together."

Landon's mouth twitched into a different smile now. Small but genuine, warming Aaron as much as one of Ria's generous smiles. Landon's fingers crept towards his, and Aaron reached his out, letting them weave together over the cold metal line.

"I've missed you," Aaron said softly.

"I've missed you too," Landon replied.

"If you need space, I'll give it to you. Know I'm here for you, always."

Landon gaped at him in disbelief. "You're on the other side of the line, in another world. You don't exist in mine."

"But I'm here, aren't I? Talking to you, seeing you."

"Perhaps you're a curse."

"Or maybe it's destiny."

"Destiny doesn't exist."

"So, I'm your destiny," Aaron joked, trying to lighten the mood.

"You said crossing this line could mean vanishing into another world, right?"

"That was the game, yeah."

Landon leaned in closer, his breath mingling with Aaron's. "But what if we both stepped forward? Met in the middle...with a kiss?"

"Could be great, could be a disaster."

"Worth the risk, you reckon?"

Aaron dropped his gaze to Landon's lips, then back up to his eyes. His heart skipped a beat. "Can I...cross the line?" he whispered.

Landon barely got out a "Yes" before their lips met, turning goodbyes into hellos, and 'I'm here for you' and 'I don't want to be anywhere else'. The kiss wiped away the space between them, both desperate to tear down the invisible barrier keeping them apart.

Landon's fingers held on to Aaron's against the cool ground, his grip firm, as if to anchor Aaron and keep him from vanishing into another world or to ensure they both remained in this one together. More than a game now, more than crossing lines or breaking barriers, this was about finding where they both belonged.

Aaron got lost in the kiss in a way he never had at the Barbican Centre. But this time, he didn't feel lost at all. For the first time, he felt as though he had found something.

When they finally parted, Aaron's laughter came light and easy.

"Hey," he greeted Landon as if meeting him all over again.

"Hey," Landon murmured.

"Still in one piece?"

"Were we ever?" Landon rested his forehead against Aaron's. They were so close that Aaron's vision merged, leaving Landon looking like a real-life, one-eyed Mike Wazowski. "Okay. Let's give *this* a shot."

Aaron's smile grew. With his thumb, he stroked the back of Landon's hand, which was warm despite the chilly air. "You said no promises, but maybe we can add one more rule to your playbook?"

"What's that?"

"Be honest with me about what you want and what you don't. I never want to overstep. You define your comfort zone, not me. Understand?"

Landon looked taken aback, but he agreed with a nod. "Aaron, you were never a distraction. You actually gave me a reason to quit searching for one."

"I know. I listened to the podcast."

Landon tensed up. "Ria."

"Yeah. You're great."

"Just talking rubbish."

"I like it. I mean it. But...'Say It Right' by Nelly Furtado?"

Landon shrugged. "Hey, I'm gay and living with Nyle, who's even gayer."

Aaron chuckled. He'd missed wandering around the house and hearing the songs Nyle played at full volume.

"Speak of the devil," Landon said. "Nyle's planning a horror movie marathon tonight. We take a drink every time someone flinches. Fancy joining?"

"That sounds tragic."

"Exactly." Landon pulled Aaron up to standing. "Come on, let's go."

They left the tunnel and made their way through the streets of Greenwich, hands clasped, comfortable in each other's silence.

As they neared their destination, Aaron said, "Landon?"

Landon turned, a question in his eyes.

Meeting his gaze, Aaron continued, more confidently than ever, "You, too, are a bonfire."

🎵 Untitled

[Now playing » Podcast, Ep. 35—Untitled—Don't Listen to Me]

As a man, saying 'I've been raped' is difficult. You know, there's a shame that comes with saying out loud that you've been violated by another man.

We grow up with these ideas about being masculine, right? We're told we can't show weakness. We shouldn't cry or act in any way that people might call 'sissy'. It's like from the get-go, we're taught to always put up this front of being tough.

For the longest time, I kept questioning myself, my own weaknesses. But over time, here's what I figured out. Being vulnerable, that's not a weakness. In fact, it's a kind of strength. Owning up to it means nobody else can use it against you.

So now, I don't have any trouble saying, "I've been raped."

No one's ever ready for something like abuse, but what comes after, dealing with all the fallout, is a whole different ball game.

You can do a lot of therapy, but nobody can prepare you for the guilt that hits you the first time you think about wanting to fuck another man. Like, shouldn't you now hate every man on Earth because of what happened? Shouldn't the very thought of dealing with a penis make you sick?

Nobody tells you that the trauma will stick around forever. There won't be any magic dick to cure it. And don't let anyone feed you that line about 'trauma makes you stronger' because the truth is trauma messes with your head. With trauma, there are no winners, only survivors.

It sucks to always be on high alert, to be knocked sideways by a panic attack over the smallest thing. It could be a smell, a place, a touch, or just a word. Sometimes, I wish I could turn it all off and have a normal—even if it's boring—sex life.

It's frustrating having to make a checklist of 'can do's' and 'can't do's' every time. But I've learned that one bad experience shouldn't, and definitely must not, define everything else. We're allowed to be scared, but we also need to allow ourselves permission to trust again.

Life's going to throw you good days and bad days, good people and bad people, good sex and bad sex. But here's the thing. You're still here. Healing might seem impossible, but moving forward—that's something you can do.

Having someone around can make a huge difference. Not to fix you, but to lean on when things spin out of control when those demons come knocking. It's okay to cry, to feel hurt. But let's try to get back up every time. Take a hot shower, push aside those dark thoughts. Don't let the ones who hurt us keep that control.

I know I can't erase those bad memories and scars, but I'm working on stacking up enough good moments to outweigh the bad ones. Just because someone took something from us without asking, doesn't mean we can't still give freely when we want to.

And I still have a lot to give.

Chapter Thirty-Two

Stay

[Now playing » Heaven is a Place—Amber Run]

In the following month, things shifted quite a bit.

Community payback was behind them, and since Aaron and Landon had officially become an item, they spent more time together. Sometimes just the two of them, others in good company. But with Landon's big day in court on the horizon, Aaron thought it better to give him some space.

That was why he stayed at Aunt Olivia's rather than moving back in with Landon. He still hung out at his place most of the time, though, so not much really changed except for where he slept. They'd both agreed to take it slow, sticking to kisses and occasional touches here and there. No sex. And while it was nice being that close, more often than not, it left Aaron yearning for more. The more time he spent with Landon, the stronger his feelings grew.

Things had shifted within Landon's family, too, particularly with Luzanne. She worked on mending fences with Landon. It was baby steps, but the lack of snide remarks and more frequent family dinners were promising signs.

On the eve of Landon's testimony, Nyle decided to cheer his cousin up with a low-key get-together at their house. The whole gang was there—Maeve, Ria, Fell, even Luzanne and Jean.

They'd been having a laugh over board games, accompanied by Fell's craft beers and crispy fried chicken. Lo-fi tunes playing in the background kept the atmosphere calm and relaxed. As the evening winded down, people began to head off.

Maeve was the first to make a move. "Right, I'm off. See you lot later!"

Nyle and Fell left next. Luzanne and Jean, who'd been pretty cosy all night, slipped off to their room without much fuss.

"I'll help you tidy up," Ria suggested, gesturing to the aftermath of their game night—plates, glasses, and cards everywhere.

Landon got up to lend a hand and bumped his knee against Aaron's. The quick touch was enough to make Aaron jolt and accidentally whack his toe on the table.

"Everything all right?" Ria asked, sounding worried.

"Yeah, I'm fine," Aaron lied, ignoring the throbbing in his toe. He picked up a card from the floor and handed it to Landon. "You missed one."

Their fingers brushed for a second, sending a tingle up Aaron's spine.

"Right, I'll sort the dishwasher," Landon said, heading to the kitchen.

Watching him go, Aaron took another gulp of his drink. Maybe he'd had one too many of Landon's killer cocktails. "I might need to stop with these. Can't be hungover tomorrow."

"You know they're non-alcoholic, right?" Ria grinned. "Landon's a wizard with spices, makes them taste boozy. He calls it the 'Placebo'."

Aaron twirled the empty glass in his hand, thinking back to when he first tried one at his surprise party. He'd believed the cocktails were part of the reason he was seeing Landon in a new light. Turns out, he'd been stone-cold sober the whole time.

"Excuse me a sec." Aaron darted off to the kitchen where Landon was busy at the counter. "You're a dick," he blurted out as he got closer.

Landon placed the last dish down and turned with a mock-serious frown. "Easy with the compliments, or I might get emotional."

"That cocktail you make." Aaron gestured with the glass still in his hand. "It's non-alcoholic, isn't it?"

"Yeah, it's a mocktail."

"So, you knew I was making a fool of myself at the party when I told you how beautiful you are."

Landon nearly choked, trying to stifle a chuckle. "Not my fault people can be easily tricked. I never said it had booze in it. You just assumed."

"You could've mentioned it though."

"Why? Would it have made a difference?"

Aaron thought back to that night, the irresistible draw he felt towards Landon, a feeling that was just as strong now. No, it wouldn't have changed a thing.

With his heart pounding, he edged closer, fixated on Landon's lips. Everything inside him screamed to bridge the gap with a kiss.

"Heading off," Ria called out from the doorway. "I'll see you two tomorrow."

The sound of the front door closing echoed through the corridor, signalling they were now alone.

"Aaron..." Landon grasped his chin, tilting his face up to meet his gaze. "I'm sorry if I've been off lately, but it's just that—"

"You don't have to apologise. It's okay."

"No," Landon said, shaking his head. "It's not okay. I'm all over the place about tomorrow, and I hate feeling like this. I should be over it by now."

"Hey." Aaron covered Landon's hand with his own. "You're allowed to struggle, even when you're getting better."

"And where'd you nick that bit of wisdom from?"

"Lottie might have mentioned something like it."

Landon offered a half-smile. "So, you're warming up to her?"

"Not exactly, but she's not entirely useless."

"Good to hear. I did tell her you weren't going to be easy."

"Wait, you've been talking to your therapist about...me?" Aaron asked, his curiosity piqued.

"Doctor-patient confidentiality," Landon replied, kissing him.

It was a quick peck, but it coaxed out a soft moan from Aaron. Landon stepped back and released Aaron's hand.

"Should I head off?" Aaron asked, inching towards the door. He didn't want to overstep.

"Stay." Landon's tone was soft yet firm.

"All right." Aaron finished up with the dishwasher and turned it on. "I can stick around for a bit, catch the last train."

"No." Landon's hand found Aaron's waist, holding him close. "Stay with me tonight."

Aaron paused, searching Landon's eyes. He wanted to spend the night with Landon more than anything else in the world, but he wanted Landon to want it too. "Are you sure?"

"Yes."

Their next kiss started off gentle and slow, but it quickly heated up, growing more passionate, almost desperate, as if they couldn't get enough of each other.

"Let's go to my room." Landon took Aaron's hand and practically raced up the stairs.

As the door clicked shut, everything else seemed a million miles away. Downstairs, the faint hum of music and distant chatter of people drifted in from the street, mingling with the rustling leaves outside the window. But in that room, it was just them, shielded from the world yet exposed to each other.

Landon pushed him towards the bed, kissing him like it was the end of the world and this was their last shot at it. They didn't bother about turning on the lights, left with just the moonlight and the glow-in-the-dark stars.

"No third rule tonight," Landon whispered near his ear, sending a shiver down Aaron's spine.

It took him a moment to grasp what Landon meant, mainly because he was still dazed by how Landon was nuzzling into his neck. "You mean…"

"You can touch me anywhere. Everywhere. You decide."

Landon's fingers trailed up Aaron's arms, halting at his wrists. He guided Aaron's hands up between them, close to his face, a silent invitation to take the lead.

Aaron quivered slightly as he brushed back that rebellious curl from Landon's forehead, then let his hands drift down to Landon's shoulders and chest. Even through the fabric of the hoodie, he could feel the tension in Landon's muscles and the quickened beat of his heart.

"You don't have to prove anything," Aaron murmured. "Not to me, not to yourself."

"I know." Landon took a deep breath, his eyes searching Aaron's. "I want this."

That was the green light they both needed. Their hands started exploring freely, shedding clothes until they were both bare under the duvet, wrapped up in each other.

Aaron wanted this too.

He savoured every inch of Landon's skin, tracing tattoos, and scars, and freckles.

"I want you," Landon murmured, reaching over to the bedside table. The sound of crinkling foil made Aaron's pulse quicken.

"Are you sure?" he asked again.

Landon's confirmation came with a gentle kiss, followed by the soft caress of their noses brushing together. Their foreheads met, and Aaron closed his eyes. He opened them again as Landon's warm hand settled on his chest, fingers splayed against the thrumming of his heart.

"Afraid of the dark?" Landon joked, but his voice trembled.

"Never been. You?"

"Not when I'm with you. I trust you."

Aaron snorted, his hands twitching. "I'm not sure what to do."

"Well...if it makes you feel better, neither am I."

They stifled a nervous chuckle, but their kiss swept away any fear.

Skin against skin, heavy breaths, greedy touches, and messy kisses, their barriers melted.

And they fused.

It was more than physical. It was the whispers, Landon's steady hand on his heart, the other on his back, holding him close, refusing to let go. It wasn't just their bodies laid bare before each other—it was their scars, their very souls, exposed and intertwined.

It didn't last long. Aaron should have expected it. All the intense emotions they'd been holding back burst forth. But as quickly as their union peaked, Aaron sensed the shift.

A shadow crossed Landon's face, his eyes clouding with distant thoughts.

Trauma and inexperience didn't mix well. Much like alcohol and painkillers.

"Landon..." Aaron reached for him, wanting to bring him back. Taking Landon's hand, he placed it over the long scar on his abdomen. "It's okay. It's you and me, here and now."

"Aaron..."

"We're in your room; you're safe." He laced their fingers and placed their hands on the bedhead, touching the indentation in the wood. "I'm here with you. No one's going to hurt you."

"Stay."

"I'm not going anywhere." Aaron planted a kiss on Landon's forehead and gently pulled away from him.

Landon's next words were a soft murmur, nearly drowned out by the heavy air, but Aaron could swear he caught a whisper of "Never leave again."

As they snuggled under the blankets, it felt like more than just getting into bed. It was like coming *home*. Aaron's eyelids grew heavier by the second, but before sleep took him, he gazed up at the starry ceiling and smiled.

He'd found it. His happy thought.

Tori was right. Neverland wasn't a physical place but a state of mind, somewhere in that sweet spot between dreaming and waking, where reality itself seemed like a dream.

And Aaron had just been there.

With Landon.

Chapter Thirty-Three

The Trial

[Now playing » Can't Break What's Broken—The Hunna]

When Aaron woke up that morning, his heart fluttered at the sight of Landon asleep next to him—still comfortably naked, with his right cheek squished into the pillow. The duvet, a crumpled mess, barely covered them, exposing most of Landon's skin.

Aaron followed the trail of ink across Landon's body, pausing at words near his hip that read, *This thing of darkness I acknowledge mine.* He made a mental note to eventually learn the stories behind each tattoo.

Turning back to Landon's face, Aaron smiled at the view; Landon looked so peaceful. It wasn't often Aaron got to see beauty like this, not with all the tough stuff life had thrown at him. But right there, watching Landon sleep, one word summed it all up for Aaron: beautiful.

He shivered pleasantly at the memory of last night. It had been a big step for them. He hoped it was the start of something more.

Just then, Landon stirred, and directed a half-grumpy, half-sleepy glare at him with the one eye not buried in the pillow.

"Hey," Aaron whispered, not wanting to break the quiet morning spell.

"Hey," Landon grumbled back, still groggy.

"Sleep well?"

"Nah, not really. My mind was racing all night."

"About what?" Aaron shifted to his side and inched a bit closer to Landon's warmth.

"Just...us. We had sex."

"I know," Aaron said, deepening his tone to put on his best impression of Landon. "I was there." He even added a touch of seriousness and a hint of posh accent.

Landon pinched him on the hip. "Okay, first off, I do not sound like that. And second, will you ever stop parroting? It's not attractive."

Aaron grinned. "But it was good, right?"

Landon paused, then nodded. "Sort of, yeah. It's the first time I didn't feel like throwing up halfway through, so...yeah, thanks for that."

"Uh...you're welcome?"

"It's a good thing." Landon caressed Aaron's cheek, his knuckles brushing under his eye. "How about you?"

"It's always good with you."

"That's cause your bar's set pretty low, and you don't have much to compare it against."

"You know it's not that." Aaron placed his hand on Landon's chest, his fingers tracing the tattoo of the ECG line with a semicolon. He'd been curious about it since the first time he'd seen it. "What's the story behind this one?"

Landon glanced down, then up again to meet Aaron's eyes. "It's about my choice, to stop or go on. I chose to keep going, like a sentence that doesn't end."

A twist churned in Aaron's stomach. Despite everything, Landon was still here, still pushing on. "You're strong. That's why I like you so much. You make me want to be better."

Landon pulled a face. "I'm not strong. I'm still...broken."

No, he was far from a broken thing, even if someone had clearly tried their best.

"You may be broken, but you're still beautiful. And brave. And you'll be brave today too. I know it."

"That makes one of us. I'm scared as fuck. Having to stand up there, all those eyes on me, everyone knowing—"

"They'll know that Green is a scumbag who deserves to go to prison."

"It's going to be hell."

"No," Aaron said firmly. "*We* are going to give him hell. You can do this. You're not on your own."

Landon went silent, then placed his hand over Aaron's, right atop the tattoo near his heart. "Aaron," he started with some hesitation, "This...us...it might not always be like this. Last night was great, but next time, I might still push you away, or—"

"Hey," Aaron cut in softly, easing his hand from Landon's grasp to brush over the closely shaved hair at the back of his head. The subtle prickliness tingled against his fingertips. Landon leaned into the caress, almost kitten-like. "Let's take it step by step. We've got all the time we need to work through this. Just focus on today, on what you've got to do."

Landon sighed deeply, then closed the distance between them with a tender kiss. In an instant, the world outside faded away, leaving only the intimate space they shared.

"How about breakfast?" Aaron suggested. As he attempted to swing his legs out from the tangle of sheets, Kat pounced onto the duvet to nibble at his toe. "When did she come in here?"

Landon reached out to pet her. "She's sneaky."

"Seems she takes after her *dad*," Aaron quipped, finally freeing himself from the bed's grasp.

They dressed quickly and headed downstairs. In the kitchen, Nyle looked as if fresh out of a spa, with his bathrobe on and hair wrapped up in a towel. Busy chopping fruit for his yoghurt and granola, he brightened up when he spotted them.

"Morning, *lovebirds*," he greeted with a big smile. "Heard some interesting noises last night...though I must say, it was over pretty quick."

Aaron coughed, feeling a bit hot, while Landon nonchalantly flipped Nyle off with his tattooed middle finger.

"Hey, I'm always here if you need some tips," Nyle said, brandishing his knife with a grin. "As the resident gay guru, I'm offended you guys didn't ask for advice. I could give you pointers on making it last longer, best positions, relaxation techniques...you name it."

"We'll pass, thanks," Landon replied, heading straight for the coffee machine.

"Just offering my expertise," Nyle called after him. "I'm all about helping the newbies to our rainbow club."

"I've been part of that club since I was eight," Landon shot back.

"Yeah, but he might not have." Nyle nodded towards Aaron.

"I'm not gay," Aaron stated firmly.

Nyle looked surprised for a second, then quipped, "Honey, even if you're bi, that's still part-time gay."

Jean, popping in from around the corner with Luzanne, added, "I agree."

Aaron and Landon shared a look that said they were both over this conversation as everyone gathered around the table.

Back to his fruit cutting, Nyle leaned over the counter towards Aaron. "So, how's your fibre intake? It's key for—"

He was cut off by the clank of the milk pitcher on the counter. Landon glared at Nyle in a way that said *enough*.

"Welcome home," Nyle chuckled. "Welcome back, both of you."

*

During the Tube ride on the way to court, Landon seemed lost in his bubble, headphones on, fingers often drifting to where his lip piercing used to be, or fidgeting with his suit jacket. Getting him to swap his usual gear for a suit, lose the piercings and leave his Docs at home hadn't been a walk in the park, but it was necessary for the court appearance.

Walking out of the station, Aaron and Landon strolled down the street together, close but not too close. Aaron kept to himself, thinking his presence alone was what Landon needed for now. Ria, Nyle, and Luzanne would be at the courthouse, too, but they'd agreed to meet there directly. Landon wanted it to be just the two of them—their own little calm before the storm kicked in.

They'd almost reached the courthouse when Landon stopped suddenly in his tracks, his hand clutching at his chest, panic written all over his face. Aaron could practically feel the waves of anxiety coming off him.

"Landon, breathe," he murmured, stepping closer but careful not to touch. He knew that even a small touch might be too much for Landon to handle right now.

"I'm trying," Landon gasped, his fingers clumsily working at the top buttons of his shirt in a desperate bid to get more air.

"Hold on. I'll be right back." Aaron sprinted back the way they'd come.

He spotted a Japanese fast-food restaurant and bolted over. He scooped up a couple of wasabi sachets, not even stopping to catch his breath before racing back to Landon.

Aaron found him exactly where he'd left him, propped against the wall, his hand rubbing his chest, trying to ease his breaths.

"Close your eyes and open your mouth," Aaron instructed with the wasabi sachets hidden in his fist. "Do you trust me?"

"No."

"Landon..."

Reluctantly, Landon complied, and Aaron popped a bit of wasabi on his tongue.

Landon's face scrunched up. "Should've known," he muttered.

"It worked, didn't it?"

Landon nodded, still grimacing.

"Okay, look for five things you can see."

Landon's eyes darted around before settling back on Aaron's face.

"Four things you can touch."

Landon fiddled with his tie, slid his fingers over the buttons of his jacket, then brushed his hand against the wall. For the fourth item, Aaron held out his pendant.

"You sure?" Landon asked.

"Tori would've liked you," Aaron said, holding back the words *because you're my happy thought*. "Now, three things you can hear."

The everyday sounds of the city filled the air. So, Aaron was taken aback when Landon leaned in and rested his ear against Aaron's chest.

"Two things you can smell."

Almost doglike, Landon sniffed his way up Aaron's shirt until the tip of his nose tickled behind Aaron's ear. "You used my coconut shampoo."

"Got curly hair, too, don't I?"

"Not like mine."

"One thing you can taste."

Landon made a face. "Like I can taste anything after that wasabi," he grumbled, but his breathing had evened out. He stepped back, a small smile on his lips. "Thanks for that."

"Feeling better?"

Landon did up his shirt buttons and straightened. "Let's do this."

Together, they faced the courthouse building, squared their shoulders, and walked towards whatever awaited them.

*

The courtroom felt as cramped and tense as a PE changing room before a big school match.

Aaron, wedged between Landon and Ria, found his shirt collar tightening into a noose around his neck. Behind them, Nyle and Luzanne offered silent support.

Landon fiddled with his tie, twirling the end around his fingers. Aaron had to stop himself from reaching out to hold his hand.

The man who'd been haunting Landon's nightmares sat right there, separated only by a glass wall. Well-dressed, clean-shaven, hair styled perfectly, he might have passed for harmless to anyone who didn't know better. But Aaron saw the man for what he was—a wolf in sheep's clothing. Despite how the media had tried to gloss over it, Aaron hoped the truth would finally come out.

When they called Landon to the stand, Aaron glanced at him, trying to pump a bit of courage into him. He'd tried his best to be strong for Landon's sake. But inside, he was just as jittery, clutching the little rabbit plushie in his pocket, practically squashing it flat from all the squeezing.

Landon approached the witness stand without a glance at the crowd. He kept his eyes fixed on his hands as if they were the only things in the room.

"Mr. Bailey," the prosecutor's lawyer started, her voice steady. "Could you please confirm your period of residence with the Greens?"

"Yes," came Landon's soft reply, almost lost in the quiet room. "Two years. Started when I was thirteen."

"And it was during this time, while under their care, that you experienced abuse at the hands of your foster father?" she continued, her tone gentle but firm.

Landon nodded, his fingers twisting together.

"Please, answer verbally, Mr. Bailey," the judge interjected.

Landon swallowed. "Yes."

Despite being prepared, Aaron knew the questions were difficult for him, but they had to be asked—the answers were key to helping the jury grasp how serious and long-lasting the abuse had been.

It all changed when the defence lawyer, sharp in her tailored suit, strutted up and started grilling Landon. "Mr. Bailey, it appears you've had quite an unsettled upbringing. The son of a single mother turned drug addict, no dad in the picture, and shuffled around the foster system since you were three. *Twelve* different families."

She'd stated each point as if ticking off a grocery list. But it was her emphasis on the number of families that made Aaron uneasy.

"Your case workers labelled you as 'problematic'," she continued, "with aggressive behaviour and a tendency for theft. Yet, the Greens welcomed you, funded your education at a top boarding school, and paid for your clothes and all other expenses. Is that also correct?"

Again, Landon nodded but immediately followed with a cracked "Yes."

"You've never stayed in any other place longer than a year, and before your time with the Greens, such financial support was unfamiliar to you. Would it be accurate to state that you benefited from their generosity for as long as you could?"

"Objection, relevance!" Landon's lawyer exclaimed. But the judge let it slide, and the atmosphere got even tenser.

Leaning in like a hawk eyeing its prey, the defence lawyer continued her line of questioning. "Why, then, if the environment was as abusive as you claim, did you remain there for an extended period? Why not leave as you had with previous families?"

Landon clenched his hands in front of him. "I was a kid. I didn't know any better. I believed I had no other option."

Whispers rippled through the courtroom.

"Why come forward now, after all this time?" she pressed. "Opportunism, maybe? Inspired by Mr. Thompson's allegations?"

"No." Landon's voice rose, his fists pounding against the stand. "It wasn't easy coming forward. I was ashamed and scared, and I thought no one would believe me. But after Ian..." He paused, his eyes locked with the lawyer's, clearly avoiding looking at the man who haunted his past. "After what happened to him, it wasn't about shame anymore. It was guilt. Guilt for not backing him up. Guilt for keeping quiet too long. I can't let him control me anymore." He finally turned to face the man he was accusing. "He has to pay for what he's done to me, to Ian...to all of us."

"So, payback is what you're after, isn't it, Mr. Bailey?" The lawyer grinned like a Cheshire cat, seizing on Landon's unfortunate choice of words. "Your allegations are severe, particularly against a respected figure who's helped many children in challenging circumstances, like your own. And yet, after the Greens, you seem to have had quite the struggle. With a criminal record and a recent community payback sentence, your trajectory appears troubled. How does this reflect on your character?"

"That's not—" Nyle piped up from behind Aaron, but Luzanne was quick to hush him. The judge called for quiet from the public.

"And regarding Mr. Bailey's financial situation," the lawyer pressed on, "his employment history includes a series of low-paying jobs like waiter, bartender, and his latest stint as a tattoo assistant, terminated due to bad attitude. This paints a stark contrast to your life with the Greens, does it not? Might jealousy or financial need be motivating factors?"

"I want justice, not money," Landon nearly shouted, his frustration palpable.

"Yet financial gain would be advantageous, wouldn't it? Isn't it true that you tried to get a loan for your own tattoo studio and failed?"

Aaron's breakfast threatened to make a comeback. The lawyer's game was clear as day—paint Landon as a money-hungry opportunist. It was a sly move, and Aaron worried if it would work.

But Landon's lawyer was quick to counter. After a confirming nod from Landon, she dived in. "Let's not overlook Mr. Bailey's scars, both physical and emotional. Contrary to the insinuation, Mr. Bailey did reach out for help, only to be ignored. His self-harm is a direct result of the abuse he suffered during that time. Mr. Green took advantage of a vulnerable child instead of protecting him. He used gifts to buy silence, grooming him. As a recently turned teenager, how was Mr. Bailey to know better when those tasked with his care failed him? His aggressive behaviour wasn't a flaw. It was a loud cry for help."

The defence lawyer pounced on every word, twisting Landon's story, trying to cast doubt. Aaron's stomach was in knots. This was more than a trial; it was a battle for Landon's truth.

As soon as his testimony was over, Landon bolted out of the courtroom. Aaron, along with Ria, Nyle, and Luzanne, trailed behind him. Out in the corridor, Landon slumped against the wall as if he'd just gone ten rounds in a boxing ring.

"Fuck it! I knew it'd be like this. They're trying to paint me as some fucking gold digger." He groaned. "This was all for nothing."

Aaron moved closer, pausing before touching Landon's face. After getting a slight nod from him, Aaron cupped his cheeks. "Hey, no matter what happens, you stood up and spoke your truth. That's what counts."

"But what's the use? They twisted everything. And Ian... It's like we're fighting shadows."

"It does matter, Landon," said Ria. "You're not fighting this battle alone. Remember, we're with you every step of the way."

"And us too," a voice piped up from behind.

They all spun around to see two guys approaching.

Landon's eyes widened. "I thought you weren't going to testify?"

Nyle peered at them curiously. "Who are they?"

Landon introduced them briefly as other foster kids who had been in the same home after him. Ian had reached out to them, too, but they hadn't been keen on testifying.

One of the guys spoke up. "Honestly, I was scared and feeling ashamed. But hearing what you said in your podcast...it kind of inspired me."

Landon turned to Aaron, but Aaron shook his head.

"It was Nyle's video," the other guy added. "He talked about supporting his cousin and mentioned your podcast. After we heard it, we felt like we could do this too. As Nyle always says, you have to shine for others, right?"

Landon stared at Nyle, expression unreadable. Then, he strode over.

"Look, Lanny, I'm so—" Nyle began, but he didn't get to finish. Landon cut him off, wrapping him in a fierce hug that was part tight embrace and part near-suffocation.

"Thank you," Landon said, muffled against his cousin's shoulder.

"Oh my God." Nyle was clearly fighting back tears. "Lanny, I love you so much."

Landon chuckled awkwardly and patted Nyle on the back as they pulled apart.

"You can't say it back, can you?"

"Just know that I do," Landon replied.

"See, told you being an influencer can make a difference."

"Never doubted it. Actually, despite our different tastes in fashion, I've always looked up to you."

Nyle put a hand on his chest, over his heart. "Wait, you look up to...me?"

Landon nodded, scratching behind his ear. "Remember Aunt Jane's posh wedding? The only other time I was stuffed into a suit like this." He rolled his eyes. "Everyone was trying so hard to look perfect, pretending we weren't just getting by on welfare. But you, you went into a massive fight with your mum and dad over that bright pink outfit because they said it was *too gay*."

Nyle laughed. "Hey, it was bang on trend!"

"It was hideous," Landon continued. "Still, you wore it anyway, with such confidence. That day, I thought, 'This guy has balls. He doesn't give a fuck about what others think. That's how I want to be.'" He hitched up his trousers to reveal his clover-patterned socks. "Since you gave me my first pair, I've always worn funky socks. The weirder, the better. They're like a little reminder to be brave and just be me, like you are."

As Nyle's eyes welled up again, this time with a joyful smile, he glanced at the two guys standing nearby. "We're going to bring him down, Lanny. I promise you."

Chapter Thirty-Four

Home

[Now playing » How Far We've Come—Matchbox Twenty]

"Guilty," announced the foreman, handing down a five-year sentence to David Green.

"Take him away," the judge commanded.

Aaron took a deep breath as Landon's shaking finally stopped. He knew this wasn't the end, just the start of a long road to healing for Landon. But it was still a win, a big one.

Once they left the courtroom, Ria, Nyle, and Luzanne were up for celebrating, but Aaron sensed that wasn't on Landon's mind. So, they politely declined and went their separate ways.

"How about we go somewhere?" Aaron suggested, back at the house, as they changed into their usual clothes and shoved their suits away.

"Where to?" Landon asked.

"Trust me. I know a place you'll like."

Landon muttered a subdued "All right" and tagged along with Aaron.

*

The gardens at the retirement centre were still a work in progress, yet the cherry tree showed off some shy blossoms.

"I thought our community payback days were over?" Landon quipped.

Aaron smiled as they neared the tree. He lifted a branch so they could get a closer look. The sweet scent of the flowers wafted around them. "Check it out, it's starting to bloom."

"Can't believe it," Landon observed, sounding surprised. A small smile tugged at his lips.

"You were the one who gave it a chance when nobody else did."

Landon brushed his fingers against a blossom. "Guess I did, didn't I?"

They stood there, admiring the tree. It had taken a lot of effort, but the results were beautiful.

"Muhammad must be so proud," Aaron said.

"No, not him. This one's for the founder's daughter, Lily. It's like she's still around, isn't it?"

Aaron touched his pendant, then let his hand drift to Landon's arm, thinking about the rose petal tattoos under his sleeves. In every new bloom, in every line of ink, memories and legacies persisted, never truly fading away.

Just then, a loud rumble came from Landon's stomach. They hadn't eaten anything since breakfast.

"How about we get something to eat?" Aaron suggested, and Landon nodded in agreement.

Eventually, they found themselves sitting on a pebbly stretch along the riverbank, munching on burgers and fries with a view of Canary Wharf.

Mid-bite, Aaron ventured, "Can I ask you something?"

"You just did," Landon said but invited him to continue.

"What landed you in prison?"

Landon paused, taking a sip of his soda. "Stole my mum's car."

"That got you locked up?"

"Well, I also may have used it to rob an ice cream shop."

"But you hate ice cream."

"Exactly why."

"So, car theft and ice cream? That's it?"

Landon hesitated. "And I sort of assaulted the arresting officer. Oh, and they found drugs on me."

Aaron tried not to laugh. "Are you fucking with me?"

Landon stared back, deadpan.

Aaron tried to wrap his head around it. "You're serious? You did all that?"

"Googled what crimes would get me sent down. Wanted to make sure."

Aaron shook his head, still in disbelief. "Okay, one more question. Why do you hate ice cream?"

Landon's grip on the paper bag tightened, and he dropped his gaze to his sneakers. "Every time after...he'd take me for ice cream. Like a reward or something."

A lump formed in Aaron's throat, making it challenging to gulp down the rest of his drink. The weight of Landon's revelation hit hard. Why had he asked? He grabbed another handful of fries from the seemingly bottomless bag, wishing he could shove the question down there with them.

"I'll never get why this fancy burger place gives you such a heap of fries," Aaron said, trying to lighten the mood.

Landon shrugged. "It's their thing, isn't it? Makes you think you're getting a bargain, even though it's no cheaper than the average fast-food place."

"Then why didn't we just go there?"

Landon chuckled, rubbing the back of his neck. "Felt like spoiling myself."

"With burgers? If you were after a treat, we should've gone for a steak."

"Hey, I might get some money after all of this, but I'm not exactly loaded."

Aaron hummed in agreement, munching on the last of the fries.

"Shall we head back?" Landon made a move, but as they got up, Aaron gently caught his arm.

"Wait..." He fished out a folded paper from his jeans and handed it over. "I'm a bit early, but think of this as your birthday present."

Landon took the paper with hesitation. Reading it, his eyes widened. "A lease for...a tattoo studio in Camden?"

"You're too good to be an assistant," Aaron said with a warm smile.

Confusion flickered across Landon's face. "But how did you..."

"Turns out my parents had a life insurance policy. It's...quite a bit."

"And you used it for this?"

"Not all of it," Aaron said casually, trying to downplay the significance.

Landon eyed Aaron. "What's the catch? What do you want back for this?"

"It's a gift," Aaron assured him.

"Aaron." Landon made it sound like both a question and a statement.

"Think of it as an investment, a thank you for all you've done for me."

Landon shook his head, a slight smile playing on his lips. "You're too trusting sometimes. It's sweet you see it as an investment, but in the real world, investments are not a gift."

"How do you mean?"

"If you're serious about this being an investment, let's treat it properly. You're the money man, and I've got the skills. Let's make it more than a kind gesture. Let's be partners."

Aaron laughed softly. "Business partners?"

"Yeah. Even though you know shit about running a business and even less about tattoos."

"Guess you'll be the boss then, showing me the ropes. And who knows? I might even become your tattoo assistant."

"That's not a bad idea. Your sketches, they're pretty good, you know."

Aaron hummed, thinking about those he'd done lately. Landon had been the one to nudge him back into drawing, even suggesting creating designs inspired by Australia, stars, and the planets—a tribute to Tori, kind of like what they'd done with the cherry tree.

Landon read the lease agreement again, his face lighting up in the same special way when he was absorbed in sketching a new tattoo design. Aaron felt like the luckiest person in the world, being the only one who got to witness these moments. Landon was beautiful when he smiled.

"You can..." Landon whispered, answering an unspoken question in Aaron's gaze. "You can kiss me."

Aaron didn't hesitate. In a heartbeat, he closed the gap between them.

The remnants of their recent meal mixed on his tongue—cheese, bacon, and the fizzy sweetness of the soda. It was an unusual combination, like tea and cigarettes, bourbon and custard, mint and coffee. But as their lips met and their breaths mingled, it felt right.

It was them. And it was perfect.

Epilogue

[Now playing » Home—Gabrielle Aplin]

SIX MONTHS LATER

Aaron's cheek scars tingled, a sure sign rain was on the way.

He tugged his earphones into place and yanked his hood low as he and Landon slipped into the Barbican Centre's multilevel maze one last time. They loved getting lost here.

Settling atop their usual spot on a low wall, the lyrics of "Something Just Like This" washed over them. Legs tangling together and mouths pressing quickly, they kissed against a backdrop of running fountains and the lively playground.

In less than twenty-four hours, they'd be in Australia, spotting koalas and who knew what else, maybe even catching the Southern Lights. It felt unreal that this trip was finally happening.

Their moment was broken as the music stopped abruptly—a call coming through on Aaron's phone. Nyle's photo popped up, snapped at Pride, all heart-shaped glasses and glitter.

"Ignore it," Landon whispered, his breath warm against Aaron's neck, lips brushing along his jaw.

Aaron narrowed his eyes playfully, giving Landon's knee a gentle squeeze through the rip in his jeans. "Bet he's wondering when we're heading back. Did you catch his mopey face yesterday?"

"He's being dramatic. It's only a month, after all. He'll survive."

"Like you survived without me?" Aaron snickered. "We've already agreed you'd spend your days recording gloomy podcast episodes and recommending '90s music."

"I'd watch my mouth if I were you, especially perched on that wall. One little nudge…"

"It's not that high."

"High enough to cause permanent damage."

"You wouldn't dare," Aaron said, assessing the crowd. "Too many witnesses. They'd arrest you on the spot, and this time, you wouldn't get away with just community payback."

"I've been to prison before." Landon feigned a push, then drew Aaron in for another kiss.

"Thanks for coming to Australia with me. I'm not sure I could've done this alone."

"You've thanked me enough. And who would miss a chance to see Australia?"

"You, apparently, with all those horror videos about spiders and snakes you sent me."

"Just doing homework. We need to know what's out there, especially if we're going off the beaten track to scatter your sister's ashes."

Aaron grasped the pendant, feeling its reassuring weight. This was his way of bringing Tori to the places she'd always dreamt of.

As Aaron's phone fell silent, Landon's vibrated into life.

Without even checking it, Landon answered, "What now?" A pause, then a frustrated, "Yes, we'll be back. No, we don't need more beer. And for fuck's sake, Nyle, they do have it in Australia." He sighed, pocketing the phone.

"What do they have in Australia?"

Landon shot him a look. "Trust me, you don't want to know."

"Don't tell me Nyle's thrown another party?"

A small smile played on Landon's lips. "You know him."

Aaron chuckled, then rubbed his neck. His fresh tattoo itched more than the scars.

"Don't scratch it," Landon warned gently.

"I'm not a tattoo regular like you."

"Stop whining. That chest piece of yours is going to be a long haul. We've got quite a few sessions lined up."

"As in…days?"

"Months. Good things take time."

"Or maybe you get distracted too easily," Aaron teased, thinking back to their first tattoo session. Not one drop of ink had graced his skin that day; they'd gotten busy in entirely different ways.

Aaron's phone buzzed again, but this time, a message from Aunt Olivia flashed on the screen, asking if he had everything he needed for his trip. He'd since moved back in with Landon but was seeing her more than ever, especially on Sundays, when they'd started a new lunch tradition. Sometimes, Landon joined them; other times, it was just the two of them. Aaron loved it.

In reply, he sent her a picture of the notebook she'd given him the first time he attempted the trip, along with one of Landon, captioned, *Got everything I need.*

"Ready to go home?" Landon hopped off the wall and offered his hand to Aaron.

Home. Though he'd been sharing a room with Landon for months, the word still made him pause. Standing, he grasped Landon's fingers.

Side by side, they navigated the Barbican's stark concrete jungle. As they strolled past rows of dull, identical buildings, Aaron observed the climbing plants that clung to the harsh walls.

He used to see them as stubborn intruders in a cold, unwelcoming world. Now, he saw resilience: they carved out their own space, splashing bursts of green against the grey. Much like him and Landon.

Maybe their feeling of not fitting in wasn't about the wider world but more about the people who'd raised them, those who only pretended to understand. Finding where they belonged was about connecting with people who resonated with them—the fighters, the survivors, the misunderstood, those who wore their distrust like a badge.

Not looking for a hero or a fix. Just something to hold on to, someone to share it with.

They were fractured, sure, no gold filling their cracks, but that was what made them real. That was what made them beautiful.

As Aaron and Landon stepped into the house, a buzz of chatter and laughter from the living room greeted them. The moment they popped their heads in, the noise dropped for a second.

Nyle, scooching over on the sofa, invited them to join in. Before Aaron knew it, he was right in the heart of the familiar rumpus. Pinching a few crisps from the coffee table, he slumped beside Landon, struggling to keep a straight face at the scene before him.

Nyle was in the middle of a heated discussion with Maeve about which film to watch, Ria and Fell were on snack and beer duty. On the floor, Luzanne and Jean were having a giggle, trying to play with Kat and feed her some treats.

When Aaron first met this lot, he labelled them as eccentric misfits. But now, they were his chosen family.

And home was waking up to the scent of Landon's brewing coffee, Nyle's vibrant shades, and Kat purring on his lap. It was Ria's warm laugh, the songs Fell made him listen to at the vinyl shop, and regular check-ins from Aunt Olivia. It was a cupboard full of quirky mugs, the never-ending supply of peppermint tea, and a fridge door plastered with funny sticky notes and lots of photos.

Playlist

Peter Pan Was Right – Anson Seabra

Somewhere I Belong – Linkin Park

Something Just Like This – The Chainsmokers, Coldplay

All These Things That I've Done – The Killers

Pumped Up Kicks – Foster the People

Monster – dodie

Turn – The Wombats

loneliness for love – lovelytheband

Kids In The Dark – All Time Low

Dangerous Night – Thirty Seconds To Mars

Pluto – Sleeping At Last

Heaven is a Place –Amber Run

If You Want Love – NF

Apocalypse – Cigarettes After Sex

We'll Never Have Sex – Leith Ross

Home – Gabrielle Aplin

Acknowledgements

This novel is very close to my heart. It's taken three years of living with these characters, pushing through doubt, rejection, and rounds of rewriting. Now that it's finally here, it's no longer just mine. It's yours too.

First and foremost, thank you to my husband—my best friend, my anchor, my home. You've listened to me ramble about this story more times than I can count, read one too many drafts, and never once complained. Your patience, your belief in me, and your love carried me through every stage. I'd be lost without you.

To my mum and dad, who became the most enthusiastic sales team for my first book, especially my mum, who has fought every battle for me and is the strongest person I know. Thank you both for your pride and unwavering support.

To my big sister, who's always been there to take care of her little pain-in-the-neck sister. Your kindness and every small act mean the world to me.

To my friend Kavya, who cheered me on when I needed it most. Though you're far away now, you're close to my heart.

To those who've inspired me—whether directly or indirectly—you're in these pages more than you think.

To my Italian readers, who embraced this story from the very beginning and stayed with it through the entire process. Your encouraging messages kept me going on the hardest days.

To my beta readers, for sharing invaluable feedback that made this better.

Thank you to my editor, Elizabetta, who saw Aaron and Landon for exactly who they are—two rough diamonds with aching hearts—and guided this book to its final form with the care it deserved.

And lastly, to you, dear reader. And to all the queer kids out there—those still searching, still healing, still wondering if there's a place for them. I hope this story finds you, wraps around you like a blanket, and reminds you that you are not alone.

About the Author

Born in Boston (USA) and raised in Naples (Italy), Jessica has always had a desire to explore beyond borders, leading her to live in Japan, the Netherlands, Germany, and now the UK. These experiences have given her a deep appreciation for different cultures and a sense of being a true citizen of the world.

Writing is her way of making sense of things—a space to explore the complexities of identity and belonging. During the pandemic, she rediscovered this passion, leading to the publication of her first YA novel in Italy, *Love is a Mess*, which won the Italian Wattys Award in 2021.

For the past 11 years, Jessica has called London home, and the city's rich diversity inspires her to dive deeper into LGBTQ+ themes in her stories, with a special focus on the asexual spectrum, reflecting her own experience as demisexual.

When she's not writing, Jessica brings her creativity to the fintech world as a digital product designer. She's also on a mission to perfect the art of sourdough baking and stays busy as the chief tin-opener for her two cats.

Email
hello@jexyla.com

Facebook
www.facebook.com/jexyla

Twitter
@jexylawrites

Website
www.jexyla.com/author

Instagram
www.instagram.com/jexylawrites

Pinterest
www.pinterest.com/jexyla

TikTok
www.tiktok.com/@jexylawrites

Spotify
www.open.spotify.com/user/t0ch2qjhfbdldbkrlc502n406?si=25d91c9
4dc384af6

Connect with NineStar Press

Website: NineStarPress.com

Facebook: NineStarPress

X: @NineStarPress

Instagram: NineStarPress

BlueSky: NineStarPress

Threads: @NineStarPress